BEHIND THE WALLS

BEHIND THE WALLS

A Harper Jennings Mystery

Merry Jones

This first world edition published 2012
in Great Britain and in the USA by
SEVERN HOUSE PUBLISHERS LTD of
9–15 High Street, Sutton, Surrey, England, SM1 1DF.

British Library Cataloguing in Publication Data

Jones, Merry Bloch.
  Behind the walls.
  1. Women veterans–Fiction. 2. Iraq War, 2003–
  Veterans–Fiction. 3. Post-traumatic stress disorder–
  Patients–Fiction. 4. Cornell University–Employees–
  Fiction. 5. Antiquities, Prehistoric–America–Catalogs–
  Fiction. 6. Blessing and cursing–Fiction. 7. Suspense
  fiction.
  I. Title
  813.6-dc22

ISBN-13: 978-0-7278-8118-2 (cased)

All Severn House titles are printed on acid-free paper.

Severn House Publishers support The Forest Stewardship Council [FSC],
the leading international forest certification organisation. All our titles that
are printed on Greenpeace-approved FSC-certified paper carry the FSC logo.

Typeset by Palimpsest Book Production Ltd.,
Falkirk, Stirlingshire, Scotland.
Printed and bound in Great Britain by
MPG Books Ltd., Bodmin, Cornwall.

To Robin, Baille and Neely

Acknowledgments

In writing *Behind the Walls*, I had support and encouragement from lots of people, too many to list. But special thanks to:

my agent, Rebecca Strauss at McIntosh and Otis;

my editor, Rachel Simpson Hutchens at Severn House Publishers;

my fellow Liars: Greg Frost, Jon McGoran, Jonathan Maberry, Don Lafferty, Kelly Simmons, Marie Lamba, Dennis Tafoya, Keith Strunk, Solomon Jones, Ed Pettit, Keith DeCandido;

my friends and family, especially Robin, Baille and Neely.

October, 1989

The crate was smaller than most, simply marked 'Utah'. No dates, like all the others. No specific dig sites either. Odd; Professor Langston was obsessive about labeling his collection. Maybe the labels were inside, taped to the lid? Or maybe they'd been lost.

Carla Prentiss sighed, glanced at her watch. Almost four. Without a list, there probably wouldn't be time to identify and catalogue the contents before sunset, and she didn't want to be caught there after dark. The professor's rambling old Victorian mansion was spooky enough in daylight. The place had been built in the early twentieth century by some hermetic silent movie star whose name she couldn't remember but who, in his paranoia, had designed the place with secret passages and hidden vaults, setting it deep in the woods outside Ithaca where, even now, it had no near neighbors. When he'd offered her the assistantship, Professor Langston had told her with some pride that his house was probably haunted.

'Haunted?' she'd parroted.

'Its inhabitants have led, shall we say . . . uncommon lives.' He'd smiled, wheezing heavily as air forced its way through his dense nose hairs. 'In the twenties, a young woman – a starlet named Chloe Manning – simply disappeared during a visit. Some say she's still in the house, wandering the passages in the walls.'

Carla had blinked at the walls of the study. Wondered if the bookshelves concealed secret doors. And bodies.

Under his white, unruly brows, Langston's eyes had twinkled, amused. He'd lowered his voice to a gravelly whisper. 'Some years later, a maid suddenly fell or jumped – or was pushed – over the balcony. Broke her neck. And then, in the fifties, well . . .' His eyes had narrowed, drifted across his study.

'What?' she'd pressed him. 'What happened in the fifties?'

He'd drawn a dramatic breath. 'Well, these things happen, even today.'

What things? She'd waited for him to explain.

'Sometimes men run amok. They snap and release pent-up aggressions on to their family members.'

'Professor, what happened?'

'Well.' He'd cleared his throat, reached for a pipe. 'The man of the house – Fredericks was his name. One night, he simply hacked his wife and three children to death. Damaged the walls a bit, too.'

Carla had felt a chill, held her breath.

'But it worked out well for me; I was able to acquire the place for a very reasonable price afterwards.' Professor Langston had smiled slyly. Pleased with himself.

Carla, of course, didn't believe in ghosts or haunting. As an archeologist, she believed in history. In science. And so, despite the professor's grisly tales, she was thrilled at the opportunity to work with him, cataloguing the massive and disorganized collection of artifacts he'd accumulated in digs from Peru to Pennsylvania over the course of some five decades. Now in his seventies, Professor Langston had decided to write his will. And the Archeology Department, hoping that he'd leave a generous part of his conglomeration to the university, had offered to pay a graduate student to help him get it organized and itemized.

And that graduate student, Carla Prentiss, welcomed the income that came with the assistantship, not to mention the chance to see – to actually touch and examine – rare Pre-Columbian relics. So she overlooked the dusty cobwebs, eerie history and damp chill of the house. Not for the first time, she shook off the sense that she wasn't alone, and focused on the crate in front of her.

Utah.

An hour before dark. Maybe there would be time to do this one crate, depending on what was inside. Probably, it wouldn't take long. It wasn't heavy, might not have much in it. Glancing again at her watch, she reached for a lever to pry up the lid. As she wedged the tool in-between slats of wood, the light shifted. A shadow fell over her from behind.

'Professor?' She turned, expecting to see him. But, of course, he wasn't there – Professor Langston hobbled with a cane. Made thudding sounds as he walked. Carla listened, heard no footsteps. Nothing. Just her own breathing and the silence of dust.

Uneasy, Carla surveyed the storage room. Saw nobody, just rows of metal shelves holding oddly shaped packages. Stacks of wooden crates and cardboard barrels lining the walls. The door slightly ajar.

The row of cut-glass windows, revealing slivers of orange and red treetops, a gray cloud crossing above them.

The cloud – that was it. It must have blocked the sunlight for a moment, casting a shadow, darkening the room. That was all. She needed to relax.

Reinserting the lever into the crate, Carla pushed down on it to force up the lid. Her stomach growled with the exertion, complaining that she'd skipped lunch. Reminding her that it was her turn to cook dinner. Curried chicken with apricots. She could almost smell it.

Or no – wait. The smell wasn't her imagination. Nor was it curried chicken. What was it? She sniffed the crate where she'd loosened the lid, got a whiff of wood shavings and musty air. She straightened, sniffing, but couldn't figure out the source of the scent, so she continued her work. Inserting the lever on the other end of the crate. Pushing until the lid came up with a squeak of resistance. Or was the floor creaking? Carla looked around again. The smell was stronger. Musky and warm. Smoky. Sweet. Like incense? Or cheap cologne?

She thought of that starlet – Chloe somebody? The one who'd disappeared years ago, whose ghost might live in the walls. Oh God, was she smelling Chloe's stale perfume?

Ridiculous. Even so, the hairs on Carla's neck stood on alert, and she shivered at the idea. Probably, she reasoned, the odor was drifting up from downstairs. One of the professor's sons must be burning incense or scented candles. Or some exotic wood in the fireplace. That was all.

Calmer, Carla turned back to the crate just as another shadow fell over her. Not a cloud, this time. No, this shadow flickered from over head. And something darted above her – a bird? Lord, was there a bird trapped in the room? Cautiously, Carla looked up to see a tiny creature, flapping its wings, disappearing behind a beam high on the ceiling.

Damn. A bat? The house had bats? Cringing, she reached for the light switch and flipped it on. Examined the ceiling again. Saw no sign of the thing, couldn't see where it might have escaped. But, fine. Bats were harmless. They ate bugs, didn't they? Weren't they a sign of a healthy ecology? In an old house like the professor's, they probably weren't unusual, probably came out as the sun went down. No reason for alarm.

A little on edge, Carla continued her work. Carefully, she lifted the lid, set it on the table beside the crate. And looked inside.

When the first blow struck, she went down hard, her head banging the table. She tried to get up, but she was dizzy, blinded by pain. Carla huddled, protecting herself, trying to escape sharp swiping blows. Twisting, she had the impression of a large cat – a jaguar? Or no. A man? She crawled, kicking, and, even as her flesh tore, she told herself that the attack was not possible. There was no such thing as a man who was also a cat. But this not-quite-man-not-quite-cat kept ripping at her. Digging at her chest.

Fading, Carla had three final thoughts. The first was that she never should have stayed to open the Utah crate.

The second was that she was having her final thoughts.

The third was that, damn, she wouldn't get to have that curried chicken.

October, 2011

At first, they didn't hear the banging. Maybe they mistook it for loose garbage cans clattering around in the driveway. Or maybe it got lost in the screaming howls of wind that gusted against the house, buzzing through cracks in the window frames, drowning out all other sounds.

Vicki Manning, clearing dinner plates, waited for the wind to subside before speaking. 'Wow. That was almost as loud as Trent's snoring.'

Harper Jennings laughed, nodding. She'd heard those snores; Vicki's husband could shake walls when he slept.

'Need. Putty. Fix.' Hank Jennings put down his wine glass. He'd cooked again, had become quite adept in the kitchen in the last year. 'In. Sulate. Before winter.'

'Put it on the to-do list.' Harper picked up a salad bowl, planted a kiss on his cheek on her way to the kitchen sink. She had become accustomed to Hank's speech; he had aphasia due to brain injuries from a fall from the roof. Most of the time, she understood his meaning perfectly, and she'd convinced herself that his speech was steadily improving.

Vicki took Hank's dish. 'The pasta was yummy, Hank. Thanks.' She'd been eating with them on Tuesday nights while Trent taught an evening class. 'You should open a restaurant—'

Her voice was drowned out by rapping sounds and another anguished groan from the windows. Tree branches blew against the house, scraped against glass panes.

Hank shook his head. 'House com. Plaining. Old. Arth. Ritis.'

Indeed. The house was old, over a hundred years. And he and Harper had been renovating it, by themselves. To Harper, the process seemed endless, as if every job they completed led to ten more. But, with Hank's aphasia making him unable to teach, the endless work wasn't so bad; rehabbing gave Hank a focus. Something positive to work on.

Vicki poured herself the last of the wine as Harper washed pots and pans, gazing out the window into the darkness. Hedges, firs,

branches of the oak tree bent to the wind. Night came early, felt
stark and dangerous. But lights from the fraternity house next door
spilled into the yard, defining shapes. Reminding her that she was
safe, that the shadows held no snipers. That she was home in Ithaca
not back in Iraq, surrounded by war and terror.

'Where's a towel? I'll dry.'

'There was one on the—' She stopped mid-sentence, interrupted
by loud banging. It didn't sound like the wind. It came from the
front door.

'Trent maybe?' Hank turned toward the sound. The dish towel
was draped on his shoulder.

'Can't be,' Vicki glanced at the clock. 'He's still teaching.'

Harper grabbed the dish towel off of Hank, tossed it at Vicki as
she headed for the door. The banging grew louder, more rapid. Urgent.
Harper hurried, hearing shouts.

'Harper? Are you in there?'

She didn't recognize the voice.

Harper stopped beside the door, cautious. Old instincts, trained
responses.

'Who?' Hank came up behind her, limping slightly.

Harper turned on the porch light, peered through the window. And
saw Zina Salim. Zina Salim? Really? Why? But there she was, her
hair flying in the wind, her dark eyes wide. Her fist raised to pound
some more.

Harper swung the door open, and Zina rushed in, watching over
her shoulder, repeating, 'Thank God. Thank God. Couldn't you hear
me? I thought you'd never answer.'

Harper was speechless. But what was Zina Salim doing there? She
and Zina weren't friends; they politely tolerated each other. Within
the Archeology Department, they were staunch rivals, earning their
PhDs under the same professors. Competing for assistantships, fellow-
ships and teaching assignments, attention. And annoyingly, whatever
Harper applied for, Zina Salim seemed to get. She was politically
connected, the darling of the department – especially of Professor
Wiggins, the graduate coordinator. There had been rumors, and more
than once, Harper had wondered if a romance were involved.

'Thank God, Harper,' Zina breathed, rushing into the house.
'Thank God you're home.'

'Come. In.' Hank welcomed her, scanning the front yard before
shutting the door.

Zina was trembling as Harper led her into the living room, where Vicki stood staring, sipping her wine. 'Here, sit down. What happened, Zina? Are you OK?'

Panting, Zina sank on to the sofa, covered her face with her hands.

'Zina?' Harper watched her.

Zina hugged herself, silent and shivering. She seemed small, childlike. Harper pulled an afghan off the arm of the sofa, wrapped it around Zina's shoulders and sat beside her. Zina stared warily at Vicki.

'This is our friend, Vicki Manning,' Harper reassured her. 'Vicki, this is my colleague, Zina Salim.'

'Warm get. Now.' Hank threw some logs into the fireplace. Added some kindling. Zina watched him, transfixed, fingering an ornate bangle bracelet.

'What's wrong with her?' Vicki mouthed.

Harper shrugged, rolled her eyes. She thought Zina coy, manipulative. Affected, with her British accent and aristocratic attitudes. For everything she did, she seemed to have an ulterior motive. Harper didn't trust her, doubted she'd reveal her actual purpose for coming over. But clearly, she was frightened.

Hank's fire blazed, toasting the room. Zina watched the flames, became more collected. 'Better now?' he asked.

'Thank you,' Zina attempted a smile. She slipped her bracelet on and off, nervously. 'This is so nice of you, opening your home to me.' She spoke in a sweet, controlled tone. 'I'm better now. Probably I was overreacting. I mean, obviously, I was. Just being silly. I hope I didn't interrupt your—'

'What happened, Zina?' Harper cut in.

Zina looked away, stared at the fire. Harper, Hank and Vicki stared at Zina. Moments passed. Finally, Zina turned to Harper.

'Harper,' her eyes were doubtful. 'Do you believe in the Nahual?'

'The Nahual.' Harper repeated.

Zina nodded, eyes shifting.

'In what?' Vicki asked.

'Shape-shifters.' Harper watched Zina, tried not to smirk.

'No – I know it sounds crazy. That's why I said I was overreacting. It was nothing—' She attempted a laugh, failed. Started to stand.

'Uh uh.' Harper grabbed her arm, pulled her back to the sofa. 'You're not leaving until you explain what the hell you're talking about.'

'Tell us.' Hank took a seat by the fire, waiting.

Vicki stepped closer. Zina's face reflected the fire. She looked from one to the other and finally caved, sinking back against the cushions.

'You'll think I'm making it up.'

'Just tell us.'

She drew a breath. Let it out. Drew another. And began. 'It was . . . I was at work. At Langston's house.'

'Cataloguing?' Harper had applied for that assistantship, a plumb opportunity to document the late professor's expansive Pre-Columbian collection. But Wiggins had selected Zina. Of course.

'Yes. Cataloguing.' Zina pushed hair off her face, still playing with her bracelet. 'But when the sun went down, the air – all of a sudden, it shifted. It actually moved. I felt someone there. Behind – or maybe in front – of me. I heard owls hooting. Dogs barking. And I smelled something – like incense. Smoky and musky . . . And then wings were flapping—'

'Wings?'

'I swear. Like the wings of a bat.' Zina nodded, her face ghostlike, flickering orange. 'And boards – the floor was creaking. Someone was there. I looked but couldn't see anyone. And then, real low, I heard growling – soft and threatening, like a large cat about to pounce.' She stopped, checking their faces as if afraid they'd laugh at her.

Three faces watched her in firelight, not laughing.

'Then the lights flickered and suddenly – they went off. I stood, ready to run, but I smelled the thing in the dark. I couldn't see it, so I turned, feeling for it, and then something brushed my face – something furry. It was right up next to me – it growled right into my ear, so close that I felt its breath on my neck. I *smelled* it, like raw meat. I don't know what happened next. I ran – flew out of the room and down the steps, out of the house and into my car. Before I knew it, I was speeding back to town. On the way, I saw your lights were on . . .' She looked at Harper, then Hank, then Vicki. Back at Harper. 'You all think I'm nuts, don't you?'

Everyone shook their heads, no. Politely. Even sympathetically.

'Of course we don't.' Harper knew all about panic, wasn't about to label it 'nuts'. She put a hand on Zina's shoulder. 'Whatever happened, real or imagined, you're safe. It's good you stopped here.'

'I did not imagine it.' She sat up straight, panting again.

'Breathe,' Harper ordered. 'Take deep slow breaths.'

Zina gazed around the room. Met their eyes directly, one pair at a time. And she took deep breaths. 'It was real,' she insisted. 'But they don't know the significance, do they?' She motioned at Vicki and Hank.

'Significance of what?' Vicki asked.

'Of the animals that were there. The bat is a sign of death. The owl represents the underworld; it's a messenger of the dead—'

'Oh, come on, Zina,' Harper interrupted. 'That's just mythology.'

'And the large cat – the jaguar – is the most revered and powerful of all animals. A symbol of power.'

'Since when? Sorry. That's just—' Vicki began.

'It's symbolism.' Zina insisted. 'Each of the animals has meaning. And I was surrounded by powerful symbols of death.'

For a moment, nobody spoke.

Finally, Hank stood. 'Get drinks. All of. Us.' He headed for the kitchen.

'So? What do you think? It couldn't really have been a Nahual. There is no such thing, right?' Zina blinked at Harper.

'No. Of course there isn't,' Harper tried to answer as if the question were rational. Obviously, Zina had been frightened. But was she seriously asking if she'd encountered a Nahual?

'So how do you explain what happened? If not a Nahual, then what was it?'

'Here's what I think. You've been working alone in that spooky old mansion. The wind was howling, the boards were creaking, and the moon was full. You know about the house, what's happened there, so your imagination was predisposed to think scary thoughts. In the dark, it took off—'

'No, Harper. I swear to you. It was *not* my imagination.'

Harper tilted her head. 'Zina. Are you seriously saying that a bat or an owl changed into a jaguar and growled at you?'

'OK.' Zina's cheeks were ruddy from the warmth of the fire. 'OK, no. I mean, I know better. Even so, what I told you was real. It happened.'

'Zina.' Harper's voice was flat, definite. 'Whatever happened, it wasn't a Nahual. There is no such thing.'

Vicki lowered herself on to the cushioned chair beside Harper, leaned over. 'Will you please explain what you guys are talking about?'

Harper turned toward Vicki. 'Remember that research position I applied for – the one where the professor died, and they needed someone to document his collection of artifacts?'

Vicki nodded. 'Of course I remember. You were pissed that they passed you over and gave it to the bitch you think is sleeping w—' She stopped short, her mouth forming an 'oh'.

Harper cleared her throat; Zina stared at the flames, handling her bracelet. She didn't seem to have been listening. 'Anyway, Zina got the position. She's been working on the collection for a few weeks, all alone in the professor's isolated old house.'

'So the floors might creak by themselves,' Vicki suggested. 'And with nobody living there, animals might have moved in—'

'How do you know there's no such thing?' Zina was still focused on Harper's comment. 'I mean, maybe there is. Because if it wasn't a Nahual, then what was it? How else can you explain it? Wings flapping, a big cat growling, fur and claws – and that smell . . .'

For a moment, Harper almost laughed; she thought Zina must be kidding. But no. Zina showed no signs of humor. 'Zina. Shape-shifters are mythological creatures. They're legends. Nothing more.'

Zina looked away, back into the fire.

'Shape-shifters?' Vicki asked. 'What?'

'They called them Nahuals. Pre-Columbians believed in shaman-like creatures that could take almost any form they wanted. They could change into men, large cats, dogs, deer, bats. Owls. Whatever shape they needed to protect their people or defend their territory—'

'Or their possessions.' Zina's voice was low. 'Their artifacts.'

'Seriously, Zina,' Harper began. 'Try to be—'

'Hot. Rum. Buttered.' Hank carried a tray of mugs and spice cookies.

The fire crackled; the drinks were warm and boozy. And Zina, warmer and relaxed by the rum, repeated her story to Hank.

'Ghost,' he concluded. 'Pro. Fessor. Haunting. House.' His eyes twinkled playfully.

Vicki grinned. 'Of course – he's probably changed his mind about donating his precious relics and wants to scare Zina away.'

'Cut it out.' Harper didn't see humor in Zina's fear. 'Nobody's haunting anybody. Nobody's shifting shapes. It's just – suggestion.' Harper put down her mug, thinking of the best way to explain. 'Look, Zina – it's like I said before. All those stories about the house, the history of the place – that's what's haunting you, nothing else.'

'Stories. What?' Hank asked.

Harper picked up a cookie and crossed her legs. She looked at Zina. 'You want to tell them?'

Zina emphatically shook her head, no.

So Harper began. 'In 1989, when Professor Langston first decided to will his collection to Cornell, he hired a young woman to catalogue it. One night, just before Halloween, the research assistant—' Harper stopped as the wind screeched through the windows, interrupting, as if to prevent her from going on.

'The research assistant got mauled to death,' Zina finished when the wind subsided. 'And the killer cut her heart out.' She didn't look at Harper. She set her bangle bracelet down on the table, picked up her mug and gulped hot buttered rum.

'Well, we're not sure about her heart. But, yes, she was killed.'

'No. She was *mauled*. As if by a jaguar. Or a mountain lion. And her heart was dug out. Get your laptop,' Zina insisted. 'Let's Google it and I'll show you.'

In moments, the four were huddled around the screen, reading newspaper accounts of a mystery over two decades old.

Carla Prentiss had been found early Halloween morning, set out at the end of the professor's long, wooded driveway, positioned as if on display under a tree. Her wounds were extensive, and there was a lot of blood, so much that at first police didn't notice the hole in her chest where her heart should have been.

'See that?' Zina crossed her arms. 'They took her heart, the same way Pre-Columbians took human hearts—'

'But that's my point,' Harper interrupted. 'You got spooked by that horrible old crime. It's almost Halloween again – the anniversary of that murder. And you had that story in the back of your mind—'

'Read on,' Zina interrupted. '"Because of the missing heart, Professor Langston speculated that the murder was designed to resemble the work of a mythological shape-shifter who would sacrifice the hearts of enemies to the gods, or eat them to acquire their strength."'

'Yuck, they ate them?' Vicki winced.

'Read it for yourself.' Zina went on. 'Even Langston thought there was a Nahual—'

'Bull. Shit,' Hank interrupted. 'No such. Thing.'

Vicki was still reading. 'Hmm. It says that, for a while, police suspected the professor's Brazilian housekeeper. Oh, wow. He was having an affair with her, and she was jealous of the attention he paid to the dead girl. And there was another suspect – a kid who hung around with the professor's sons. His family pulled him out of school and sent him abroad.'

'OK, Vicki. We get it.' Harper was watching Zina, saw her biting her lip, holding her stomach.

'No.' Vicki wasn't finished. 'Wait, listen. That house – wow.' She looked up from the computer screen. 'Did you know about the family that lived there before the professor? The dad killed his wife and kids. With an axe. And he slit his own throat.'

Hank leaned over her shoulder, reading.

'And before that, a silent film actress disappeared there. Wait – oh, man – did you know the house has hidden passageways—'

'Vicki, enough. You're not helping.' Harper closed the lid of the laptop; the articles disappeared.

Hank scowled. 'Was reading.'

Zina cowered.

'OK,' Vicki sighed. 'I get why you're scared, Zina. That house has some bad karma.'

'Karma? Oh please, Vicki.' Harper was dismissive. 'It's just an old house, like this one, just bigger. The professor raised his family there – three sons, right? A couple of them still live around here. Nothing out of the ordinary has happened there in what? Twenty years? More? Not since the murder.'

'Maybe that's because the professor locked the collection up. No one's even looked at it since that assistant got killed.' Zina curled herself into a ball. 'Until now.'

The fire crackled. Harper began to argue, but Zina cut her off. 'No – now I've gone and messed with the relics again. So that shape-shifter thing that killed the last researcher is back. And, I swear, whether you believe me or not – if I hadn't run out of that house tonight, they'd have found my body tomorrow with my heart cut out, just like hers.'

The fire crackled, but for a while nobody spoke.

Then Vicki tried to help. 'But Zina. Think about it – that murder was so long ago. The killer would be an old man by now – if he's even still alive.'

'A Nahual doesn't age—' Zina began, but the wind moaned again, drowning out her voice.

When it stopped, Hank stood. 'Get. More rum.' He collected their cups and went to refill them.

'Actually, Vicki's right.' Harper chewed another cookie, 'Carla's murder might not have had anything to do with the relics. Someone might have just made it look that way.'

'Come on, Harper. Why would they do that? Who would follow ancient rituals and cut out someone's heart, just for fun? It has to be about the artifacts. They're cursed – lots of relics are. That's a known fact.'

'She's right,' Vicki agreed. 'Remember that story about Montezuma's gold? Trent and Hank told us about it. The gold was cursed, too.'

Harper scowled. 'Vicki, that's ridiculous. That's just a legend.'

But Vicki ignored her, turning to Zina. 'Back in 1910 or so, divers found a skeleton, deep in a lake. The thing was sitting up at the entrance to a cave, as if he were guarding it – I think it was somewhere in Mexico.'

'No, it was in Three Lakes Canyon,' Harper corrected. 'In Utah. And that story is bull, besides which it has absolutely nothing to do with the professor's collection.'

'Yes, it does. It's an example of how stuff can be cursed, Harper. People thought the skeleton was guarding gold, so they dug a tunnel to excavate it, but they all came down with a mysterious fever and died.'

'No, Vicki.' Harper closed her eyes, sighing. 'The only fever that those people got was *gold* fever. Nobody died.'

'Yes, they did.' Vicki sat up straight, eyes wide; her voice husky and low. The room was in shadows except for the fire, and its light flickered, dancing ghostlike on her skin. 'Then, divers went down to look but came up, terrified, refusing to go back. They said they'd been chased away by translucent figures without oxygen or diving gear. Spirits, protecting the gold. One diver swore that a figure had tried to choke him, and when he took his gear off, they saw hand marks on his neck—'

'More rum!' Hank bellowed.

Harper jumped; Zina gasped. Vicki let out a shrill yelp. Startled, Hank juggled the tray, trying not to spill the drinks as the women dissolved into bouts of laughter.

'What?' He steadied himself. 'Scared crap. Out of me.'

'Sorry, Hank,' Vicki caught her breath. 'There's a lot of that going around.'

'Nonsense,' Harper insisted. 'Zina, pay no attention to Vicki's story. Gold is just a metal; relics are just old things. And whatever happened to you tonight, there's a logical explanation. No curse or spirit or Nahual was involved.' She grabbed another mug of rum and took a drink.

By the time Harper walked Zina to her car, the wind had died down. The night was quiet. Music no longer blared from the fraternity house next door.

'You're sure you want to go with me?' Zina asked. 'You don't really have to. The professor's sons usually come around in the daytime, and I'll be sure to leave before dark.'

'No. I'd love to come. I've been dying to see his collection.'

An awkward silence reflected that Zina had gotten the position that Harper had wanted.

'You know, you should have gotten the position. They only gave it to me because of my family. The business.'

'Business?'

'My family trades antiquities, so Professor Wiggins thought I'd have more experience handling relics. I mean, I've worked with them since I was a child.'

Oh really? 'Well, it doesn't matter. I'd just like to see it.'

'You realize that nothing is actually on display. All the pieces are packed up. I go box by box, identifying things, piece by piece. And half of the items aren't where they're supposed to be.'

'But Zina, maybe being there together, we'll be able to figure out what happened tonight.' Harper was sure that something tangible – maybe just the noise of the wind or a flicker of a shadow – had frightened Zina. That her imagination had taken over only after some real event had triggered it. 'Look, I've had a lot of experience with fear—'

'Oh, right. With Iraq and all.'

Harper nodded. Yes. With Iraq and all.

'But this is different. It's not a war – it was something unearthly. Unnatural.'

And war was earthly and natural? 'The point is that fear sets off reactions that aren't always appropriate or rational. If we explain what frightened you, you might not be afraid of it any more.' Lord, she sounded like Leslie, her shrink.

Zina looked away, into the night. Unconvinced. 'I know you don't believe me. But it was there. It was real.' She turned to get into her car, but Harper stopped her.

'Look, Zina. We don't know each other very well. But I've had my share of scare. And I can tell you that perceptions – what we think is happening – can be misleading.' Harper recalled a white flash, a blast, the feeling of flying through the air. Closed her eyes to shove the memory away. 'Just because something flies like a bat and has fur like a cat doesn't mean that it's a Nahual.'

Zina met her eyes, seemed defeated. 'Thanks for tonight, Harper. I know you mean well. And I'll be glad for your company tomorrow. But please don't try to convince me that I imagined everything. I was there. You weren't. I know what I know.'

With that, she opened the door of her electric-blue Smart Car, got in and drove away. Harper watched until the tail lights faded into the night. Then she went back to the house, finished clearing up. And noticed Zina's silver bangle bracelet on the coffee table.

Oh well. Harper popped it into her bag. She'd see Zina in the morning; she'd give it back to her then.

Vicki left after the dishes were done. And a while later, Harper finally crawled into bed, curling up against Hank.

'Think?' he asked.

Think? Harper considered the question.

'Zina.' Hank clarified.

Oh. 'I'm not sure. But clearly, something spooked her.'

'But bat. Cat. Man? Nuts.'

He was right. Zina's story sounded nuts. Then again, Harper, suffering from Post Traumatic Stress Disorder, had seen ambushes, explosions and suicide bombers, had smelled gunfire and heard shots fired where there had been none, and her flashbacks had seemed real, as real as the bed she was lying in. As real as the silence of her reply. Hank's dismissal of Zina's perceptions felt personal, as if he were somehow dismissing hers, as well.

'What. Say. Your mind.'

'Just because you don't perceive something, Hank, doesn't mean it's not there.'

In the lamplight, she saw his eyebrow raise. 'Nahual? Hoppa. Really.' His eyes danced, laughing. Mocking?

'No. I don't mean a Nahual. But something.'

'Shadows.' Hank chuckled. 'Hallow. Ween. Ghosts. Nerves. Stories. Just.' He put his arm around her, kissed her forehead.

'It seemed real to her. She was terrified.'

'Nothing. Her mind. Weak. Zina.'

Wait, Zina was weak? Because she'd been frightened by her own mind?

'Sleep. Love.'

Harper leaned up, returned his goodnight kiss. And lay there, not sleeping, not moving. Cuddling against Hank, she tried to disregard both the weight of his judgments and the heaviness of his arm.

By morning, Zina was mortified. Goodness. Had she really gone running to, of all people, Harper Jennings, the person who probably disliked her more than anyone else in the entire Archeology Department, and told her – admitted to her out loud – that she'd been scared off the Langston property? That she'd thought she'd encountered a Nahual? Really? Oh my. If that got back to her family, they'd kill her. And, if it got around the department, she'd never get over it. The gossip would ruin her career before she even started it. Rumors would fly. She'd be the brunt of countless pathetic not-even-funny jokes. She imagined them. 'What "shape" are you in today, Zina?' Or 'The Jaguar agency called; your Nahual's ready.' Stupid, stupid jokes.

OK. Never mind. She'd been in worse situations. She'd correct this one before it got out of control. Go to work and act as if nothing had happened. Actually, she'd go early and be there, fully composed and engrossed in her work, when Harper arrived. Goodness, how had she ever agreed to allow that woman soldier to come to work with her? As if she needed a combat officer to protect her and hold her hand. As if she couldn't manage on her own? Everyone knew Harper had wanted the Langston job, that she'd been jealous when Wiggins had given it to Zina. And now, Harper might use this incident to make it seem that Zina needed her help. Well, nothing doing. When Harper arrived, Zina would make light of the night before. Yes – she'd avoid being the brunt of jokes by laughing; she'd make fun of herself before anyone else could. And she'd be immersed in her work, too busy to do more than briefly show Harper around, pointing out the stacks of crates, letting her ogle a few relics. Then she'd send her on her way. Making it clear that she was in charge.

Zina showered, dressed, ate a stale donut, and got into her little blue Smart Car, trying to recover some sense of dignity. There had to be logical explanations for everything that had happened. It had to have been the darkness. Creaking floors were normal in old homes. As were bats. And the lights? Well, the wind had probably blown down a wire. And the wind might even explain the feeling of fur – might have blown small pieces of fiberglass insulation into the room. Or, more likely, a cobweb or some packing paper had blown against her skin in the darkness. The wind, after all, had been terrible; tree branches had been blown down, now lay scattered on the road.

Her panic had simply been an overreaction. All she could do now was damage control. She'd explain it to Harper and hope the woman was decent enough to keep it to herself, not make her a laughing stock. But that wasn't likely; if the situation were reversed, she would certainly think the story was hysterical and share it with everyone. Oh dear.

The whole way to the Langston house, Zina considered what she'd say to Harper. How she'd convince her that she was fine, that her behavior the night before had been no big deal. That she'd been more amused than frightened – yes. That was it – she'd say that she'd stopped by Harper's house to share an odd but amusing anecdote. Like, would you believe it? Langston's house has its own Nahual. Haha. Isn't this a good spooky story for the week before Halloween?

She turned off Route 96 on to the long dirt road leading to the professor's driveway. About forty yards up, she stopped. A huge branch had toppled, blocking the way. Damn. She sat for a moment, considering her options. No way she could go around it; even her tiny car wouldn't fit between its top end and the trees. She could wait there for Harper; they could ride her motorcycle the rest of the way. Or she could park right there and walk the mile or so to the house.

Finally, Zina decided to get out and try to move the branch, to shove it just enough that she could drive around it. And if that didn't work, if it was too heavy, she'd park and walk.

Moving to the thinner end of the branch, she lifted her feet, stepped carefully through the tangle of twigs and lingering yellow leaves, took the central stem into her hands. She realized that moving without tripping on the foliage would be difficult; it might have been easier to grab the heavier, less dense end. Somewhere close, she heard the hooting of an owl. And, in the periphery of her vision, she saw something move. A man? No, something that looked like a big cat.

When her phone rang the next morning, Harper was straddling her Ninja, checking to make sure she had Zina's bracelet with her before leaving for Professor Langston's. She almost didn't answer it. But her new ringtone, the sound of a gong, kept chiming, and she realized the call might actually be from Zina. Maybe she needed to change the time. So, opening her storage compartment, she pulled out her big leather sack and felt around inside, finally locating the phone.

'Is this Harper?'

Not Zina. A man. Not a familiar voice.

'Who is this?'

'Is that you, Harper? Lieutenant Harper J. Reynolds of the United States Army?'

Harper tried to ignore a sudden rumble of gunfire. She took a breath. Looked around at her house, the gazebo in the yard. 'Who's calling?'

'Don't tell me you don't recognize my voice, Lieutenant. Honestly?'

She didn't. Or damn, no – maybe she did. It was smooth, liquid. Not quite deep enough. Sounded like – Burke Everett? But they hadn't talked in years, not since before the explosion had killed her patrol and sent her home, half dead. Why was he calling now? And how had he gotten her cell phone number? 'What's up, Everett?'

He laughed, triumphant. 'See that? I knew you wouldn't forget me.'

'It's not for lack of trying, trust me.'

'Same old Harper – still a ball-buster. How the hell are you?'

Harper looked at her watch. Almost nine. But the time made no sense; her mind whirled, trying to make sense of the voice in her ear. Images blurred. The air changed, felt dry and sandy, and she had the urge to check her bag for her gear – ammo, knife, goggles, sun block, water bottles, baby wipes . . .

'You survived that suicide attack – I knew that. But how are you now?'

How was she? Burke kept talking, not waiting for an answer. Harper tried to process what he was saying, but his words were too fast, made no sense. She pictured him in uniform, heard him whining about the heat. Or the flies. Or the dust. Or the duty, whatever was bothering him at the moment. Burke Everett? After all this time?

'. . . because, I'll tell you what – I'll be in Ithaca Thursday. Day after tomorrow. It would be great to see you. You know, to catch up.'

What? No. No, it wouldn't. Harper swallowed. 'I don't know, Burke. I'm pretty busy—'

'Actually, thing is – it's kind of important. I need to talk to you about something. How's dinner Thursday night?'

Wait. Dinner? 'Burke, I'm married.' The words popped out of her mouth, unplanned. As if she'd assumed he'd wanted a date. Harper felt her face get hot.

Burke was laughing. An unpleasant, high-pitched sound. 'Well, congratulations. But I'm not asking for your hand. Just for dinner.'

'I didn't mean—'

'How about drinks then? A beer. Or lunch. Or coffee. Or frozen yogurt.'

'What do you want to talk to me about?'

He paused. 'It's not for the phone. Seriously. It's big. And I need to talk to you in person.'

A squirrel raced by, ran up a tree. Harper stared after it as it disappeared into dwindling orange leaves. In Iraq's stark sands, she'd missed the trees, the colors of summer and fall. She pictured it, that final patrol. Watching a car speed up to the checkpoint. Seeing a woman in a burqa crossing the street. And then, the sensation of flying through heat and fire. She remembered it clearly, even the smells of smoke and burnt flesh, but her memories were just that: memories. Not flashbacks. Everett's unexpected voice had stirred up the past but hadn't entirely revived it. It wasn't engulfing her. At least, not yet.

'Harper? You there?'

'Yes.' Well, sort of.

'I'm just asking for half an hour – an hour at the most. You'll understand when we talk.'

She didn't answer. She tasted sand, felt it coating her sweaty skin. Heard Burke's voice only vaguely. Maybe she'd been too hasty deciding she wasn't having flashbacks.

'. . . wouldn't bother you after all this time . . . wouldn't have come all the way from Milwaukee . . .'

'Fine.' Harper closed her eyes, bit her lip, concentrated on the pain of teeth puncturing skin to avoid falling into the past.

'Fine?'

'Yes. Fine. I'll meet you Thursday. Three o'clock. Ithaca Bakery.'

'Great, Harper. I'll be there—' Burke began. But Harper ended the call, tossed her phone into her bag and zoomed off on her Ninja before he finished his goodbye.

Harper roared downhill through the edge of town, heading out along Lake Cayuga, thinking about the phone call. Trying to figure out what Burke Everett wanted. In the war, he'd been a wimp. A tall, lanky guy, always keeping his head down, bucking tough details. Complaining even about the easy ones. Not someone she'd want protecting her back. Not someone she'd spent much time with.

So why was he calling her now? It had been – what? Seven? Eight years since she'd seen him? What could he want?

Harper didn't want to think about Iraq. Didn't want to remember. She'd spent years trying to recover from her injuries, still had a bad leg. Not to mention the flashbacks. She'd been better lately, not having as many. Leslie, her shrink, had helped, had shown her how to diminish their intensity, employing scents, sensations or sharp flavors to keep focused on the present. She wondered if Burke Everett had flashbacks. No, probably not. Burke hadn't risked much, usually had soft duty, chauffeuring visiting brass through the Green Zone or base camps. He'd never been wounded. Had never seen his buddies blown up by IEDs or suicide bombers. Again, Harper saw the woman crossing the street, approaching the detail of soldiers at the checkpoint. White heat flashed, and Harper felt herself fly.

But this time, she was flying past the lake, not through the air. And the noise was the engine of her Ninja, not bursts of explosives. She needed to stay grounded. In the moment. To focus on colored leaves. Traffic. The cloudless sky and crisp air. Anything except Iraq.

Her mind, however, remained on precisely that. The past. And the unexpected reappearance of someone she'd almost forgotten. Someone she'd chosen not to stay in contact with. Why had Burke Everett called? What could he possibly want? Harper was so intent on those questions that it wasn't until she turned on to the unpaved road leading to the professor's long rocky driveway that she gave a thought to Zina and the relics, the reason she was there, racing along a darkly overgrown path in the middle of nowhere.

She hoped that Zina would be waiting outside, that she wouldn't have gone into the house alone after her panic the night before. On the other hand, maybe Zina felt better, wasn't as shaken now that it was daylight. Looking up the curved narrow road through the trees, Harper tried to spot the house up ahead, wondering about its history. The missing actress, the murdered family. The dead research assistant. Zina's fear.

Engrossed in her thoughts, Harper sped ahead. She almost didn't notice a mass of electric blue just off the narrow road, half hidden by trees. Almost didn't bother to glance back to see what it was, a color that didn't belong. Almost didn't turn and go back to investigate.

But when she did, she barely recognized the heap of mangled metal as the little blue Smart Car that had been Zina's, smashed against a thick old oak.

Harper jumped off the bike and raced to the wreck, shouting, calling Zina's name. She tore through trees, around shrubs and over undergrowth. Twigs snapped underfoot like sniper fire, but Harper ignored them, kept moving until she could peer through tangles of foliage, broken glass and twisted metal. Only when she saw what was left of Zina, her blood-drenched body slumped beside the car, her eyes fixed on nothing . . . only then did she stop and stay still.

The air smelled of oil and blood. Harper stared; sweat poured down her torso. And somewhere, guns began firing. Men cried out. No, she insisted. Not now. But, even as she told herself that the fighting around her wasn't real, that it was a flashback, she ducked low to the ground, dodging bullets, feeling them whizz past her ears. Guns popped. Smoke clouded her vision. Someone screamed. She reached for her weapon, couldn't find it. Realized that, damn, it must be back with her gear. So half crawling, half scooting, she made it back to her Ninja, pulled out her leather bag, reached inside for a pistol, found a phone. Dug some more. And pulled out a lemon.

A lemon? She blinked at it, forcing herself to remember what it was doing in her gear. A voice deep in her head commanded: *Bite it*. Bite it? The lemon? But wait – a woman was crossing the street, her hand reaching inside her burqa, and a green car was speeding toward the checkpoint. She knew the explosion was coming, needed to warn the patrol . . . *Bite it!*

Harper jammed the lemon into her mouth and chomped; sour acidic juice spilled on to her tongue, startling her. Overpowering her mind. Making her focus on taste. On the moment. And suddenly, the checkpoint, the car, the woman suicide bomber – the war faded away, leaving Harper alone on the wooded path to Professor Langston's, a phone in her hand, a lemon in her mouth. And, a few feet away, Zina, dead, huddled beside her car.

Lights and sirens. Sirens and lights. Harper sat on a large rock, watching as police and firemen and medical technicians scurried around. The coroner's van pulled up. A tow truck. A television crew. She didn't know what to do, where to be, so she stayed off to the side, huddling. Trying to understand what had happened. Zina had to have been speeding, must have lost control of her car and hit the tree. Must have crawled out, injured, and died. But why had she been speeding? What was her hurry? Was she being chased, maybe? Here? On this unpaved back road? Something nagged at her about Zina's body. She was almost sitting up. And there was so much blood. Not much, if any, inside the car. None visible on the seat. What had caused her to bleed so much?

A man wandered over, balding, maybe in his forties. Tall, lanky. Prominent cheekbones. Wearing jeans, a tweed blazer. He nodded in her direction, stood watching the commotion. Hands in his pockets.

'Hell of a thing.' He didn't look at Harper, kept his eyes on the wreck.

Harper didn't answer. But he was right; it was a hell of a thing.

Finally, the man turned to her. 'Angus Langston.'

Langston. One of the professor's sons? Angus held out his right hand. As if introducing himself at a social function.

Harper shook the hand. It was large and lean, smooth-skinned. 'Harper Jennings.'

Police and EMTs huddled around Zina's body.

'So, Ms Harper Jennings, they tell me you're the one who found this? You called it in?'

Harper nodded.

He nodded, silently watching the scene. After a while, he looked at her. 'Well, if you don't mind my asking, Ms Jennings, what exactly brought you here to this spot this morning?'

Harper opened her mouth to reply, but Angus continued. 'Being as this is private property. A private road. Which would make you a trespasser.'

Wow. Harper's mouth was still open. She closed it, stunned. Zina was dead, her body still crumpled beside battered blue metal, and this guy was bothering her about her presence on his property? Slowly, deliberately, she stood to her full five foot three-and-almost-a-half inches, assumed an officer's stance.

'You live here, Mr Langston?' She used her most authoritative military voice. Had to arch her neck to meet his eyes. 'In the professor's house?'

Her tone surprised him; he took an instinctive step back. 'No, I stay in the cottage. But where I sleep isn't your concern. The house and property belong to me and my brothers.' He shifted his weight, eyed her. Lost some bluster. Looked away.

'Look, I'm aware that this is private property,' Harper continued. 'But I am not trespassing. I was invited here.'

His eyebrows rose. 'Really. Because I sure don't remember inviting you. And I doubt my brother invited you—'

'Actually, I was invited by the woman over there.'

Angus crossed his arms. 'Well, that's interesting. Because the fact is, that woman didn't have the right to invite anyone here. It's bad enough she was here, wandering around. Which by the way, she didn't have the right to do. Now she's brought you. Next, everyone and his uncle Fred will be here.'

'Hey, Mrs Jennings? Harper?'

Harper turned. Saw a face from the past. Detective Charlene Rivers. She shut her eyes, opened them again. Still saw the detective approaching, walking across the road. Not a flashback. Rivers was actually there. Oh God. Memories swirled: a student jumping out of a window. Another, dead on her front porch . . .

'I saw your Ninja over there.' Rivers smirked. 'I thought I was done dealing with you.'

Harper nodded. 'Good to see you, too, Detective.' She rubbed her eyes, pushing away bloody memories. She hadn't had contact with the Rivers since that debacle with stolen drugs over a year ago.

'Who's your friend?' Rivers eyed Angus Langston who introduced himself just as another news van pulled up the road.

'Aw, hell,' he scowled. 'Who the fuck let them on the grounds? Doesn't anyone understand the words "private property"? What's next? Rock bands? Concession stands? What is this, goddam Woodstock?' He stomped off toward the television van.

'Friendly guy.' Rivers watched him, turned to Harper. 'So tell me. What are you doing here? You know the victim?'

Wait, the 'victim'? Harper drew a breath. Looked across the road to the empty coroner's gurney awaiting Zina's body. And, as she began to answer, remembered that Detective Rivers was in homicide.

What was a homicide detective doing at the scene of a car accident?

Rivers and Harper walked along the road, heads down, voices low, as Harper summarized the events of the night before. Gravel crunched underfoot; the air smelled of dry leaves. 'So basically, you're saying that your friend was afraid for her life?'

'I guess. But she wasn't entirely rational, at least not at first. She thought a Nahual was after her. But Nahuals aren't real.'

'So you think it's just a coincidence that the very next morning she's dead?'

Harper shrugged, shook her head. She had no idea. 'Detective, what are you saying? That Zina was murdered?'

Rivers stopped walking, looked back at the crash site. 'Truth is, I don't know what I'm saying. I have to wait for the coroner's report before I draw any conclusions. All I know is I heard the dispatch that there was a fatality out at Langston's, so I came out to see what went down.' She looked at Harper. 'You know about this place? The history?'

'Some.'

'Then you know what I'm talking about. This dead woman was a researcher for the university. Just like the last dead woman way back in – I think it was eighty-nine? That's the kind of thing that sends alarms bells off in my head. I don't believe much in coincidence.'

Somewhere nearby, an owl hooted. Odd. An owl, in daytime? Weren't they nocturnal? Owls were supposedly one of the Nahual's favorite shapes. Ridiculous. But maybe not to Zina. In fact, maybe Zina had seen an owl – or even a deer or a fox. Or a large cat. Maybe she'd thought the animal was the shape-shifter again, coming after her, and she'd panicked, smashed her car into a tree. It was possible.

Damn. Harper should have arranged to drive with her, not to meet her at the house. If she had, Zina would still be alive. Far away, guns fired; Harper felt snipers watching her from the shadows. She scanned the ground for IEDs. The detective was still talking.

'. . . press will go bonkers, especially now at Halloween time with all the ghosts this house supposedly has. So I wanted to see for

myself. Find out what really happened. And, frankly, after talking
to you, I'm not happy.'

Oh dear. 'Why?'

The detective shifted her weight, sighing. 'Harper. People do not
normally freak out and claim that someone's trying to kill them.
And, even when they do, they don't normally die within hours.
Unless someone was really trying to kill them.'

Oh. That was why.

'No. My gut tells me this car accident is wrong. This woman
didn't just floor her gas pedal and drive into a tree. And, superficially?
Her heavy bleeding from the chest, those wounds seem wrong for
a car accident.' Rivers sighed, shook her head. Looked at her feet,
then back at the car. 'No. I can't prove it, at least not yet, but this
woman, Zina Salim? I'd put money on it: she was murdered.'

Rivers had been right about the press. Instantly, the news media
focused on Zina's death, presenting it not as a tragic accident, but
as just the most recent of a long list of bizarre occurrences at the
old house. By the six o'clock news, tales of the missing actress, the
fallen maid, and the murderous father gone amok were resurrected
along with that of the mutilated former research assistant. Anchors
indicated that the huge house was haunted or cursed, noting that
none of the current owners actually lived in it, speculating that they
didn't dare reside under its roof.

Hank was not pleased. He turned off the television, glowering.
'Dead. Fault. My.' His eyebrows furrowed.

Trent had stopped by for Happy Hour. He poured Scotch. 'I'm
not sure I follow. You're saying it's your fault that the woman drove
into a tree?'

'Came here. Help. Asked.'

'Stop it, Hank.' Harper felt bad enough without Hank's help. 'This
isn't on us. What were we supposed to do? I was going with her to
the house. I was on my way—'

'Not. You, Hoppa. I. Man. Can't.' He swallowed his Scotch and
stood. Eyes fierce. 'Can't. Man. Do.' His fist tightened. 'No use.'

'That's not true—'

'What's he saying?' Trent broke in. 'That he's useless? Come on,
Hank – you're strong as an ox—'

'There was no way either one of us could have foreseen or
prevented what happened.'

'—you've come a hell of a long way since last year.'

Harper and Trent spoke together, reassuring Hank, but he wasn't listening. He turned and stomped away, wobbling slightly.

Harper was on her feet, following, calling. 'Hank – wait.' She caught up to him, took his arm.

'No, Hoppa.' He resisted, pulled himself away. 'Me. My. Self. Lone.'

Harper let him go, and hugged herself, stunned. Hank had never before pushed her away. Her chest hurt when she took a breath. Trent walked over to her, concerned, smelling of Scotch, asking if she was all right. And as she lied, nodding, and saying, 'Of course,' they heard the front door slam.

Trent poured himself another Scotch. 'What's going on? He's not himself.'

Harper wasn't sure what was going on. But she didn't want to discuss the possibilities, not even with Hank's best friend. She sat on the sofa, picked up her glass.

'Are you two all right?'

What? 'Of course – yes.' The question surprised her. Did Trent think there were problems? Did he know something she didn't? 'Everything's fine.'

'Well, it's got to be tough.' Trent stared into his glass.

Tough?

'Hank and all. Now. You didn't sign up for this life.'

Really? What was he saying? Trent had been there when Hank had fallen off the roof. Before that, he'd been Hank's colleague in Cornell's Geology Department. They'd been inseparable, had taught, consulted, conducted research, published articles, even climbed mountains together. But now, Hank could barely speak and had trouble moving on his right side while Trent had become a tenured professor, secure in the lifestyle to which Hank had aspired. And Trent thought that was 'tough'?

Harper's jaw tightened. 'He gets frustrated.' So did she. Frustrated, sad and tired. The day already seemed endless, and it wasn't even dinner time.

Trent drank. 'But he seemed to be doing so well.'

'He *is* doing well, Trent.' Her tone was sharp. 'He's doing incredibly well.'

Silence.

'I didn't mean that he wasn't doing well.' Trent tried again. 'I just meant I've never seen him resentful about his condition before. Not that I blame him – he has every right to—'

'He's adapted amazingly well.' Harper wasn't going to discuss Hank behind his back. 'He's entitled to take a moment.' She tried to convince herself. Remembered the shock of his bear-like body shoving her away.

'Of course. We all need that sometimes.'

The moment strained; Trent had come for a drink with Hank, not awkward and self-conscious exchanges with Harper.

'Well . . .' they both said it at the same time. Both stood.

'I ought to get home.'

'Vicki must be waiting.'

A quick hug, and Trent took off. Harper sat on the sofa, drinking Scotch, until half an hour later, when Hank reappeared.

'Eat.' He went into the kitchen, took out some eggs.

Harper followed, started chopping onions and tomatoes. Neither of them mentioned Zina or the part they had or hadn't played in her death. Neither referred to Hank's stomping out of the house. They cooked an omelet, ate it quietly and washed up. But they had no real conversation, and Harper, unwilling to be pushed away, didn't even try to touch him for the rest of the night.

Emails and text messages regarding Zina's death flooded the Archeology Department, whose faculty and graduate students assembled in Goldwyn-Smith Hall on Wednesday morning to share their shock and sadness, and to discuss the prospect of a memorial service. They met in a lecture hall, about twenty people huddling in a couple of rows surrounded by a hundred empty seats. Professor Wiggins, Zina's advisor, began by extolling Zina's spirit. Phillip Conrad, a PhD candidate, said he'd arrange to have the service held in the Annabel Taylor chapel. Professor Schmerling, temporary department chair, offered to provide an organist and a tenor. Marge Thomas, one of the secretaries, volunteered punch and cookies.

Harper's attention drifted; she hadn't slept well, tormented by images of Zina's mangled body and disturbed by Hank, who'd tossed and kicked all night. She didn't volunteer for any of the committees, didn't offer to read or to select readings, or to order floral arrangements, or to help print a program with Zina's photo and biographical material. She felt distant from the others, unable to participate. And when the meeting finally broke up, she was the first one out the door, dropping a twenty into the memorial fund; it seemed a trivial amount, but it was all she had in her bag.

'Harper – hold up a minute, would you?' Professor Schmerling called to her from the front of the lecture hall.

She stopped, felt caught. Like a kid trying to skip class. 'Of course.' She turned and smiled, watching him approach. Wondering what he wanted.

'Do you have a couple of minutes?' He looked troubled. Weather and life had carved lines deep into his face, and his half-lenses rode tentatively on the middle of his nose.

Actually, she'd promised Hank she'd take him shopping for work boots. 'Of course . . .'

'Because – here. Let's sit.' He led her to a back corner of the hall, away from the others.

They sat. He looked at her closely. His eyes were dark, probing. Harper tried not to squirm.

'So, how are you doing? I understand you were there, at the, uh, scene. You found her; correct?'

Oh Lord. He wanted details? That's why he'd stopped her? Harper nodded. 'Yes. But I'm all right. Thank you for asking.' She started to get up.

'Wait! Sorry, that's not actually what I want to discuss – although, believe me, I do care about how you're doing; don't misunderstand. I imagine it must have been quite terrible to find a colleague that way. Or anyone, really. It would have had to be . . .' He fumbled with words, reddened, looked away. Folded his hands. 'Nonetheless. Well. As they say: life goes on.'

Harper had no idea what Schmerling was trying to say. 'Yes. It does.' She didn't know how else to respond.

He looked at her again, smiling sadly. 'Good. I'm glad you agree. Because, under the circumstances, what I'm about to say might otherwise seem, well, indelicate.' He paused, cleared his throat. 'Harper. I'd like to know if you're still interested in the Langston research assistantship.'

The Langston research assistantship? Harper's mouth opened. Speechless.

'I'm aware that you'd applied for it last summer, but that it was assigned to Ms Salim. But now that she's unfortunately – that is to say, tragically – unable to complete it, I'm . . . The department and the university are hoping you'll be willing to take over.'

Harper's head tilted; her mouth dropped. 'Professor, Zina just died yesterday. She hasn't even been buried.'

'I'm aware.' He stiffened. 'Do you not think I'm aware of that, Harper? I told you it would seem indelicate, didn't I? Nevertheless. The fact remains that Professor Emeritus Langston has left the university his entire priceless collection of Pre-Columbian artifacts, gathered over a distinguished fifty-year career, and, regardless of your or my own personal grief and sympathies, that collection still requires the careful and meticulous attention of a knowledgeable, qualified person so that it can be documented accurately for probate, insurance and tax purposes.' He stopped for a breath.

Harper didn't move. She watched him for a moment. 'With all respect, Professor, what's the hurry?'

Schmerling cleared his throat again. Crossed his legs. Looked over at his colleagues and students lingering across the lecture hall. Finally, he faced Harper. 'I'll be completely candid, but our conversation is confidential, agreed?'

She agreed.

'There has been some . . . reluctance among the Langston family to adhere to the terms of the professor's will.' He paused. 'Speaking plainly, the sons are planning to challenge it. They're claiming that Langston was ill, physically and mentally impaired when he drew up the will, that he left his collection to the university while suffering paranoid delusions, and so on. Naturally, their claims are completely without merit, but the university would like to be aware of exactly what is included in the collection, given that the sons have access to it until we actually take possession of it, which we want to do as soon as we can, but might not be able to do if the sons contest the will. In fact, any day now, they might even prevent us from examining the collection because it's on premises willed to them.'

Harper thought of Angus Langston, his indignation that she was on his property.

'So, as insensitive as it seems to press onward, the sooner the cataloguing can be completed, the better. As you know, the terms of the assistantship are generous – your tuition and fees would be covered completely for the term. Professors Hayes and Wiggins would advise you. Frankly, Harper, you're the best-qualified candidate for this. The university needs your help. All else aside, it's a golden opportunity for you, and I'd consider it a personal favor if you'd accept.'

He watched her, waiting. Did he expect her to answer here? Right now?

'Have I overwhelmed you?' He smiled. The lines on his face deepened, became crevices.

'Just a little.' Harper tried to absorb what she'd just heard. She wanted the assistantship, but so soon? Wouldn't grabbing it so quickly be like profiting from Zina's death? 'It's a lot to take in.'

'Not really. All you need to think about is the work itself. Documenting the collection. Any chance you're still interested?'

God help her and Zina forgive her, yes, she was interested. Extremely, avidly, passionately interested. Pre-Columbian symbolism was a focus of her dissertation – the only part of her PhD still to be completed. Of course, definitely yes, she wanted the position, was thrilled at the chance to accept it, to see and examine and touch precious rare artifacts. She couldn't imagine them, couldn't wait to begin. And couldn't say so, not there at the meeting to plan Zina's memorial. Harper sat perfectly still. She opened her mouth, but words wouldn't come out.

Professor Schmerling waited. Cleared his throat. 'Well, I understand that you'll want to think about it. Especially under the circumstances . . .'

Harper nodded, relieved.

'Why don't you sleep on it? Let me know tomorrow? Or as soon as you can?'

She nodded again. What now? Was she supposed to thank him? It didn't seem appropriate, since the offer had resulted from Zina's death. And he'd labeled it a 'personal favor'; she shouldn't thank someone for asking her a favor. Still silent, unable to figure out what to say, she stood when he did and grabbed her bag.

'I'll call you tomorrow, Professor,' she managed. And hurried for the door.

Harper had walked to campus that morning, feeling restless. In the morning, sunlight had sparkled on red and orange leaves; the breeze had been gentle and warm. But the walk home, just an hour later, was different. The sky had darkened with heavy gray clouds, and the air chilled her. Not only that; the long walk had stressed her left leg. Her war injuries tingled and ached, her leg threatening to cave under her weight.

Slowly, carefully, she made her way to the Suspension Bridge, heading home, replaying her conversation with Professor Schmerling. Absorbed in her thoughts, Harper paid little attention to the Big Red band, practicing for the weekend's Homecoming, marching toward her across the Quad. Students gathered along their path, listening, singing. Sometimes cheering. Harper took a breath, not in the mood for marching bands or team spirit or fun. Even so, as she walked away, she found herself moving in time to a fight song. Drumbeats marking her steps, urging her on.

Crossing the bridge, she didn't make her customary stop to take in the view of the gorge. Didn't pause for even a glance at the rocky walls or gurgling stream below. She simply wanted to get home and talk to Hank about the offer. To think about it someplace quiet and calm.

Approaching her house, though, she realized that it would be neither. Rock music blared, electric and grating, from the fraternity house next door. Members were outside, decorating for Halloween, hanging skeletons from trees, building a fake cemetery in the yard. Planting plastic hands beside Styrofoam headstones, making it look like the dead were clawing out of their graves. Frat boys tottered around, imitating Zombies. Partying. Starting the Homecoming/ Halloween weekend on Wednesday morning.

'Beer?' One called to her in greeting.

Harper smiled, waved. 'Too early for me.'

'Early? I thought it was late – we're still going from last night.' He grinned, turned away.

She limped to the mailbox, took out a pile of mostly junk mail and headed to the house, wondering if Hank was ready to go boot shopping. Noticed an envelope hand-addressed to her.

Postmarked Atlanta. Who did she know in Atlanta? She stopped for a moment, staring at the envelope as if it would explain itself. Not recognizing the handwriting. Then, stuffing the rest of the mail into her big leather bag, she opened it.

Inside was a newspaper clipping. Harper unfolded it, saw an obituary column. With one notice circled: Peter Murray. His picture was there, looking handsome and young. In uniform.

Harper froze, staring at the photo, reading and rereading, trying to understand. Peter Murray. He'd died on October fifth, 'suddenly'. Suddenly? What the hell did suddenly mean? A car crash like Zina? An overdose? A heart attack? A gun to the head? What? She pictured him, back in Iraq, hanging out with Burke Everett. Pete was polite, a gentleman. Almost an anachronism. Opening doors for women, offering his jacket in the cold. Never sitting until women sat. Never cursing or telling a dirty joke in mixed company. Blushing when she did both. Pete Murray was dead?

Harper stood in the front yard, oblivious now to the music blaring next door, not noticing the raucous frat boys rough-housing not twenty feet away. She was absorbed, reading and rereading a death notice. Remembering Burke's call. His insistence on seeing her. Obviously, the call and the death were connected. In fact, Burke had probably mailed her the obituary. Probably wanted to talk about Pete, his death. But that made no sense; he could talk to her about that on the phone. Why did he need to come all the way to Ithaca? Burke was from Milwaukee. How could he have mailed the envelope from Atlanta?

Nothing made sense. Not the letter, not the call, not the offer from Schmerling, not Zina's death. Harper was puzzled, troubled. Her leg throbbed; she needed to sit. To collect her thoughts. Heading into the house, she held on to the obituary as she set the mail and her leather sack on the foyer table.

'Hank – I'm back.' She passed the living room, limped down the hall. Passed the kitchen, looked in. Didn't see him. Heard nothing. 'Hank? You ready to go?' she called again, approaching the study. No Hank. Where was he? Oh God – had something happened?

Her heart skipped, and she saw him again, lying in the hedges, his head cracked and bleeding . . . But she kept moving, out of the study, up the stairs, past the nursery, the spare room, going into the bedroom.

'Hank?' she stopped at the door, staring at the bed.

Hank didn't answer. He just lay there, his face blank, watching her.

'What are you doing in bed? It's noon. We're supposed to go get you new boots?' She went to the bed, sat beside him. Rubbed her nagging leg. 'Are you OK?'

Hank stared ahead at nothing. 'Fine.'

Obviously, he wasn't. His eyes were dull, not twinkling.

'What's wrong? You never stay in bed all day. Come on.' She stopped rubbing her leg, tugged at his arm.

He didn't resist. Didn't react at all. When she stopped tugging and let it go, his arm dropped like a stone.

'Hank? Stop. You're scaring me. Get up.'

He blinked, not moving. 'Get. Up.' He finally repeated. 'Why?'

'Why?' Harper sputtered, searching for a reply. But she couldn't find one. Because, other than to follow a conventional routine, there really was no reason for Hank to get up.

She sat on the edge of the bed, silent. Seeing his point of view. Why, after all, should he bother? What was there for him to do? He didn't drive any more. Had trouble walking long distances. Didn't work. Couldn't even do chores, given his weakened right side. Maybe he was sick of going with her to the grocery store or the farmer's market. Of tinkering alone on the house, laying tiles in the bathroom and painting walls, remodeling the house. Of being disabled. Of not being able to speak and live his life the way he wanted to. And, if he were sick of all that, no one could blame him.

She pictured him, the old Hank. The way he'd been before the accident. A hiker, a swimmer, a runner. An athlete in top physical condition. She looked at him now, lying slack against his pillows, felt a familiar pain ripple through her. God, she missed him.

And if she missed the old Hank, Hank certainly must miss him more. The man had every right to mope. When he'd fallen, he'd lost everything: his career as a professor, his ability to speak, his agility, his goals . . . hell, his sense of self.

Harper moved closer, lay down beside him. Listened to his breathing.

'We're lucky.' She lifted his hand, kissed it.

He turned his head, scowling doubtfully. 'Not. So. Much. Useless. Should have. Died.'

His answer stung. He wished he'd died? Really? No matter what he'd lost, they still had each other. Wasn't that worth living for? Harper remembered her fear at almost losing him. Watching him fall from the roof. Seeing him unconscious. Waiting through the days of his coma, the weeks of intensive care. The months of intense therapies – physical, speech, occupational, psychological, experimental. And suddenly she felt not just gratitude, but almost painfully intense joy that he was still there, warm and alive, alert enough to be depressed by his condition. Well enough to mourn his lost self.

'But we are lucky.' She propped herself up on an elbow. Touched his stubbly cheek with her free hand. Turned his head and planted a kiss on his lips. 'We have each other. And I love you,' she whispered, kissing him again. 'Even more since I almost lost you.' And again. 'Even more since I see how strong you are, every day.'

And she kept it up, kissing his mouth, his cheek, his neck, his chest. Moving down his body and not stopping until he wrapped his arms around her and lifted her to meet her mouth with his. Even then, she didn't let go. She hung on to him with all her strength, as if her love could pull him out of his grief and sadness and make him want to live.

It seemed to work, too, even though it didn't get him out of bed. They lay there together, tangled in each other's arms, legs entwined, Harper's clothes lost in the sheets. Bodies relaxed, eyes closed.

'Mad.' Hank finally sighed. 'I. Can't man. Be.'

'If you were any more of a man, you'd kill me.' Harper grinned at him.

He didn't smile. 'Man. Keeps. Safe. Prot. Tects.'

Of course. This mood was about Zina. That he hadn't been able to help her.

'Friend. Your. Asked help. From.' He paused, licked his lips. Struggling with words. 'I was no help. Now dead.'

Harper kissed his shoulder. 'It wasn't your fault, Hank. Nobody could have predicted what happened.'

'No. Not able.' His body tensed as he repeated. 'Not able. Me. Not. Self. Gone.' His tone was factual, flat. Not maudlin. Not emotional. He kissed her forehead.

Harper wanted to console or encourage him. But what could she say? That he was wrong? That he hadn't changed, that he was still fit and strong and could do whatever he wanted? Enter triathlons? Compete in Iron-man? No. The truth was that his life had changed. A lot. Resting her head on his shoulder, she sighed, feeling helpless. Searching for words. Finding none. Harper lay silent, wondering if either of them would ever get out of bed.

But they did get up. Soon, Hank made an announcement: 'Food.'

In a flash, he was on his feet and in the shower. Then downstairs, cooking. It wasn't until Harper was halfway through a stack of pecan and banana pancakes that she thought about the events of the morning. The envelope containing Peter Murray's obituary. And the offer of the assistantship from Professor Schmerling.

She wanted to talk with Hank about both. But, given his earlier mood, she didn't expect that Hank would welcome either topic. At the moment, mentioning Pete, yet another dead acquaintance, didn't seem like a good idea. But maybe Hank would see the assistantship as a good opportunity, despite the reasons it was available. Maybe she just had to present it positively.

'Pancakes are incredible.' She chewed, assessing his mood. He seemed less bothered. But his eyes seemed altered, as if looking inward. Lacking their usual laughter.

'Secret.' He swallowed. 'Batter.'

Really? She tasted it now, a trace of liquor. 'Cognac? You're a genius.'

'No.' He shook his head. 'Magi. Shun.'

Good. Hank was feeling better. So why was she hesitant about talking to him? Usually, they were completely open with each other. She should just go ahead and tell him about the offer; Professor Schmerling wanted a quick reply. Harper took a breath, swallowed. Opened her mouth to speak.

'Boots.' Hank began at the same time.

'Hank, there's something I—'

'Go buy? After we. Eat.'

Harper paused. 'Sure. As soon as we're done.'

'Hoppa. What? You were saying?'

Harper put her fork down. Looked at her plate. She might as well just tell him. 'Professor Schmerling took me aside after the meeting this morning.'

Hank chewed, listening.

'He wanted to talk about Professor Langston's collection. He said Langston's family is contesting the professor's will – something like that. So the university wants the collection documented before the lawyers put a halt to it. Which means as quickly as possible.'

'And?' Hank's eyes darkened. He stopped chewing.

'He asked me to take over Zina's job.'

Hank's eyes were cold, stone-like. He didn't move. Didn't say anything.

'He apologized for offering it so soon after Zina's death. But the work needs to be done, and he needs an answer.'

Hank remained silent.

'Look, it would pay my tuition for the whole semester. And I'd probably be able to apply some of the work to my dissertation research.'

Still nothing from Hank.

Harper kept talking. 'The thing is, someone has to do it. And I'm the most qualified of the available grad students, and it's an unbelievable opportunity to work with those actual artifacts, even though, obviously, it's terrible what happened.'

'Know. You.' Or maybe, 'No. You'?

'What?'

'Do. What you. Want. Will.'

Harper crossed her arms. 'What's that supposed to mean? I'm talking to you about it because I want to know what you think before I do anything—'

'No. You. Know. Already made mind. Up.'

'Not true. That's not fair.'

'OK.' Hank pushed his plate away. 'Hoppa. You want my oh. Pinion?'

'Of course I do.'

He scowled, crossed his arms. 'Job. Not good. Bad. Karma. Juju. Vibes.'

'Seriously? Karma? Juju? Vibes? How about shape-shifters? Nahuals? You didn't mention *them*.'

'See. You did know. Do what. You want. Told you. Thoughts. My.' He stood, picked up plates.

'Hank, am I supposed to turn down a great opportunity because you think its bad luck? Because of superstitions? You know we can really use the money.' Especially now that he wasn't working, but she stopped short, didn't say that. Didn't have to.

'Not money only. About.' He turned to face her, dishes in each hand. 'Choice. Yours. Not mine. I'm hus. Band. Not your boss.'

He was right. If he told her not to take the job, she'd resent him for trying to control her. She needed to decide on her own. And, actually, she had. Talking about the artifacts had reminded her how badly she wanted to work with them and convinced her to accept the assistantship.

Harper followed Hank, carrying cups to the sink. Then, as he washed the griddle, she put her arms around him and squeezed. He allowed it, but didn't stop washing. Didn't return the hug. Harper moved away, wondering if she'd been wrong to tell him about the offer. If he was getting depressed again. If her new opportunity was reminding him of his own lost ones. Still, she had a right, even a responsibility to accomplish as much as she could. In fact, she ought to call Schmerling and make it official. Find out when she would start.

She started into the hall to get her phone. But Hank turned off the water, dried his hands and came with her.

'Boots.' He announced. 'Go and buy. Now?'

And they did. Heavy-duty Timberland's. They joked about the frat boys next door. Discussed the music, costumes, Halloween candy, the weather, what they'd have for dinner. But Harper didn't tell Hank about Pete Murray's obituary, and for the rest of the day, made no mention of Zina or the assistantship.

Vicki's hair was darker. She'd rinsed it again, a bluish shade of maroon. 'Are you fucking nuts?' Coffee splashed out of her cup as she set it down, gaping at Harper.

Harper bit off the tip of a bacon slice.

'You're crazy. There is *no* way you should take that job.' Apparently Vicki agreed with Hank.

'Too late. I already called him to accept.'

'So? You can call him back.'

'Why? Vicki, it's a great position. I get to work with actual relics and—'

'And the last two people who did that are dead, Harper. How is it that you do not get that?' Vicki shook her head, looked out the window of State Street Diner where they'd met for breakfast.

'No one's going to hurt me.' Harper shoveled a wad of French toast into her mouth. Chewed. 'Look, you yourself said that whoever killed that researcher twenty some years ago is either old or dead now. And—'

'I said that to calm Zina, who is now dead. Dead, Harper. I saw how scared she was about working there. And now she's dead.'

Vicki sounded like Detective Rivers. 'In a freak car accident. It had nothing to do with the research assistantship.' Besides, Harper was a trained combat officer; she could take care of herself.

Vicki sputtered. 'You asked my opinion. I gave it.'

'The university needs the documentation.'

'If the university is so hell-bent on documenting that collection, they can move it to university property and post security guards.'

'They can't take it anywhere until the will is settled.'

'Fine. Then let them wait until it's settled.'

'But the brothers might mess with it unless it's catalogued. Besides, settling the will could take years; who knows where I'll be then.' Clearly, Vicki, a dentist, had no idea how rare an opportunity Harper had been offered. Not a clue how thrilling it would be to work with rare, Pre-Columbian treasures.

'What did Hank say?' Vicki stuck her chin out, a non-verbal challenge.

Harper hesitated.

'I knew it. Hank doesn't want you to do it either.'

'I didn't say that.'

'Then tell me. What did he say?'

Harper mumbled her answer. 'Basically, he said it was up to me.' Well, not really. Really, he'd indicated that she wouldn't listen to his opinion. That she would do what she wanted to do regardless. That, once again, he felt powerless.

Vicki shook her head again, leaning on her elbows, watching Harper. 'No one who loves you wants you to do this.'

Harper hid behind her coffee cup. They were silent for a while. Finally, a gong rang inside Harper's bag. Harper reached in, dug around for her phone.

'That's your new ringtone?' Vicki frowned.

The gong continued while Harper rifled through keys, flashlight, water bottle, Zina's bangle bracelet, wallet, baby wipes, pens, tampons, chapstick, sunblock . . . Damn, where was her phone? Maybe it was Professor Schmerling's office, calling about paperwork. Or maybe Burke Everett was canceling their coffee date.

But when she finally found her phone, caller ID announced Ithaca Police Dept. And by the time she answered, the caller had hung up. She tried to return the call; it went to the switchboard. No way to find out who'd called.

'The cops are calling you?' Vicki wiped her mouth, dropped her napkin on the table. 'Why? Something about Zina?'

'Vicki.' Harper was losing patience. 'How can I possibly know why they're calling? No one was on the line.' She stared at the phone, trying to dismiss her ominous feelings. Telling herself that the caller hadn't been Detective Rivers. That Rivers' instincts hadn't been right; the Coroner's report hadn't indicated that Zina had been murdered. That the police didn't need to talk to her again.

But neither her feelings nor Vicki's chatter would let up. 'Something's wrong, Harper. You know what? I'm thinking maybe Zina's accident wasn't just an accident.' She paused. Then added, 'I'm thinking the police don't want you to take that position either.'

Harper was early for her appointment with Leslie. She'd been seeing her less often – every other week. Now that her flashbacks seemed under control and Hank's health had stabilized, she didn't feel an intense need for a therapist. Until today. Today, she couldn't wait for Leslie to open the door to her cozy, candle-scented, plant-filled inner sanctum with its green leather sofa and steaming sweet teas.

Waiting, she sat, breathed evenly, tried to clear her mind. To think of nothing. Not sure how to do that, not able to picture 'nothing'. So she envisioned an empty room, but Zina appeared inside it, her chest blood-soaked – no. She took another breath, started over. Closed her eyes. Counted, focusing on the numbers. One. She saw it, '1', straight as a spear, strong as an impaling rod. Great. She'd counted all the way to one.

Harper stood, began pacing around the tiny waiting room. Heard Detective Rivers saying that people didn't usually spend the night fearing for their lives and coincidentally end up dead the next morning. Heard Vicki telling her not to take the assistantship, Hank withholding his support. Hank. She worried about him. He was changing. Harper walked in circles, literally spinning. When would Leslie open up? What time was it, anyway?

Finally, the door swung wide, and warm green eyes and a cup of hot spicy chai greeted her. Harper took her place on the sofa beside Leslie and spewed words. About Zina's death. About the assistantship. About Hank.

'He was just lying in bed. Hadn't showered or shaved. He said he didn't see any reason to get up.' Unexpected tears welled in Harper's eyes. 'Which sounded like he didn't see any reason to live. He said he wasn't a man any more. That he couldn't help Zina, couldn't protect her or anyone else.'

Leslie tilted her head, nodded slowly.

When Harper blinked, a tear rolled down her cheek. She swatted at it, despised crying. 'I reminded him that it wasn't his fault, what happened to Zina. And that we're lucky that he survived. And that we still have each other. '

Leslie said nothing.

'And he seemed all right again, for a while. But when I told him about the assistantship, he got distant again. He said that the position was bad luck, but that it didn't matter what he thought because I'd do what I wanted to do anyway. As if his opinion was irrelevant. And the truth? The truth is he was right; I took the position even knowing he didn't want me to.'

Harper stopped. Realized that she was whining. These weren't survival issues. They were trivial, in the scope of life's calamities. What the hell? Why was she sniveling about her husband's moods, her job opportunity? She was tougher than that, Army strong. Not a self-pitying sniveler. And yet, here she was, sniveling the hell out of her hour with Leslie: oh, poor me. Look at what a bad time I'm having.

She began to back off, change the subject.

'No, Harper. Don't try to gloss over this. It's important.'

It was?

'Fact is I've been waiting for something like this to come up.'

Really?

'Sadly, the catalyst was the death of your friend, which we also need to talk about. But one thing at a time. First, let's focus on you and Hank.'

Oh dear. 'OK.'

'Frankly, I think it's a good thing that he's expressing his feelings. Given all that's he's been through, don't you think his attitude has been a little too positive this last year?'

Maybe. Yes, actually.

'Look, Harper. After his accident, the two of you went through incredible stress and anxiety. Both your lives changed dramatically, but – face it, Hank's changed far more than yours. He suffered physical losses like his speech, and professional ones like his professorship. Beyond that, he's inevitably coping with psychological and emotional issues. He's a strong guy, but he's still only human. How has his injury affected his sense of self? His identity? The fact is that Hank needs to rediscover himself and find out a new way to be Hank.'

Harper nodded. She'd known all that. She thought Hank had been working it out, that he'd find his new path with time. 'He's been dealing with all that. It's been over a year, and so far, he's been fine.'

Leslie paused, pursed her lips. 'Hank's had a lot of physical healing to do. That took his energy for quite a while. And you've said he's pretty macho, right? So I imagine he'd fight his emotions. He wouldn't let himself admit how powerless he feels, or how depressed. I mean, would he?'

No. Definitely not. Harper should have known, should have anticipated Hank's emotional reactions to his accident. After all, she'd been terribly depressed after her injuries in Iraq; she was still suffering Post Traumatic Stress Disorder. Why should she expect Hank to be any less vulnerable?

Obviously, because she'd wanted him to be. She'd wanted to believe he was basically unchanged. Still the old Hank.

Leslie went on. 'The fact is that to fully recover, Hank needs to go through this phase. He needs to see himself as he is, to mourn what he isn't any more, to accept what he's lost. He can't really heal or integrate what happened without allowing these feelings to emerge, however sad or angry or frustrated they may be. So in a way, it's a healthy sign that he's not pretending any more that everything's just dandy. He's admitting his emotions, and that's a big step toward coming to terms with what's happened.'

So Hank's depression was a good thing? Harper thought of his losses. Remembered him preparing a lecture, hiking up a mountain trail, setting up a tent in the woods. Whooshing past her downhill on skis . . . No. She couldn't go there. That Hank was gone.

The hour was almost up. Harper's chai sat untouched on the coffee table.

'Next time, we'll need to talk about your friend's death and that assistantship. But about Hank – given his tough exterior, I'd bet that he's struggling a lot more than he's letting on. I'd keep a close eye on him.'

She would?

'Make sure he knows that help is available. It's good that you remind him how important he is to you, but he's dealing fundamentally with himself, not your relationship. You can't fix it for him, Harper.'

Leslie's voice was soft but firm. She waited for her comment to sink in. Then added, 'I can refer him to someone. If he's willing. If he'd go.'

Oh God. Did Leslie think Hank was seriously in a crisis? That he needed professional help? 'What are you saying?'

Leslie paused, her eyes steady on Harper's. 'What I'm saying is this: you love this man. You helped him survive. Now, he's got to want to.'

On her Ninja, Harper roared down the hill, letting the chill air slap her. Thinking about Hank. How insensitive she'd been. How oblivious to his feelings. She'd been wrapped up in their life, getting it back, having him home. Continuing her PhD program as if he'd never been hurt. Pretending he was fine. How selfish of her. How superficial. How lonely he must feel.

Well, she'd make it up to him. She'd encourage him to explore new options. Maybe suggest he see a therapist? She pictured it. 'Hank, Leslie has a referral for you. A colleague who can help you.'

He'd resent it. He'd glare. Maybe snarl. 'You think. Need. I. Damned. Shrink?' And stomp out of the room. Slamming the door.

No. Better to be supportive. Wait and see.

Harper stopped for a red light. Looked around the intersection. Pedestrians crossing. Cars waiting. Leaves scattering the street, golden and red. The sky pillowed with purple clouds, foreshadowing winter. She closed her eyes, collecting herself. Focusing on the moment.

Almost time to meet Burke Everett. Damn, she hadn't even mentioned him to Leslie. Or Peter Murray's obituary. Who had sent it? And why?

The light changed. Harper rode, taking a long route to the Ithaca Bakery, concentrating on motion, the wind on her face, the chill of the air. Trying to think of nothing.

Burke had lost his swagger. He dashed into the Ithaca Bakery, looking over his shoulders, glancing out windows. Drawing attention to himself by trying not to. Spotting Harper at a table near the door, sliding into the seat opposite her.

'We should move.'

Not, hi. Not, good to see you. Not, you look great.

'Move?'

'To the corner.'

He was on his feet, leading the way. Harper followed. Burke positioned himself where he'd have the greatest view of the area: against the wall, facing the room, windows nearby. He looked around, satisfying himself that no one was watching him. Not the table of students across the room, not the elderly man reading the paper, not the guys behind the counter, not the construction workers buying coffee.

Finally, Burke's eyes stopped wandering, settled on Harper. 'You look good.'

'What's going on?' She pictured him back in Iraq. Complaining about the rations. Or the ninety-second showers. Or the heaviness of his gear. Complaining. Always. 'Why are you so jumpy?'

He snickered. 'So much for foreplay.'

'You didn't come all the way from Milwaukee for foreplay.'

'No.' He looked around again. Shifted in his seat. 'Thanks for meeting me.'

Harper riveted her gaze on him. He was practically quivering. 'You hear about Murray?'

Burke's eyes looked away, darted side to side. He hunched forward. Lowered his voice. 'You got the obituary? I sent it while I was there, down in Atlanta. For the funeral.'

Why was he whispering? The funeral was no secret. Burke seemed downright paranoid. Was he having a breakdown? Some vets had trouble adjusting to civilian life, lost their grip. He looked thin, gaunt. Maybe he should eat something. Aromas of fresh bread, sugar, chocolate and cinnamon surrounded them, closing in.

'Why don't we get some food?'

'No – don't get up. Just let's stay here a while.' More looking around. At the door. Out the windows.

'So you drove here all the way from Atlanta?'

He nodded. 'Couldn't risk buying a ticket. Look, I can't stay long. Gotta keep moving.'

'Burke.' Harper leaned back. 'I've got to say it: you seem – nuts.'

He let out a harsh, cough-like laugh, made a nervous, twitchy nod. And looked around again. 'Don't hold back, Harper. Tell me what you really think.'

'Why do you keep looking around? Are you paranoid? You think someone's following you?'

'Shh – not so loud.'

'Burke. No one's listening.' She picked up the sugar dispenser, looked underneath, pointed to the bottom of the glass. 'See? No wires. No bugs. No one's here but you and me.'

She wondered if he was dangerous. Delusional people could get violent. She readied herself, sat alert just in case.

'It's not a joke, Harper. Not after Pete. But you're right; I can see where you're coming from. I'm on edge.' His leg bounced, vibrating the table. 'But I'm not crazy. I swear.'

Harper said nothing, doubtful. Wondered what her responsibilities were, what she should – or even could do for him.

'You got to believe me, Harper; you're one of the good ones. I mean I think about the people I've known. There aren't many I can trust. No matter what, though, even in the worst times, I always knew – right from the beginning back in Iraq, at that camp outside

of Mosul – I could count on you. I knew that the first time I saw
you.'

He did? Harper tried to recall meeting Burke. Pictured him
sweating in his T-shirt, filling a Humvee's gas tank, swatting at flies.

'That's why I came to you. I swear this thing is out of control.
People are fucking killing each other.'

Harper watched him. 'Burke. I'm thinking you need to sign yourself into a VA clinic. Get some meds.'

'Fuck I do.' Another quick look around. 'OK. Let me explain.
James Henry Baxter. Remember him? Our detail?'

Their detail? The walls of the bakery faded; Harper recalled sweat
and sand coating her skin, the grumble of a Humvee's engine, a hot
white rocky road stretching out ahead. An ambush. Yes, she remembered. She'd been in charge of the special detail, driving the colonel
around Iraq. 'Sure. What about it?'

Burke smirked. 'We thought we lucked out, getting assigned to
light duty escorting Baxter. A real plum. You, me, Maurice Shaw,
Pete Murray and Rick Owens.'

The detail had lasted just one week. They'd taken Colonel Baxter
around so he could attend meetings, befriend local leaders, boost
troop morale, inspect projects and sites. Except for one minor skir-
mish, it had been nothing memorable.

'Turned out the duty wasn't so light – with that ambush. We saved
the Colonel's life.'

OK. So what? They'd saved the Colonel from a ragtag bunch of
insurgents who'd tossed explosives at their caravan. It hadn't been
all that difficult or memorable.

'Shaw never came home, you know. IED.'

Harper hadn't heard. 'Shit. I didn't know.' A flashback rumbled;
she saw a burst of white, felt herself flying on to the top of a burnt-
out car. Lifting pieces of her sergeant off of her belly. She bit her
lip hard, grounding herself with pain. Focused on the smells of
cinnamon and baking bread. Burke was still talking.

'. . . and now, Murray's bought it.'

Murray? Oh, right. The obituary. 'What happened? The obituary
didn't say.'

'Because they think he fucking killed himself.'

What? Pete Murray? He'd been in her unit. Handsome, in a gingery
freckled way. And good-natured, a gentleman even in war. Saying
please and thank you even when asking for rounds of ammo.

Promising to have people over for sand-free Sunday pot roast when
they got home. Never ever cursing, careful to say 'gosh' instead of
'God' . . .

'His mom found him on the end of a rope in her garage.'

Pete Murray had hung himself? Wow. But then, lots of war veterans
had invisible emotional and psychological wounds. Maybe Pete had
PTSD. Lord knew that could be deadly. If she hadn't found support
– if she hadn't met Hank and found help from Leslie – who knew
what would have happened? Maybe she'd have hanged herself, too.
Post Traumatic Stress Disorder could rip your mind apart. Could be
lethal.

'At least, that's what they say. But you and I know better.'

What? 'Wait. You're saying he didn't hang himself?'

'You knew Pete. He wouldn't impose on his family that way. No,
he would never off himself. Listen, Harper – you were Baxter's
temporary assistant. Think back. There were five of us in that detail.
Two are already dead. And one is the Colonel's personal
secretary.'

Interesting. Nice gig. 'Rick Owens? Owens works for the Colonel?'

'He's his fucking personal butt kisser. Which leaves just the two
of us loose.'

Loose? What the hell was he talking about?

'I'm getting some coffee. You want anything?' She started to
stand.

'Wait.' Burke grabbed her arm, stopping her. 'Remember when
he – when Baxter left? How we loaded the helicopter?'

Vaguely.

'Remember he had us transfer a bunch of crates?'

She thought back, felt the heat, the dust. Heard the Humvees'
motors. The deafening whirr of the helicopter's blades. And she saw
the men: Owens, Everett, Murray and Shaw loading it with supplies.
Knapsacks. And stacks of boxes.

'I remember. So?'

'So great. Would you testify to that?'

Testify? What? 'Burke.' She tried to sound non-judgmental. 'I
don't have a clue what's going on with you, but – honestly. You need
help.'

'Listen to me, Harper. Put it together,' Burke sputtered. He still
held her arm, tightened his grip. 'Jesus Christ. What do you think
was in those boxes?'

She shrugged. 'Supplies?'

His eyes were too bright. 'Guess again.'

Not supplies? What was Burke thinking? That the crates held drugs? Or – oh God – stolen artifacts? She'd heard about priceless ancient relics being looted from Iraq . . . But no, that was ridiculous. The Colonel's crates had been legit supplies. 'Burke, this is bullshit. Get help.' She removed his hand from her arm.

His whisper was raw. 'You know that Baxter started his own foundation. It sponsors some serious organizations. Militias and such. Survivalist stuff.'

Really? Harper doubted it; Burke was unbalanced. If he was right, Baxter's activities were surprising. Maybe even disturbing. But it was his right to sponsor organizations, wasn't it? This was a free country.

'Not just your usual survivalist groups, either. I'm talking dangerous people. People infiltrating high places. People who make all those skinhead militia extremist freaks look like your grandma's Canasta club.'

Actually, Burke sounded kind of like a dangerous extremist freak himself. What had happened to him? And why was he so fixated on Colonel Baxter?

His eyes gleamed. 'And now, guess what? Baxter is running for the United States Senate. State of Tennessee.'

So what? Again, even if it was even true, what difference did it make? What did he expect her to do about it? 'Burke. Seriously. What point are you trying to make?'

'Harper – he's funding the campaign with his own cash. Don't you get it? He's spent a few million so far.'

And? Wasn't that his right? 'So?'

Burke's eyes darted from the window to the door to Harper. 'Baxter didn't get rich on a military salary. And he didn't inherit any big money either. His dad was a high school history teacher. And he didn't marry money.'

'How do you know all that?'

'The Internet – you can find shit out about anybody.'

Harper sighed. She wanted to get Burke help but didn't think he'd allow it. 'So you're saying what? That Baxter got his money from Iraq? That he stole something?'

Burke smiled. 'Bingo.'

'What did he steal?'

He tilted his head, scowling. 'Money. Harper – the US sent billions over there to be used at the discretion of the military.'

She knew about it. Everyone did. The Commander's Emergency Response Program was set up to provide cash for local programs and projects. Funds were supposed to turn enemies into friends, sponsor local initiatives, counter the root causes of instability and marginalize extremist groups.

'Literally, billions are missing. Tons of crates filled with hundred dollar bills.'

'So you think Baxter dipped into CERP and he's using that money to fund his campaign?'

'And his lifestyle. And his foundation. Believe me, our Colonel is one ambitious and dangerous dude.' He looked around again.

Harper frowned. It was no secret that CERP funds had been badly managed. But Burke had no evidence. He was irrational, pooling together unrelated events, jumping to conclusions. 'I don't know—'

'You think I'm nuts.' His leg wouldn't stop twitching. 'Believe me – I thought it was fucking nuts, too, when Pete called to talk about it. But a couple weeks later, boom – Pete shows up on the fucking end of a rope. This is for real, Harper. A lot is at stake. You and I are in danger.'

'No, Burke. I don't—'

'We're the only ones left who knew about the theft!'

'Except that I didn't know about it. In fact, I still don't—'

'That doesn't matter, don't you get it, Harper? He *thinks* you know. Or that you *might* know. And he can't afford to have anyone knowing or even *maybe* knowing. That's why he hired Rick. He bought him off.'

Burke's eyes popped, pupils dilated. There was no point trying to reason with him. Harper let him go on ranting. When he finished, she simply asked, 'Bottom line, Burke. What do you want from me?'

He let out a long sigh. His eyes drilled into hers. 'I need to know that you'll back me up.'

Back him up? 'Back you up how?'

'I'm going to expose him. So if and when the time comes, I need to know you'll confirm what happened with the boxes. Testify that we loaded all that cargo at the Colonel's orders.'

'Burke, I'm sorry. I'm not agreeing to do anything until I'm sure what's going on. Because, frankly, I see not one real piece of evidence to back up your accusations. In fact, the only evidence I see here indicates that you need help and some serious meds.'

'I swear, I'll get you evidence.'

'Aren't you married, Burke?' She interrupted, redirected his attention. 'How's your wife?'

Burke's eyes narrowed. 'How'd you know about that?'

'About what?'

'Who told you?'

'Nobody told me anything. I'm just asking—'

'She threw me out. Said it was the war.'

Harper nodded, unsurprised. 'Sorry. Maybe she was right. You should get help.'

'I'm not fucking nuts, Harper.' His gaze pierced her.

A man in a tan suede jacket walked into the bakery, looked around. Talked on his cell phone. Went to buy a Danish.

Burke stiffened, eyeing the man. 'Gotta go. It's not safe. Look – I get that you won't believe me until you see proof. But at least be cautious, will you? Oh – and don't tell anyone you saw me. Don't even mention my name.'

'Burke, that's—'

'Harper, you and I are the only witnesses left. We're liabilities. I'm not fucking with you – Rick's his lackey. And Pete's dead. That's evidence enough, isn't it? That should show you how big this is.' He stood, whispered in her ear. 'I'll explain more next time we meet.'

'What makes you think –' Harper began, but Burke darted away before she could finish her sentence – 'that there'll be a next time?'

The Ninja sped back up the hill, found its way to Stewart Avenue, then up to College Town. Seeing Burke Everett had rattled her. Brought back images Harper didn't want to see. She fought with her memory, focusing on shops windows filled with Halloween decorations: jack-o'-lanterns, skeletons, witches, ghosts. Reminding herself that pedestrians, not checkpoint patrols, stood at intersections; that students toting backpacks, not soldiers lugging heavy gear, occupied the sidewalks. Snipers weren't aiming at her; IEDs weren't buried in the road. Harper raced ahead, trying not to think of Burke Everett or their time in Iraq. But as she crossed the bridge toward campus, she distinctly saw the woman in a burqa standing beside the street. And, oh God. She recognized her. Had seen her before.

Knew what she was planning. And this time – even if it killed her – this time, she would stop her . . .

Harper swerved, made a U-turn, got off her bike. Set out on foot, chasing after the woman, and, locating her, Harper raised a weapon, confronted her. Ordered the woman to put her hands on her head and get on the ground. But the woman stood there, defiant, unmoving. Harper repeated her orders. Asked if the woman understood English. Gradually became aware of voices behind her. People crowding around . . .

'She has a bomb,' Harper warned. 'It's hidden in her burqa. Stay away – she'll detonate it!'

Nobody responded. Nobody ran to help. Nobody seemed concerned. They stood still, watching her. Tittering. And laughing.

Harper blinked, looked around. Slowly, the sand of Iraq faded, became the concrete of Ithaca. The soldiers became students. Oh God – her gun turned into a flashlight. And the woman – the suicide bomber? Her burqa was flowing, long and black. She stood outside a hookah shop, an inanimate mannequin dressed like a Halloween witch. Complete with broom.

Oh God. Harper felt her face burn. She hadn't had so severe a flashback in more than a year. Faces surrounded her, leering, questioning, mocking.

'Look out – the mannequin has a bomb.' Someone snickered.

'What is she on?'

'Whatever it is, I want some!'

'Cut it out – she's mentally ill.'

'Right. Listen to the Psych major.'

'Seriously.' Someone touched her arm. 'Are you OK?'

Harper took a step back. Looked at the faces. Oh God. 'Fine.' Another step back. 'I was just – I'm fine.' She fled to her bike, set it right, jumped on and sped away, feeling eyes on her all the way across campus until, ignoring the graveyard, pumpkins and skeletons in the yard next door, she finally made it home.

Hank looked up from a soup pot. His eyes were twinkling like usual, and something smelled wonderful. 'Chili.' He told her. 'Veggie.'

'Yum.' Harper tried to smile. Tried to stop trembling and act normal. She kissed him, asked how he was.

'Mood. Better.' He stirred in some cumin. 'Busy. Helps.'

He was talking about his feelings. A good sign.

'You?'

Harper looked away. He wanted to know how she was. What should she say? That she'd just had a humiliating flashback? Or endured a crazy visit with paranoid Burke Everett? Or accepted Zina's assistantship, about which he'd had serious reservations? No. She couldn't risk talking about any of those things, at least not yet. Hank was feeling better but his mood was probably still fragile. She didn't want to upset him and send him into another bout of depression. 'I'm fine. I had a busy day, too.'

He nodded. 'Good. Stuff done?'

He assumed she'd been in the library, gathering research for her dissertation. It was where she should have been. 'Not a whole lot. I wasted time.'

He shrugged, tasted his chili. 'Some days. Happens.'

'Need any help?' Harper took out her phone, texted Leslie: *Can U C me? Bad flashback.*

'Salad. Make.'

Harper took out a bag of pre-washed lettuce, a bag of walnuts. Maybe it wasn't really a relapse. Maybe her PTSD wasn't getting worse; she'd just been reacting to seeing Burke again, and the flashback had been like an allergic response. A case of emotional hives; embarrassing, but not really a big deal. Her face reddened at the thought of the witch in College Town. The crowd staring at her . . .

'Today. Nahual here.'

What? Harper looked up, saw Hank's playful smile. She crumbled blue cheese into the salad bowl. Why would he ask that? 'A Nahual. You saw one?'

'Yes. True.'

'Not funny.' What was he doing? Why would he make light of Zina's fears? Was he mocking a dead woman? No, Hank wouldn't do that. So what was he doing? Harper began slicing an onion.

'Want. To meet. Him?'

Really? 'You're asking if I want to meet a Nahual?' He was going to introduce her to a shape-shifter? Harper looked at him, confused.

Hank turned off the stove, stepped over to her, took the knife from her hands and set it on the counter. When she turned, he engulfed her in his arms and kissed her.

'Hoppa. I am. Nahual.' His breath tickled her ear. 'Shift. My shape.'

Oh my, Harper thought as Hank pressed against her, and, feeling what he meant, she laughed out loud. It was funny. Hank was joking, must really be feeling better. And so, despite her troubling day and unsettled thoughts, she accompanied him upstairs, hoping that Hank's depression was easing and that his big warm body would comfort her. Or at least for a while, empty her mind.

Afterwards, eating dinner, Harper intended to tell Hank about her day. But every time she began, she stopped herself, heard Leslie warn, 'He's probably struggling more than he lets on.' Was he struggling? She watched him eating, spooning up his chili with gusto.

'Something?' Hank felt her watching him.

'No.' She smiled. 'Not really.' A lie. Why not just blurt out the truth, that, after taking the assistantship despite his objections, she'd had a disturbing visit from a paranoid guy she'd served with, followed by her worst flashback in a year?

'Know you. Tell me. What?'

Damn. Hank was no fool; he knew something was bothering her. But she heard Leslie warn that Hank was vulnerable: 'I'd keep a close eye on him if I were you.' Harper wasn't sure how stable Hank was, didn't want to send him spiraling back into feelings of power-lessness and depression. He was watching her, waiting for an answer.

'It's been a long day, that's all.' Not a lie. That was true. Harper took a sip of wine. Avoided eye contact.

'Talk. Me.' He ripped off a chunk of fresh bread. 'Want?' He held the chunk out.

'Thanks.' Harper took it, stalling by spreading butter on it. Maybe she should just tell him part of what had happened. Maybe about the assistantship. But that might start a whole chain of anguished conversation about Zina's death and bad karma and danger, would no doubt depress him again. Better if she began with Burke Everett's visit and his insane claims about the Colonel; after that, she could tell him about her flashback.

'OK? Chili?' Hank watched her. No doubt wondering why she was so quiet.

'Delicious.' It was, too. Rich and spicy. But why was she making small talk? She needed to be open and talk to Hank even if it might affect his mood. She took a long sip of wine. Drew a breath. Opened her mouth, ready to begin. Chickened out. 'Where'd you get the recipe?' What was wrong with her?

'Book. But changed. Improvised.'

Wow. He'd just said, 'improvised'? That might have been the biggest word he'd managed since his accident. 'You're an amazing man, Hank.'

He winked. 'Not bad. Nahual. Too.'

She met his eyes, returned his grin. Oh God. What was she doing? Playing happy housewife after publicly attacking a mannequin?

Harper took another gulp of wine. Blurted, 'I had a visit today. From a guy I served with.'

Hank broke off a piece of bread. 'Wow. The blue. Out of?'

'Pretty much. He looked me up because another guy we knew there – Pete Murray – died. Hanged himself.'

Hank frowned, stopped buttering and looked at her. But his eyes sparkled, alert. Not depressed.

She swallowed more wine, measuring Hank's mood, deciding that he was fine. It was all right to continue. She was about to tell him about Burke's conspiracy theory that Colonel Baxter had stolen millions from Iraq's CERP funds to start his own extreme political movement, that he'd killed Peter Murray for figuring it out. That he might kill Burke for the same reason. And might come after her.

'The guy – his name is Burke. He's got lots of issues. Seems paranoid.'

Hank frowned. 'How?'

Harper was about to explain all about Colonel Baxter and Burke's theories. And she would have, too, but just then, the doorbell rang.

The fraternity next door was celebrating in anticipation of the weekend: the rare and spectacular simultaneity of Homecoming and Halloween. The smell of beer and marijuana permeated its yard, drifted through the neighborhood. Detective Rivers had beeped her siren and flashed her lights, just to give them a scare, had watched the brothers scurry for cover, disappearing into bushes, turning lights out inside the house. When Harper opened the door, she was still shaking her head.

'Year after year,' she sighed. 'It never changes. The government ought to give up already and make all that stuff legal. Make it a lot easier on us cops.'

Harper wasn't sure exactly what Rivers was talking about. 'Come in,' she held the door open.

Rivers looked haggard. 'I called you earlier, Mrs Jennings, but you didn't pick up. So I thought I'd stop by.'

Harper swallowed. 'We're just eating. Join us? Want some chili?' Her heart rate sped up a notch. Why had Rivers come over?

'I shouldn't—'

'How are. You?' Hank stood at the kitchen door, remembered the detective from the drug incident a year earlier. 'Come in. Eat.'

'Good to see you looking so well, Mr Jennings.'

'Hank. Call me.' He led her into the kitchen.

Harper filled another bowl with chili. 'Something to drink, Detective?'

'Water, thanks.'

The three of them sat at the table. Rivers marveled at the chili. 'Delicious. Who's the cook?'

'Hank.'

Hank beamed. 'Chef. I'm good.'

'You sure are. This is perfect.'

Harper refilled her wine glass. Drank. What the hell was Rivers doing at their dinner table? Why were they sitting around chatting like old friends?

Rivers swallowed. 'So.' She turned to Harper. 'I hear you've taken that Langston assistantship.'

Damn – Harper hadn't formally told Hank yet. She glanced at him, caught his frown. Did he think she was hiding her acceptance? 'That's right. I accepted it just this morning. How did you find out so fast?'

Rivers smirked. 'Mrs Jennings, I'm an investigator.' She lifted her spoon to her mouth, chewed. 'Frankly, between you and me, I'm not thrilled with your decision, given that the last two research assistants were murdered.'

'Murdered?' Harper echoed as Hank said:

'What?'

Hank dropped his hunk of bread on to the table. Stopped eating. 'Oh damn. You didn't know?'

Harper saw Zina, sitting in the woods, blood-drenched and lifeless.

'I tried to call and give you a heads up, but by now, I assumed you'd heard.' Rivers looked from one stunned face to the other. 'I guess you haven't seen the news.'

No. Not since the morning paper.

'Well, it's been reported all day. It'll be on the eleven o'clock news and tomorrow's headlines.'

What would?

'Zina Salim's death was no accident. Definitely a homicide.'

Harper swallowed. Stiffened. 'But I thought the crash . . .?'

'No. The crash didn't kill her.' Rivers paused, put down her spoon. Cleared her throat. 'We don't know why the car hit the tree. Maybe she was driving fast, being pursued by someone. Or dodging something, so she lost control of her car. But when Ms Salim got out of the car, she wasn't bleeding much, if at all.'

'So? Then?' Hank's voice was hushed.

'So then someone killed her. And they posed her body upright, in a sitting position.'

Harper swallowed wine, remembering the last research assistant, the one from twenty-odd years ago. Hadn't her body been propped up, seated like a sentry?

Even so, she couldn't accept it. 'Maybe the crash caused Zina's injuries. Maybe she fell or crawled out of the car and tried to get up but couldn't and died in a sitting position.'

Again, the detective paused, dabbed her mouth with her napkin and looked directly at Hank, then at Harper. 'Well, I suppose that would have been a possibility. Except for one thing.'

'What?' Harper looked at Hank; his face was blank. Puzzled.

Rivers pursed her lips. 'The fatal injuries weren't caused by the car crash. This murder is exactly like the one from 1989.' She met Harper's eyes. 'Zina Salim's body was mutilated. The killer took her heart.'

They washed the dishes in silence. They both knew the implications. Had discussed them at length with Rivers. Harper rolled the conversation around in her mind.

'What do you think it means?' Rivers had addressed them both.

Hank had been silent, waiting for Harper to answer. Knowing what she'd say.

'I have no idea.' Harper had condensed her comments. 'But in many Pre-Columbian cultures, taking hearts was an accepted practice. Victors cut them out of vanquished enemies. Priests would sacrifice the hearts of conquered warriors to the gods.' She'd stopped, leaving it at that.

'Go. On.' Hank had pressed. 'Tell eating them.'

Oh Lord, really? Why was that relevant?

Rivers looked puzzled. 'Eating?'

Harper sighed. 'Well, it's not proven. But, yes. Some scholars theorize that Pre-Columbians believed that a person's strength was located in the heart. So, to acquire someone's strength, they took the heart out and . . . ate it.'

She'd cleared her throat, tried not to think about the fate of Zina's heart.

Rivers had folded her hands on the table. 'So this heart-taking is Pre-Columbian in origin.'

Harper had shrugged. 'It may be. But we can't be sure—'

'Pre-Columbian, just like Langston's relics. The ones that both victims just happened to be working on when they were killed.'

Harper had nodded.

'Is it common knowledge about the hearts? Would lots of people know about this practice?'

'Not. Lots.' Hank shook his head.

'But it's no secret,' Harper added. 'Anyone who's read about Pre-Columbian history would know. Or traveled and visited ruins. Or studied—'

'OK. I get it,' Rivers cut her off. 'So there's a select group who'd see the connection. But they don't have to be experts or scholars like yourself.'

Like herself? What? Had Rivers been implying that she'd had something to do with Zina's death? Harper had bristled, straightened her posture. Prepared to defend herself.

But Rivers had simply sighed and asked Harper and Hank to let her know if they had further thoughts concerning the murder. Then, thanking them for the chili, she'd taken off, advising Harper to be careful working with the relics. 'Remember, two women have already died at that place.'

Silently, Harper and Hank finished in the kitchen. It wasn't until they were in bed that she finally spoke. 'Just so you know, I was going to tell you I'd taken the assistantship. I just didn't—'

'You can. Still. Quit.'

She took his hand. 'I know.'

'Will you?'

She probably should. Under the circumstances, no one would blame her. 'I promised Schmerling I'd do it. They're counting on me.'

'Schmer. Ling would. Understand.'

'But I can't just quit – I haven't even started yet.'

'Can turn down. Murderer. Loose.' He lay on his side, facing her, his eyebrows furrowed. 'Zina. Saw Nahual. Sensed danger.'

'Her imagination ran away with her.'

'She's dead, Hoppa. Not imagined. Killed. Real. Job bad. Karma. Evil.'

There he was with his bad Karma Juju Hoodoo Vibes again. 'Hank, don't even pretend to believe in superstitious mumbo—'

'Places. Things. Can. Be bad.' He didn't smile. Seemed serious. But how could he be? Hank was a geologist, had a PhD. Had traveled all over the world. How could he believe that locations could possess 'good' or 'bad' vibes?

Obviously, he must not mean it literally. He must just be worried about her. 'It's OK, Hank. I can take care of myself. I'm not like Zina – I'm Army. A trained combat officer. I mean it – bring it on. Let her killer try to mess with me – I'll take him down in a heart-beat.' Oops. Wrong expression.

'Damn Hoppa.' Hank wasn't impressed. He sighed. 'OK. But. With. I'm going.'

Really? He'd go with her? And do what? Hold her hand? Hang around bored all day? 'How about this: I'll go and assess the situation. If it seems even the least bit dangerous, you can come along—'

'No, this how about? Come. Me. Along. Assess. With. You.' He sounded adamant.

'It's not necessary.' She leaned over and kissed him. 'But thank you.'

'Hoppa.' He wasn't backing down. 'Dead. Serious.'

He was right. It was serious. Harper saw Zina's slumped, blood-soaked body. Why was she making light of the danger, ignoring Hank's concerns? Maybe he was right that she should turn down the assistantship, forget about working with the relics. She pictured herself at Langston's – personally examining rare, never-displayed ancient artifacts, documenting them, holding them in her hands. Making tangible contact with a culture lost centuries ago – how could she explain to Hank the thrill she felt even thinking about it? No, she didn't want to give up this opportunity, wouldn't be so easily scared off.

'Killer. There.' Hank persisted. 'Zina. Nahual saw.'

'What are you implying? That an actual Nahual was protecting the artifacts, that he killed Zina and took her heart? Because that is utterly beyond ridiculous.'

Hank didn't reply. He lay back, folding his hands on his chest, staring at the ceiling, leaving Harper to think about her attitude. Was she being foolish? Was there, as Detective Rivers suspected, a connection between Zina's terrors of a Nahual and her murder the very next morning? Had someone been stalking her, someone she'd mistaken for a shape-shifter? And, if so, what was his motive? Did it have to do with the collection? Was everyone who worked with it going to be targeted?

Maybe. Even probably.

Damn. Hank was right. She should at least let the murder investigation proceed before recklessly putting herself in danger.

'OK. You win. I'll talk to Schmerling.' She sighed. 'I'll tell him I don't want to work there unless he can guarantee it's safe.'

'Hoppa. For real.' Hank raised an eyebrow, doubtful. 'Promise.'

Harper bit her nail, and her voice was husky with resentment. 'Promise.'

She lay back against her pillows, but she tossed, picturing crates filled with carved vessels and masks, figurines of marble, silver and gold. And when she finally drifted off, she dreamed of an immense ebony warrior, poisonous serpents emerging from his mouth, his helmet and the twist of his belt.

The memorial service was well attended. The chapel in Annabel Taylor Hall was full. The press was there, as was the entire Archeology Department, along with members of the press, a number of university bigwigs, including the Provost, the Chancellor, the Dean, and a slew of people who hadn't even known Zina, who were simply curious about the murder.

Harper sat with other graduate students, between Philip Conrad and Stacey Cohen. As a small choir sang Amazing Grace, Philip leaned over, whispering, 'Sad about her family, isn't it?'

It was? 'Why?'

'Well.' He looked around. 'She has four brothers and family living in New York. Not one of them came.' He shook his head, disapproving. Covered his mouth with his hand as he whispered. 'They wouldn't have any part of this. Flatly refused. They said it was a matter of honor.'

Honor? Why? Getting murdered was dishonorable?

'I don't get it. It's about women in their culture or their religion.' He stopped abruptly as the singing ended and the chapel hushed.

A pastor led the twenty-third psalm, then invited people to speak. One of Zina's housemates read a poem. 'I Did Not Die,' she recited. 'By Mary E. Faye. Do not stand at my grave and forever weep. I am not there. I do not sleep . . .'

Another housemate talked about how ambitious and smart Zina was, how she'd overcome the constraints of her family and fought to establish her own identity on her own terms. The third one broke down and couldn't read, so someone volunteered to read her notes, in which she promised never to forget Zina, her strength, and her spicy couscous dishes.

Harper listened, moved by the statements, wondering why she'd never seen in Zina the qualities extolled by her friends. Maybe she'd been foolish to resent her, competing against her instead of getting to know her.

Professor Wiggins stood and talked about Zina's commitment to Archeology. He confessed to being awed by her uniquely powerful and determined spirit. His affect seemed wrong, almost joyous, and his comments were followed by awkward silence until Phil got up and talked.

Phil described first meeting Zina, being intimidated by her dark, enchanting beauty, and trying to impress her with his knowledge of Indian culture, only to find out later that her family was from Syria, and that he must have sounded idiotic.

Finally, Professor Schmerling gave a eulogy, praising Zina's initiative, persistence and talent. He closed by inviting everyone to mingle and honor Zina by informally sharing their memories. One of Zina's friends played the Beatles' 'Blackbird' on the guitar as people filed out to the lobby where Marge, the department secretary, was serving cookies and punch.

'That was nice.' Tears swelled in Stacey's eyes, threatening her mascara. 'You did a great job, Phil. You lightened it up.'

'Someone had to. Especially without her family here.'

'Yeah. That's terrible.'

Phil picked up a piece of shortbread. 'You have to give her credit, though. Standing up to them.'

'Standing up to them?' Harper had no idea what they were talking about.

'Yeah,' Stacey sniffed. 'Her housemate Sonja, the one who read the poem—'

'I talked to her while I was arranging this,' Phil interrupted. 'I

wanted to include Zina's family, but Sonja told me that was out of
the question. That they'd told her she was dead to them.'

'What? Why?'

Phil sighed. 'Long story.'

'They arranged a marriage for her—' Stacey began.

Again, Phil cut her off. 'She said they did it for business. They're
into international importing and exporting. Art, antiques, high-end
collectibles – that kind of stuff. Apparently, to promote their interests,
they promised Zina to a wealthy client back in Syria. She'd never
even met him.'

'Never mind he was thirty years older than she was and had two
other wives. Can you believe it? Zina was accomplished and independent, getting a PhD from an Ivy League university.' Stacey was
incensed. 'And her family was forcing her into an arranged polyga-
mous marriage? Positively medieval.'

Harper agreed.

'Zina refused, of course,' Phil added. 'She wouldn't go back to
Syria, wouldn't meet with her brothers in New York, wouldn't agree
to the marriage. She flat out defied her family, which evidently
infuriated them. I assume that's why they wouldn't attend the service.'

Harper didn't know what to say. Zina had been stronger, far more
complicated than Harper had imagined.

'And that's the least of it.' Stacey swallowed a bite of sugar cookie.
'Sonja said that by refusing the wedding, Zina had dishonored her
family. And she was worried there would be consequences.'

Consequences? Like what? They'd ground her? 'What consequences? They couldn't force her to get married.' Could they?

Stacey looked at Phil. Phil looked away, shrugged. 'Harper,' he
said, 'in some cultures, women represent the honor of the family.
Being dishonored isn't taken lightly.'

Harper blinked, as if snapping back to consciousness. Of course
– she ought to have realized, having dealt with some of those cultures
during the war. She knew what he was about to say even before the
words left his mouth.

'At the time, Sonja assumed "dead" was just a figure of speech.
But Zina told her otherwise. Because she'd dishonored her family,
she was literally dead to them. And, if they ever saw her again, or
if she ever tried to go home, they'd kill her.'

An honor killing? Harper pictured Zina, her confident, assertive
attitude. Her ambition. And her lifeless, bloodied body. Was it possible

that her own relatives had murdered her for defying them? For shaming them?

Harper had first heard of such things while in Iraq. Incidents where family members – brothers, husbands, fathers or even mothers – killed their sisters, wives or daughters for shaming them. For not being virgins. For falling in love with the wrong man. For trying to get a divorce. For going out alone in public, dressing and behaving too 'westernized'. She'd heard about these killings and maimings of women, but, in Iraq, she'd never personally encountered any.

But now there was Zina. Was it possible that Zina had been killed by her own family? Harper couldn't imagine it. And yet, it was possible. Maybe even likely.

'Do the police know about this?' she began.

Phil nodded. 'I told them myself – and I know Sonja did.'

'I mentioned it to that woman detective who came to the Archeology office.'

So Rivers knew about the honor killing possibility. Why hadn't she mentioned it?

'So is it true you're taking over Zina's assistantship?' Phil asked. 'There's a rumor—'

'Lovely memorial, wasn't it?' Professor Schultz, a member of Phil's dissertation committee joined their cluster, and Phil began chatting him up. Stacey went to refill her punch.

'Harper.' Dean Van Arsdale suddenly approached, Professor Schmerling at his side. 'Thank you for stepping up on the Langston project.' He put a hand on her shoulder and squeezed. 'Especially in these circumstances – we all appreciate it. Myself especially. Good luck with it.' He flashed some teeth and kept moving, releasing her shoulder in order to extend his hand to someone else.

Oh dear. How awkward – she'd promised Hank she'd turn the position down. But Professor Schmerling was still standing there, handing her an envelope. 'Contract, detailed instructions and the keys to Langston's,' he said. 'Return all four signed contract copies to my office any time next week. And again, thank you.' He nodded, started to walk off.

'Wait – Professor? I need to talk about this.' She held out the envelope, trying to return it.

Schmerling kept nodding, walking away. 'Call me with any questions. The instructions are quite clear.' The Dean joined him, pulled him away.

Harper stood in the middle of the crowded lobby, holding the envelope, surrounded by the buzz of conversation, thinking of the assistantship and how embarrassing it was going to be to turn it down. But how could she complain? Embarrassment was nothing compared to what Zina had endured. She thought of Zina's last minutes. The horror of knowing that her own flesh and blood were taking her life – if, in fact, they had. But it made sense, didn't it? The family wouldn't even come to her memorial service; maybe that was because they were responsible for her death.

It was too much, too awful. Hoping for quiet, Harper stepped outside but was immediately assaulted by blaring brass and pounding drums. The Big Red Band paraded down College Avenue, promoting the next day's Homecoming game. Life and football went on as usual, not even pausing for a woman's murder.

Harper closed her eyes, leaned against Annabel Taylor's wall, absorbing the vibrations of the band, holding the envelope with the contract and the Langston keys. Damn. She'd promised Hank she'd turn it down, but according to Phil, everyone in the department had already heard she'd taken it. And Dean Van Arsdale and Professor Schmerling – the whole university was counting on her to get started. She pictured rooms filled with relics. Mysteries of time preserved in boxes. She opened the envelope, took out the keys. Looked at them.

She could just go over and glance at the collection. Just take the briefest peek. What would be the harm in that?

No – what was she thinking? She'd promised Hank she wouldn't go until she was sure it was safe.

But that was before she'd known about Zina's family. Now, it seemed that Zina's death had been an honor killing, that she'd been killed by her own relatives. In that case, there was no danger to anyone else. What would be the harm in just stopping by?

She could just go look at it. Not actually begin work – merely peek at a few pieces. See how Zina had left things. What the place looked like. How it was set up. She'd spend just two or three minutes – at most five.

She'd call Hank and let him know that it was safe, that he didn't need to worry – maybe just send a text message to avoid a discussion. Harper dug around her bag, pushed aside the flashlight, her wallet and Zina's bracelet, located her phone. Saw that she'd missed some calls. Good God, three voicemails from Burke Everett.

The lunatic was stalking her. She played back his first voice message.

'Harper – I'm being followed. You might be, too. Keep your eyes open and be careful. I'll be in touch.'

The next: 'Harper, they know I'm here. Watch your back. They've figured out I came here to see you. So they know you know what I know – sorry I put you in danger.'

The last: 'I have to ditch my cell. They're tracking me on it. I'll call you when it's safe.'

Burke had completely lost it. Wherever he was, he needed help. Lord. She hoped he wouldn't harm anyone. Hoped he'd call again so she could get him to a hospital.

The last message was from Leslie, her soothing voice agreeing to could see Harper at four o'clock.

Good. Four o'clock.

It was hours away. She had plenty of time.

Before she went to her Ninja, Harper sent Hank a text. *No need 2 quit! Will explain. Making a stop. C U 2ish.*

Then, dropping the keys and phone into her bag, she headed to her motorcycle and roared away. She had gone all the way to the Langston's long private driveway before the question came to mind.

If her family had killed Zina, why had they taken her heart?

She didn't have an answer. She'd never heard of it being part of any honor killing before. But then, she was no expert on the subject. Maybe it was symbolic in some cultures. Harper was still considering the missing heart as she confronted the yellow police tape still draped across the drive, blocking the road to the Langston house. Police and the press had been gone for some time; evidence had been gathered and removed. But the tape remained, wrapped around the area where Zina's body and car had been found. Harper didn't want to mess with the police, so she got off her bike and walked it through the trees around the taped off area, parking it near the house.

Up close, the place was much larger than she'd imagined. Like some once grand and elegant hotel. Rambling and endless, hollow and forlorn. Haunted, even. Odd that Zina hadn't mentioned that paint crumbled on the porch pillars, that wood rotted on the frames of windows and double doors. A riser was missing on the front steps. The roof sagged. Parts of the house literally seemed to be crumbling. Well, never mind. Harper was well acquainted with worn-out floorboards and loose shingles; she and Hank had been renovating their own old house for years. And in Iraq, sometimes, living conditions made this place look like five star luxury. So, undaunted, Harper left her Ninja and plowed through ankle deep fallen leaves toward the house.

Climbing the front steps, she reached into her bag for the house key, found her cell phone instead, thought briefly of calling Hank, decided that there was no reason to; she'd be on her way home in a few minutes. Finding the key, she unlocked the elaborately carved double door, stepped inside. And sneezed.

Dust was everywhere. Clouds of it. Specks as large as snowflakes. She saw it floating around her, illuminated by light beaming from the windows. Harper looked around the foyer, saw a high, rounded dome with a heavy crystal chandelier, a spiral staircase, marble floor, ragged Oriental rug.

Harper noted the worn carpet leading to the second floor. The faded wallpaper, curling at the corners. To her right, walnut panels and closed doors. Corridors leading to various wings of the house. To her left, another corridor, and the entrance to a cluttered living room, the surfaces of sofas and chairs buried beneath journals and publications. A large marble fireplace gaped from the opposite wall, filled with burned wood and ashes, surrounded by stacks of firewood.

Harper was tempted to explore the publications – the professor probably had a treasure trove of archeology literature. But that was his personal property; besides, she couldn't wait to get a look at the collection, which her instructions said was on the third floor, at the east end of the building. In seconds, she'd gone up the spiral staircase to the landing, then up another flight of steps to the floor above. Then down a long hallway, passing door after door until she came to an arch that divided the east wing from the core of the house. On the other side of the arch, she confronted the collection.

No one had prepared her for what she saw. Not Professor Schmerling, not Zina. No one. When she entered the east wing, Harper stopped, gaping at the dozens of pine crates stacked in the hall. She stepped around them, looked into the first room she passed. Saw a few worktables, a computer. Shelves of small cases, notebooks and more boxes.

The next two rooms were loaded wall to wall with various-sized containers and boxes. Harper gaped, overwhelmed. The collection was huge – far larger than she'd imagined. She stepped into the last room, squeezing between rows of mid-sized cartons, noticing that each had a note taped to it. She stooped to read one:

Early/Middle Mohica, Loma Negra, 300 BC–300 AD. 6 ¾ inches high. Copper warrior mask, slight damage. Est. $5000–$7000.

Really? She had to see it. Box cutters were all over the place. Harper took one and slit the seal of the package. Opened it. Began removing the packing material wadded up inside—

'Excuse me!'

Harper jumped, sent the box cutter clattering to the floor.

'You want to tell me what you're doing in there?'

A man stood in the doorway, glaring. At first she thought it was Angus. His hairline was receding like Angus', and he was thin and tall. Same prominent cheekbones. But this man had a ponytail. Wasn't Angus. Another of the professor's sons?

Harper's heart was still somersaulting. She took a breath. 'Sorry if I startled you.' Actually, she was the one who'd been startled. 'I'm here from the university.'

'The what? You're fucking kidding me.' He shook his head. 'Those sons of bitches don't waste any time, do they? That last one isn't even buried yet.'

Actually, Zina was going to be cremated. But Harper didn't explain that; she got his point.

'Well, go ahead. Knock yourself out – make all the lists and labels you want. But you're wasting your time.' He watched her for a moment, must have realized he'd been acting belligerently. Backed down a notch, nodded at her. 'I'm Jake Langston.'

Harper breathed. 'Harper Jennings.'

'So you're a grad student like the last one – like Zina?'

'Yes. Same department.'

Jake reached into his vest, pulled out a pack of Camels, offered her one with tobacco-stained fingers. Lit up when she declined. 'I'll share something with you, Harper Jennings. It doesn't matter how many lists you make or pictures you take. The university isn't getting any of this collection. Not one single arrowhead. Everything here belongs to my family.'

Oh great. Jake was going to argue with her about the professor's will? Get into details of the lawsuit? Harper didn't want to hear about it, had no part in the dispute. She just wanted to take a look at the mask in the box she'd opened. 'Look, I'm just here to document—'

'Even so. You ought to know what you're getting into. The will that leaves the collection to the university is, excuse the expression, a piece of shit. My father didn't have a clue what he was doing when he wrote it. For the last few years, his mind was gone. He was senile.'

'But I thought he made the donation decades ago.' Back in the eighties, before the first research assistant had been killed.

Jake exhaled a smoke ring, shook his head. 'No.'

'But wasn't there a research assistant—?'

'Yes, Carla. Pretty Carla.' He picked a shred of tobacco off his tongue. 'I was in my first year of college, fantasizing about asking her out. I was too shy, of course. Still, all of us tried to catch her eye. Angus, Caleb—'

Caleb?

'He's the oldest. Married, lives in Oregon.' Jake smiled, shook his head. 'But Carla stole my heart.' He stopped, cleared his throat. 'Sorry. Poor choice of expression. But all of us were smitten. Even Angus' friend, Digger. And Digger wasn't easily impressed.'

Why was Jake telling her all this?

'You know, they never found out who did it. And now, Zina's dead, too.' He looked at Harper too steadily. For too long. As if testing her reaction.

Harper met his eyes. Stared back. Wondered how well he'd known Zina. Obviously, well enough to call her by her first name.

Finally, Jake looked away. 'My father was still teaching back then; Carla was one of his research assistants, and he assigned her to inventory everything. For insurance purposes, I guess. But his will? No. He wrote that a few months before he died, when he had dementia. Otherwise, he'd never have given everything away.'

Harper chewed her lip, not sure what to say. She eyed the open box, trying to glimpse a bit of copper. Wished he would leave.

But Jake didn't leave. He stood there, tall, gangly. Middle-aged skin loose under his jaw. Spewing smoke into dust-filled air. 'It's obvious how confused he was – you can see for yourself. Father was always meticulous. He kept neat, careful records, labeled everything.' Jake let out a harsh, ragged cough. 'But the last few years, as his mind went, he took relics out, repacked them someplace else but didn't write down or remember where. Then he'd search for them. I'd come by to check on him and find an artifact worth fifty thousand in the laundry basket – or worse, in the washing machine. Some never turned up. You'll see how it is. Clutter and chaos. The collection – hell, the whole house – is a portrait of Dad's confusion.'

Oh dear. How sad for Professor Langston. Harper imagined him digging through the myriad of packages, searching for a priceless artifact he'd placed beside his frozen peas. 'Poor guy.' She meant it.

'We took care of him, my brothers and I. We kept him from harm. Then he died, and guess what? He left us nothing. Just this pathetic old house that needs more repair than it's worth. But the collection worth millions – the relics he spent his life gathering? That, he left to the university. To strangers.' Jake shook his head. He took a final long deep puff of his cigarette, crushed it against a wooden crate, leaving an ash mark. Stuck the stub into his pocket. 'Father wasn't in his right mind. He got manipulated, plain and simple.'

Maybe it was true. Harper had no idea. Either way, it wasn't her issue. The open box beside her gaped, teasing, inviting her to look inside. But she felt awkward with Jake standing over her, claiming the contents rightfully belonged to him. She cleared her throat, leaned against a stack of crates, crossed her arms. Smiled. Hoped he'd move along.

Jake didn't budge, didn't say anything. Seemed comfortable right where he was, took out another Camel, lit up in silence.

Damn.

Harper fidgeted, ran her fingers through her hair.

Jake blew smoke rings.

'You live here?' she finally gave in, broke the silence.

'Seriously? Here?' he scoffed. 'No, no. I have a place down the road. My brother Angus lives on the property, though. In the guest house.'

'I've met him. He accused me of trespassing.'

Jake grinned. 'That's Angus. He's our guard dog. Protects our domicile. He and Digger – they love these relics. When they were young, my father took them along on digs. In fact, that's how Digger got his nickname. His love for all things archeological. But no. Nobody should live in this old thing. The plumbing's shot. Wiring's fried. Roof leaks. Stairs are loose, and there are rotting boards all over the place. Walls about to collapse in on the passageways.'

Passageways? 'It's true about those?' Harper remembered the story about the film star – that actress who'd disappeared in them.

'Quite true.' Jake grinned. 'This house has false walls, hidden doors, secret passages. Vaults. Trapdoors. Tunnels.' His grin didn't fade as he winked. 'Be careful where you step and what you touch.'

Harper told herself she should leave, come back another time when Jake wasn't around. But no. She had a legitimate job to do, shouldn't let him interfere with it. She needed to check out the work Zina had done, see her notes and how she'd left things. Besides, she wasn't willing to leave without seeing even one single relic.

'Well, I'd better get started here. Get some stuff done,' she reached for the box.

'Like I said, knock yourself out.' Jake remained where he was, leaning against the doorframe, watching her.

Harper felt his stare as she turned away and reached for a handful of packing material. 'I won't stay long. I just need to get myself oriented.'

He was quiet.

She set the material on the top of a crate, took out another handful. Looked into the box, still didn't see the mask.

'Well, remember what I said: be careful. Watch your step.' Jake's voice sounded different, kind of thin.

'Thanks,' Harper turned to say goodbye, but Jake wasn't there. She went to the door, into the hall, over to the stairway. Didn't see him anywhere. Gooseflesh rose on her arms. She hadn't seen him leave; Jake was simply gone.

Probably she'd been so engrossed in finding the mask that she hadn't heard him go. But finally, he was gone and she could explore the collection. She went back to the box, dug in with her hands, feeling for a mask.

Finding nothing.

She pulled out clumps of packing material, let it drop to the floor, until the box was empty.

Nothing.

Oh God. Jake must have been right. The professor must have tampered with his collection, moving pieces around, relocating them, misplacing them. The mask could be in the microwave. In a shoebox. Under a cushion. Who knew? What a nightmare. Not only was the collection larger than she'd imagined; it was also completely disorganized. She gazed around at the boxes and crates, realizing how much had to be done. It could take months or even years to sort things out.

Sighing, Harper headed down the hall, back to the room with the computer. Maybe Zina had left useful notes. Booting up, she looked around. The room was pristine, dust-free. The shelves held cleaning chemicals, disposable smocks and gloves. And a row of notebooks. Harper took one at random, opened it. Saw the name on the inside of the cover: Carla Prentiss.

Oh dear. The handwriting, the book belonged to the first research assistant. She turned the pages, scanning lists of crate numbers and itemizations of content. Harper couldn't believe the relics listed – objects thousands of years old, representing the craftsmanship and symbols of Pre-Columbian cultures, most in perfect and near-perfect condition. Vessels. Bowls. Masks. Figurines. Oddly, several pages of the logbook indicated that a few items were missing. Maybe the professor hadn't been as competent and organized as Jake thought. Maybe he'd been misplacing relics even back in the eighties.

Harper replaced the notebook, sat at the computer. Found Zina's records. They were scant; she'd only been working a short time. Probably had spent most of her energy getting organized, setting up the computer file, arranging the crates. Like Carla, Zina had approached the artifacts box by box, labeling each with a code number. Like Carla, she'd itemized their contents as she'd proceeded, comparing actual content to that listed on the lids or sides of the boxes. And, like Carla, she'd found disparities.

Relics listed on the boxes were not always found inside. Missing from Crate A-1 was a ten-inch high Mayan gold figure of a turtle with the Maize god, AD 900–1200, valued at $70,000. From Crate A-3, a Honduran vessel, mosaic marble, eight and a half inches tall, a thousand to fifteen hundred years old, value $55,000. Harper read on. Saw that out of seven crates and twenty-four items Zina had catalogued, four items were missing.

Strange. But probably not a big deal, Harper decided. Over the years, the professor had probably removed some of the items – might have put some on display, sold some or donated them to museums. Her job was to make a record of what was there, not to explain what had been done with what wasn't. She'd simply follow Zina's technique, code each crate, open one at a time, record the contents. Indicate any discrepancies.

Saving the file, she shut down the computer and turned to the stacks of boxes, noting the labels: A-1, A-2, A-3. Zina had made it to A-7. For a moment, Harper felt her presence, imagined her working there alone at dusk. Saw a bat flap out from the rafters, heard the wind scream through the walls, watched the lights flicker and go out. She could understand how Zina's imagination had taken off, how she'd panicked. Even now, in daylight, the massive house was eerily quiet. Stacks of boxes cast ominous shadows and concealed dark corners, and the air seemed bathed in a haze. Harper shook her head, refusing to acknowledge the chilly draft on her shoulders. Reminding herself that she ought to get going. She had to get home. Had only a few minutes to peek at relics.

But where should she begin? Actually, she'd already opened a box. The one without the mask. Maybe she'd just go back there and look through that stack. Or she could just stay here and continue with the crates Zina hadn't looked at yet. That made more sense.

Harper took a lever and jimmied it under the lid of an unlabeled large pine crate. She pushed down, loosening the lid a bit. Moved the lever along, shoving it into the gap, pushing on it, repeating the process until one side of the lid had lifted up. Then she started on the opposite side, inserting, pushing, reinserting, pushing, until, finally, the lid came off.

Underneath, on the inside of the lid, was a list of contents. Harper didn't bother to read it; her hands were already sifting through shredded fabric and papers, feeling for smaller packages. Closing around a carved Styrofoam container. Lifting it, carefully. Unwrapping the tape. Removing the Styrofoam. Gasping.

Staring.

She was just over a foot long. Clay with a dark patina. Probably Proto-Classic. Harper cradled her in her hands, admiring her. Picturing the artist as he formed her, never imagining his work would endure, connecting him to people over two thousand years later. Harper checked the list inside the lid of the crate; yes, the piece was Proto-Classic, created between 100 BC and 450 AD. And its estimated worth was – oh dear – $70,000.

Harper's hands trembled as she laid the figurine on the black fabric, photographing it from different angles. Then, replacing it in its Styrofoam bed, she wrapped fresh tape around it and set it back into the crate. She really should go. Soon. After she looked at just one more piece.

Again, she reached into the packing, retrieved an item. Unraveled the tape, opened the Styrofoam casement. This time, she found a late-Classic jaguar – a guardian effigy, made between 550 and 950

AD. In perfect condition, multicolored, two feet high. It had a thick collar, claws, bared fangs. And stood on its rear haunches, its front legs flexed. The lid listed its value at $65,000.

Harper's hand fished in the crate, pulled out another package. Unwrapped it. Discovered a Chimu silver beaker, shaped like a human figure in a loincloth and headband. Made between 1100 and 1400 AD. Worth $8,000.

She couldn't stop. Photographed and logged them and moved on to the next crate. Used the lever to open it. Pulled out a golden Teotihuacán mask, made around 450 AD, worth around $85,000. A Mayan polychrome vessel, decorated with detailed images of humans and animals, made around 600 AD. Valued at $70,000.

Harper was agog. Completely absorbed. She stopped replacing the relics, arranged them instead on the worktable, surrounding herself with the artistry of lost cultures. Lost times. She examined one then another, then returned to the first, admiring the craftsmanship, the combination of utility and symbolism in each piece. The pristine quality of the pieces, their thousands of years of undamaged existence. Rapt, she pictured the people who'd owned them. Their belief in the power of animals – jaguars, turtles, owls, deer, bats. And men mystical enough to take those forms. She picked up the jaguar, felt the inspired awe of the artist worked into the sculpture's smooth sinews.

It wasn't until the room darkened that she realized she'd lost track of time. Harper stood and looked out a window, saw the sun disappearing behind the tree line. What? How could the sun be setting already? What time was it? Disoriented, she looked for a clock. Saw none. Where was her bag with her phone? Damn. She'd left it in the other room when she'd been talking to Jake, needed to go get it and leave. But no – she couldn't just leave, not with all those relics lying exposed on the table; she had to put them away. Where was the light switch? She scanned the walls, found one. Flipped it, but no light came on. She looked up, saw a blackened blown-out bulb hanging from the ceiling between the rafters. Damn. Carefully, Harper worked in fading light to pack up the array of precious masks, vessels and figurines. She squinted through increasing dimness to fit them into their snug individual packing, and set them into their proper crates. How had she gotten so engrossed in the collection that she'd forgotten the time? Lord – Hank must be worried. Must wonder where she was.

Finally, the last artifact was safely in its crate. Harper hurried down the hall to get her bag, noticed again how quiet the house was. Palpably, deathly quiet. She moved alone through shadows, aware of Zina, picturing her there in the dark, imagining creatures closing in on her. Bats. Cougars. Harper kept moving, rejecting the sense that someone was watching her. That time had slowed. That it was taking forever to move a few yards down the hall to get her bag. She picked up her pace, nearly tripped as a floorboard sagged under her weight and the ankle of her war-ravaged left leg twisted. Damn. Pain shot through her. She shifted her weight, stopped. Winced. Saw a shadow shift behind some crates. No, ridiculous – it was she who'd wobbled, not the shadow. Even so, her heart rate picked up. Harper looked around, tense and alert as she half hopped, half ran down the cluttered hall to the storage room, grabbed her bag, and flew through the arch, down the hallway to the stairs through deepening darkness. Looking over her shoulder, braced for the unknown, she scolded herself. She wasn't afraid of the dark; she'd survived places far more frightening than a creaky old house.

Still, as she left the Langston place, Harper thought she heard the distant hoot of an owl, was sure she saw someone rustling among the trees. She told herself it was Angus or Jake. Even called their names.

No one answered.

Harper hurried to the Ninja. Heart pounding, trying to reign in her imagination, she told herself she was not smelling incense, was not seeing a bat fluttering above her. But her hands shook as she tossed her bag into the storage compartment, pulled on her helmet, jumped on to her bike and roared away, tearing right through the police tape, determined to be off the property and home before dusk became night.

When she got to Ithaca, stopped at a red light, she finally pulled her phone out and looked to see what time it was. Almost five thirty. What? Lord, she'd been at Langston's for four and a half hours? Appalling. And confusing. OK, she'd stayed longer than she'd planned, had gotten involved with the relics, but – four and a half hours?

Damn. She'd also missed a bunch of calls, hadn't heard her phone ringing down the hall. She played back the first voicemail.

'Where. Hoppa? OK?' Oh boy. Hank hardly ever called, didn't feel comfortable on the phone. Must really be worried.

The next call began. 'Harper, it's four fifteen.'

Oh God. Leslie. Harper had forgotten all about their four o'clock appointment. Had missed it entirely.

'Are you coming? Give me a call.'

Harper's face got hot, mortified. Leslie had done her a favor, squeezing her into a busy schedule as an emergency, and she'd simply *forgotten* to go? She thought about the flashback, remembered standing on the sidewalk, trying to arrest a mannequin. No question, she needed to see Leslie. Needed to call and apologize. Reschedule. Oh man.

The light changed, but Harper stayed near the curb, listening to the rest of the messages. Hank had called again. 'OK you? Hoppa? Call me.'

Oh dear. How could she explain herself? She'd apologize. Admit that she'd been selfish . . .

But a man's voice whispered from the phone. Hoarse. Raspy.

'Be careful, Harper. They almost got me today.' Burke Everett. He was panting. Possibly hurt? 'They might come after you, too, so watch your back. I'm trying to lose them, but they're everywhere and—'

Harper sighed, pushed the 'end' button. She had enough on her mind without Burke's paranoid ranting. She'd screwed up, needed to get home and make amends, first to Hank, then to Leslie. She sped through dark streets, planning what she'd say, how she'd explain. Not noticing the rented black sedan closing in on her until it almost ran into the Ninja. At the last second, Harper realized the car wasn't going to slow, and she swerved right, nearly smashing a parked car, flying past it up on to the sidewalk, avoiding a startled pedestrian walking his corgi. Barely righting her bike and stopping as the sedan sped away.

'Did you see that?' she sputtered.

'What's the matter with you? You could kill somebody,' the man scolded. 'Keep that thing off the walkway.' Scowling under the streetlight, he turned and walked away.

Harper stared at him, then the street. She took several slow deep breaths, muttered some curse words, and walked the Ninja through parked cars, on to the asphalt, climbed on and rode home. Finally, prepared to gush apologies on to her husband, she pulled into her driveway and noticed that, though the fraternity next door was decorated and blazing with light, the windows of her house were completely dark.

Harper parked her bike and stood for a moment, chewing her lip, watching the house. Picturing Hank sitting inside, alone in darkness, deep in another bout of depression. Maybe drinking? And it was her fault – she'd known his moods were fragile; Leslie had warned that he was struggling emotionally.

And then, she'd disappeared on him. She'd said she was coming home, but hadn't, reminding him, once again, of how dependent he was, how powerless he felt. He couldn't reach her by phone. Hadn't driven since his accident, so couldn't go looking for her. Couldn't figure out where she'd gone, why she hadn't returned. Could only sit and wait, helplessly.

Oh God. She'd really messed up.

But, hell, she'd only been gone a few hours. Was that a crime? Was Hank so fragile that he'd panic if she spent one single afternoon somewhere without telling him? And if he was indeed that fragile, how long could he – how long could either of them – stand it?

Music blared from the fraternity. *The Monster Mash.* A Halloween oldie. Oh Lord. It was going to be a long party weekend. Homecoming Saturday. Halloween Sunday. Hank's depression every day . . .

But she was getting ahead of herself, making assumptions – she needed to go inside and talk to Hank. Turn on some lights. Apologize. Taking in a deep breath, Harper straightened, took her bag out of the Ninja's storage box and started along the row of Hemlocks toward the house. The music had changed. The trees, the ground, and Harper's nerves vibrated to *Bad Moon Rising.*

Harper let herself into the house, turned on the light in the entranceway. Called out Hank's name. Heard no answer. Tossed her bag on to the hall table and saw light spilling from his office near the back of the house. She hurried toward it, eager to see him. Passing the kitchen, she realized she'd underestimated him. She'd been wrong to think he'd so easily fall apart and mope, sitting alone in the dark. Hank was strong, resilient. He was in his office, no doubt, reading some obscure geology journal article on his computer. Everything was fine; she'd apologize for being late, for losing track of the time. And he'd understand.

'Hank?' She approached his office door. Again, Hank didn't answer. Didn't come out to meet her. Harper stopped, listening to his silence, remembering his accident, his fall from the roof. She closed her eyes; saw him sliding over the shingles, falling. Hitting his head against concrete. Oddly, in the same moment, she saw a black sedan close in on her Ninja, nearly hitting it . . . Felt the surge of the motorcycle as she swerved away just in time . . .

'Hank!' Still she didn't move. She stood at the door, calling his name louder this time, again picturing the car coming out of the darkness, straight at her. Deliberately. Accelerating. Aiming? Was it possible that Burke was right? Were people actually coming after her? Had they already been there – was Hank all right?

'Hank?' This time, her voice was edgy and ragged. She thrust herself into the office, scanning the desk chair, the big leather easy chair, the carpet, the corners . . . 'Hank,' she called as she spun around, looking again. 'Hank,' she repeated over and over. First as a question, later as a wail. But Hank didn't appear. Nor did he answer.

Oh God.

Harper went through the house, quietly now, turning on every light as she went. Hank wasn't in the kitchen. Not in the powder room, dining room, living room. Harper's chest tightened; breathing was an effort. She kept seeing his accident, watched him fall, over and over. No, she wouldn't go there, wouldn't relive it. Needed to stay in the moment. To find Hank. Climbing the stairs, to the dark second story, she felt a sharp pang in her stomach. Clutched it. And heard Leslie's voice: 'He's struggling more than he lets on . . . I'd keep a close eye on him if I were you.'

Harper stopped, suddenly chilled. Shivering. Again picturing Hank alone in the house, depressed. Unable to reach her. Feeling abandoned and hopeless . . .

No. Ridiculous. Unthinkable. Hank would never hurt himself. Never. Not ever. No.

Still, Harper remained on the steps, unable to move. Unable to shake her icy paralysing fear of what she might find at the top of the staircase.

'Hank?' Her voice this time was thin. Broken.

He probably just dozed off, she told herself. Probably was asleep.

Unconvinced, her feet refused to move, and she had to force them up the final few steps. Had to push herself on to the landing, down the hall into the bedroom.

Where she found Hank.

He was standing by the window, staring out at the fraternity. His back to her.

'Hank?'

He didn't answer. Turned slowly to face her.

'Didn't you hear me?' Harper was annoyed. 'I've been calling your name – why didn't you answer?'

His voice was low. 'Why didn't *you*? Answer? Phone.'

Harper switched on the light. Hank was still in his robe. Unshaven. Hadn't gotten dressed all day.

'Called you.' Hank glowered.

'I know – I'm sorry. I didn't hear the phone.' He hadn't gotten dressed again. Had he stayed in the bedroom all day? 'Look, I'm sorry. I messed up. I got involved with the Langston project – it turns out Zina was most likely killed by her own family. Some kind of horrible honor killing. But, if that's the case, there's no danger to anyone else, and I might as well take it. So I went over just to take a look for a few minutes, and I lost track of—'

'Friend came. Here.' Hank's eyes sizzled. He wasn't even listening. 'Burke. Iraq from.'

What? 'Burke? Came here?'

'Told me. You saw him.'

Damn. What had Burke done? Had he shown up at the house and told Hank the whole cockamamie story about Colonel? That his militia was out to assassinate them both? No wonder Hank had been upset when he couldn't reach her.

'I told you about him, remember? Burke's got some serious mental issues. I guess the war messed him—'

'Not told me. Burke's story. About. Not told me. Zina's job. Took. Lots. Hoppa.' Hank didn't move. He stood at the window, broad shoulders stiff. Jaw tight. 'Why? Don't trust. Me?'

'That's ridiculous.' Harper wanted to go to him, touch him. She took a step forward, but stopped, held back by his glare. 'Of course I trust you.'

'Then tell me. Now.'

Oh God. Where to start? 'OK. Burke came into town. We met for coffee, and he started making wild accusations about some guys we knew in Iraq. He's paranoid.'

'And?'

And?

'Burke. And. What else?'

What else? 'Oh. You mean the assistantship?'

He stared, didn't reply.

'OK.' She swallowed. Took a breath. 'I know I told you I'd turn it down. But that was because of the murder, right? But this morning, I found out about Zina's family – they thought she'd disgraced them by refusing an arranged marriage and probably killed her.'

'And? Also?'

'Also what?'

Hank stepped forward, a towering, lumbering infuriated bear. His mouth twisted into a grimace. 'Also. About. Us.'

Us?

'Not tell me. Not talk to me. Not trust. Not good. Not. Us.'

Oh God. 'Hank – how can you say that? We're good. I do trust you . . .'

He moved past her, toward the door.

'OK. Lately, I've held things back. But the only reason I've done that is that you've been depressed. I haven't wanted to upset you—'

'Depressed. Me?' He spun around more quickly than she'd thought he could. 'Think. So?'

'Yes, but I get it – you have a right to be.' She stepped toward him. Again felt the invisible wall. 'I understand you have to work through your feelings after everything—'

'Think I can't. Manage? Need my. Wife. Protecting. Me?'

'Of course not, don't even—'

'Think. I'm not. Strong. Man?'

'—suggest that!'

'Maybe. Hoppa.' He turned, walked out of the bedroom. 'Maybe. Right.'

Harper followed him down the hall, talking to him. Telling him to stop. To sit down and talk. But Hank ignored her. Pulling off his bathrobe, he pulled on jeans, a jacket, stepped into his new boots, stopped at the door to point to the hall table.

'Burke. Phone. Number,' he said. Then he left.

Harper started after him, opened the front door, but stopped. What was she going to do – wrestle him to the ground? Force him back into the house? She bit her lip, refused tears. Hank was going through a phase, wavering between sadness and anger, just as she'd done after her war injuries. His moods were natural, inevitable. And he needed to work through them on his own. She hadn't helped by going AWOL that afternoon, but he'd forgive her in time. They'd talk. He'd be all right. They'd be all right.

Wouldn't they?

She stood in the hall, facing the door, hoping he'd come back inside. After all, Hank wouldn't go far. Would he? She watched the door.

Damn. Harper couldn't help it. She hurried after him on to the front porch; *Season of the Witch* blasted from next door. But where was Hank? She looked around. Scolded herself for upsetting him. She was supposed to be there for him, helping him through this crisis. Instead, she'd gone off on her own without even telling him, just to look at some relics – well, some incredible relics. But she hadn't even considered how he'd feel . . .

Nearby, through the music, she thought she heard the revving of a car's engine. And suddenly, Hank's Jeep, parked for months in the garage beside the house, zoomed in reverse down the driveway into the street, jerked into drive and sped away.

Harper stood in the middle of the front yard, chilled and ankle-deep in leaves, her mouth hanging open. Hank hadn't driven in over a year, not since his accident. His right side was weaker than the left. Would he be able to steer? To control the gas and brake? Damn it. What was he doing?

Cursing and worried, she ran to the street, saw tail lights disappear around the corner. Stood there, staring. Considered taking off after him on the Ninja, pictured catching up with him, how he'd react. Not difficult to figure out: he'd be furious. Would feel emasculated, as if she didn't think he could manage on his own.

Amplifiers screamed, 'Must be . . . must be . . . the season of the witch!'

Harper trudged back to the house and slammed the door, refusing, absolutely refusing to cry. She paced. Took out the Scotch. Walked away from it. Paced some more, feeling helpless and furious about being helpless. Worrying about Hank. Pouring a drink. Staring into the glass as she drank. Seeing Hank fall from the roof, hit his head . . . No. Refusing to relive that. Closing her eyes, thinking of Leslie . . . Oh God. She needed to call her. That was, if Leslie would even speak to her after her missed appointment.

Quickly, unsteadily, Harper dug her phone out of her bag, made the call. Got Leslie's voicemail, of course. Left a message apologizing, saying she'd gotten caught up earlier but really needed to talk, asking her to call back. Hearing herself sound needy.

Damn. Harper stood in the front hall, phone in hand. Where had Hank gone? She pictured him driving, taking a turn too fast, losing control of the car. Thank goodness it was a Jeep, sturdy. Not likely

to get totaled if he crashed. Unless it rolled into the gorge. Or the
lake. Harper clutched her phone, walked in circles, waited for Leslie
to call. Get a grip, she told herself. Hank is fine. He's just proving
himself. Testing himself. He'll come back, having shown that he can
still drive. He'll be in a better mood. She needed to calm down, be
patient.

But she couldn't. Tossing her phone on to the table beside her
bag, she noticed a piece of paper there. A number was scrawled on
it. Burke's number. Lord. She'd almost forgotten about him, how
he'd shown up at her house, gotten Hank all riled up. Furious, she
made the call, waited for him to pick up so she could yell at him.
But he didn't pick up. A computerized voice told her to leave a
message at the tone. So she did.

'What the hell's wrong with you, Burke?' The words flew out,
unplanned. 'What did you say to my husband? Did you share your
genius theory about Colonel Baxter? Did you say that he's trying to
kill us? Have you completely lost it? Did you not happen to notice
that my husband has his own problems? Could you not realize that
maybe you should leave him out of your damned paranoid bullshit?'
She paused to catch her breath, composed herself. Lowered her voice.
'Here's the deal, Burke. Don't . . . do not bother me or my husband
again. Ever. Don't come over, don't call. Don't send obituaries in
the mail. Just take your frickin' conspiracy theories and sign yourself
into a VA hospital. Get help. But go away.'

Harper felt a pang. Pictured Burke, how jumpy and pathetic he'd
been, almost twitching with fear. The guy was sick; he hadn't deliberately caused harm. She was being too harsh, didn't want to be
cruel.

'Sorry, Burke,' she softened. 'It's just too much right now. I've
got my own stuff, can't help you with yours.'

And then she hung up.

Waiting wasn't easy. Harper waited on the front porch, on the living
room sofa, at the kitchen table. She poured another finger of Scotch,
blinked at it, gulped it down, poured another. Left the glass on the
table. Walked up and down the hall, looked out windows, sat down,
stood up, went to her phone, picked it up, thought of calling someone
– but couldn't decide who. Leslie again? Vicki? Detective Rivers?
What would she say? That she was frantic, almost hysterical because
Hank had left their property?

Even she could hear how irrational that sounded. Clearly, she was overreacting. Didn't need to be frightened. Hank was fine. Would be fine. But she kept seeing him fall off the roof. Kept imagining him crashing the car. She put the phone down, tried to ignore the rumble of gunfire closing in on her. Too late . . . Suddenly, to her left, something exploded; burning air scalded her face, and she smelled burning flesh, heard screams of pain. Started to run for cover – no. Damn it. She fought back. Closed her eyes. Wouldn't, couldn't allow a flashback. But the bullets still flew. Whizzed past, barely missing her head. Ducking, hunkering low to the ground, Harper dashed back to the base – or maybe the kitchen? She grabbed a grenade from the cold drawer in the arsenal, and bit off the pin. Dug her teeth in. Instantly, the grenade's sharp sour taste jolted her, banishing the battleground. Returning her to the moment where she stood by the refrigerator, holding a half-eaten lemon.

Even so, her skin still burned. Her lungs felt raw, and she tasted copper. Danger reared up and roared, but no matter how much she wanted to, she didn't know how to confront it. Not this time.

This time, the battle wasn't hers. It was Hank's.

So Harper stood and sat and stood again in her kitchen, downed another glass of Scotch, poured another. And waited.

At ten before two in the morning, Hank pulled into the driveway, parked the Jeep in the garage. He came in, looking frazzled. Relieved, Harper didn't say a word. She just ran to him.

'Sorry.' Hank seemed straighter. Taller.

'No. I am.'

'Both. Should. Be.'

He was right. They broke apart, stood awkwardly near the front door.

'Want a drink?' By then, she'd had more than a few.

'No. Late.'

'We should talk.' She needed to apologize, explain. Tell him about Burke, the assistantship – about her selfishness.

'Not now, Hoppa. Sleep.'

He headed to the stairs. Acted like nothing had happened. Harper was drained and exhausted. Unable to let go.

'I was worried about you.' She followed him.

'Why?'

Why? Really? 'Because you were upset. And you haven't driven since—'

'Fine. I'm. Fine.'

They went upstairs, got ready for bed. Harper stayed close to him, needing to connect. Uneasy about his silence. But Hank simply got into bed, rolled over and turned out the light. Harper snuggled against him.

'No kiss?'

He turned and kissed her. A dutiful peck on the forehead.

'Uh uh.' She pulled his face to hers, kissed his mouth.

But even though he lay facing her, their arms and legs entwined, Harper felt his distance. In seconds, his breathing became deep and even. Harper tried to but couldn't relax.

'Hank?'

'Huh.'

'Where did you go?'

Hank didn't answer. Softly, he began to snore.

Harper had just fallen asleep when the doorbell rang. She opened her eyes, looked around. The sun blazed through slats of the bedroom blinds. Clock said nine thirty. Hank's side of the bed was empty.

Oh God. Harper jumped out of bed, raced to the window, looked outside for the Jeep. Saw it there, right where Hank had parked it, inside the open garage – thank God.

But where was Hank?

'Harper?' Vicki's cheery voice floated up the staircase. 'Get your lazy butt down here!'

Damn. It was Saturday morning. She and Vicki usually had coffee during the week. But this was Homecoming; Trent was attending a brunch, glad-handing alumni to stimulate contributions. Vicki didn't want to go, so she'd offered to come by with scones.

'What, were you out partying all night? Get up!' Vicki called.

Harper groaned. She ached all over, didn't feel like getting her butt anywhere but back to bed. Her left leg ached as she dragged herself to the bathroom; the rest of her complained as she splashed water on to her face and moved her toothbrush around her mouth. The face in the mirror was blotchy; her hair clumped into tangled blonde stumps. Harper stuck her tongue out at the reflection, ran her fingers through the tangles, and plodded down the stairs, looking for Hank.

Finding Vicki. She'd dyed her hair again. This time, too dark. Almost black.

'Where's Hank?' Harper looked down the hall, toward the kitchen.

'Wow. Hello to you, too.'

'Have you seen him?'

Vicki nodded at the front door. Harper went to the window, looked out.

Hank was in the front yard, raking leaves. What? She stood, frozen, watching. He was off balance, his movements short. But they were steady. Persistent.

'Are you sick?' Vicki came up behind her, frowning. 'You look terrible.'

Really? 'Hank took the Jeep out last night.'

Vicki's mouth dropped. 'What?'

Harper kept watching him, amazed. 'He drove. He was gone for hours, alone. In the middle of the night. I have no idea where he went. He wouldn't tell me. And now, look.' She pointed at the window. 'He's . . .'

'He's raking. He had half the yard done when I got here.' Vicki stood beside Harper, watching Hank. She shrugged. 'So. This is all good, right?'

It was?

Harper turned to Vicki, about to tell her about Hank's moods, but her voice choked and her eyes had filled. Why? What was wrong with her? Hank was fine, working outside on a brisk October morning. Recovering, testing his capabilities. Getting a renewed sense of self. She should be glad.

'Oh, Harper.' Vicki hugged her. 'You've been a soldier through this whole ordeal. Thanks to you, Hank's come back from hell. Look how strong he is. He's out there, pushing himself. Not giving up. You guys are going to be fine – both of you.'

Harper gazed out the window. Watched Hank work the rake, pulling leaves into speckled heaps of red, yellow, orange.

Vicki seemed convinced that there was no problem. That Hank's exertion was unremarkable, a positive sign of progress. She led Harper to the kitchen. Freshly baked scones – a variety of cinnamon nut, chocolate chip and cranberry orange – were set out on a plate near butter and honey and jam.

'So.' Vicki poured coffee. 'Hank's driving again. Doing lawn work. He's full of surprises. What do you think he'll do next?'

Vicki meant well, but Harper tensed. Grabbed a scone, forced a smile. 'I can't even guess.'

Leslie hadn't called back yet. And Harper needed to talk. Vicki knew Hank well; she'd probably have insights as to his moods and behavior. Would have ideas about how Harper should respond.

'What do you think?' Vicki primped her chin-length hair. 'You like it?'

Harper thought it looked witchy, appropriate for Halloween. 'It's different.' She shrugged. 'Something new.' Two days ago, it had been auburn. Vicki was constantly changing her look.

'Different good? Or different bad? Maybe I should cut it real short—'

'No, it's good. It's a change – it's fun.' Kind of. 'Look, Vicki. Can I talk to you? About something . . .'

'Of course you can talk to me. What a question. What's up?' She bit into a chocolate chip scone. Crumbs tumbled on to the table.

Harper took a breath. Didn't know where to start. Maybe she should back up to yesterday, her visit to Professor Langston's house. As soon as she began, Vicki stopped her.

'Wait. You took that assistantship? Are you crazy? After Zina was killed there? I thought—'

'No. It's OK. Turns out, her family probably did it.' Harper explained that Zina had refused an arranged marriage. That it was likely she'd been the victim of an honor killing.

Vicki's eyes widened. 'Wait. You're saying her own brothers killed her?'

'Maybe. Or an uncle. Or her father – even her mother.' Harper began to move on. 'Anyway, when I got there, the collection—'

'Hold on.' Vick shook her head. Bit her lip. 'Her own *parents* might have killed her?'

'I know. It's horrible.' She pictured Zina's slumped, mutilated body. Blinked the image away. Picked up her coffee. 'But the thing is that, if they did it, then Zina's death wasn't a random murder. Which means there isn't some crazed killer out there.'

Vicki shook her head. 'Imagine.'

'And if there's no crazed killer out there, there's no reason I shouldn't take the assistantship. So I decided to accept it, and I went there to get—'

'No wait.' Vicki frowned. 'Remember the night before she died, when Zina came here, terrified of that newel—'

'Nahual.'

'Whatever. Do you think . . . maybe she had real reasons to be afraid. Maybe somebody was actually there – one of her brothers or her father might have been stalking her, and she thought it was a nowl.'

'Nahual.' Harper didn't want to dwell on the murder. She wanted advice about Hank and had mentioned the honor killing theory only to explain why, instead of turning down the assistantship, she'd gone to Langston's where she'd lost track of time and not come home, infuriating Hank, setting him off on a rampage of unpredictable activity. 'Anyway, I'm sure the police are—'

'Did Zina ever mention the arranged marriage? Did she talk about problems with her family?'

'No.' Harper sighed. 'Not to me. But we weren't close. Vicki, can we please talk about—'

'What about her roommates? Did she tell them? Did she say she was afraid of her family?' Vicki swallowed coffee. 'Because, I mean, if it were me, I'd carry a gun and mace and pepper spray. I'd be petrified – wouldn't you?'

Harper chewed her lip, impatient. 'Yes. I'd carry a damned arsenal. But can we come back to this? I want to tell you what hap—'

'Hold on a second, OK? We'll talk about whatever you want, but this is important.'

'And what? I'm not?' God, had she just said that? It sounded whiny and petulant. Like a jealous kid. She bit into a scone.

'Don't be stupid.'

'I'm not being stupid.' Her mouth was full. 'I just want to talk to you. A lot's been going on.'

'Fine. A lot's been going on with me, too. I haven't told you about the drama in my office now that Pam's leaving.' Vicki was a dentist and Pam was her office manager. 'Or about Trent's promise to stop drinking and join AA. But Trent and I and Hank and you can wait until we talk about Zina.'

Harper put the scone down, wiped her hands. 'We aren't going to accomplish anything by—'

'I didn't say we were. But honestly, Harper. We were with her the night before she died. So I want to talk about it, OK? Can't you put your devastating, earth-shattering problems on hold for just five minutes?'

Her devastating, earth-shattering problems? Vicki was mocking her? Really? Harper's jaw tightened. She was tempted to say or do something regrettable, maybe hurl the rest of the scones at Vicki's perky little nose. But she refrained. Zina's death wasn't a topic to be glossed over; it deserved respect and attention. So, calming herself, Harper picked up her cup. Sipped. Sat silent, stiff. Drummed her fingers on the table.

'So here's my thinking.' Vicki leaned forward, elbows on the table. 'From what I've heard, Zina wasn't carrying any weapons. Was she?'

'No.'

'Not even scissors or a steak knife. Not one thing to protect herself?'

'No.' Harper bit off a chunk of scone, unsettled. Wondering what mood Hank was in. Why he hadn't even said 'good morning' before going outside.

'So?' Vicki seemed to think her point was obvious. 'So, I think that means that Zina wasn't afraid of her family. She didn't believe she was in danger.'

'Well, I guess she was wrong.' Harper drew a breath. Maybe she was being selfish to want her issues to take precedence over Zina's. Maybe Vicki was right that discussing the murder was more important. Even so, Harper drifted away, thinking about Hank, how she should approach him. What she should say. She looked out the kitchen window. Didn't see him. Wanted to go outside. To talk to him.

Vicki went on. 'But, obviously, she knew her family and their beliefs. She had to know—'

'Maybe she didn't take the beliefs seriously, Vicki.' Harper finished her coffee. 'No one had any reason to think her family would commit an honor killing until after the murder.'

'Well, that's just weird.' Vicki held her cup, sat straight. 'Imagine you come from a family – from a culture – that dictates the death penalty for certain acts. And you knowingly commit one of those acts. Can you imagine not considering that? Not taking precautions to protect yourself?'

'No, I can't.' Neither could she imagine Zina's mindset, her background and its conflicting values. 'But we're Westerners. We really can't know what Zina was thinking. We can't comprehend being part of a culture where women get killed for having relationships with men. Or wearing make-up. Or going out alone, or—'

'But Zina wasn't a fool. She was a bright woman. Worldly.

Educated. And yet she seems to have been oblivious to the dangers of going against her culture.' Vicki broke off a piece of scone, toyed with it.

'What are you saying?'

'I guess I just don't want to believe her family would, you know . . . do that.'

'You'd prefer it if a random stranger had killed her?' Harper didn't want to consider that possibility.

'You know what?' Vicki chewed slowly. 'I would. Yes.'

Harper felt a chill, pictured the moment Zina realized that her own flesh and blood was taking her life. She imagined meeting the killer's familiar eyes, searching them for compassion, feeling cold steel pushed through her body . . .

Harper stood, went to rinse out her coffee mug, realizing that, yes, she no longer wanted to talk about Hank. Compared to Zina's death – the betrayal by her family – she and Hank had no problems at all. She looked out the window, saw Hank pushing a wheelbarrow filled with leaves. A year ago, he'd struggled even to walk. Now, he was doing yard work. And driving the car.

Vicki had stopped talking, was waiting for a response. 'Harper?'

'Sorry.' She had no idea what Vicki had been saying. But, suddenly, watching Hank, she thought she knew why Zina hadn't been afraid. She'd known the culture and its rules, but had been too close to her family to see them objectively. Zina had underestimated the people closest to her, hadn't grasped the extent of their passion or the depth of their resolve.

Zina made a fatal, though not uncommon mistake.

'I have to go out,' Harper ran to the closet and pulled on a fleece jacket.

'What? Harper?' Vicki stood up, gaping. 'I thought you wanted to talk!'

'Not now. Don't have time.' Harper hurried to the door. 'Sorry to run off. Just leave everything, OK? I'll clean up later . . .' And she was out the front door, rushing over to Hank.

He looked up as she approached, didn't say anything. Nodded, as he balanced carefully and pulled the rake, gathering leaves. Harper went to a pile a few yards away, ordered her left leg to bend, and, despite its complaints, began picking up arm-loads, dropping them into the wheelbarrow. When it was full, she rolled it to the back of the house, tossed them over the fence on to the floor of the woods.

Then she returned to the front yard, repeated the process. Again and again. And again.

At some point, Vicki came out, looking confused. 'So. I guess I'll go.'

Harper picked up some leaves, wiped her brow. 'OK. Yeah. I have to do this. Thanks for the scones.'

'Trent. Say. Hi.' Hank called.

Vicki wandered off. 'Dinner Tuesday?' she shouted.

Harper nodded, waved back. 'Bring dessert!'

At some point, Harper noticed that her left leg was seriously throbbing. But she didn't give in, wouldn't stop until Hank did. And Hank wouldn't stop.

It took a few hours to clear the front lawn. Finally, they returned the wheelbarrow and the rake to the garage.

Hank was sweating, flushed with exertion. But his eyes twinkled with energy. And as he put an arm around her, he was smiling. 'Talk. Now.'

Harper's phone was ringing when they went inside, but Harper let it go, interested only in talking to Hank. He led her into the kitchen, poured coffee. Two mugs. Sat at the table. Waited until she sat. Met her eyes. The twinkle had faded.

'I was mad.'

'I know.'

'I was. Wrong.'

'No. You had a right to be mad. I was wrong. I should have called and—'

He put a hand up. 'Me first. Talk.'

OK. Harper lifted her coffee, took a sip.

'I've been. Thinking. Hoppa.'

She waited.

'Whole year now. I've. Not had a. Life. Too much on. On you. Leaned on you. Burden.'

'No, you've never been—'

He covered her lips with his finger, hushing her. Harper wanted to assure him that he had never been, never could be a burden, but he wouldn't let her speak.

'Me first. Talk first.'

OK.

'Hoppa. You.' He stopped, took a breath, rearranging his lips and tongue. 'You need your life.' He swished coffee in his mouth, moistening it. Swallowed coffee. 'To do. Your thing. Go where you want. Not worry. Poor. Hank.'

What? Harper's chest fluttered a warning. 'But I don't—'

'No. Listen.' Again, he stopped her. 'Change. We need. We. Both need change.'

Harper's throat tightened. Her hand rose to her mouth. What kind of changes? What was he saying?

'I can't be. Any more. Pris–prisoner.'

A prisoner? 'You haven't—'

'Not your fault. Not about. You. About. Me.'

Her stomach flipped, heart raced. Was Hank giving her the old 'it's not you it's me' line? Dumping her? No, of course not. He couldn't be.

'I need to. Go. Work. Do. Man be.'

Harper couldn't move, couldn't breathe. She sat riveted. Frozen.

'You do.' He strained to form the syllables. 'What you want. Where. And when. You want.'

Was this really happening? Was Hank telling her to just go wherever she wanted? Tears filled her eyes, blurred her vision.

'I need also. Need to go. Drive. Do. What I want.' He paused, watching her. Not looking quite like himself. Altered in some way. Hank, but not Hank. He inhaled. 'Indy. Pendent.' Exhaled.

Harper's eyes swam. Do not cry, she ordered herself. You are stronger than that. You love this man, and if he's dumping you to prove he can be independent, that sucks. But at least sit up straight and show some spine. Harper sat up, but blinking, she sent a single fat teardrop spilling on to her cheek. She slapped it away.

'Crying? Don't.' Hank reached out, touched her face. 'Not bad. Change. Good. Both. For us.'

Really? Harper's chest hurt when she breathed. She crossed her arms, bracing herself. She wondered what she could say. Whether she'd even be able to speak, with her throat so choked.

'The truth. I'm saying. Not. Pretend.' Hank who wasn't quite Hank paused to lick his lips. Moved them around as if limbering them up. This was more than he'd said at one time since his accident. 'You need, Hoppa. To tell truth, too.'

Hold on. Was he saying she hadn't been honest with him? 'What are you talking about?' Instantly, hurt became anger, and Harper's finger rose, jabbing the air. 'I have never lied to you, not ever. About anything.'

'No.' His eyes were steady, his voice grave. 'But truth not said. Same as lies.'

Harper felt as if he'd slapped her, covered her cheek. 'Hank, I have not hidden the truth!'

'Burke.' One syllable. It struck like a thunderclap. 'And took Zina's. Job.' His voice was a low rumble. Or no – was that gunfire?

Harper heard shots, felt the ground explode as she scanned the area for something – anything to fend off the flashback. She saw napkins, jam. Leftover scones. A butter knife. Picked up the knife, pressed it deep into the palm of her hand until sharp pain pushed the encroaching battle away, grounding her. She closed her eyes, wincing, and made a fist.

'Told me. You weren't taking. Job. But took. It.'

Harper listened, heard no guns. Looked around for snipers, saw only her kitchen walls. Focused. 'We've already been over this, Hank. I was going to tell you about all of that, but I didn't get a chance. Let me explain everything now—'

'Missing point.' Hank cut her off.

What point? 'No. You said I'm not truthful. But that's not fair; I haven't tried to hide anything from you.'

'Me either.'

'You? You mean you're hiding things from me?'

'No. Just do. Now. My thing. Own. Like you.'

Harper pictured him backing out of the driveway in the night. Staying out for hours. Raking the leaves. Doing things without her for the first time in over a year.

'Two lives. Do own things. Each. Apart.'

'Apart?' Her voice wobbled.

His eyes hardened, held on to hers. 'Each. Hoppa. I love. You.' He paused. 'But we can't. Like before. Be. Need change. Big.'

Harper drew a breath. She understood Hank was going through dramatic changes. But did that mean he wanted to separate? Was he breaking up their marriage in order to prove he could be independent? And who put him in charge of dictating what was to change? Was he saying that things had to be his way or no way, putting her on some kind of ultimatum, a wife probation? Well, no thank you. That wasn't going to fly. She stood, pushed her chair away from the table.

'Listen, Hank. It's my turn to speak now. Maybe I've screwed up. Maybe I've done something – or a bunch of things – that really pissed you off. But I have never ever deliberately hurt you or stood in your way. I have been your staunchest ally since I married you. I love you. If that's not good enough, then fine. Be as independent and apart as you want. Do your thing. You want change? You got it.'

She spun around, accidentally knocking the coffee mug off the table. Heard it shatter on the floor. Heard Hank call, 'Hoppa, wait – look. Hand. Bleeding,' as she sped from the room.

He stood, yelling, 'Hoppa, stop. Come back – please!' But Harper didn't hear him; she'd already left the kitchen and was halfway to the door.

Burke Everett hadn't shaved in a couple of days. Kept the hood of his sweatshirt up, concealing his face. Moved around College Town, never staying in one place long, crashing overnight in some apartment with a bunch of stoners, half in Halloween costumes where nobody knew who anybody was. Spending the day trying to blend in with scruffy potheads who hung out around there. Keeping his eyes open.

So far this morning, he'd seen three of the Colonel's people. Three that he was sure of: two in a black sedan. Christ, they might as well have carried a sign announcing themselves. One was subtler, hanging out near a pizza shop. His shoes had given him away, all laced up with their military shine. With tattered jeans? Really? Did they think he was stupid? At least they hadn't spotted him – so far, he'd seen them first and disappeared.

Meantime, he'd tried to reach Harper, even had gone to her house to warn her. But she'd been out, and her husband, well. No point telling him anything. There was something seriously wrong with that dude. Big guy, good-looking, but he moved like a wounded gorilla. Couldn't even talk. Maybe he was one of those brain injury guys. Burke had heard that a lot of guys got head wounds from IEDs, got all kinds of weird afterwards. Harper had called afterwards, left a pissed-off message, telling him not to come to the house. Probably she was embarrassed about the guy, trying to shield him from people. Burke understood. Harper was one of the good ones, all about being strong. Being loyal.

Which was probably why she hesitated to take a stand against the Colonel – he was her superior officer. She probably couldn't believe a man of his stature could be so corrupt. Well, she was wrong. And,

by the way, speaking of loyalty, Burke was Army, too, wasn't he?
Where was her loyalty to him?

Someone bumped smack into him, walking fast. Fuck – he hadn't
seen the guy coming. If that had been one of them, he'd be dead.
Just like Pete. Time to move on. Burke kept his head down as he
walked. Time to get out of town. Leave them here, crawling all over
Ithaca looking for him. His car was parked off Stewart Avenue, and
he headed that way. Watching over his shoulder. Feeling eyes on him.
What was that guy doing across the street, just standing there as if
smoking a cigarette? Why was the guy looking at him? Burke quick-
ened his step. The guy didn't follow. Didn't make a call. False alarm.

At the corner, he turned sharply, suddenly, watching to see if
anyone was on his tail. Some chick, yakking on her cell. He stood
against the wall, watching until she passed. Then backtracked. She
didn't follow. Didn't even glance his way.

But those guys were good. Might have tag teams. The chick might
right that second be telling her contact on the phone where he was
headed. Burke slipped a hand into the pocket of his sweatshirt,
clutched his 9 mm. Felt better. Life was better with a Beretta. He
chuckled; not a bad slogan. He should send it to the company. Maybe
they'd buy it from him. But first, he had to get out of town. Kept
his head down. Kept walking.

Harper's hand was bleeding. Her palm was wet and sticky, a small
incision right smack in the center. Who knew a butter knife could
break skin? And who cared? It was only fitting that she'd bleed after
what she'd just heard. Harper sped to the door, aware that Hank was
coming after her, calling her name. But she didn't stop, couldn't. She
grabbed her bag from the front table and kept moving, not stopping
for Hank, the sharp pain in her left leg, her bloody palm, the frat
guys' raucous Homecoming party revving up in the yard next door,
her phone chiming its gong sound. Smearing tears off her face, Harper
popped her helmet on, hopped on to her Ninja and rode away, aware
of Hank on the front porch, yelling words her engine drowned out.

Harper sped down the hill to the lake, barely aware of traffic or
surroundings, immune to the chilling wind in her face, aware only
of pain. How could Hank accuse *her* of not being honest with him
when he was the reason she didn't tell him things. He was the one
whose moods kept shifting, who was often too depressed or frustrated
to have a conversation. And how could he accuse her of 'doing her

own thing'? As if she hadn't put her PhD program, her friendships – her entire *life* – on hold when he'd been hurt. As if she hadn't devoted herself completely to his recovery, rejoicing about each triumph no matter how small. Coaxing him through his therapies. Cheering his progress.

Harper stopped at a red light. Looked around, saw no one coming. No cops. Went through it. Besides, who said she had to tell Hank about every single decision she made or every conversation she had? She was his wife, not his possession. She had a perfect right to go where she wanted and say and do what she wanted.

But wait. Wasn't that pretty much what Hank had said? She replayed his voice: 'You do. What you want. Where you want.' Had he been complaining about that? Or just stating a fact?

Oh God. Was it possible that she had seriously overreacted?

Harper slowed down. Replayed Hank's words again. And again. Had he been saying he wanted them to go their separate ways? Or just that he needed to be more independent, like she was? Near the railroad station, Harper pulled to the side of the road, stopped the bike. Thought.

Her phone chimed. Hank? She reached around for her bag, dug it out of the storage unit and retrieved her phone. By then, she'd missed the call. Damn. She checked missed calls, hoping to see Hank's number, but no. It hadn't been Hank. She didn't recognize the number, not even the area code. And she saw that she'd missed a bunch of other calls, too. She took out a tissue, wiped drying blood off her hand. Blew her nose. Thought about going home, what she should do. Wondered why Hank hadn't called. What he really wanted. Rubbed her eyes. Glanced at the list of missed calls.

Good God – Burke Everett had left three voicemails. Vicki had called, too, and Harper's mother, just back from a cruise. And Leslie. Thank goodness – maybe Leslie could see her today even though it was the weekend – maybe she was even free now . . .

But Leslie's message said that she was away for the weekend. At a wedding. She could see Harper Monday at noon.

Harper bit her lip, looked at her cut hand, then off into the hills. She closed her eyes and drew a breath. Monday was a long, long time away.

Burke stopped cold, looked over his shoulder. Gazed quickly across the street. Seeing no one, he turned back to his car and stared.

The thread was gone. The thread he'd hung on the door handle had fallen to the ground. Which meant someone had tried to get into his car.

They'd found it. The Colonel's people had probably booby-trapped it, attached an explosive device to it. He didn't dare stop to look for it. They had to be nearby, watching for him. If he lingered or poked around, they'd see him. No. No way he was even going to touch that car. No one was going to blow him to hell.

Burke kept walking, deciding what to do. Finally figuring out that he'd been wrong: there was no bomb. An explosion at a major university would draw too much attention. What they'd probably done was much less obvious, though just as dangerous to him; they'd put a tracking device in the car. That way, they could keep tabs on him. Follow his every move. Get to him later, with less fanfare.

But Burke wasn't going to let that happen. He walked on, not clear where he was headed. Used his phone to find a rental car office. But before they even picked up, he realized what an idiot he was: to rent a car, he'd have to use his credit card. They'd be watching for his card number, would track him that way.

In fact, now that he thought about it, he shouldn't use his credit card at all – even to go to a damned ATM for some cash. Did they think he was an idiot? That he couldn't figure out how they worked? Fuck them. His feet slammed the sidewalk. Pissed. What the fuck was he supposed to do now? He couldn't even get a fucking bus ticket without them finding about it. He felt trapped, cornered. Looked around. Lowered his head.

OK. OK. They couldn't stick around Ithaca forever, could they? He'd just have to outsmart them, stay out of sight. He needed to talk to Harper; he'd already called a thousand times, would keep calling until he reached her. She didn't want to be part of this. But she was smart, would figure out that she had no choice; she was part of it, like it or not. Just like he was. She'd give him some cash and some food. Maybe even put him up for a while. He pulled out his phone, called her again. Got her voicemail again. Damn, couldn't she just pick up her damned phone? Just once? Why did he keep getting her voicemail? It made no sense . . .

Unless the Colonel had already gotten to her.

Christ. Burke stopped walking. Put his hands over his eyes. Pictured Harper dead somewhere, murdered like Pete.

Burke had to know. Had to find out if Harper was still alive, if he was the only one left. Taking side streets, watching pedestrians, he made his way back to her house.

Harper rode around Ithaca, uphill, down again. Rode around to the stadium, heard percussion bursting from the Big Red Band, roars from the Homecoming crowd. Kept riding. Across campus, past the Quad. Through College Town. Back downhill, across town to the lake. Barely aware of traffic or her location, Harper headed to nowhere in particular, riding her way through time. Unsure what she should do. Alone.

The Ninja cut through crisp air; the wind slapped her face raw, but she kept moving, determined to go faster than her heart. Eventually, though, like a homing pigeon, she found herself approaching the turn-off to the long dirt road through the woods, the sign that said, PRIVATE PROPERTY: KEEP OUT. And without hesitation, as if that had been her destination all along, she took the turn on to Langston's place.

Slowing down too quickly, Harper felt the bike skid on pebbles and leaves. The engine was too loud, disturbed the stillness of the place, so she parked it. Decided to walk the rest of the way to the house. She pictured the crates, the hundreds of relics waiting for her, and picked up her pace. Work would help, she decided. She'd spend some time on the collection, think about something besides Hank for a while. Maybe she'd get a fresh perspective. Or at least escape the present one.

Leaves crunched under her feet. Around her, the woods were silent. Nothing moved. She wondered if Angus was around, if he'd pop out from behind a tree, challenging her right to be there. Or if Jake would appear again inside. Never mind. She had every right to be there, would simply insist that they allow her to work. She thought back to the relics she'd already seen: vessels, masks, bowls, figurines. Imagined the thrill of unpacking them, examining them.

Something rustled among the trees. Harper kept walking. Probably a squirrel. Maybe a fox. She looked around, though. Saw just foliage. Light filtering through branches. Dense clusters of trees. And one, along the road, that was missing a chunk of bark – oh God. Zina's tree.

Harper didn't stop to look. She picked up her pace, kept it up until she got inside the house. And even then, she kept moving, not letting the shadows or stillness bother her. She went directly to the third floor, along the long hall to the east wing, focusing only on her task. Determined to ignore the nagging memory of Hank's declaration of independence. His voice, repeating, 'Two lives. Do own things. Apart.'

No. She wouldn't let herself dissolve. She was strong. Would survive somehow. Fine. He wanted her to do her own thing? She would. Starting now. Tears kept filling her eyes, but she resolved to get a grip. She'd concentrate on other times, lost peoples. Escape into the past until she figured out how to bear the present.

Wiping her eyes, Harper booted up the computer, logged on to the documentation page. Picked up a crate, set it on the worktable. Methodically, efficiently, she removed the lid and checked the items listed on the crate's content sheet. Took out the packing materials. Lifted a Styrofoam packing case from the box, carefully removed the tape. Took an excited deep breath. Opened it.

And froze, staring.

The case was empty.

A space had been carved, precisely shaped to hold a vessel. But the vessel wasn't there. It was gone. Harper rechecked the content sheet, scanned the list of items for a vessel. Saw: Mayan polychrome vessel, 550–950 AD, five and a quarter inches high. Estimated value $75,000.

Oh God. Harper couldn't breathe. A piece worth that much money was missing? She looked around the room as if it might suddenly appear. Damn. But how could it be missing? The crate had been sealed. Obviously, someone must have opened it, taken the bowl and then resealed the crate. But who could have done that? The professor? Was this one of the pieces he'd moved to the laundry room?

And even if it was, how could she prove it? Would she be suspected of stealing it? Would Zina? No, that was ridiculous – anyone could have taken it. There was no security at all, no one guarding the collection. The only lock was a hundred years old, on the front door. Other than that, the place was abandoned, unprotected. They might as well put a sign up, advertising the place to thieves.

Lord. For all she knew, all the crates were empty. She scanned the stacks of boxes in the room. And suddenly thought of Jake – maybe Jake had found the vessel. Maybe he'd know where it was. Or at least, he'd vouch for the fact that the professor had moved pieces around and forgotten about them.

Harper let out a breath. Of course. The vessel hadn't been stolen, would turn up in a soup pot or under a pillow, if it hadn't already.

Still, Harper made a note of the missing piece before taking out another packing case. She was uneasy as she unwrapped and opened it, afraid it would be empty. Let out a sigh of relief when she saw that the case still held its relic: a figure of a priest with beadwork around his belt and on his headdress. Fourteen inches high. Made between 500 BC and 500 AD, estimated value of $20,000. Harper photographed and logged it. Took out the next box, opened it to find a Teotihuacán mask, eight and a quarter inches high, made about 500 AD. It was nicked slightly at the top, but still estimated to be worth about $75,000.

Harper's phone rang a few times, but she let it go. If Hank was calling, she wasn't ready to talk to him yet, and if it was someone else, she'd rather work than take the call. Harper proceeded, unpacking the crate, item by item. Logging and photographing each relic. Finding bowls and gold pieces. Another copper mask, early to middle Mohica, Loma Negra, from around 300 BC, six and a half inches high, valued at $4,000. Even damaged, its expression was mesmerizing, powerful. Merciless.

Finally, she replaced everything in the crate, marked it as logged, and made notes of the discrepancies between the original content sheet and her itemized log. In addition to the vessel, two small sculptures valued at $40,000, were unaccounted for. Might be in the professor's sock drawer.

Harper logged off the computer, noticing that three hours had passed since she'd begun working. And that she hadn't dwelt on Hank in all that time. Had been completely absorbed. In fact, she felt stronger now, and refreshed. Stable. Ready to go home and face him, for better or worse.

Walking back to the Ninja, Harper braced herself for the latter. Hank's voice had begun again, telling her that their lives were going to change. Repeating, 'Need change. Big.' And, 'Do own thing. Apart.' She refused to cry again, but her stomach churned, and she realized she hadn't eaten since early morning. Not that she had an appetite. Still, she was thinking about eating as she approached the tree hit by Zina's car. And the spot where she'd found Zina' body.

Up ahead, Harper saw the bald trunk, the dented part missing bark. She shuddered, picturing it. Had Zina's family ambushed her there? Had one of them run in front of the car, causing her to steer into a tree? She imagined them yanking Zina out of the smashed vehicle as she begged them to let her live. Harper stopped herself, didn't want to envision the killing, made herself focus on the leaves, the sound of her footsteps.

She moved through the woods, furious at the brutality of Zina's death. Closing her eyes, she reminded herself that, by comparison, her own family problems were trivial. At least she and Hank could be civil. They could solve their problems without shedding blood.

Passing the damaged tree, Harper steeled herself and glanced into the woods where she'd found Zina's body. She blinked, at first assuming she was having a flashback, seeing Zina lying there again. But the image wouldn't go away. There really was another body there. Only, this one was a man.

A big party was going on next door to Harper's house. Fraternity brothers, dates, alumni, wives. Lots of beer. A big banner, saying, 'Welcome Alumni'. A fancy buffet set up under an open tent in the side yard. A band blasted music from the balcony. Half the people were in costumes – one guy was dressed as a pirate, another as a zombie. Several were in drag. There was a chick in a way-short skirt, her top so low she might as well not have worn it, but somehow it had a badge pinned to it, and she had a cop hat on. An electric witch cackled whenever someone came too close, which was always. Skeletons and zombies swung in the breeze, hanging from trees. Fake tombstones were everywhere. A lot of noise, a rowdy half-in-the-bag crowd.

A good place, Burke figured, to fade into the background. He wandered, trying to be invisible. Pretending that his clothes were a thug costume. People stood in small clusters around the yard, yelling over the music, laughing, drinking, eating. He managed to grab a roast beef sandwich from the tent, wolf it down with a beer, smile and nod when someone said, 'Some game today, huh? Did we whoop Brown, or what?' Everything was going all right until a guy in Gucci walked up with an extended hand and suspicious eyes, introducing himself.

'Jeff Wasserman.' He moved his lips to show teeth. 'Class of oh-six.'

Jeff Wasserman asked what class Burke had been in. Burke shook Jeff's purposely too firm hand, returned the smile. Fumbled for an answer. The guy looked about his age, obviously could tell that he didn't belong there, that he'd never been at Cornell, let alone in the fraternity. Burke was dressed way wrong, didn't have a preppy blazer or an actual costume. Didn't fit. Shouldn't have taken the sandwich. The guy had probably seen him take it, pegged him as a homeless guy stealing food. Well, hell – he had to eat. And he couldn't exactly go into a restaurant or food market.

Burke decided he'd come up with some bullshit about how he'd never graduated. Had flunked out and gone to Iraq. Which would explain his clothes, right? Vets could dress in old jeans and hoodies or whatever they wanted – even at parties. Even on Halloween.

'Mike. Mike Burke,' he began. But he didn't have to go on.

'Hey, Wassy!' a guy in a chicken suit called from the porch. 'We need a legal opinion.'

And so Jeff Wasserman and his Gucci blazer excused himself and took off, leaving Burke to grab another sandwich, refill his beer and wander to the back of the house where no one would notice him. Where he could watch Harper's house and look for her or anyone else who approached it. Where the trees would shield him from anyone tailing him.

But after almost an hour, no one had stirred at Harper's house. Damn. Where the hell was she? He wondered if she'd gotten the letter he'd sent, outlining everything just in case something happened to him. Every detail was there, implicating the Colonel. He'd wanted to give it to her personally, to make sure it didn't get intercepted, but ended up mailing it. And now, Harper was AWOL. Was it because she'd read the letter? Because they knew she knew?

Burke thought of calling again. What was the point? He'd called her dozens of times, gotten no response. And he had to ditch the phone soon – his third in as many days, afraid they'd trace his calls to Harper and find him from the signal. But he couldn't buy another phone without using his credit card, so he couldn't toss this one quite yet, just turned it off. Felt his sweatshirt pocket for the Beretta as he looked around. He could feel them around him, closing in. He'd seen them that morning, a black sedan following him along Seneca, so he'd ducked between buildings, stayed away from traffic after that. Moved as he'd been trained: efficiently, invisibly. Holding them off.

But they weren't far. He sensed them, the searing beams of their eyes. Smelled the tension, the adrenalin. They might even be here, mingling with the frat boys, disguised in costumes. He checked out a guy dressed like a hula dancer. Was he packing under his leis? And the dude in the chicken suit – he could have a whole arsenal under all those feathers. Burke shifted positions, scanned the perimeter. Saw nothing definite. But he wasn't fooled. They were watching him even now. Closing in.

Harper froze, staring at the body. Dark hair, dark skin. Lying exactly where Zina had been. Looking very much like she had looked. Perfectly still.

Damn. How was it possible that there was another body there? Right there, in that exact spot. Not a week after Zina had died there.

Harper listened, looked behind her. Heard nothing, saw no one. The body was on top of a pile of leaves, as if resting against them. She edged closer, peering through the trees. Looked for a wound, for blood. Saw neither. So how had he died? Strangling? Poison? Was there a knife in his back? Oh God. Who was this man? And who'd killed him? She thought of Angus, the way he disliked having people on the property. Had he completely lost it and killed a trespasser?

Or could it have been Jake? She remembered being alone in the house with him. His anger about his father's will, about losing the collection. Maybe this guy was a lawyer and Jake had taken his revenge? Ridiculous. Jake had made her uneasy, but that was no reason to assume he was a killer. Was it?

Besides, she shouldn't be standing there, staring at a dead body. She should leave it alone, shouldn't mess up the scene. Should simply take her phone out and call the police. Except maybe he was still alive . . . Before she did anything else, she should at least find out if he had a pulse. Maybe she could help him. Maybe he was still alive and needed first aid. CPR.

Cautiously, quickly, Harper moved toward the man. Kneeling beside him, she reached for his throat, hesitating for a moment to touch him, to invade the privacy of his death. Dreading the absence of a heartbeat, the sensation of cool, lifeless flesh. But she stiffened, took a breath, and put her hand directly over his carotid artery, as she'd been trained. And, just before he sat up, yelling, swinging and grabbing at her, she saw the half-gallon of Cutty Sark near his feet, almost a quarter gone.

For a couple of hours, Burke managed to dig in and hold his position behind the fraternity. He drank beer, tried to blend in. Kept watch on the woods and Harper's house. Saw nothing. But he wasn't fooled.

He sensed their presence. Where the hell were they? What were they planning? They weren't simply going to leave him alone and go away; they were up to something. His face itched from nerves. A tic had begun in one eyelid. It was like Iraq, being on alert, not knowing what was coming.

Around dusk, the party began to wrap up. Burke thought he'd grab a final sandwich when he heard rustling in the trees. Instinctively, he dropped, stayed close to the ground. Peered into the growth. The music pounded, shook the ground. And suddenly, something large shook the foliage, darted away – damn. A deer. A fucking deer. Burke released a breath and stood up again, relieved.

Remembering the sandwich, he stepped around to the side of the house. People were drifting away. Probably, he should ignore Harper's order to leave her alone. Probably, he should go back to her house and simply knock on the door. If she was out, he could wait for her there. What else, really, was there for him to do? He had no other options – she'd have to let him stay there until it was safe. Maybe she'd even have an idea for their next move.

Unless – fuck! Again, the unacceptable possibility hit him: it might already be too late. Harper might not be home because the Colonel had already gotten to her. In which case . . . Well, in which case, he wouldn't let them take him, too. His hand closed around the Beretta. No way would he let the Colonel have that satisfaction.

The chip bowl was empty, and the potato salad was gone. Oh well. Burke grabbed his sandwich and headed out of the tent. He was taking a bite, thinking about ringing Harper's bell when he saw the guy in the chicken costume walking toward him. A cat burglar had moved in, blocking his path to the woods. OK. Time to take off. Still chewing, Burke pivoted, hurrying toward Harper's.

The guy took her by surprise, but Harper instantly shifted into combat mode, pinning him effortlessly. He didn't have much bulk, and she'd been trained. Had dropped men twice his size. She'd rolled him over, had a knee in his spine, held his arms behind him.

'What do you want?' he panted. He wriggled, still trying to free himself. 'Who are you? Let go of me.'

Harper smelled the booze in his breath. She tightened her grip. 'Hold still.'

'You want my wallet? Take it.'

'Who are you?' Actually, it was none of her business who he was.

Or what he was doing there. He was trespassing, but that wasn't her concern; the property wasn't hers.

'Get off of me.' He twisted his neck, trying to look at her.

'Answer me.'

'No, I won't answer you. I won't tell you anything until you get off of me.' He bucked.

'Hold still.'

'I will not hold still.' The guy was stubborn; even flattened on the ground, his face buried in dead leaves, he argued. Refused to give in.

Harper stayed put, but her left leg complained, didn't like bending for long periods. Soon it would throb. 'Look. I can stay here all day,' she lied. 'Tell me what you're doing here.'

'Tell me why you've assaulted me.'

Really? 'Dude. You're the one who did the assaulting. I saw you lying here not moving, and I came to help you. I was afraid you might be dead—'

'Well, now you know. I'm not dead. And I don't need your help. So just—'

'But you started swinging at me.'

'Well, of course. Naturally, I did. I was sleeping here, and suddenly you came at me out of nowhere!' He sputtered, but she felt his body relax. 'You put your hands on my neck – what would anyone in that situation do?'

Good point. In that situation, she'd have probably decked somebody. Then again, she wouldn't have been sleeping out here in the woods on the Langston's private property. Her left leg was tired of bending, beginning to throb. And she really needed to get home. 'OK. If I let you up, will you promise not to try to hit me?'

'If you leave me alone, I'll leave you alone.'

More conditions. Why wouldn't the guy just give in? Probably, she'd wounded his pride. Never mind. They both knew she'd flattened him and that he didn't dare mess with her again. She slid off his back, watched as he rolled over and sat up. He gazed at the trees. Then at her.

'So.' Harper crossed her arms. 'Who are you? And what are you doing here?'

'I might ask you the same.' He spoke formally, looked up at her with steady dark eyes. Familiar eyes.

'I'm Harper Jennings. I have a research position here.'

He nodded, then reached for his bottle of Cutty Sark. 'Nice to meet you, Harper Jennings who has a research position here.' He took off the cap. 'Would you like a drink?'

Burke didn't get far. Looking over his shoulder, he stumbled over a tombstone and hit the ground. Lost the roast beef sandwich. Regaining his balance, he reached for the 9 mm that had fallen from his pocket. Looked around to make sure no one had noticed him dropping it.

Saw a guy in a blazer approaching from his right. Recognized him.

'That him?' The chicken pointed a wing at him.

'You all right there, Burke?' The guy smiled at him. Held out an arm to help him to his feet.

Burke hesitated, feigning pain and surprise. 'Rick? What the hell are you doing here?'

Shit shit shit. They'd found him. Rick Owens, the Colonel's right hand man, was an arm's length away. Reaching for him.

Burke moaned, pretended to be unable to get up. Then, as Rick and the chicken stepped forward, he scrambled. Grabbing the ground for balance, he fumbled the gun, had to let it go. Took off in a full out run. Made it past Rick, faked a move to the left, made it past the chicken and into the woods. Heard Rick calling, 'Everett! Hey. Wait – stop!' As if they were buddies and he wanted to catch a beer.

Burke zigzagged through the trees, uphill. Slipped on leaves, nearly tripping over stuff hidden beneath them – twigs or undergrowth. His breath was ragged, his lungs scraped raw, but he kept going. Felt Rick right behind him, didn't dare slow down to look. Heard his shoes crushing leaves. Heard his panting. Ahead, Burke faced a steep incline. Damn, maybe four feet straight up. No choice, no time – he bent his knees and jumped, legs out. Grabbed a tree trunk and held on. Steadying himself, he saw the fence.

It was ten feet tall. Extended at least fifty feet in each direction. And it stood just a few yards in front of him, blocking his way.

Instinctively, Burke whirled, kicking. His heel landed in Rick's gut, and the guy folded, sounded like a dying cat. Burke spun left, didn't see anyone else. Rick was recovering, climbing to his feet, pissed.

'What the fuck's wrong with you?' He wheezed, coughed, held his stomach. 'Are you nuts?'

Burke didn't want to get trapped following the fence, needed to get back down the hill, past Rick.

'I just want to fuckin' talk to you. Have a conversation.' Rick brushed dirt off his slacks, catching his breath. Reaching into his pocket.

Burke wasn't going to wait for the gun to appear. Before Rick could say another word, he lunged straight at him, knocking him aside, and charged back down the ledge, through the trees, past the fraternity with its Halloween zombies and graveyard markers, its gaggle of costumed pot-smokers on the porch.

Burke didn't stop to look around. Was sure that Rick hadn't come for him alone, that others were nearby, lurking, about to pounce. He raced along Wyckoff, Thurston. Headed towards a bridge. Saw a gang of them coming towards him, some of them in disguises. One dressed as a clown. Really? A clown? But there were too many to take on. And Rick was behind him; he couldn't slow down, couldn't wait for Harper, couldn't rest, didn't dare. Rick was fast – Burke could hear him panting, closing in, just a few steps behind. He ran even after he'd lost his breath, even when his muscles burned. He sprinted on to the bridge, kept going even when he knew they had him. He was trapped, Rick behind him, the others ahead. Out of options, Burke looked around, grit his teeth. And did the only thing he could.

The man took a swig of Cutty. Held the bottle out for Harper.

Harper shook her head, no thanks. It was getting dark. And she had to get home.

'I have no diseases.'

Well, what was the harm? The encounter had left her jittery, and one sip wouldn't hurt, might even settle her nerves. Lord knew they'd had a rough day. Harper took the bottle, raised it to her mouth. Swallowed. Felt the heat of booze slide down her throat, warming her. She handed the bottle back.

'I am Salih.' Salih drank again. 'Salih Salim.'

Salih *Salim*? As in Zina Salim? Harper drew a breath, felt cold again.

'And, I admit it.' He stopped to hiccup. 'I am trespassing.' He blinked at her. 'Do you want to call the police, Harper Jennings? Do you think I should be arrested?'

'No. I'm sorry – I didn't realize. Are you related to Zina?' She didn't know what to say.

He tilted his head, looking at her. 'You knew my sister?'

Harper nodded. 'I . . . yes. Actually, I found her. Here.' Why had she said that?

'*You?*'

Harper nodded.

They were silent for a moment.

'And when I saw you lying in the same spot, I thought . . . Well, I thought there was another body.'

Salih nodded, 'Of course.' He gestured to a fallen trunk beside him. 'Have a seat.' Another hiccup. 'I'm afraid I'm not dead. I've simply been drinking for a while. I must have dozed off.'

Harper sat, assessing Salih. His body was beefy and long. His features fuller than Zina's, his eyes round and fiery. If Zina's death had been an honor killing, had he known about it? Had he actually committed it? Harper imagined it: Salih holding his sister while their father wielded a knife. Or the other way around. Oh God. This man, Salih – was he Zina's murderer?

Harper stiffened and glanced at the path, ready to bolt. Salih blinked, his back sagging against a tree trunk. He'd had too much to drink to be a threat. Besides, she'd already taken him down once, could do it again. And she wanted to find out more about Zina's family.

'My little sister was a rebel.' He shook his head. 'Even more than me. I – well, as you can see – I take a drink. My family doesn't approve.'

Harper said nothing.

'But Zina defied our parents. Always, from the time she was a little child. She had to do things her way. So stubborn.' He chuckled. 'There are seven of us – oops. Were seven of us. Now we are six.'

Harper nodded. 'I'm sorry.' Salih couldn't have participated in Zina's murder. Her loss clearly pained him.

'We grew up in Britain. Our parents and three brothers are still there. But our business expanded to the United States, so some of us moved here. Zina was the youngest. She came over for school, and, right away, she was American. Watching *Friends*. Or *90210*. Or whatever. Getting ideas about men, about dating. Dressing in tight jeans, showing her body. She became a different person.'

He lifted the bottle, offered it to Harper. She accepted, took a polite sip. Passed it back.

'Zina came to my house the night before she was killed.' Harper thought he might want to know. 'She was frightened.'

Salih's eyebrows lifted. Interested.

'She was working here, at the house. And she thought she was being followed.'

'So she knew she was in danger?'

'Well . . .' How was she to explain that Zina thought she was being followed by a mythological creature? 'I think working here stimulated her imagination. She thought she was being followed by a shape-shifter.'

'A shape-shifter.'

'Yes. A Nahual.' Harper explained the Pre-Columbian belief in men who could change forms to guard their land and people.

When she finished, Salih blinked at her. 'My sister believed such a thing was real? A – what did you call it? A Nahual? That this Nahual was chasing her?'

'Zina was shaken. She thought something was chasing her. I don't know why.'

'A premonition.'

Harper didn't comment.

'Do you think that's what it was? A premonition of her death?'

Harper hadn't considered that possibility. Didn't know how to answer. 'I don't know.'

'They say these things happen. That people sometimes have a sign that the end is coming.'

Harper doubted it. 'All I know is that she was frightened. Not herself. Up until then, Zina had seemed very . . . calm and realistic.' She'd wanted to say very competitive and aloof. 'Your sister was very strong willed. Very ambitious.'

'Too strong willed. Too ambitious. Forget the Nahual or whatever you call it. Her stubbornness and ambitions are what got her killed.'

Her stubbornness and ambitions? Why would he say that? Was Salih acknowledging that there had been an honor killing? Admitting that Zina had been killed because she was too Westernized? 'I don't understand . . .'

'If she hadn't been here –' Salih gazed into the trees – 'if she hadn't been working on that research position and insisting on that doctorate degree, if she'd just gone along as part of the family, helped with the business and gotten married like our parents wanted, she'd still be alive.' His voice broke; he looked away.

'You were close?' Stupid question. Obviously, they'd been close.

The man was here, where Zina's body had been found, getting drunk and fighting tears.

His shoulders sagged. 'She was my little sister.'

But Harper was confused. 'There was a memorial for her at the university. You weren't there – nobody from the family came.'

'We have our own ways of mourning.'

Harper pictured family members laundering blood from their clothes after the honor killing. 'Still. It might have helped to see how many people cared about her. You said you were close.'

'I said *I* was close with Zina. I didn't say my family was. My family is . . . We come from a different culture. I don't expect you to understand. But my sister parted ways with it. It's a long and bitter story. She defied our parents constantly. Whatever the line was, she crossed it. Many times. She embarrassed them publicly. She refused to participate in the family's business enterprises. She even refused to marry the man to whom our father promised her.'

'Well, of course she did, Salih. Nobody's parents arrange marriages for them in America—'

'My family is not American.' Salih cut her off. 'We were raised here and in Britain, but we are Syrian. Traditional and proud. Zina was part of our family. She knew our ways, but she resisted. When she turned her back on the family interests, my parents declared her dead. So there it is: why would they come to a memorial service for her when, to them, she'd already been dead for some time?'

Harper sat straight. 'What do you mean they declared her "dead"?' Had they issued her death sentence?

'I mean "dead". They cut off all ties. Including funds, even for education. I'm the only one who even talked to her. I kept urging her to make amends. To perform symbolic acts of humility and penance. I did it secretly, but I suspect my mother knows – knew.'

Again, he took a drink, passed the bottle to Harper.

'Who do you think killed her?' Harper took a sip, watching his eyes.

'That's a question, isn't it?' Salih shifted positions. 'Trust me, I think about it every minute. About who killed her . . .' He lifted the bottle, gulped booze. 'I know several who might have done it. Including close members of my family.'

Oh God. He suspected an honor killing, too? 'Are you talking about an honor killing?' Had she just said that out loud?

Salih didn't answer, didn't seem surprised or offended by the question. He took another long drink, looked at Harper with a resigned smile. 'Honestly, you want to hear the truth? Whoever did it, my sister understood why. And whoever did it, no one else will ever know.'

By the time Harper returned to her Ninja, Salih had put away much of what was left in the Cutty Sark bottle. And among other things, he had confided that he believed his family was behind Zina's murder, that despite living in the West, they still held to the old ways of their heritage. His aunt had wanted a divorce and had been stabbed to death years before – no doubt at his uncle's hand. Before Harper had thought about the time, the sun had dipped to the horizon.

Salih promised he was perfectly fine and able to drive, but Harper insisted that he leave his car parked on the main road where it was. She was sober, having swallowed only a few sips of liquor, but Salih was slurring his words and teetering, in no shape to get behind the wheel. Harper insisted on taking him to his hotel. She dropped him at the Embassy Inn on Dryden Road, and, as darkness fell, watched him wobble inside. Then, she headed home.

Oh dear. Hank. What was she supposed to say to him? Maybe she should call and let him know she was all right. Then again, if he was ready to break up their marriage, he ought to get used to not knowing how she was. A hot pang ripped through her belly, into her chest. Was Hank really doing this? Why? 'Why' didn't matter, she scolded herself. It wasn't about reasons or arguments; it was about feelings. Needs. And she couldn't make Hank need her or feel for her. Maybe Leslie was right that his healing required him to redis-cover himself. Maybe his fall had damaged not just his bones and brain, but his ego. Before she'd met him, Hank had been quite a player. Maybe he needed to prove that he could still be one. That he was still hot, could still score with the ladies – well, if so, if that was what he needed, they were over for sure. Done. No way she'd stick around for that.

Cut it out, she told herself. She had no reason to think that Hank wanted other women. She was imagining things, needed to stop.

Harper revved the engine, sped down Dryden to Hoy, along Hoy to Campus Road, Campus to East. East to Thurston. Along the way, she passed Homecoming events, parties in transition from happy hour to Halloween Eve bashes. Something was going on at the

Alumni House. Music pounded out of fraternities, sororities. Dorms. Harper kept moving, zipping past. Going home.

Finally, she pulled into the driveway. Saw the house dark. The Jeep gone.

Damn.

Harper got off her bike and stood, arms folded, feeling the chill of the night, dreading going into the empty house.

'Hey, Mrs Jennings!'

She turned, saw a kid from the frat next door. Dressed as a chicken. 'We still got some beer – come on over!'

Harper waved. Thanked him and backed off. Turned away and headed toward the house. The last thing she wanted was to hang out with drunk college kids in Halloween costumes.

Or no. Maybe not the last thing.

Inside, she turned on the hall light, took out her phone and checked her messages. Nothing more from Burke, thank God. But Hank had called. Once. An hour ago.

Harper hesitated, afraid to hear the message. What was wrong with her? Why was she scared of a damned telephone message? Squaring her shoulders, she braced herself and played it back.

'Damn. Hoppa. Answer.' That was all. Not, 'Come home. I'm worried.' Not, 'I'm sorry. I love you.' Just a curse word and a command.

She played it again. His voice sounded strained. Hank was upset.

She pushed the 'send' button, returning his call. Waited, breathing unevenly for him to pick up. Heard his phone ringing in the kitchen.

Lord. Hank hadn't taken his phone? Where had he gone without it? And when was he coming back?

Or more to the point: *was* he coming back?

Harper closed her eyes, imagining their bedroom. His half of the closet empty. His razor missing from the bathroom sink. No. He wouldn't have moved out. Not so suddenly. It hadn't – couldn't have – come to that yet.

Even so, she didn't want to go upstairs. Damn Where had he gone? She thought of calling Vicki and Trent to see if Hank was there. But if he weren't, she'd have to explain why she didn't know where he was. And she wasn't ready to do that.

Cursing, Harper flung her phone into her bag, stomped into the kitchen. Her stomach felt hollow; she'd been drinking but not eating. She opened the refrigerator, took out an apple, bit into it. Gagged.

Her stomach was empty and rumbling but her body rejected food, refused to eat. Fine. She opened a cabinet, found the Halloween candy. Ripped open a mini-bag of M&Ms, poured them into her mouth. No gagging. Her body didn't object, accepted chocolate. Grabbing a second bagful, she didn't know what to do with herself, where to be. She couldn't stay in the kitchen. Couldn't stay anywhere. Walked in circles until she finally went back outside, on to the front porch.

She watched the street for a while, saw cars drive by, none of them Hank's.

The music from next store had quieted; it was dark now, and their post-game party was over. Alumni and their wives had gone; pledges were filling trash bags and folding tables, cleaning up. A few couples in Halloween costumes lingered in the yard, drinking and smoking dope among the plastic tombstones and hanging skeletons. A guy in a hoodie darted across the lawn, activating a mechanical witch who cackled and danced.

Harper wandered off the porch, down to the sidewalk, not ready to go back into her empty house. The night air was brisk. Harper shivered as a gust of wind picked up leaves, swirling them around. Maybe she should reconsider calling Vicki and Trent. She could call just to say 'hi', not even mention Hank. If he were there, they'd tell her, wouldn't they?

Harper stopped mid-thought. Something was out there in the trees – running. An animal? No – a man. He wore a blazer and khakis, and, though he didn't seem to notice her, he was running right towards her.

Harper froze, gaping as he sped past. It had to be the darkness. She had to be mistaken. She turned, walking after him, staring into the night long after he was out of sight.

He'd been moving fast, she reminded herself. And it was dark; she hadn't gotten a good look. Even so, she could almost swear she'd recognized him. She was almost positive it was the guy Burke had said was following him: Rick Owens, from their detail in Iraq.

But that made no sense. Obviously, it hadn't been Rick. Why would Rick Owens be hightailing it out of the woods behind her house in the middle of the night? In Ithaca? Burke had colored her thinking; she was taking on his paranoia.

The wind was picking up. Harper went back to the house, hearing sirens nearby, wondered what college pranks had gone too far this time. Inside, she changed into flannel PJs and listened for Hank's car. She went downstairs to make a sandwich. Found a can of tuna, a half-empty jar of mayo. A lone bagel, not too stale to toast. Mindlessly, she went through the motions of preparing food, on alert for the sounds of tires on the driveway.

Waiting, she chewed tuna. Swallowed beer. Thought of Salih and Zina. Her family alienated enough to declare her dead. Even to kill her. Thought of the relics to get her mind off of that.

Finally, headlights flared through the windows. Harper heard a car in the driveway and couldn't help it. She ran to the door, expecting to see Hank climbing out of his Jeep.

But the car wasn't Hank's. It had red and blue lights on top, and letters on the side, spelling POLICE.

And the person walking along the path to the house wasn't her husband. It was the homicide detective, Charlene Rivers.

Hank? Oh God. Something had happened to Hank – Rivers was in homicide. Had Hank been – oh God . . .

Harper couldn't move, couldn't speak. She watched Rivers' approach in slow motion, through a haze. This wasn't real. The detective wasn't actually there. Neither was Harper. Her mind was tricking her. Snipers fired; she felt the whizz of bullets flying past her cheek. Heard men scream. Smelled smoke as Rivers took a step, then another, wading through thickened air. And then, ever so slowly, Rivers smiled.

Wait. She smiled? How could Rivers smile at a woman whose husband had just been killed?

'Good evening, Mrs Jennings.' The words were dim, distant. The smile disappeared. Rivers kept coming. Spoke again, asking a question.

Harper's heart raged against her ribs, threatened to burst through. Rivers stood facing her, watching her. Making words.

Harper strained to hear her over the roaring sounds of her blood. 'Mrs Jennings? You all right?'

She moved her head up and down, yes. Hugged herself, shaking.

'Well? Can I come in?'

Oh God, oh God. Rivers wanted to come in? Bad sign. Obviously, she didn't want to deliver bad news on the doorstep. Harper wanted to refuse her. To say, no, you can't come in. Because, somehow, if nobody told her that Hank was dead, he wouldn't be. Officially, anyway. As far as she knew, he'd still be alive. Wouldn't he?

Rivers took a step forward.

Harper's head moved again, up and down. She opened the door. Rivers went in. Harper hesitated, gripping the doorframe. Making herself breathe. Finally, she followed the detective into the house.

'Can we sit?'

Harper had to read Rivers' lips; blood rushed through her head like a waterfall, drowning out all other sounds. She was shivering violently, couldn't get warm so she pulled Hank's parka from the closet, put it on. Hunkered into it. Smelled Hank. Oh God.

Rivers was touching her arm, asking questions. Moving her lips: 'What's wrong? Are you sick?'

Harper wrapped the jacket around her. 'Chilled,' she managed.

They sat at the kitchen table, Rivers across from her. Studying her.

Harper waited, aware that time had slowed. That each moment was stretching and distorting. She heard her pulse, her lungs. She felt like screaming. Dammit, why couldn't Rivers just get it over with and tell her what happened to Hank?

Ask her, she told herself. Just go ahead and ask.

But she didn't have to. As soon as she opened her mouth to speak, Rivers reached into her pocket and took out an envelope. 'Mrs Jennings,' she began. 'I'm afraid I have some unpleasant news. There was a suicide tonight.'

Suicide?

'A man jumped off the Thurston Avenue Bridge.'

A man? Harper waited for Rivers to utter Hank's name. Why was she being so oblique? Shouldn't she be more empathetic? Shouldn't she prepare the widow for her loss, offer condolences?

'A bunch of students saw him. A man was there, trying to talk him down. The kids tried to help.'

Harper strained to listen to Rivers' details. Apparently, as the students approached, the man had tried to help him, offered him a job. But the jumper had refused, cursing and shouting that he'd never take a deal with 'that fucker'. Promising that 'your boss is going down'. Then he'd jumped.

The kids had called 911; in a matter of minutes, the body had been retrieved from the gorge.

Harper's pulse slowed. Rivers still hadn't said Hank's name. Hadn't even hinted at it. And the story – well, the guy didn't sound like Hank. For one thing, Hank wouldn't have made such coherent statements. His words would have come out differently, in short spurts. So this dead man wasn't, couldn't be Hank.

Relief washed over her, made her giddy. Hank was alive. Although, if he didn't come home soon, he might not be that way long; she might kill him herself. Where the hell was he? She pictured him out at a bar. With another woman. His head too close to hers. Damn, she needed to stop imagining—

'Mrs Jennings?'

Lord. She hadn't heard a word the detective had been saying.

'I gotta tell you, you don't seem like yourself. You might be coming down with something.'

'Sorry. I'm . . . fine.'

'As I was saying, his cell phone shows that he's called you several times today.'

What? Harper felt blood drain from her head.

'And there's another reason we think you know him. He had this in his pocket when he died.'

Rivers held up a piece of scrap paper. Handwritten letters spelled: HARPER REYNOLDS. Reynolds was crossed out, replaced with JENNINGS. And her address and phone number.

The realization hit Harper hard: it was Burke. He was dead. Burke Everett had jumped off a bridge.

Harper couldn't get warm. She wrapped Hank's parka around herself and heated up some coffee, but kept shivering anyway.

Burke was dead? Oh God.

If she'd taken his phone calls, agreed to help him, would he still be alive? Was his death her fault?

She pictured him flying off the bridge. Lying limp and lifeless in the gorge.

A detail about his death resonated in her mind. She tried to figure out what. But Rivers kept interrupting, asking questions. Wanting to know who Burke was, how Harper knew him. Why he'd been calling her.

Harper told the detectives about serving with Burke in Iraq. About his recent visit and urgent need to talk with her.

Damn you, Harper. Don't tell them another word. She heard Burke's voice as clearly as if he'd been sitting beside her. *They won't believe you anyway. They'll tell the Colonel anything you say – you're digging your grave.*

Rivers frowned. 'After all these years, Mrs Jennings? Isn't it strange that Mr Everett suddenly came all this way for a visit?'

'Not really. Another guy we served with just died. Burke came here after the funeral.' And suddenly, Harper knew what had been bothering her: Peter Murray. He hadn't simply died; he had hanged himself.

First Pete, now Burke. Both dead. Both suicides. Harper shivered.

Rivers nodded. 'I see.'

'Actually, our friend committed suicide.'

Burke hissed: *Shut the fuck up, Harper – you can't trust her. Baxter has the cops—*

'Suicide?'

Harper swallowed hot coffee. Felt it cool as it made contact with her icy gut. 'His name was Peter Murray. He hanged himself.'

Rivers met Harper's eyes.

'Also a suicide.' Rivers repeated.

Harper nodded. Hugged herself inside the parka.

'And when was this funeral?'

'Recently. A week or two ago.'

Rivers jotted down notes. Raised an eyebrow, waited for Harper to go on.

'Burke was torn up about Pete's death. In fact, he . . . he sounded paranoid. Truthfully, I think he'd lost it.'

Stop, Harper. I mean it – button your trap.

'What do you mean "lost it"?'

Harper slid deeper into the parka. 'He had a theory about why Pete died. He was positive everyone who'd served on a special detail was in danger from a retired Colonel who was having us followed.'

Shut the fuck up, Harper!

'He said that, with Pete dead, he and I were the only ones left who could bring this Colonel down – he was irrational.'

Rivers watched her for a moment, then sighed. 'Some of these military guys, they come home changed. They can't readjust. My cousin's kid is like that. Can't hold a job, doesn't want to do anything. We worry about him.'

Harper wrapped her hands around her coffee mug, trying to warm them. 'Burke said his marriage broke up.'

'See? That might have been what sent him off. What about work? Do you know if he had a job?'

Harper didn't. But she knew something else: that Burke's death was her fault. 'I told him to get lost. He was calling constantly, warning me about the danger we were in. He even showed up here at the house and got Hank upset – the guy was out of control.' She paused. 'But instead of getting him some help, I told him to buzz off. I just . . . abandoned him.'

Rivers crossed her arms. 'So you're blaming yourself for this man's death?'

Maybe. A little. Yes. 'He needed help. I didn't look out for him. I left him on his own.'

They sat in silence for a few moments, drinking coffee.

'It wasn't your job to take care of this guy.' Rivers finally spoke. 'You're not in Iraq any more; he's not your responsibility.'

But he was. He'd been one of her guys; he'd come to her and she'd let him down.

'You couldn't have known what would happen and probably couldn't have stopped it anyway.'

Harper wasn't sure about that. She nodded anyway, so the detective would stop talking.

More silence. Harper stared at her coffee mug. Saw Burke diving off the bridge, the laces of his sneakers flying.

'Well. Anything else you can share on this guy?' Rivers pushed her chair away from the table. 'Because, first glance, seems pretty open and shut.'

It did?

'Guy was having a breakdown. He was depressed, losing control. Becoming delusional. Finally committed suicide.'

Suicide. Something icy ricocheted inside Harper's chest. She pictured Burke waiting for her to call back. Not daring to come to her home because she'd forbidden it. And, while she'd been out drinking with Salih, he'd given up. Lost all hope. Gone to the bridge and jumped. She heard the thud of his landing. Shuddered. Closed her eyes.

Detective Rivers stood. 'Where's your husband?'

Her husband? The question startled her. All evening, she'd been listening for Hank's car to pull into the driveway, but Detective Rivers didn't know that – why was she asking about him? What did she know?

'You're not in great shape, Mrs Jennings. I don't want to leave you here alone.'

Harper released a breath. 'I'm fine. Hank'll be back soon.' She hoped.

She glanced at the clock. Twenty after nine. Where was Hank?

As if in answer, a car door slammed outside. Hank was back. Unless it was more cops. No. She recognized the footsteps coming up the back stairs. Hank's gait. Harper froze, couldn't move. Rivers took their cups to the sink. Getting ready to go.

The kitchen door opened and Hank burst in wild-eyed. 'Hoppa?' He looked around the kitchen. 'Happened? Police.'

Rivers sat again, reviewing what had happened for Hank. Asking what he knew about Burke. What Burke had said the day he'd come to the house.

'Jumpy. Wanted to see. Hoppa.' Hank didn't look at her. 'Wouldn't tell. Said urgent. Danger. Not. Why.'

'He was jumpy?'

Hank nodded. His eyes glowered. 'Looking. Behind him.'

Rivers sighed. 'Well, that fits.'

'Fits what?'

'What we know so far.' Rivers' eyes travelled from Hank to Harper, back to Hank. 'Mr Everett was extremely troubled. Possibly troubled enough to take his own life.'

'Self killed?'

'He jumped off a bridge.'

'Damn. But kill. Why?'

'Because of me.' Harper finally spoke. 'Burke asked me to help him. And I didn't.' Harper wanted Hank to hold her, warm her in his big muscled arms. But he didn't. Might not ever. She huddled into his parka across the kitchen from those arms, speaking to him for the first time since she'd left the house that morning. 'He must have come here looking for help again, and I wasn't here.'

'But kill self? He wait could. Or come back.'

'Mr Jennings, the guy wasn't thinking straight.' Rivers folded her arms. 'His buddy just killed himself. His marriage fell apart. He never readjusted to civilian life. He came to his old army pal but even she couldn't help him.'

The words felt like a blow to the gut; Harper let out a soft involuntary grunt.

'Not to say it's your fault. You didn't do anything wrong. Mrs Jennings, look, statistically, each year there are twice as many suicides as murders – and that number is even higher among war vets. Given all the factors I just rattled off, it looks like a cut and dry suicide.'

Harper sat silent, only half listening to the detective, her thoughts spinning. It wasn't her fault that Burke had died – was it? She didn't dare look at Hank. Wished he would do something to reassure her – move his chair closer. Take her hand. Something. And, oh God – the detective would leave soon. What would happen then? Would Hank want to talk? Later, would they sleep in the same bed? She bit her lip, looked at her hands, began her spiral again. Oh God, Burke was dead. But it wasn't her fault, was it?

Harper watched Rivers, not listening any more. But Rivers was looking at her, so she tuned in, heard: '. . . second dead body connected to your wife in as many weeks . . .'

Harper sat straight. Cleared her throat. Tuned in.

'. . . don't seem connected to each other, but they're both connected to her . . . understandable if she's shaken up.' Rivers eyed her but talked to Hank. '. . . keep an eye on her if I were you.'

Two bodies. Harper saw Zina again, her slumped body bathed in blood. And she imagined Burke, battered on the floor of the gorge. She recalled the indifferent stillness of Zina's flesh.

'Any news? Zina case?'

'Nothing I can discuss yet.' Rivers watched Harper. 'Mrs Jennings, are you OK?'

She wasn't. Zina had come to her for help and died. The same thing had happened to Burke. No question. Somehow, everything was her fault. She was toxic. No wonder Hank was done with her. Her stomach wrenched and she tasted bile. Harper stood and dashed to the powder room, about to be sick.

'Hoppa?' Hank waited outside in the hall.

Harper rinsed her face, patted it dry. 'I'm OK.' She stepped out of the powder room, drained.

Hank didn't say anything, just followed as she walked back to the kitchen.

'Are you all right?' Rivers stared at her. She was standing, as if about to go.

Harper's face got hot. 'I'm fine. Just upset – I haven't eaten much, and I guess I had too much to drink this afternoon.'

Silence. Two pairs of eyes watched her.

'I . . . I was working at Langston's. And I ran into Zina's brother. He was there, at the exact spot where I found her—'

'Excuse me?' Rivers interrupted. 'You ran into who?'

Harper felt Hank's glare. 'He was drinking, visiting the place where she died.'

The detective's mouth dropped. 'Which brother?'

'Salih. Salih Salim – musical, isn't it?'

'You discussed the murder with him?'

Well, sort of. 'A little. I mean, I said I'd found her.'

Rivers sighed, crossed her arms. 'Mrs Jennings, tell me exactly what was said.'

'He . . . actually, he thinks their family killed Zina. He suspects an honor killing because Zina defied their parents.'

'Where is Salih?'

Harper told her where she'd dropped him off, and the detective headed for the door. 'Mrs Jennings,' Rivers stopped as she was leaving. 'If Salih Salim contacts you again, let me know immediately.'

'But why? He's not the one who—'

'We've been trying to contact Zina's family since her murder. So far, we haven't been able to locate a soul. Every single one of them seems to have left the country.'

Harper waited, but Hank didn't say anything. After Detective Rivers left, he turned to the refrigerator, got out some sliced turkey and cheddar cheese. Started to make a sandwich.

A sandwich? He was hungry? Ignoring her?

Finally, she couldn't take it any more. 'Are you going to offer me one?'

He didn't turn around. 'Want?'

Her stomach still hurt, but it was empty; she'd lost her tuna sandwich. 'No cheese on mine.' Was he giving her the silent treatment? Acting as if nothing had happened? Didn't he care about Burke's death?

Harper took two beers from the refrigerator.

'Not enough. Drink. With Salih?' Hank's voice was flat.

He was mad that she'd been drinking? 'I didn't really drink that much—'

'Wrong with. You?' Hank spun around, facing her, the mayonnaise jar in his hand. 'Killer. Zina. Might be this man!'

'Salih didn't kill her.'

'You know? How?'

How did she know? Well, because he'd told her. 'He wasn't dangerous. We just talked.'

Hank replaced the mayonnaise in the refrigerator, brought two plates, two sandwiches to the table. Didn't say a word. Began eating.

'Why are you so mad?'

'Mad?' His mouth was full. 'Why? Really?'

'It's not because I had some drinks with Zina's brother. You've been mad all day, right?'

Hank fumed, chewed. 'Just walked out. You. Today.'

Well, what had he expected her to do? 'I was upset. You said we needed to be apart. So I *let* you be apart!'

'Not talked. Not said. Just left.'

'What was there to say? You want to be on your own!'

Hank slammed a fist on the table; the plates bounced. 'Damn. Hoppa.'

She blinked, stunned. Hank, with all the frustration he'd had in his recovery, had never pounded a table. Never lost control. Tears rushed to Harper's eyes. She started to get up, but Hank put his sandwich down and grabbed her wrist.

'Sit.'

She sat. Felt his hand gripping her without tenderness.

'I've had a hell of a day, Hank.'

'Too.' Or two. 'Wife walked mad out. Killed could be, like Zina.'

'Really, Hank. I was in no danger.'

'No calls. No idea. Where you—'

'I didn't know where you were either. I got home and you weren't here. I tried to call, but you left your phone in the house—'

'Got dark. Went looking.'

'—so I was waiting for you, and meantime, they found Burke—'

'Drove all over. Trent's. Ruth's. Leslie's. No Hoppa. Not anywhere.'

'—and had no idea where you were or how to find you. So how do you like it so far, us being apart?'

They both stopped, stared at each other. Hank's eyes were flames, searing her. Harper's nostrils flared. Suddenly, Hank leaned over, grabbed her head and pressed his mouth against hers, hard, expressing his fury and frustration without the need for words.

When he released her, Harper was breathless, couldn't speak. Hank glared.

'Apart. Means. Not me leaning. Always on you. Doesn't mean. Not talking.'

What? Had she mistaken his meaning that morning? Overreacted to the word 'apart'?

'OK,' she began. 'I get that you're stronger and don't have to lean on me any more. But I don't see why you're so damned mad.'

Hank glowered. 'Why? Told you. You hide. Secrets.'

'I do not have secrets.'

'Bullshit. Burke. Didn't tell—'

'There was nothing *to* tell!'

'Man was crazy. Could you have. Hurt. Killed.'

No, Burke wouldn't have hurt her – but Hank kept talking. Repeating his list of Things She Hadn't Told Him. 'You took job Zina's. Didn't tell.' Hank paused, puckered and stretched his lips, limbering them to speak. 'Found maybe out family killed. Her. Didn't tell. Now today. Left. Drank with maybe man killed Zina. Wrong.' He stopped, reworked his lips again. 'What's wrong with. You. Hoppa? Want danger? Why?'

He went on for a while, scolding, listing things she'd done that were wrong or reckless. Or inconsiderate, secretive, selfish. Harper had never seen him so exasperated, wanted to calm him down. She didn't defend herself or try to explain; that would only fuel his temper. Besides, she didn't have the energy. Instead, she nibbled at her sandwich, strangely at peace. Because despite everything – her husband's complaints, the shock of Burke's death, the horror of Zina's murder – one fact was clear: Hank didn't want to split up. No matter what else was happening or how furious he was, he still loved her. She knew that from his kiss.

Harper awoke Halloween morning, not sure if Hank had come to bed or not. She'd fallen asleep as soon as her head had hit the pillow, too exhausted to dream. And the sheets beside her were empty.

It was after ten. She'd slept for eleven hours? Lord. Harper hurried downstairs, smelling coffee.

'Hank?'

He didn't answer. He'd left a note in the kitchen. He hadn't wanted to wake her, was out running errands. Would be home about three.

Harper held the note, sank into a kitchen chair. Listened to the silence of the house. Told herself to get it together, not to be so easily hurt. This was just a phase. Hank was proving that he could be independent. Once he'd shown that he could do things solo, he wouldn't need to any more. Would include her again. Meantime, she would not waste time and energy feeling sorry for herself.

She poured a cup of coffee, gazed out at the wooded spot behind the house. In the daylight, almost bare of leaves, the trees seemed sparse. She thought of Burke. How could he have killed himself? Had he been entirely without hope? Felt trapped by his delusions? Had he imagined he was being chased by the cluster of students and that man who'd been trying to help him?

Harper wasn't sure. But she couldn't stop thinking about Burke, his calls, his death. Setting down her coffee, she went for her phone, brought it back to the kitchen. Sat and played his last messages again.

'They found my car.' His voice was ragged, whispering. 'I don't dare use it, so I'm on foot. I know you don't want me to come over. Can you meet me somewhere? Harper, it's serious. They're all over the place, watching for me. I can't use my credit cards or they'll find me. Can you get me some cash? Call me back. We're not safe.'

His next call was breathless. More urgent. 'I gotta keep moving, can't carry the evidence. So check your mailbox. They're closing in and they'll do anything to shut me up. I'm on my way to your place. It's fuckin' showdown time.'

And the last: 'Damn, Harper. Where are you? Did they get to you already? At least call me the fuck back and let me know you're still breathing.'

No question. Burke had reached out to her for help, and she'd let him down. Harper sat at the table, drinking coffee. Thought about her mailbox. Maybe he'd left something for her? She ran outside to the street, checked the box. Found it empty. Burke hadn't left anything there. He'd just been rambling.

Back in the house, she popped a piece of rye bread into the toaster oven, looked for the butter. Damn – there was no butter. No jam either. She hadn't shopped all week. Maybe Hank would go to the grocery store on his 'errands'.

Reaching for a jar of peanut butter, she glanced out the window again. Heard Burke's desperate whisper, 'It's fuckin' showdown time.'

Showdown time. Burke believed that Colonel Baxter had people looking for him. That his car had been tampered with, his credit cards tagged. But he was getting ready to take his enemies on, face to face. Was that the attitude of a man about to take his own life?

Harper didn't think so.

Then again, Burke was unbalanced. Who knew what an unbalanced man's attitudes would be?

She heard him explaining Colonel Baxter's theft. Telling her about the detail in Iraq. The cargo of stolen cash they'd loaded on to the helicopter.

It seemed preposterous. Probably, Burke had concocted it all as a way to blame his problems on somebody else, as his marriage, job and mental health were falling apart.

But Peter Murray was dead – Burke hadn't concocted that. And now Burke was dead, too. She thought of the other member of their team, Rick Owens. Had she seen him near her house?

The ding of the toaster oven jangled her; Harper spun around, grabbing her knife. Wow. Maybe paranoia was contagious. Harper took out her toast, used the knife to slap on some extra chunky. Took a bite. And thought about the only other living member of their detail. She ought to tell him about Burke.

Unless, of course, he already knew.

Thank the Lord for Google. In seconds, she'd grabbed her laptop and located hundreds of Rick Owenses. In a few more seconds, she'd found her particular Rick Owens and his business contact information in Washington DC. Rick, it seemed, was a political consultant. And if there was any truth to Burke's story, one of his major clients was Colonel Baxter, candidate for Senator.

Chewing her toast, she punched Rick's number into her cell. On the third ring, Rick's voicemail picked up. The recording was smooth, professional, positive, slick.

She pictured Rick in fatigues, covered with sweat and dust, swatting flies. Tried to put the voice with the image. Couldn't.

At the sound of the tone, she wasn't ready, hadn't planned what to say. It wasn't right to give bad news by voicemail; she shouldn't mention that Burke was dead. Still, she had to speak – her silence was being recorded. Finally, she spurted. 'Rick? Hi Rick, it's Harper – Lieutenant Reynolds. From Iraq. Give me a call when you get a chance? Thanks.'

She ended the call, after leaving her number, feeling clumsy. Had she really said that? 'It's Harper. Lieutenant Reynolds. From Iraq?' Like he wouldn't know who Harper was? They'd served together, for

God's sake. And how many Harpers did he know? Well, it didn't matter what she'd said. The important thing was that he'd get the call, return it, and answer some questions about Burke and the Colonel.

Meantime, Harper had a blank day ahead of her. She should go to the grocery store. Maybe work at Langston's for a while. She rinsed her coffee mug and put the peanut butter away, headed up to shower. She was drying off, wrapped in a towel when her cell phone gonged.

She reached for it, hoping it was Hank. Saw the incoming call number, didn't recognize it. The area code was 202. Washington DC.

Rick was calling back. Harper grabbed the phone, answered the call. 'Hey, there, soldier. How are you?' she began.

'Just fine, Lieutenant. I hope you are, as well.'

The voice wasn't Rick's. Harper's hand tightened on the phone and her chest tightened as she recognized the gravely voice of Colonel Baxter.

Why was the Colonel calling? Did he know that, minutes ago, she'd called Rick Owens? Was he responding to that call?

She heard Burke's voice, whispering a warning: *They're closing in. They're watching.* But that was ridiculous. Rick worked for the Colonel; they were probably together. Rick must have seen the message and shown it to the Colonel, who just wanted to say hello.

'Heard you got hitched.'

He had?

'Sounds like he's a good guy. Sorry about his accident.'

What? How did he know about that? 'How did you know—'

'Oh, make no mistake: I keep tabs on my people, Lieutenant.'

What did I tell you? They're watching you. A chill rattled Harper's bones; she pulled Hank's robe off the hook, put it on.

'The older I get, the more I realize how few people I can truly rely on. And I never forget a person who's helped me out – let alone saved my life.'

Or who can expose his crimes, Burke interrupted.

'Back in Iraq, you proved to be one of those people. So I've kept tabs on you from afar to make sure you're doing OK.' He wheezed as he chuckled. 'Think of me like your crazy old uncle.'

Her uncle? How creepy. Harper gathered the robe around her, covering up. That detail in Iraq had lasted only what – five days? And based on that, all these years later, he was her 'uncle'? Harper bristled.

I told you, Harper. He kept tabs on all of us because we can ruin him.

'Truthfully, sir, that's not called for—'

'Oh, trust me. It's not simply for your sake. It's for my own, as well. If a man has ambition in life, which, God help me, I do, he needs to surround himself with good people. When you find them, you're a fool not to keep them close, or at least to keep track of them in case you'll need to bring them close later. That little cadre of yours, that detail back in Iraq – you got us out of that ambush. If you hadn't, I wouldn't be here today. You proved yourselves to be people I could trust and rely upon. So I've kept track of each and every one of you, just in case.'

'Really?' Harper looked around, half expecting to see cameras in the woodwork. 'Well, then you know there aren't many of us left.'

A loud sigh. 'I know. Tragic about Peter Murray.'

Only Peter Murray? Didn't he know about Burke? 'And Burke Everett.'

A pause. 'Everett?'

'Yesterday. He went off a bridge.'

'Holy Mother of God.' The Colonel growled. He sounded genuinely stunned, dismayed. 'What in God's good earth is wrong with people? First Murray. Now Everett? Two suicides in – what? Two weeks? God almighty.'

Suicides? Harper scowled; she hadn't said it was suicide. But she guessed it was a safe assumption; probably, death by bridge was rarely anything else. 'And Shaw never made it home. So that leaves Owens and me; we're the only ones left.'

Harper heard paper shuffling in the background. People moving around. An unintelligible whisper. Then, 'Yes, Harper. Sadly, you're correct. The numbers are dwindling. Which brings me to the point of my phone call. You've heard about my Senate run?'

'Yes, Sir.'

'Harper, my opponent is formidable and it's a tough race. But I'm confident that I'll come out on top. And when I do, I'm going to need dedicated, trustworthy staffers. Rick Owens is already on board.'

Burke's voice interrupted: *Here it comes, Harper. He's going to try to sign you on. It's a pay off.*

'Frankly, my staff is off-balance. I need a strong woman's point of view. Someone who's a leader, who's smart, gutsy, innovative, articulate. And savvy. In other words: you.'

What did I tell you?

It took Harper a moment to speak. 'Colonel, I'm enrolled in graduate school. I'm about to write my dissertation.'

'I know all about it, Harper. Look. Archeology isn't going to go away if you put it off for a while. And, since your husband isn't employed, even with his disability payments, I know that you can use some income—'

What?

'—especially since graduate school doesn't come cheap at an Ivy League school like Cornell.'

'Colonel.' Harper clutched the phone. 'This conversation – you're making me very uncomfortable.'

'I understand. You've thought you were all alone and on your own. It's an adjustment to realize that you're neither. Given your circumstances, Harper, I'm prepared to go even farther. I'll offer your husband a job, too – there's plenty of non-verbal work to be done . . .'

Harper stood with her mouth open, appalled. Colonel Baxter knew all about Hank, the nature of his injuries, their finances. He'd not just been watching from afar; he'd been downright spying on them, just like Burke had said. What the hell?

'. . . believe me, I take care of my people. Come on board; you won't have to worry about another bill. I'll talk to Professor Schmerling. Dean Van Arsdale, too. They'll give you an extension on your—'

He even knew her professor? 'How do you know Schmerling and Van Arsdale?'

Another sigh. 'Harper. Like I said: it's my business to be connected. I've kept my eye on you. You're one of the people I've wanted to keep close.'

In her mind, she heard Burke: *Be careful, Harper. He's not just trying to buy you off; he's also warning that he knows everything about you, including how to hurt you. It sounds like an offer, but it's really a threat.*

'I'm a little overwhelmed here.' She felt bullied and spied upon. Tried to hide the indignation in her voice.

'Understandably. No need to answer me today. Just consider what I've said.'

'But I assure you, my husband and I don't need—'

'Harper,' he interrupted, 'let me ask you this: out of all the places in the world, why do you think Burke Everett killed himself right in the town where you live?'

'I didn't say he—'

'I think I know why. Everett came to you because he trusted you, because of the bond formed between you when you served in that detail. Owens and I saw him at Murray's funeral, and he was almost irrational. He had wild notions about the past. Tell me, did Everett share those notions with you?'

'No.' It came out of her mouth too fast. Sounded untrue.

'Really? Didn't you see him?'

'No.' Damn – the lies just kept coming. Why was she denying it? If the Colonel had been 'keeping tabs' on her, he already knew she'd seen Burke.

'You're saying you never saw him?' His voice sharpened; he knew.

'No, wait – I forgot.' She scrambled to change her story. 'When he first came to town, we had coffee. That's how I found out you were running for Senate – he told me. After that, he called a few times, but we didn't connect.'

'And? Did he seem stable? Say anything unusual?'

Don't tell him anything. He's fishing.

'Well, he was depressed about Pete. He took the loss real hard.'

'Murray's death. That's all he talked about?'

'Yes, pretty much. Why?' Harper sat stiffly on the edge of her bed, biting her lip.

The Colonel sighed. 'I understand you don't want to betray a comrade, Harper. But I can't help but think that Burke came to you for a reason. Probably to confide something he considered important. And I have to think that it's no coincidence his death took place in your neighborhood. In fact, I'm betting it was a symbolic message to you, reinforcing whatever he confided. Am I completely off base here?'

Sonofabitch. He's threatening you. Saying that my death was a symbolic warning. A message telling you how close his people are, how much they can get away with.

Harper heard whispering on the Colonel's end of the line. A chair creaking and background shuffling. Then his blustery voice again. 'Sorry – I keep getting interrupted. But that's my thinking. Terrible news about Everett. A real waste. Makes me even more determined to reach out and gather my people close. Think about what I've said, Harper. I can take care of you and your husband, and you can be of service. We both win. Sound good?'

'Thank you, sir,' Harper's jaws were clenched. Something told her not to stand up to him. Not even to turn him down flat. 'I'll think about what you've said.'

When she got off the phone, Harper stayed on the bed, replaying the conversation. Feeling invaded. Exposed. The Colonel knew way too much about her life. Was way too pushy. How odd that a man running for Senate from a state she'd never been to, a man she hadn't seen or heard from in years and had served with for only a few days – how odd that such a man would spy on her for years and call right after Burke's death to offer jobs for her and her husband.

It made no sense at all.

Unless, as Burke said, the Colonel was trying to buy her silence about what happened back in Iraq.

Harper thought back to the detail, loading cargo on to the Colonel's helicopter. Had those crates been loaded not with supplies, but with millions in stolen hundred-dollar bills? Was that why the Colonel had kept an eye on everyone who'd worked that detail? Was it possible that, for all his seemingly irrational paranoia, Burke had been right? Why else would the Colonel take time out of his busy campaign, just a few days before the election, to suddenly call her and out of the blue offer her a job?

Because he thinks you know the truth and he wants to scare you silent.

'Shut up, Burke.' She said that out loud. Good God, what was wrong with her, hearing Burke's voice in her head? Answering it? Enough. She needed to get away, out of the house. Harper pulled on jeans and a heavy sweatshirt, grabbed her phone and bag. Hesitated for a moment, long enough to text Hank: *See you later*. No need to give details; he hadn't given her any.

She was in the driveway, about to climb on to her Ninja when Detective Rivers pulled up. Oh God. What now?

'Your friend wasn't at the hotel when we got there, Mrs Jennings,' she called as she got out of the car.

Her friend? Oh, Salih.

'No one by that name was even registered.'

'But I dropped him there . . .'

'Might have used a false identity. Fake name on the credit card.'

Really? 'I don't know why he'd do that.' She felt as if she knew him. As if they were friends.

Rivers looked off into the woods behind the house. 'Well, it's probably not all that complicated. In my experience, people use false IDs when they're up to no good.'

'Detective, Salih didn't kill his sister.'

Now Rivers looked at Harper. 'You know that for sure?'

Of course not. 'He was terribly upset about her murder. He didn't seem capable of—'

'I looked into the honor killing theory, Mrs Jennings. Lots of times, people kill their relatives even though they love them. They see the murder as a sacrifice necessary for the good of the entire family. A man might feel obligated to kill, let's say, his sister. It would be his duty. That's not to say he wouldn't then deeply mourn her loss.'

Harper tried to imagine Salih cutting Zina. She couldn't. Salih hadn't done it. Had he?

'These are people from a different culture. Different rules. If the brother did it, he thought he was doing the right thing. And his family will respect him for it. But I doubt we'll get the chance to find out for sure. Salih wasn't at the hotel, and the family's cleared out of their place in New York.'

A breeze scattered leaves around their feet.

'I don't suppose he told you where he was going from here?'

Harper shook her head. 'Sorry.'

'Damn. Looks like this one's going cold.' Rivers frowned. Didn't leave. Just stared past the garage at the trees behind the house.

Harper wanted to get going, sensed that she wouldn't want to hear whatever Rivers was going to say next.

'You or your husband own a Beretta, Mrs Jennings?'

A Beretta? 'No.'

'We asked the frat boys next door. Odd. None of them claimed it either.'

'I'm sorry – I'm not following you.'

Rivers shook her head. 'Of course you don't; I haven't explained. The fraternity boys were cleaning up after their party, and one of them found a gun by a ledge uphill back there – unregistered. So we're asking if it belongs to anyone in the area.'

Harper nodded. 'Well, it's not ours.'

'I didn't expect it would be. The only prints on it belonged to the suicide victim.'

Burke? Why would Burke's gun be in the trees behind her house?

'And that leaves us with a conundrum, Mrs Jennings.' Rivers'
brown eyes narrowed, and she crossed her arms. 'How would you
rather die, by jumping off a bridge or taking a bullet in the head?'
Seriously?

'Because, between you and me? I can't see why a man who had
a loaded gun in his possession would go to all the trouble of climbing
on to the wall and jumping off a bridge.' She paused. 'Of course,
his gun was all the way back here. Maybe he dropped it. Couldn't
find it. Still. Something about this one doesn't seem right.'

Burke had had a gun? Not a surprise, given his state of mind.
But, as experienced in combat as he was, Harper knew that he
wouldn't have accidentally dropped it. He would never have lost his
weapon; someone must have taken it. Must have ambushed him.
There must have been a struggle, and he must have dropped the gun
as they fought. Harper envisioned it; saw Burke running for his life,
heading in the dark on to the Thurston Avenue Bridge. Feeling
trapped there. Climbing on to the ledge.

But that was ridiculous. Students had seen him jump. They'd tried
to stop him.

And they'd said someone else had tried, too. A man had been
there, talking to Burke.

And Harper had seen a man run past her – a man who'd looked
a lot like Rick.

Stop, she told herself. You're imagining things. Buying into
Burke's delusions.

But what if Rick had been there, had struggled with Burke back
in the trees. What if Burke had dropped his gun and run off, and
Rick had followed, running right past her? What if they'd confronted
each other on the bridge, and Rick had not been talking Burke down,
but had been threatening him?

No question: rather than surrender, Burke would have jumped.

After Rivers drove off, Harper rode around town, replaying snip-
pets of conversations with the Colonel, Hank, Salih, Burke. And,
finally, with Rivers. Memories fragmented and bumped each other.
She was finding Hank's abrupt note, then hearing about Burke. Then
finding Zina's body. Or drinking with Salih. Or listening to the
Colonel.

She thought of Rivers' reaction to Burke's fears of Colonel Baxter.

Rivers had scoffed. 'Let me get this straight. The man is running
for Senate from the state of Tennessee?'

Yes.

'And supposedly, he stole millions of dollars from Iraq, yet he's never been accused or even suspected of this theft.'

Again, yes. Harper had explained that she was just repeating what Burke had told her.

'And this guy, Baxter – he's suddenly having everyone who served on your detail killed in order to prevent potential accusations that, even if they were made, nobody could prove?'

Harper had agreed that it sounded crazy; she hadn't believed it either. But then, Burke had died. Peter Murray had died. And the Colonel had suddenly offered her a job.

'He what?'

Harper had told Rivers about the phone call. The Colonel's too intimate knowledge of her life.

Rivers had shaken her head. 'Mrs Jennings. This is all – well, no question, it's odd. Nevertheless, other than an unexpected job offer and your buddy's unsubstantiated claims, there's no evidence that Colonel Baxter has broken any laws. Am I right?'

She had been. Unless Burke actually had possessed the proof as he'd claimed. But even if he had, who knew where it was? Harper rode her Ninja, airing her mind out, trying to think of other things. Like where Hank was. Or no, not that. And not about Zina and Salih, either . . .

She refused to think about them even as she pulled on to the turn-off that led to the only place where she could find stillness and peace, where she could escape. She parked the Ninja not far from the spot where she'd found Zina's body. When she heard the gong of her phone, she grabbed inside her bag, hoping it was Hank. Fumbling, she grabbed her flashlight instead of her phone. Then her wallet. When she finally pulled the phone out, she saw that it wasn't Hank at all. She recognized the number on the screen, though. It was Richard Owens.

He knew that the Colonel had called her. 'I'm following up.' He sounded smooth, cheerful. Like a political consultant, not a hitman.

'There's nothing to follow up on, Rick. He made an offer, but I'm not interested.'

'Hell, Harper. You called earlier – I got your message.'

Right – why was she snapping at him? He was just returning her call. 'I wanted to tell you about Burke.'

'Yeah, Baxter told me. It sucks, doesn't it.'

It did.

'But the very fact that you called me, that proves you still feel connected.'

Connected?

'That's what Baxter and I want to point out to you: we three share history. We're linked, like family. Look, I know the Colonel pretty damn well. He's a good guy. He comes across a little too strong. But he's for real, I swear.'

For real? As real as Burke's 'suicide'? Harper wasn't sure about Burke's death, but she didn't want anything to do with Rick. She started toward the Langston house. No way she was letting the Colonel or his people anywhere close to her. Even a punk like Rick.

'Listen, Harper, I'm actually not far from you.'

Harper stopped walking. He wasn't far? So that man she'd seen running – had it really been him?

'I had to visit a big backer in Rochester, and before I head back south, tell you what – I'd love to sit down with you.'

Oh no. Harper tensed. Heard Burke warn: *Don't let him.*

'I can come by, catch up, and we can iron out the specifics of your offer.'

What? 'You mean today?' Harper looked around, as if Rick would walk out of the woods.

'Sure. How's this afternoon?'

'Sorry. Can't today, Rick. I'm . . . busy.'

'Busy? It's Sunday. And Halloween. What are you doing, trick or treating?'

'I'm working.' None of your business.

'Working? On what?'

Seriously? 'It's archeology stuff. Nothing—'

'You're on a dig?'

'No. I'm documenting a collection of—'

'OK. So you're on campus? I can come by.'

'No, I work at a professor's house. Off campus.'

'So, I've got a car – how far away will you be?'

Man, he was pushy. Why was he pressing so hard? 'Rick. It's not going to work. Besides, like I said, I'm not interested in working for the Colonel.'

'At least hear me out before you make up your mind. No harm in listening, right? Are you at work now?'

Good God. 'Yes. I am. And I've got to get back to it. So—'

'OK. I get it. I know when I'm shot down. Hey. Good to talk to you, Harper. Catch you later.'

Harper stood on the gravel road, baffled. Irritated. What was Rick's problem? Why had he been so persistent? Was he the Colonel's duty officer? Had Rick sent people to quiet Burke? And Murray? Would he come after her next? She looked around, saw nobody among the trees. Of course she didn't. Colonel Baxter was ambitious, overbearing. Possibly dishonest. But a killer? Doubtful. Even if he'd stolen the money, he wouldn't assassinate every potential witness. He was a renowned public figure with a distinguished military record. The idea of him putting hits on people – well, it was absurd.

Enough. She wasn't going to think about them now. In fact, she wasn't going to think about anything that was newer than Pre-Columbian. Tossing her phone back into her bag, she closed her eyes. Took slow deep breaths. Relaxed her shoulders. Felt the stillness of the air and the trees. Opened her eyes again.

The gray sky sent soft light through the branches; yellow and copper leaves speckled the ground. The air smelled of crispness, of autumn. Harper walked on, her shoes crunching pebbles, crushing leaves. One step. Another. Gradually, though, she noticed another sound – soft and muted. Echoing her steps. She stopped, listening. Looking around. Bracing herself to fight – was someone following her? One of the Colonel's people?

Silence. Then a breeze skittering through the trees. Damn. Now, she was the paranoid one; Burke's fear had infiltrated her psyche. *You shouldn't be alone*, she heard him warn. *They're all around, watching. Closing in.*

'Shut up,' she muttered, walking on, feeling an ache in her left leg, hearing the sound again. Deciding that it wasn't actually a sound; it was more like imperfect timing, as if her footsteps were slightly out of sync with the noise they made.

Harper kept going, reaching into her bag, searching for her pocket knife, finding her flashlight and phone, her water bottle. Pretending not to notice the sound, she tried to identify its direction. And when she did, even without a weapon, she spun around to face it, adopting a combat stance.

A young buck stood among the trees. Bambi? That's who'd shaken her up? She exhaled, shook her head. Noticed the odd coincidence: deer were the Pre-Columbian symbol of the Seventh Day. And it was Sunday – the seventh day of the week. Chills skittered up

Harper's spine even as she dismissed the fact as meaningless. Big deal. So she'd seen a deer on a Sunday – Pre-Columbian beliefs were fascinating but had no basis in reality. After all, they were nothing but myths. Deer symbolized many things: they stood for the hunt; they were the rescuer of the moon goddess. And they were a favored shape taken by Nahuals.

The deer lifted its head and met Harper's eyes, stared right at her, directly, as if challenging her. But of course, it wasn't doing anything of the kind. Deer were meek; deer didn't challenge. The creature was probably terrified, frozen in fear. Harper stood motionless, watching it, recalling Zina raving about a Nahual. Swearing she'd encountered a cat-man-bat-owl . . . Deer?

No. Absurd. Still, for a long moment, neither of them moved. The deer watched Harper; Harper watched the deer. A stand-off. Harper assured herself that the deer would not change forms and turn into a hunter. Wouldn't come after her heart. A Nahual hadn't killed Zina; there was no such thing as a Nahual, and Zina's family had killed her.

Still, the animal was large. Muscular. And its eyes were steady, holding her gaze. Harper told herself to get moving, asked herself why she was in a staring contest with a four-legged furry opponent. Decided that she would end it. Breaking her stare, she took a deliberate step forward and looked at the path ahead.

A few steps later, Harper turned to look back. She didn't see the deer, but she heard an odd sound for daytime: the mournful hoot of an owl.

Inside the house, Harper went straight upstairs, through the main house to the east wing. She needed to work, to focus on concrete items and tasks. So she hurried to the workroom with the logbooks, cameras and computer.

And saw that the boxes had been moved.

She'd left the crates that she'd already itemized and labeled neatly arranged in stacks. But they weren't stacked any more; they stood side by side at odd angles, sloppy and disorganized. Harper stood at the door, surveying the room, her senses on alert. The intruder might still be around, hiding behind stacked boxes. Silently, she reached into her bag, feeling for cylindrical shapes, sifting through granola bars, water bottle, pens, pocket knife, tampons – until, finally, she retrieved her flashlight and slowly stepped into the room, aiming the light into dark corners behind the hodgepodge of boxes. Finding no one, she moved out, down the hall, searching each shadowed room. Nobody was there.

Could she be mistaken? Had she been so upset that she hadn't actually left the boxes as neatly arranged as she'd thought? No. Absolutely, no. She clearly remembered separating the boxes she'd examined from the others, leaving them in order, clearly coded. Stacked neatly one on top of the other.

One of the brothers must have been there. Angus or Jake – both resented her presence. One of them must have come in to see what she'd done, messed around with the boxes, probably to annoy her. Well, they'd succeeded. Now that the boxes had been tampered with, she'd have to reopen them and confirm that the contents were still there as she'd logged them, undisturbed. Damn.

Harper shoved her flashlight into her belt, went back to the work-room. Put on the protective gloves and got to work, rechecking the crates one after another, confirming their contents, redoing what she'd already done. Finally, when she'd made sure everything was intact, she re-stacked the boxes neatly in the corner and lifted a new crate on to the worktable. It had a mark on the side: Utah. She reached for the lever to pry the top up. Opened it. And stared.

Nothing was in the box. Not even packing material. OK. There could be a lot of reasons it was empty. The professor might have removed everything. Or the contents could have been loaned out to a museum. Or broken during shipping, or sold. She read the list fastened to the inside of the lid. Three vessels and a gold mask were supposed to have been in the container. The note said nothing about lending or selling the relics.

Harper did the only thing she could; she added the items to her growing list of missing relics. Then she resealed the empty box, placed it in the corner with the others she'd examined, and opened another crate. Lifting the lid, she hesitated, worried that this box might be empty, too. But it wasn't. Wads of packing material cushioned individual casings. She pulled each out carefully, and opened them, one by one.

There were seven Narino ornamental gold pieces from around AD 750. Each with dramatic projecting human faces, valued at $15,000.

A detailed avian sculpture from 2200 BC, thirteen and a quarter inches high, decorated with a double row of onyx knobs, valued at $10,000.

Two early classic Veracruz warrior sculptures from about 300 AD, with black skin, elaborate ornamental clothing, even detailed helmets. Valued at $15,000 apiece.

The final object on the contents' list was missing. A Honduran marble vessel from the Ulua Valley, early post-classic period, about 1000 AD. Eight and one eighth inches deep, with geometric patterns and a projecting feline face with open mouth and jaguar fangs, handles in jaguar forms. Valued at $55,000.

Damn. The most valuable and intriguing piece in the crate was missing. Harper looked inside again, found only packing materials. The vessel wasn't there. Why were so many pieces missing? Even if the professor had been absent minded, could he have removed all these missing pieces? Could he really have stashed unique $55,000 treasures in his soup pots?

Harper stared at the empty crate, frustrated. Too many important pieces were simply not accounted for. Someone would probably have to search the house, look under cushions, behind books. Even inside those legendary hidden passageways, if they existed.

Under the work light, the gold ornaments glowed. The warriors stood strong. Photographing them, Harper calculated that, according to the listed insurance estimates, even without the vessel, this one box contained about $130,000 worth of artifacts. She glanced around the room. Counted fourteen crates. The hallway and other rooms held dozens more. She did some rough math, estimated that the collection was worth several million. Possibly tens of millions.

Lord. She'd known that it was valuable. But now, adding up the estimates on the itemized lists, she couldn't quite grasp the numbers. Or the incredible fact that she had the opportunity to actually put her eyes and hands – well, her gloves – on such rare and high-priced relics.

Carefully, Harper made a note of the missing vessel; recorded and verified the presence of the other objects. Then, before repacking them, she studied each piece. Felt their textures and weights, studied their detail and aesthetics. She held them, sensing the presence of their creators, as if the hands that had crafted the pieces could reach across centuries, touching her through their work. Who had formed these gold ornaments? Or clothed the figurines? Had the bird sculpture signified the soul of a dead warrior? She was examining its wings when, suddenly, her concentration broke. Harper sat up, alert. Hearing – no, *feeling* – someone coming up the stairs.

No one's there, she told herself. But her instincts knew better. She'd had this sense many times in Iraq; it wasn't a sound or a visual. In fact, it wasn't anything with a name – just a certainty that someone was approaching. Maybe it came from a stirring of the air or the beating of a heart. But it was a certainty that she'd learned not to question, that had saved her life more than once.

Silently, Harper slid off her stool. Grabbing the lever, she stepped toward the door. And didn't even breathe.

Rick Owens walked past the 'No Trespassing' sign, proud of himself. He'd played Harper like a fiddle, got her to tell him everything he needed to know without her suspecting a thing. In fact, she probably thought she'd brushed him off. No way she had a clue that he was right here in Ithaca. Let alone, not far behind her on the road, following her Ninja.

He stopped to admire her bike. Not a bad choice for a female. Nice chrome—

Rick spun around, hearing a rustle in the bushes. Saw a squirrel scampering up a trunk. Rolled his eyes at his own jumpiness. He continued along the gravel path, his sneakers almost silent. Not that anyone would hear him; the place was deserted. Well, except for Harper. She was here. The Ninja said so, and so had her cell phone. Nice to have connections who could trace calls.

But he wouldn't have any more fuck ups. Not to brag, but despite what had happened with Burke, he was good. Efficient. Persuasive. He'd get the job done, according to plan. He'd show her how urgent things were, how the country was at war – not just war like the public ones in Iraq or Afghanistan or the rest of the hot spots. No it was fighting another, almost invisible war; one much more destructive and insidious than those others. One being fought right here at home, quietly, untalked about. A war that was eating the country from its gut, taking it down. The only hope was strong leadership by someone who could get people off their asses, inspire the military, mobilize the general public, close the borders. Make America strong again. A country not to be messed with.

First, this infernal, internal cancerous war had to be won. And Harper could be – no, she *needed* to be part of it. She had to choose a side. Step up. Not like Murray and Burke. Rick pursed his lips, felt the soreness of their loss, the betrayal.

For a few minutes, he hung back in the darkness of the trees, scouting out the front of the monstrous old house. The place was like a damned hotel, seemed wide as football field. But no problem; he'd find her. He could move like a shadow, disappear into dust. And he'd done his homework on Harper, on this place. Had studied the unsolved murder that had occurred here on this very site a week ago. The way the woman had died. The location, the position in which Harper had found her.

It was almost as if someone had set that murder up to make his worst-case scenario easy for him. Not that he'd have to take Harper out; his mission was to persuade, not necessarily eliminate her. Even so, combat images he'd tried to erase kept reviving themselves, popping into his head. Like the open eyes of a dead Iraqi boy, their look of disappointment. Rick blinked, trying to shake the boy from his mind, but he heard familiar screams and rifle fire; saw a leg in the middle of the road, smelled burning rubber and flesh. He rubbed his eyes. Felt the ground shake. Sweat rolled down his back, and his arms tingled from the vibration of his machine gun. Finally, he slid into a crouch beside a tree trunk, grounding himself against its rough bark.

When the images faded, he sat for a moment, recovering. Then, making sure he was safe, he checked his watch. He'd lost half an hour. Damn. Recovering, he looked over his shoulder, made sure no one was around, and darted to French doors at the side of the house. Jimmied the lock. Swung the door and snuck in. All of this in less than fifteen seconds.

Rick checked the pistol in his pocket. He wouldn't need it, of course, but kept it at hand always, even when he slept. Just in case. He moved silently across the house, along a long hall to the foyer. He wandered through the first floor, looking for Harper. There were way too many rooms. A library or study. A formal living room, a dining room that could seat dozens. A big room with a high ceiling, completely empty. A huge kitchen, divided into three large rooms. A laundry room and servants' quarters. Rick turned and went back to the stairs. Harper wasn't on this floor; he was wasting time.

He started up the staircase, his hand on his pistol, prepared. He took the steps quickly, invisibly, without a sound. Wandered through the second-floor bedrooms. One after another, like a damned dormitory. There had to be a dozen, some empty, some cluttered with random junk, a few full of heavy, old bedroom furniture.

And lots of dust. As he exited the first bedroom, Rick barely stifled a sneeze. Shit. The fucking dust was up his nose; he'd caught the sneeze this time, but the damn thing would come back. He stepped into a corner, rubbed his nose against his sleeve, pressed his nostrils with two fingers, waiting for the tickle to subside. Damn dust anyhow. He hated the stuff, had fought in it, slept in it, eaten it . . . In Iraq, it had coated every inch of him – even the crack of his ass. That dust had been hell, but it was sand dust. Clean. Not like this dust that smelled of old age and decay. And death. Like that saying: dust to dust.

When he was sure he wasn't going to sneeze, Rick continued, easing from room to room, checking each even though he was sure Harper wasn't in any of them. He'd developed a clear image of where Harper was, sensed her presence the way he used to sense an unseen silent insurgent. Rick took his time, relishing the hunt, using old skills. Verifying his instinct that Harper was upstairs.

Finally, he moved to the stairway, glided up the steps. Followed his instinct to go east. Crept along the long hallway to the arch, saw wooden boxes stacked in the hall. Headed for the room with a light on. His heart rate picked up, his breathing shortened; he smelled Harper's scent above his own sweat. Rick felt his weapon in his jacket pocket where he could get to it, but reminded himself this wasn't going to be a battle. It was going to be a conversation between friends. And, even if it went wrong, compared to combat, this was nothing. This would be a piece of cake.

Slowly, Harper moved away from the worktable, gripping the lever. Who was there? Probably, just Jake or Angus. Nobody to worry about. Still, she was careful to be silent as she stood at the door, peering into the hall. A man was coming up the stairs. Wearing a camouflage jacket.

Her glimpse was quick, but she saw he wasn't Jake or Angus. He was shorter. Beefier. Familiar.

Harper moved into the hall. 'Rick?' She glared at him in disbelief. 'How – what are you doing here?'

Rick froze, mouth open, eyes darting. Instinctively, his hand went to his pocket, quickly relaxed and moved away. Harper recognized the reflex; Rick was carrying a gun.

'Harper. Surprise!' He forced a grin, took the final two stairs and headed towards her, his arms wide for a hug. 'You look terrific. Great to see you.'

Harper didn't return the smile, didn't allow the hug. Her scowl stopped Rick mid-step, yards away.

Rick sighed, looked at the lever. 'Wow. What were you going to do with that?'

'Knock your brains out.'

'I guess I shouldn't have surprised you.'

'I told you on the phone I couldn't see you. Did you miss that? Go away, Rick.' She turned to go back to the workroom, dismissing him.

'Seriously? After all this time, that's all you have to say? "Go away"?'

Harper didn't answer.

'OK. You're right. I'm too pushy.' He followed her, stepping around stacks of crates to get in the door. 'But it's important that we talk. Critically important.'

Harper moved through the aisle between stacks, returning to her spot behind the worktable, sat on her stool. Put the lever down. Folded her hands like an angry schoolmarm. 'Fine. You have two minutes. What do you want?'

Rick smiled, opened his mouth to answer. But she cut him off. 'No – no, wait. First, I want to know how you even knew where I was. What did you do, follow me here?'

He lost the smile. 'I had to do what I had to do.'

'And how did you get in?'

Rick met her eyes.

'Really. You broke in. What did you do, break a window?'

He grinned. 'No. I'm better than that.'

'What the hell do you want?'

'I had to see you. To convince you to join us.'

She tilted her head. 'This is about Baxter. His job offer?'

'He needs to know you're with him, Harper. He wants you on his team – our team. Look, you and I are the only ones left from our detail. He trusts us. He feels indebted because we risked our lives to save his.'

'That was war. It was our duty.'

'He's personally committed to us. And he wants to bring us together again as a team. He's authorized me to increase his offer – name it, Harper. What would it take to bring you on board?'

Burke's voice echoed, warning her. *He's trying to buy you off. Tell him to fuck off.*

Harper shook her head. 'You know what, Rick? I'll tell you what I told him: I'm not interested in working for him. So you're finished here. Bye, now. Have a safe trip home.'

Harper picked up one of the gold ornaments, began repackaging it.

'Harper, let me tell you about Baxter's plans for the country. Will you at least listen? All he wants to do is bring you on board. Think of him as a rich uncle, who wants to make your life easier.'

'Why would he want to do that?'

'Because he takes care of the people who've helped him get to where he is.'

'Lovely.' Harper heard Burke cursing. 'Please give the Colonel my best.'

She carefully sealed the package, wrapped it in tape, set it back into the layer of foam in the crate. When she looked up again, Rick was gone.

She listened for the sounds of his steps on the stairs, heard nothing. Rick was stealthy and he was wearing sneakers, but still, she should have heard a creak in the floor, a brush of fabric against wood. But she heard nothing. Harper sensed his presence, knew that Rick was close. Probably just outside the door, in the hall. With a gun in his pocket – or in his hand. Why wouldn't he leave?

'Rick?' she called to him. 'I know you're out there.'

He didn't answer.

Cursing, she grabbed the lever, waiting. Certain that Rick would reappear. And in a matter of seconds, he did.

'I can't leave.' He stood in the doorway. 'I made a commitment to recruit you. I can't accept a "no".'

Harper stood. Rick came closer, his hand near his pocket. Harper anticipated his movements, bracing herself. What did he intend to do, shoot her? Or convince her to jump off a bridge?

Harper waited, silent, not moving. Rick came closer, a smile slithering across his face. 'All he wants is your loyalty.'

'Rick,' she decided to be frank. 'I didn't have a clue about our detail's real purpose or the money Baxter stole until Burke explained it to me.'

Rick scrunched his face, scratched his ear. 'What are you talking about?'

'Even now, I don't know for sure what happened. But no way I'm risking that it might be true. I'm not taking a pay-off "job" from a thief who betrayed his own country. Baxter may have bought you, but he can't buy me.'

Rick sighed, leaned against the wall. Dropped pretense. 'How can you be so fucking naive, Harper? Baxter did what he did *for* his country. So he'd be in a position to get it back on track.'

'Spare me, Rick. Just go before I call the cops.'

'The cops? What, because I broke in? Seriously?'

Harper looked him in the eye. 'Tell me you didn't force Burke to jump. Tell me you had nothing to do with Pet—'

Rick cleared his throat, bent his knees and suddenly leapt up on to the worktable, crouched among the priceless relics, pointing his gun at her head.

Before Harper had a chance to react, he frowned. 'Harper, I really can't accept another "no". Are you sure you won't reconsider?'

Harper froze.

'Put that down.' Rick meant the lever.

Harper let go of the lever and eyed the muzzle, mind racing. He could easily have killed her. Could kill her even now. He had the advantage, had taken her by surprise. So why he wasn't he shooting her?

Probably, he didn't intend to shoot her. So what did he want? For her to accept a pay-off from Colonel Baxter? Was it really that simple? Or was it more – maybe the relics? Was Rick there to steal them? Had he already stolen the missing pieces? For the Colonel? After all, the Colonel had stolen all that money in Iraq – maybe he was also stealing relics?

'Come on, let's go. Let's talk.' He faced her from the tabletop. 'I don't want to hurt you, Harper.'

'What the hell, Rick?'

'I'll do whatever it takes to convince you to accept Baxter's excellent offer. Can't I persuade you to rearrange your schedule and find some time?'

She eyed the gun, thought of Burke diving off the bridge. Had Rick held a gun on him, too? Had he forced Burke to jump? Did he plan to stage her suicide, as well? Good God, stop thinking, she scolded herself. Just take the asshole down. Get the damned gun.

Finally, her training resurfaced. Harper took a breath, centered herself, leaned back, and crashed her forehead directly against Rick's, sending him flying backwards on to the floor. Relics rolled and rattled, even fell. Were they broken? Harper couldn't stop to look.

She dashed around the table and crates, pouncing on Rick as he scurried to his feet.

Something hard – probably his gun – smacked the side of her head. Pain stunned her; darkness and white light flashed in her skull, but she wasn't down. Harper grabbed his ankles as he tried to run, pulled at his shoes. A sneaker came off in her hand; she tossed it aside, pulled his foot with both hands. He hit the floor with a sharp slap. Half crawling, Harper came at him, but he rolled, bent his knee and slammed his leg full into her chest, launching her backwards. Harper flew. And flying, she suddenly smelled smoke, heard an explosion, waited to land on top of a burned out car. To see pieces of the guys in her patrol scattered in the street, on her stomach – no. She couldn't get sucked into a flashback. Even as she sailed through air, she struggled to anchor herself in the moment.

The impact of smacking into the wall accomplished that, jolting her into the present. Proving that she was not in Iraq, but at Langston's house. Landing not on a car but against a wall. And bouncing off of it without a weapon, facing a former comrade who, though wobbly, still held a gun. Half dazed, breathing heard, she readied herself for his approach.

'Fuck.' Rick grunted as he stepped closer, pointing the gun at her. 'Settle down. I just came to talk. Just listen to what I have to say.'

Harper waited, hunched, feigning injury. As soon as he came within reach, she swung her strong leg, trying to kick the gun away. She missed, felt the momentum of her foot crunching ribs, heard the simultaneous roar of pain and blast of pistol.

In a final surge, Rick charged forward, falling against her, knocking her against a wall panel. Which gave way under her weight. Harper tumbled through it, falling into darkness. The fall probably lasted just a second, maybe two. But in that time, Harper had several distinct thoughts. First, she wondered if she'd been shot or even killed, and if she was falling into hell. Next, she recalled Hank falling off the roof, wondered if his fall had seemed this endless. Finally, she felt a pang of unbearable sorrow, picturing Hank and realizing that, if she were dead, she'd never ever see him again.

Rick stumbled to his feet. Bitch had knocked the air out of him, broken his fucking ribs. Dazed, he realized his left calf stung. And it was bleeding. Fuck. Fuck. Fuck. She'd fucking made him shoot himself in the leg?

Where was she? Where the fuck was she? Forget about the Colonel's plans – he'd blow her cute fucking little head off.

But she wasn't there. Rick turned in circles, rotated, swinging the gun up and down, back and forth. Looking behind the boxes, even though she hadn't been anywhere near them.

It was like she'd disappeared. Like she'd gone right through the wall.

Maybe he'd passed out and she'd run off? Damn, had he let her get away? No. He was sure. The gun went off and he'd hit the ground, but he'd gotten right up again. No lost moments. He would know if he'd been unconscious; wasn't new to battle or wounds. Still, where the hell was she?

Rick stumbled around, gun still dangling from his hand, trying to think. One thing was sure: he needed to stop bleeding or he'd fall down and die right there. Needed to make a tourniquet. Turned in circles, confused. Fumbled around, wincing, groaning. Reaching hurt; moving any part of him hurt. Even breathing. She must have smashed six ribs. Might have sent one into his lungs.

Damn. Blood was pooling in his sneaker, the one he still had on. He leaned against the wall, dragging his wounded leg because it buckled when he put weight on it. Finally lowered himself to the floor and managed to steady his torso while his arms unbuttoned his jacket and pulled his T-shirt over his head. He slapped himself in the face. 'Do not pass out,' he said aloud as he bit a hole in the shirt. Blinking, shaking his head, refusing the darkness that tried to wash through his head, he ripped the shirt into strips, rolled his pant leg up, exposing the wound. The bullet had gone at an angle, passing through the muscle, going in the back of his calf and out the front. Bleeding like a motherfucker. Damn T-shirt strips kept stretching. He had to keep tightening them, yanking, annoying the wound, and the damn thing killed. Well, he was no pussy, could take the pain. Still, this shit was messed up, shouldn't have happened. As soon as he got the bleeding under control, he'd go find Harper and settle this. Miss PhD. Miss I-don't-want-a-job-in-Washington, even for Baxter. Miss I'm-better-than-you-are, too-good-even-to-hear-you-out.

Rick tightened the tourniquet, took off his remaining sneaker. Leaned against the wall just for a second, to regain his wind. No

matter what it took, he'd show her, once and for all, how wrong she
was.

The impact of landing reverberated through her body. Each bone,
each nerve had its own collision and reaction. Harper couldn't move;
pain jolted her limbs, her back, her skull. Worst of all, she couldn't
see. Oh God – was she blind?

'Help.' She screamed, but her voice was a croak. 'Somebody!'
She tried again but began to cough. Her ribs raged with each cough,
and she tasted blood and dust. Finally, her body quieted, and she lay
still, her breath ragged, hearing nothing else. Seeing nothing but
blackness.

After a moment, she yelled again. 'Hey, Rick!' Her voice was
stronger now. 'Rick! Can you hear me?'

No answer. Maybe he was dead? Had been shot in the struggle?
Damn. Why couldn't she see? Panic surged in her belly. Maybe the
blindness was temporary. From the blow to her head when she hit the
ground. Maybe it would pass. Meantime, she couldn't just lie there;
she needed to get up, told her legs to bend, her head to lift. But her
parts didn't care what she said, refused to obey. Harper lay back,
staring into the dark, felt it creeping into her head, wandering through
her veins, seeping over her thoughts, and finally carrying her away.

Sitting there, his leg on fire, Rick realized the mess he was in. Even
if he found Harper, he probably wouldn't be able to get through to
her and get her to sign on. But now, if he dispatched her, it wasn't
going to look like a suicide with his damned blood all over the
hallway. And he wasn't strong enough to clean it up. Let alone to
set the scene. He was in shit. Deep in shit.

Grimacing, he reached for his phone. The Colonel would send
someone to pick him up, help him out. Karl, the guy who'd helped
him tail Everett – he must still be in town. Should have come along
on this job, too. They'd underestimated its difficulty.

His hands were bloody, left marks all over his Blackberry as he
made the call.

But before anyone could pick up, he pressed 'end'. Closed his
eyes, put his head back, cursed. What the hell was he thinking? Was
he really going to call the Colonel and tell him that he'd fucked up
yet again, even let the target get away? Oh, and by the way, that
he'd shot himself?

From the beginning, the Colonel had made it clear; there was no room for failure. Too much was at stake. People were with him or they weren't. No middle ground. His Senate seat was a critical phase of a history-making plan. No one – certainly not Rick – would be considered valuable enough to jeopardize it with scandal or worse. If Rick admitted to screwing up, the Colonel would no doubt send Karl, but not to rescue him.

Rick struggled to his feet, grunting, deciding to do what it would take to survive. His wound wasn't all that bad; he'd seen plenty worse. He had to keep focused, on task. Had to find Harper and get his job done. If they found her outside, maybe hanging from a tree, they might not come inside for a while. Might not see the blood right away. He'd have a chance to come back and bleach the place later.

Limping, he stuck the gun back into his belt, pocketed his phone. Where the hell had she gone? He checked behind the crates again, searched every room on the floor, gazed down the stairs. But before going down them, he had an idea. Rick went back to the wall where he'd last seen Harper and began tapping, listening for hollow sounds.

When Harper opened her eyes again, she saw nothing. Her sight had not returned. Oh God. She stopped breathing, felt her chest tighten. Do not panic, she commanded herself. Do not panic? Really? She couldn't see. Wasn't sure where she was or how badly she was hurt. Or how long she'd been there. Or if anyone would ever find her. She listened, called out.

'Hello?'

Hollow, empty silence.

'Anybody?' Darkness swallowed her voice.

OK. Enough. Time to get up and find a way out of there. Except that she couldn't quite get up. Could barely lift her head. She was dizzy, shivering. Her thoughts broke apart incoherent, fragmented before she could grasp them. She closed her eyes again, smelled old wood, dirt. Mildew. Mold. And thought of Leslie, how she'd helped her to remember things through hypnosis. Relax, she heard Leslie's voice in her head. Let the tension out of your feet, your legs, your thighs. Breathe slowly, from your diaphragm. Gradually, Harper replayed what had happened. She saw herself upstairs, working with the collection. Upset that so many pieces were missing. She'd been about to pack up and go when – out of nowhere – Rick had shown up with a gun in his pocket.

She remembered his claim that he just wanted to 'talk'. But his
weapon had spoken for itself. She remembered headbutting him, but
everything after that was a blur of blows and kicks until she'd
slammed a hallway wall, and – what? Gone right through it? Had
she fallen through a wall?

Harper replayed the fight, not sure her memory was right. After
injuries, people often had memory gaps or distortions. But she was
certain. She'd hit the wall and *passed right through it*.

How was that possible? Besides, if she'd broken through a
wall, wouldn't she have just landed in the next room? Or in a
closet? How had she fallen down a whole story or two – into
nothing?

Something tickled her memory but wouldn't show itself. Her
mind was swollen and foggy, and she closed her eyes, trying to
control her shallow breathing and quell her jagged pulse. And,
all at once, a memory surfaced, and Harper knew exactly where
she was.

The tales about secret passageways in the Langston house weren't
just lore; they were true. The wall she'd hit must have been a false
panel that led into a passageway, and it had given way, sending her
into a hidden corridor. She thought of the stories about the passageways. The one about an actress who'd never been found. Harper
shivered.

Never mind. That was just a story. She pushed herself up on to
her elbows. Damn. Her head and back pulsed with pain. Something
warm and wet – had to be blood – oozed down her face; she
touched her head, found the source. A gash on her temple. Vaguely,
she remembered getting hit there. Asshole Rick had slugged her
with his gun. Harper put her hands on the ground, pushed, managed
to sit up. Checking her body, part by part, she found no breaks,
no bullet wounds or other cuts. Slowly, she bent her legs and
climbed to her feet. She stood unsteadily, unbalanced in the dark.
Suddenly dizzy, she crouched again, steadying herself. Her
thoughts were tedious and muddled, the darkness disorienting.

Relax; she replayed Leslie's voice. *Breathe.*

Harper inhaled. Concentrated on breathing. Thought about Burke
and Murray. The Colonel offering her a bribe. Rick coming at her
with a gun. After a moment, she straightened her back, winced in
pain. And cursed as she stood again.

Blind or not, she was going to find her way out of there. And when she did, she'd settle things with Rick Owens. And Colonel Baxter, too.

Damn. The whole wall sounded hollow. As if there were a room or empty space behind it. Harper must have known, must have escaped through a hidden door. Rick looked up and down, felt the panels, trying to open the thing. He pressed against it. Pushed on the top, the bottom, the middle, trying to find a latch or a hinge. He backed away, examining the wall from a different vantage point, trying to see if the molding looked uneven. He moved up close, pressing his cheek against the plaster, trying to find tiny inconsistencies in the texture.

Nothing.

Shit. He had to find her. He stood still, staring at the wall. Picturing what was on the other side. Of course – probably, it was a secret room, and she was in there hiding. Maybe huddling in fear? Breathing heavily? He leaned against the wall again, holding his breath, listening. Hearing nothing. Fuck.

But she was in there. She had to be. People didn't just disappear, and there was no place else she could be. Rick leaned against the wall and called, 'Harper. I know you're in there. It's no use.'

Listened again. Heard no movement. Damn. The woman was smart, well trained. She could probably stay there for hours. Maybe a couple of days. The only way to get her out would be to go in and get her. Fine, no problem. Surely, he could break through a flimsy old wall.

Again, Rick tapped the plaster, this time listening not for what was behind it, but for what was in it. Deciding it was neither too sturdy nor too thick, he stepped back, leaned away and pounded the thing with his fist. And recoiled, howling, having overestimated his strength. Whimpering, he saw flashing lights, felt pain shooting through his hand and arm, along his bones. He cradled his hand, cursing the thin swatches of plaster that had splintered and fallen to the floor.

OK. He needed something heavier. A tool. There were tools in the room where he'd found Harper. His leg throbbed, resenting the walk, but he limped back there. Found a hammer on the shelf – exactly what he needed. Encouraged, Rick felt more optimistic. Actually had a glimmer of hope as he made his way back to the wall.

Harper knelt, feeling her way around. There was a boarded wall a few feet away on either side of her; the floor felt like wood, only grainy. Was it dust? She patted her way ahead, but – damn. Something sliced her fingertip. What the hell? A knife? She pulled her hand away, sucked blood from the cut. Cautiously, she put her hand back, felt the thing. Something smooth with a jagged edge, like a broken dish. A shard of – oh God. A shard of pottery? A broken relic?

For the first time since she'd seen Rick, Harper thought of the relics. She'd left them unpacked on the worktable, out in the open. Exposed. And when she'd fought with Rick, some had been knocked over, might have been broken. Oh God. Had a piece of one gotten caught in her clothing? Fallen with her? Gently, she felt the piece, avoiding its sharp edge, trying to identify its shape and texture. But the fragment wasn't definite enough. She couldn't be sure. Damn – was it part of the bird? Or one of those exquisite warriors?

Harper set the piece down, gaped into darkness, seeing nothing. She turned the opposite way, say the same nothing. Nothing. Do not panic, she ordered herself. Think. Make a plan. But wait, was something slithering around her ankle? Oh God. She kicked air, slapping her ankle, shaking off whatever it was. If it was anything other than her imagination. But, damn, it felt like a snake. She kicked again and stomped the ground, smashing whatever it was. If it was. Were there snakes in there? Spiders? Rats? Who knew what creatures were creeping around in the darkness? Harper told herself to take charge. Make a plan. But how? What could she do? She was trapped behind a wall – inside a hidden, secret, possibly unknown passageway. Not only that. It was completely pitch dark. She had no idea which way to turn, how to get out. And if she found her way out, Rick and the Colonel's other lackeys would be waiting for her.

Harper's muscles tensed. Her stomach lurched. She smelled blood and burning rubber, heard gunfire. Men shouting. Flies buzzing around her eyes . . . Damn. She bit her tongue sharply, grounding herself in the moment. She couldn't afford a flashback; the situation was already bad enough. She needed to focus and find her way out. Because, except for Rick Owens who no doubt wanted to assist her in a fake suicide, nobody – not a single soul – knew where she was. She was on her own.

Fine. If she couldn't see, she'd feel her way out. Hands on each wall, she took baby steps in a randomly selected direction, exploring the ground ahead with her toes, slowly testing the solidity of the ground before shifting her weight. After a few steps, her shoe bumped something; she stooped to feel what it was. Found something straight and long. Not her lever. Something shorter, smoother. With a knob at the end.

Her flashlight! She actually squealed with joy as she grabbed it. She'd forgotten about it; it must have fallen from her pocket. But here it was. Oh God. A miracle. Her flashlight.

The walls seemed liquid, as if they were swaying. Rick knew better. He'd been hurt before, knew the signs. Damn Harper had knocked him flat and he'd hit his head. Plus he'd lost blood. It wasn't the walls that were swaying; it was him. Not to worry, though. He'd been hurt worse. Even now, he could hear the explosions ringing in his ears. Could see Humvees burning, smell charred flesh. No, this was nothing. No ambushes. No IEDs. No snipers waiting to pop him. Even half conscious, this was still a piece of cake.

The hammer seemed awfully heavy. He was losing strength. Even so, he swung at the wall, hit the spot where he'd cracked the plaster. Sent more chunks flying. Swung again. Again and again until, finally, a small blotch of darkness appeared. He'd broken through to the other side.

Encouraged, he kept the hammer going, slamming the wall, breaking off pieces of plaster and lath, widening the gap. When the hole was baseball sized, he leaned forward to peer through it. And lost his balance and nearly fell when the entire panel gave way, swinging open. Rick pulled back, stumbling. The panel snapped shut.

Apparently, he'd accidentally pressed the spot that opened the door. He blinked, trying to identify it. Pressed the panel. Nothing happened. Pressed it again, a little to the left. Then to the right. Then higher, lower. Frustrated, he punched the wall. The door swung open. Before it could snap shut, Rick put his shoulder there, holding it open. He looked inside, expecting to see Harper somewhere in the room. But Harper wasn't there. Neither was the room. Rick gazed into the space behind the wall and saw a well of black, nothing else.

He looked down, saw a rotted staircase, collapsed on to itself. Couldn't see how deep the hole was. 'Harper?' he yelled. His voice disappeared into darkness. He coughed. 'Harper – are you OK?'

Of course she didn't answer. Was too stubborn. Would die before she surrendered an inch. Well, fine. He'd do it her way. But he couldn't stand there, wedged in the doorway. And, if he moved away, the wall would close again. He had to get down there, but what if he couldn't get the fucking wall to open again?

For a few seconds, he stood, considering his options. Looking for something to stick into the doorway to stop it from shutting. Seeing the crates. Contemplating ways to shove one into place without letting the door close. He leaned his torso toward the stack of crates, pressed his fingers around the closest one. Tugged. It inched forward. His leg screamed with the exertion, the shifting of weight. But he kept it up, leaning, pulling until the crate toppled off the stack, close enough for him to slide it against his leg. He held the door open with his back, moved the crate against the molding, careful not to drop it into the gaping darkness. And he stepped away.

The wall snapped against the crate, knocking it back into the hallway.

Fuck. Fuck fuck fuck. This was taking way too much time. Frustrated, Rick grabbed the hammer and smacked the wall again and again, widening the hole. He smeared sweat out of his eyes with bloodstained hands, but kept at it until the gash was big enough for him to lean inside. He fished his penlight out of his belt and cast a thin, powerful beam through the gash in the wall, aiming straight down.

Saw the rotted staircase. Scattered broken boards on the floor below. He moved the light, trying to see where Harper had landed, how far she'd fallen. How badly she'd been hurt. If maybe she was dead. He squinted, straining to see.

'Harper?' he yelled.

No answer. No body. Where was she? Had she somehow gotten away? God, if she talked to the press, his ass was grass. Rick listened, heard nothing. Couldn't be sure. Again, the darkness prevailed, engulfing his call and inking out his feeble ray of light.

Her flashlight wasn't strong, and its beam was narrow. But it reassured Harper that she wasn't blind; when she turned it on, her panic subsided. She could actually see a few yards ahead. Visibility wasn't great, but she was able to orient herself enough to know that she was in a tunnel. The floor was of panels and planks coated with thick patches of what seemed to be sawdust and littered with broken boards and debris. At her feet were shards – probably one of them had cut her finger. In the dim thread of light, she saw what looked like a shattered relic – something with a mosaic pattern? And she remembered the missing vessel. Mosaic pattern, with a jaguar head.

Harper stooped, began collecting various chips and pieces, trying to reassemble them, but stopped herself. What was she doing? Was she crazy? She needed to find her way out of there. The relic – if it even was a relic – could wait.

Gently, Harper moved the pieces to the side of the path and stood again, moving the skinny beam of light, scanning her surroundings. Beside her, against the wall, was a decayed stairway, a rotted platform at its top. There must be a hidden entrance up there; she must have passed right through it. Which meant that, even though it had seemed like more, she'd fallen just one story. And that she must now be on the second level of the house.

A narrow, hollowed-out passageway extended ahead of and behind her. Nothing moved in either direction. No visible snakes. Maybe spiders? Oh Lord, she hoped not. She flashed the light along the floor, then upward. She saw no spiders. But she stood gasping, swallowing air, staring at bats. Dozens of them. Hanging upside down from every exposed rafter like leaves from an oak tree.

OK, she told herself. They're just bats. Harmless. Good for the environment. They ate bugs, probably spiders, too. Besides, they were sleeping. And blind. If she left them alone, they wouldn't even notice her.

Harper moved the light, trying not to disturb them. Deciding not to look at them, to pretend they weren't there. Realizing that the bats were good news: if they'd been able to get inside the passageway, there must be an opening. Which meant a way out. She needed to stop gawking at the fauna, move her butt and find it.

She walked on, hearing a harsh sudden bang. Then another. Pieces of plaster loosened from the overhead wall, fell to the ground behind her. For a heartbeat, she thought of calling out; maybe someone had come to rescue her. But no – more likely, the person up there was Rick, incensed that she'd eluded him. He was coming after her, rabid enough to demolish the wall. Harper moved forward, picking up her pace, aiming the light on the floor ahead as her eyes grew accustomed to dimness, discerning more detail.

A dozen yards ahead, the passageway split into two. She stopped, considering: right or left? Which way should she go? She closed her eyes, trying to sense the exit, picturing the layout of the house. Probably, she was between walls of the bedrooms on the second floor. Which meant she had no idea which direction would be better. She pointed her finger, whispered, Eeny meeny miny mo. From the darkness behind her, she heard Rick calling her name. His voice sounded close, tore at her like a claw.

Harper veered right, hurrying. Several steps later, she thought, damn. Maybe I should have gone left.

Rick pressed his shoulders against the wall and stuck his head through the hole, the penlight in his mouth. The light was weak, but he could see the floor. She simply wasn't down there.

But how could that be? How could she have survived that fall? He turned his head, moving the light, thinking that maybe she'd crawled a few feet away before collapsing. But she wasn't there.

Fuck. What was he supposed to do now? Obviously, he couldn't admit that he'd let her get away. Obviously, he had to find her.

But how? She was somewhere inside the fucking *walls*. He stuck his head back in the hole, this time examining the space. Beyond the decrepit stairway, there appeared to be a passageway, a tunnel. And the walls beyond the stairs were fairly smooth. OK.

Rick smiled, relieved. He'd go down there after her. Even with his damned leg, it wasn't that far. All he had to do was attach a rope up here and rappel off the wall. Except that, damn. He didn't have a rope.

Think, he told himself. But his thinking was blurry, messed up. He couldn't keep his mind on one topic for very long. Probably, he needed water, orange juice. Something to offset his blood loss. Whiskey. Rye. Bourbon. Anything. He looked around the hallway, hoping to find a Coke, saw crates. What the hell was in all these crates?

And then it occurred to him: he could use them to climb down into the hole. He could drop them down, one at a time, until they piled up into a mound, like a mini-mountain. He could ease on to them and climb down to the tunnel floor. Genius. Absolute genius.

First, he had to make the hole wide enough and high enough. It took many more slams of the hammer, but he pulled away large wads of the wall. Then he went for a crate. It was lighter than he'd expected, light enough to heft it up to the opening, shove it through, hear it fall. He got his penlight, flashed it down. The crate had come apart, revealing piles of shredded foam. Damn. Well, it was a start – he'd probably need to toss in a couple dozen to make a high enough mound to climb onto. He'd better hurry. Harper had a head start, and his leg was slowing him down.

Rick limped to the crates, picked up another, brought it to the hole, shoved it through, let it go. Listened for the crash. Went for the third, repeated the process. Felt dizzy, but kept going. Army Strong, he told himself, and he moved back and forth, lifting and dropping boxes, losing count of the number. Driven by the knowledge that he couldn't let Harper get away. At some point, he peered through the hole and saw a mess of wood and packing stuff all over the floor. Not high enough. Nowhere near high enough. So he kept on tossing boxes until, finally, he realized he had no choice: he had to rest. Just for a minute.

Rick leaned against the wall beside the remaining crates, leaned on one to ease down to the floor. His leg was still oozing through the tourniquet. The pain had moved beyond the wound, occupied his head, his back. He'd be OK, though, in a minute. He needed just a minute to rest, and he'd be OK.

Harper faced a wall. A blank, flat plaster wall. She flashed the light up and down, refusing to accept that, after wandering through twists and turns, thirsty and sore, she had come to this: a dead end.

But it couldn't be a dead end. Why would someone go to all the trouble of building a secret passageway only to have it lead nowhere? They wouldn't, would they? And yet, here it was. A tunnel leading to nothing.

But wait. A blank wall was the way she'd gotten in there. Maybe this was the same thing, a fake obstruction. A secret door. She felt it gently, pressed on the corners, the middle. Nothing gave way. She pushed harder, leaned her back against it and shoved with her whole body, rammed it with her shoulder. Nothing happened. The wall was just a wall.

Harper leaned against it, sinking to the floor, flashing her light back along the path she'd just taken. Wondering how long she'd been walking. How long her flashlight batteries would last.

Oh God. What if they died? She'd be blind again, engulfed by thick black air. Buried in it. She turned off the light. Sat in the dark. Closed her eyes, frustrated, spilling tears. Her left leg throbbed; her head pulsed pain. She'd lost track of time. Lost her sense of direction. What if she'd been wandering in circles? Or tangled in false passages leading to dead ends? She might never find her way out.

She thought of Hank. Of never seeing him again. Of dying here, unseen, inside walls. Harper's body tensed. She ran her arm across her blood-smeared face, refusing to let herself cry. She needed to get a grip. After all, she was resourceful. Trained to overcome the harshest conditions and survive the most hostile environments. She could certainly survive in a decaying old mansion.

Besides, she probably wouldn't have to find her way out. Any minute, someone would come and find her. When he'd seen that she hadn't come home, Hank would have gotten help. Would have sent for the police. Detective Rivers was probably right that moment talking to Angus and Jake, who would know all about the tunnels and how to get around in them. Any minute, one of them would climb in and get her out.

Unless Rick found her first.

She listened for him. Earlier, she'd heard violent smashing. But not for a while. Now, sitting still in the pitch darkness, she heard nothing. Or wait. Something? Were those footsteps? Grunts? Dragging? Was someone there? Was it Rick?

She stopped breathing, strained to pick up the faintest hint of sound. And then, suddenly, a burst of music. Not just music. Meatloaf. That song, 'Paradise by the Dashboard Light'. The girl was singing that she had to know if he'd love her forever, that he had to tell her right now.

Harper got to her feet, trying to locate its source. Was it coming from behind her? Back in the tunnels? Through the wall ahead? Why couldn't she be sure? She turned in circles, listening, unable to determine a direction. Each way she turned seemed wrong.

'Let me sleep on it,' Meatloaf sang.

Maybe it wasn't real. Maybe that was why she couldn't locate it. Maybe the music was in her head. After all, she hadn't seen anything but a dim swatch of light, hadn't heard much except her almost silent footsteps in God knew how long . . . Minutes? Hours? She had no idea. And sensory deprivation could cause hallucinations; she'd learned that back in psych class. So maybe she was hallucinating now. Creating Meatloaf in her mind because her mind needed to hear something.

Then again, maybe she wasn't.

Which would mean that someone was actually within hearing distance. If she could hear them, then they could hear her. She yelled, 'Hel—' and stopped halfway through the word. What if it was Rick blasting the music, luring her to him with a friendly sound so he could ambush her?

Well, fine, she decided. If it was Rick, she'd deal with him.

'Hello?' she bellowed. Her voice swam into empty air, drowned by the music. 'Can anyone hear me?'

The girl answered, repeating that she had to know right now.

The music sounded real. But Harper had endured countless flashbacks that had seemed real; she was well aware that the mind could play incredible tricks. Even so, she couldn't stay there, at a dead end. Had to move, to keep searching for a way out. She turned the flashlight back on and started down the tunnel, away from the wall. She stopped, though, when she saw a bent nail on the ground, and she knelt slowly, wincing in pain to pick it up. It wasn't as sharp as her pocketknife would have been, but the nail was pointed enough to carve an 'X' on the wall.

From now on, at least she'd know if she was backtracking. From now on, she'd leave a trail.

Rick pushed himself to his feet. If he fell asleep, he was a goner. He might die right there. No, he had to find Harper, complete his job. His sweat chilled him, and he shivered. His leg was on fire. Vaguely, he noticed his phone on the floor. It must have fallen from his pocket; he'd get it in a minute. But first, he went back to his task, shoving boxes through the secret door until, finally, the pile was close enough to stand on. He secured his gun in his tool belt, took the hammer for good measure, grabbed his penlight, and lowered himself into the hole.

The stack was unstable, composed of broken and off balanced crates, and it gave way under his weight, sending him sliding to the ground. A howl escaped his throat; a jolt tore through his leg. He landed on his ass, legs akimbo, and lay panting until his body stopped reverberating. Thinking, even as he shook with pain, about his phone. That it was still out there on the floor. That he'd forgotten to pick it up. Fuck.

Gradually, his nerves stopped screaming, and he rolled to his side. Light from the open door was dim; he turned on his penlight, looked around. Saw a tunnel extending ahead and behind him. Saw some broken pottery a few steps away. Harper had been there, had gathered the pieces.

Leaning on a broken crate, Rick climbed to his feet. His leg wound was bleeding again, so he played with the tourniquet, tightening it, grimacing. His hands wet and slipping, he rested for a moment, allowing the pain. Snapped a yard-long board off a broken crate to use as a walking stick. Then, gripping his stick in one hand, his gun in the other, his penlight in his mouth, he set out after Harper.

Almost instantly, music began to blare; he couldn't tell from where. Really? Music? Fucking Meatloaf? Shit. He stopped for a second, absorbing this new development. What the hell did it mean? Was someone else in the house? Were they having a damned party? Wonderful, all he needed were more complications. Witnesses. As if this job hadn't gone to hell already. Now, he'd have collateral damage, too? He'd have to take care of extraneous people? This day just got suckier and suckier. Fuck fuck fuck.

Rick limped ahead, moving in the direction of the broken pottery. Furious about the music. How was he supposed to listen for Harper when someone was blasting fucking Meatloaf?

On the other hand, when he found her, the music would cover screams and gunshots.

Every few steps, he had to stop to steady himself, fight the dizziness. Overcome the gnashing pain. But relentlessly, he kept on. Until, goddammit, the tunnel split.

Of course it did. Everything else was fucked up, why wouldn't the tunnel be, too? Rick felt like shooting the walls, blowing the whole damned place up. He needed to get it together; he was better, smarter than to lose it. He needed to psyche out his prey, that was all. OK. Which way would she have gone, right or left? He closed his eyes, pictured Harper standing there, choosing. She would go right; he was sure of that. She was right-handed. And she'd been wounded on her left side. To her, left was vulnerable, so reflex would make her go right.

But she was smart, too. Wouldn't choose her first impulse. Would know he'd psyche her out.

Rick clutched his gun, leaned on his board, flashed the penlight ahead. And went left.

Harper's mouth was dry, parched. Beyond thirsty. But she kept on going, stopping every few yards to scratch the walls with an 'X.' Taking a route different from the one she'd taken earlier. Listening to identify the direction of the music, to move towards it. But the tunnel moved in its own complicated directions, twisting, turning, moving up and down ramps, taking her through stretches where the ceiling lowered and the walls narrowed. Once, she had to move sideways, couldn't fit through any other way. What if the ceiling collapsed? What if she were buried alive there? But she kept on. Had no choice. Behind her was a dead end.

At some point, as abruptly as it had started, the music stopped. Harper called out, hoping whoever was there would hear her. 'Hello? Can you hear me? Is somebody there?'

She kept calling, listening. Heard no reply. Fought tears. Kept walking, marking the wall. Her body became numb, her steps automatic, zombie-like. She stopped thinking, stopped being afraid. Motion, motion and breathing were the only constants. For a while, she counted steps, then lost track. Couldn't remember whether she was on one hundred twelve or twenty. Vaguely, it occurred to her that all the exits might be hidden like the one she'd fallen through. That she might have passed a dozen of them without knowing it. How could she find a door if it looked like the rest of the passageway? She couldn't. She'd wander forever, trapped in the walls. She wiped away more tears, this time of exhaustion. Told herself that the exits must have some marker. That they would have to. Harper walked on slowly, shining her light on ceilings and walls, looking for irregularities. Symbols.

The passageway veered around a corner. She flashed the light above her head, to her left and right. Finally, she aimed it straight ahead. And then the hallucination began.

It had to be a hallucination. Couldn't be real.

But there she was: a woman in a fur coat. Curled up on the floor, her head lolling forward, as if asleep.

It's sensory deprivation, Harper warned herself. She's not there. She's like an oasis in the desert; your mind is creating her. Harper closed her eyes, held them shut. Opened them again. The woman was still there.

Oh God. Someone was actually there. A person, maybe trapped like she was. Maybe hurt. Harper rushed to her. 'Miss – miss? Are you all right?'

Harper knelt, touched the woman's shoulder. Aiming the light on to her head.

Slowly, as if deflating, the woman caved in. Before Harper realized that her coat was empty, the woman's head rolled off of her shoulders, her hair falling free, her skull tumbling to the floor.

His leg raging, Rick wondered if people could go insane from pain. Decided that, of course, yes, they could. Briefly, he wondered if he was going insane right then, breaking down a wall, hobbling down some hidden corridor, hunting a woman down so he could kill her. It definitely sounded insane. But it wasn't; it was war. And when fighting a war, a little insanity never hurt.

Besides, he could take the pain. Pain was nothing, just a physical reaction. Nerves sending impulses to the brain. He was trained. He could overpower them. But it was tough; he could imagine those impulses getting stronger, taking over his mind. Pissing him off. Sending him on a rampage where he'd kill anything that breathed. Maybe even himself.

He walked on, angry at his pain, leaning on his cane, blinking rapidly to steady himself. His gun got too heavy for his hand, and his lips were tired, aching from holding the penlight. He put the gun back into his belt, used the gun hand to hold the penlight. There. That was better. Oops. His balance was off. He stumbled, would have fallen if not for the walking stick.

The corridor again veered sharply to the left, sloped down gradually. The air became chilly and damp. The walls became more clay than plaster; the planks of the floor covered rocks and earth. Obviously, the path had led him underground. The further he walked, the louder the music seemed. Damn. What if he didn't find Harper, but walked right into a damned Halloween party?

He stopped, considering what he should do. Wondering if Harper had already found the party, if they'd called the police. Damn.

He looked behind him, considered going back, climbing out the hole he'd made, finding Harper another time. Maybe waiting for her at home. She'd have to go home sometime; he could wait for her, and bang bang, do the job in two seconds.

That was probably the smart thing to do. Rick didn't relish the trek back up the passageway, but he turned, started back. Went about ten yards when, bam, the music stopped. And from somewhere – he couldn't tell where – a woman called, 'Hello? Can you hear me? Is somebody there?'

Harper was close. He stood alert, waiting for her to yell again. But when she did, he still couldn't identify her direction. Except he was sure she wasn't behind him; he'd have seen her. Unless, back at the fork, he'd taken the wrong turn. Maybe he should have gone the other way. Damn. His leg pulsed, distracting him. OK, he'd keep going forward for a while. If he didn't find her in like ten minutes, he'd go back to the fork and start over.

Rick smelled something smoky, musky. Maybe a fire? Oh God, was the house burning down? No, the scent was too mild. Almost like incense. Odd. He crept forward, sniffing, his skin itching, nerves prickling. His instincts on red alert, warning of danger up ahead, probably Harper. He stayed close to the wall, edging forward. Coming to a dead end – no, not a dead end. Too late, he noticed the sudden drop, the ladder leading straight down. Rick fell, landing hard on his leg, letting out a shattering yowl.

Instantly, someone pounced on him, pressing an arm against his throat. Rick swung and punched, couldn't breathe. Fuck. He tried to reach for his gun, but his arms were pinned, couldn't move. Damn. The fucker was choking him. Who the hell was it? Rick thrashed and twisted.

Even with his desperation and pain, his mind raced, able to get his bearings. A cave-like room. A ramp that led up to daylight. A table covered with small packages. And finally, as darkness overtook him, a creature above him unlike any he'd seen before; it had fought like a man, but had feathers like a bird. And the head of a wild cat.

Harper jumped, howling, and ran backwards around the corner. Heart pounding, swallowing air, she stood for a moment, hugging herself. The woman wasn't, couldn't have been real. The body had to be a creation of Harper's own terrified, sensory-deprived mind.

Finally, her breathing quieted, her heart rate slowed. Prepared to see an empty hallway ahead, she rounded the corner, flashed the light. And saw the skull, patched with blackened leathery skin, lying on the path. A champagne bottle on its end beside her, along with a crystal glass. The fur coat draping a decomposed skeleton against the wall.

Oh my God. Harper stared, remembering the stories about the house. Trying to recall a name – Carole? Camille? No – Chloe. Chloe Manning. The glamorous silent movie actress who'd disappeared during a party in the Twenties or Thirties, whose body had never been found. Until now. Harper stood, staring at the remains, doubting her own perceptions. After all, people had supposedly searched the passages for the actress and never found her. How could Harper have chanced upon her?

Unless she, too, was hopelessly lost.

Harper imagined the woman stumbling in the dark without a candle or flashlight. How long had she wandered around? Had she been drugged? Too drunk to know what was happening? Had she screamed, pounded the walls in despair and panic? Passed out? Never mind. It was too late to worry about her; she'd been dead for almost a century. And now, Harper was as lost as Chloe Manning had been. Very irretrievably lost. Was the body an omen? Would she share Chloe Manning's fate? Would she die there, alone?

She thought of Hank. Wondered how long he'd search for her. When he'd give up. If he'd have her declared dead so he could marry again. A hot stab of jealousy surged through her, resenting his new wife. Oh God, would she really never see him again? Damn. Was this really how she'd die? Sniper fire whizzed past her head, a bomb exploded nearby. Harper smelled smoke, heard screams of the wounded. And something else: from faraway, she heard Hank's voice. Calling her. 'Hoppa!'

How sad. How pathetic. She was so desperate, so without hope of ever seeing him again that she was manufacturing him. Hallucinating. She heard it again: 'Hoppa!'

'Hank? I'm here!' she called, knowing that he wasn't really there. That she was calling to her own imagination. Even so, she stared into the tunnel and pictured him coming for her, emerging from the darkness with his powerful, uneven gait, bearing a flaming bright torch, his eyes reflecting the fire.

'Hoppa!'

'Stop it,' she scolded her mind, aching for Hank. Sorry she'd ever argued with him.

Stop it. She pinched herself, concentrated on the sharpness of the pinch, then on the ache in her leg, aborting the hallucination with pain. Pleased that she could feel it. Pain, after all, meant there was still hope: unlike Chloe Manning, she wasn't dead. Yet.

Don't look at her, Harper told herself. Just mark the wall and keep going. She kept going, but couldn't help looking back, aiming her light one more time on the remains of Chloe Manning, her skull staring from the shadows, watching Harper leave.

Her throat was parched. Don't think about it, she told herself. Don't think about Rick or the Colonel or Hank or anything. Just walk.

She walked. She marked the wall. And walked and marked the wall. Maybe it wasn't really for a long time. Maybe it was only a few minutes. Half an hour that felt like days? She had no idea. Time could be misleading. Like darkness. She felt like collapsing, or at least like sitting for a while. Didn't do either. The passageway kept changing. Now it turned at right angles, zigzagging. Somehow she'd gotten off her original path, which had been relatively straight. Now, there were right angles, as if she were moving around the perimeters of rooms. As if she were in between them. She tapped on the wall, wondered if she could kick through. Decided to try. Stopped, put her weight on to her weak left leg and slammed the wall with her right. The impact sent her flying to the ground, cursing. White pain reverberating through her right leg.

But she kept going. After a while, the ground sloped down, probably leading to the first floor. Harper sped up; there had to be an exit down there. Had to be. The slant made moving easier, quicker. And suddenly, the passage became damp, cooler. She smelled earth. Must be underground? Yes. The walls had become rock and clay. Damn. And after a while, she smelled something sweet. Mold? No, muskier. Spicier. More like incense? A few steps later, she heard voices and almost screamed with joy.

Except she didn't. She crouched against the wall, listening. Making sure that Rick hadn't sent for reinforcements. That she wasn't walking right into his arms.

'I'll go back later,' a man said. 'Maybe there's something else even better.'

'Asshole.' This voice was gruffer, deeper.

'It wasn't my fault. She was right there.'

'Stop making excuses for yourself, will you? You fucked up.'

'I know that. Don't you think I know that?' The first man again, whining.

Silence. The scent of smoky incense was stronger.

'I paid you a week ago. Our customers expect delivery tonight. Trust me, we don't want to piss them off.'

More silence.

Harper crept forward, leaned around a corner, expecting to see them. Saw a blank wall several feet ahead. What? Where were the men? She inched closer to the wall, trying to hear the voices, and stepped forward, setting her foot down on empty air. She swam, arms flailing and grabbing at the wall as she shifted her weight, hopped backwards, lost her balance and landed on her butt. She sat for a moment, catching her breath. Shit. She'd almost fallen into a gaping hole at the end of the passageway. Soft golden light rose from the opening. Harper shut off her flashlight and rolled on to

her belly. She lay flat, crawled to the edge, peeked down. Saw a
cave-like room, dimly lit with lanterns. A man, pacing. And, directly
under her, limbs sprawled, lying not far from a rope ladder, she saw
Rick.

Rick was looking right at her, but didn't move, didn't let on. Had
he seen her? Harper waved her hand, watched for a reaction. Saw
none. Rick's eyes remained fixed, and he lay perfectly still. Oh God.
Was he dead? Maybe not. Maybe he was just hurt. Dazed or unconscious. But who were those men? Couldn't they see him lying there?
Why weren't they helping him?

She strained to hear their conversation.

'. . . figure out who he is and how in God's name he got here.'

'There are dozens of openings.'

'You know that. But how did he? How did he even know that
there are passageways?'

Silence.

'You have no idea? Either one of you? Because other than the
three of us, who could possibly know?'

'We don't know any more than you do, Joe.'

'Great. Just great.' Joe growled. 'So some random burglar just
happens to break into this house? Just *happens* to find a passageway?
Just *happens* to drop in on us today, right when we're about to make
a serious delivery?'

'So what are you saying, Joe? That this guy's a spy? Someone's
been spying on us?'

'It sure looks that way. But he couldn't be in it alone. Somebody
sent him. Somebody who wants part of the take.'

'No, wait.' The guy who wasn't Joe argued. 'Except for us, who
could that be?'

Silence.

Harper inched forward, trying to get a better view of the room,
to see who was in there. Missed a comment or two.

Then heard Not Joe say, 'You serious?'

'I am.'

'Really? The blonde from the university?'

She froze, not daring to breathe.

'Not all alone,' Joe reasoned. 'But obviously she knows the dollars
these pieces can bring in, so she might have made her own deal. Or
it might be the other way – this guy might have come to her with
a deal.'

'And they spied on us to find out about the tunnel. It makes sense. Except what happened to his leg?'

'Who knows. Perhaps she double-crossed him?'

'Well, we'll never know, thanks to Chief Catfeathers over there. That guy sure isn't going to tell us.'

Harper looked down at Rick. His eyes hadn't moved. For sure, he was dead.

'For your information, I hardly touched him. Guy was half dead to begin with – look at all the blood on him.'

'You went at him like a rabid hyena. We should have talked to him.'

Harper looked down at Rick. A blood-drenched rag formed a feeble tourniquet around his leg. His eyes gazed her way, not blinking.

'Well, since we're speaking of mistakes, genius, let's get back to yours.'

'I already told you, Joe. It wasn't my fault.'

'So whose fault was it? Mine? His?' Work boots paced into Harper's view. Then out. 'Shit. All right, it doesn't matter now. We've got a situation here. What am I supposed to tell them? That my idiot supplier fell down a shaft and broke a one-of-a-kind priceless pot for which they've prepaid fifty-five thousand?'

Fifty-five thousand? Harper strained her neck, leaning over the hole to see more of the room. Saw a table stacked with Styrofoam packing cases like the ones up in the crates. Were they relics? She tried to count them, got to nine.

'We can refund their money.' The guy who wasn't Joe suggested.

These guys had stolen relics and were selling them. Of course. That was why so many were missing from the collection. The professor hadn't misplaced them as Jake had said. The missing pieces removed by these guys. Was Angus one of them? Was Jake? Were they stealing what they believed should have been their legacy?

Suddenly, right below her, Rick began to slide across the floor.

'Oh no,' the man who wasn't Joe groaned.

'What's he doing? Hey, what the hell are you doing?' Joe barked.

Rick's arms splayed over his head as someone dragged him by the feet, moving him out of Harper's line of sight.

'Shit. Does he have to do that again?' Joe asked. 'What the hell's the matter with him?'

'Let's not bother him.' First guy sounded edgy. 'Just let him do his thing. You don't want to start something with him.'

'He's fucked up,' Joe said. 'Seriously. He needs help.' His voice sounded familiar. Slightly accented.

'You think I can't hear you?' A third voice. Kind of throaty. Also familiar?

'You're talking about me as if I'm not here. I can hear everything you're saying.'

'Good. I'll say it to your face. You fucking need to go someplace and get locked up. You're ill. It's sick, what you're doing.'

'I appreciate your opinion. But you have no inkling what you're talking about. I'd advise you not to speak to me.'

'Really, Digger? You're telling me what I can do?'

Digger? Wait. Jake had talked about Digger – had said he was Angus' friend. Was this the same 'Digger'?

'Move away. You're interfering with the rite.'

'Rite? Are you serious? You look like a fucking chicken.'

'You're speaking out of ignorance. And as a priest, I can't be bothered with your opinions. This rite is essential for our continued success. It strengthens us.'

'It does, does it?' Joe was unconvinced.

'It does.'

'It's not his fault.' The first guy spoke up. 'The old guy got him started.'

'Neither of you can possibly understand.' Digger sounded winded. Probably from dragging Rick.

'He's being doing this since the eighties.'

'Since the eighties?' Joe's voice again. 'Shit. How old were you then? Like ten?'

'Fifteen. Digger was sixteen.'

'No, I started younger. By sixteen, I'd performed a dozen rituals.'

'Bullshit! We'd have heard if—'

'I began with a dog.'

'You did what? Fuck you, Digger – that was you? You fucking killed our dog?'

That had to be Angus.

'Not his spirit. That still lives within me. The professor didn't realize what I was doing until my fourteenth – which was Carla.'

Carla? Harper drew a breath. Carla Prentiss. Langston's murdered researcher. Angus' friend killed her?

'What is he talking about?' Joe scoffed.

'The old guy used to take us on digs. Digger was fascinated by the old rituals, how they were done.'

'Shit. You're saying you killed that girl?' Joe sounded stunned.

'Not killed; sacrificed.' Digger corrected. 'She was a virgin. A pure offering.'

'And the professor knew?'

'Well, he figured it out. Quietly arranged for his protégé here to be sent on a long vacation to the Happy Home.'

'It was a private academy. My parents thought it best that I study abroad.'

'Whatever. I can't believe you killed my fuckin' dog.'

Harper thought she must have misheard. Because she could swear that the third guy, Digger, had just admitted that he had killed Carla Prentiss. And Angus was down there, explaining the past to Joe. She pictured him at the site where she'd found Zina. Had he acted as if he'd killed her? Or maybe Jake had done it. Maybe it hadn't been an honor killing at all. She shivered, recalling being alone with him in the house. The way he'd lingered. But the men were still talking.

'. . . and the professor chose me as his assistant. He taught me the mystical secrets and rites of the ancients.'

Harper edged sideways, craning her neck, stretching to see them. Saw two pairs of legs in jeans and work boots. No faces. Nobody else.

'So now you're what? The high priest of fuck-upness?' Joe mocked. 'I'll tell you what, Father Fuckup: stop what you're doing. I warned you the last time, and I'm warning you again. Stop it. Now. Hey – I'm talking to you, you sick—'

Harper heard a clank. A scuffle. Pushing? Stumbling? The first guy yelling: 'Settle down, both of you. Jesus. You'll break everything. Get it together, would you? Anybody remember why we're here? Joe's got a delivery to make.'

A pause. 'Don't you ever fucking touch me again, you hear me?' Joe was breathless, his voice wind and thunder.

'Actually, I'd prefer not to have any contact with you whatsoever. But I promise you this: if you attack me again, my physical touch will be the least of your problems. I'll gather all the powers and—'

'I swear to you, I'm going to rip your fucking powers right out of—'

'Enough!' The first guy intervened.

Silence. Harper smelled tension and incense.

Joe broke it. 'So what do you think? She still up there?'

She? Oh God. Harper ducked away from the opening. Had they seen her? Were they looking up at her? Wait, of course not. They had no idea she was there. Besides, if she couldn't see them, they couldn't see her. Even so, Joe was talking about her. Who the hell was he?

'She must be. Isn't her bike still out there?'

'Yeah. Was when I got here, anyway.'

Lord. They'd seen her Ninja, were definitely talking about her. And she was convinced, almost sure that two of them were Angus and Jake.

'What's she doing, sleeping up there?' A pause. 'Oh shit.'

'If she was mad enough to shoot *him*—'

'She might be dead up there.'

'—what do you think he did to *her*?'

Silence.

'Should we go see? If she's alive, we could talk to her about this guy.'

'No, not now.' Joe grunted. 'Focus, would you? First, we've got to make this delivery. Even if she's dead up there, we don't have time to go looking for a suitable replacement piece right now. So here's what we'll do. I'll tell them their vessel got damaged in transit. I'll offer to make it good with another piece of equal or greater value. Which you will supply.'

'That ought to work.'

'But, I'll tell you this, Butterfingers,' Joe went on. 'If they don't go for it, it comes out of your pocket.'

'The hell it does.' The first guy raised his voice. 'I'm not paying for—'

'Really? Well. Then you better hope they'll go for it.' Joe's voice rumbled, dangerous.

A pause. Then the first guy mumbled, 'Whatever.'

'So, are we done here, ladies? Let's load up.' Joe's voice called from farther away. 'That means all three of us, Your High Priest of Poultry Feathers.'

The first guy lowered his voice, urging, 'Come on, leave that for now. We got to move this stuff. Besides, aren't you supposed to do that in daylight?'

'It's almost daylight.' The third guy bristled. 'But he has no respect. He's an ignorant non-believer who doesn't understand even the most basic aspects of the spirit world. And yet, he continually challenges me.'

'Gentlemen,' Joe called. 'We got a date. Move it!'

There were grumbling replies, but the voices faded, too difficult to understand. In a few moments, Harper heard doors slam, a car drive off, and then no sound at all.

Harper waited. Still heard nothing. And decided to move.

Cautiously, she got to her feet, lowered herself down the rope ladder to the open space below. Light flowed in across the room. She squinted, covered her eyes. Looked again. Saw a dirt ramp leading up out of the room. A dark sky, black trees above the open exit.

A dark sky? Harper blinked, disoriented; she'd arrived in the middle of the day. How long had she been there? Wait – one of the men had said it would be daylight soon. So she'd been inside all night?

Oh God. Hank must be frantic. But where was he? Why wasn't he here, looking for her? Never mind; it wasn't the time to think about Hank. Harper ran for it, not even looking to see if any of the men were still there. Passing the table, she noticed that the packages were gone, loaded up for delivery. She dashed toward the ramp, aware of each breath, of the effort of each step. Of her exposure and vulnerability. She ran, oblivious of her wimpy leg, ignoring her exhaustion and pain, made it to the bottom of the ramp where she lowered her body, hugged the wall, peered up, actually inhaling fresh air again.

Seeing no one, she started up the ramp, but stopped and turned, headed back inside. No matter what he'd done, she couldn't leave Rick there without checking; she needed to be sure that he was definitely dead. Squinting in the dimness, she turned, scanned the room.

Rick was lying against the wall on a pyramid of rocks that resembled an altar. A pile of colored feathers lay on the floor beside him, and all around him, scented oil burned in small pots. Primitive painted images covered the wall: a deer. A dog. A bird. An owl. A jaguar. A man with a jaguar head. Harper stepped closer.

'Oh God.' She stopped breathing and stared.

Rick's shirt was ripped open. And his chest sliced in an X, the skin pulled back above the heart.

Harper ran in a haze, cool dew misting her face, leaves crunching underfoot. She glimpsed trees as she sped past them, vaguely aware that she'd emerged far from the house. That the ramp had led her to a familiar spot – exactly where she'd found Zina's body. But then she was on her bike, roaring away, hoping the cops would stop her for speeding and take her away.

But they didn't. She raced along the highway, through Ithaca and up the hill, around campus and, turning on to Hanshaw Street, she saw the police cars in her driveway. All the lights on in her house.

She spun on to the property, dropping the Ninja on its side as she slid off. She ran, calling Hank's name.

The front door was open; she flew inside, shouting, 'Hank?'

In the living room, she scanned faces, searching for his and found it in a cluster. Hank was on his feet, coming to her, reaching for her. 'Hoppa!'

Harper jumped into his arms, relieved. And she stayed there, pressed against him until, gradually, she became aware of other voices, other people. Vicki. Trent. Detective Rivers. Uniformed police. Everyone was asking questions. 'Harper, where have you been?'

'Are you all right, Mrs Jennings?'

'Good God, she's covered with blood!'

'We've been so worried . . .'

Hank raised a hand, stopping them. 'Hoppa. Sit.' He started for the sofa, but Harper pulled him back.

'No – no, we have to go back. To Langston's. Rick's dead, and these other guys . . . One of them killed Carla. And they're selling the relics!'

'Mrs Jennings.' Detective Rivers stepped forward, put an arm around her shoulders. 'Breathe.'

Everyone stood around her, a circle of staring faces. Harper looked from one to another. Vicki's eyes were swollen and red; she'd been crying. Trent's were liquid and boozy. Hank's – Hank's were steady and dark, making her want to stay there, lingering in their heat. But Detective Rivers led her to the sofa, made her sit.

'Slowly now. In complete sentences. What are you trying to say?'

Vicki dabbed the cut on her head with a damp washcloth. Trent offered her a Scotch. She took it, her hands trembling. Took a gulp with a parched throat, coughed at the burn. Remembered how thirsty she was. Vicki brought water and more damp towels, dabbed at Harper's face even as she drank. Harper repeated herself, insisting that Rivers go with her back to Langston's. Explaining that a man had been killed there. That she'd encountered a group who were trafficking illegal antiquities.

Rivers wanted more details. She asked questions. Who had been killed? Harper was impatient. Why did she need to explain now? Couldn't they talk on the way? But Rivers wasn't moving, so Harper told her that the dead man was someone she'd known in the army, that he'd been stalking her. That he'd been sent to kill her. That he'd probably killed Burke Everett and Pete Murray, another guy they'd served with.

Rivers was frowning.

Harper hurried on, explaining that men at the house were stealing the relics. That one of them was called Joe and another might have been Angus. Or maybe Jake. But either way, one was Angus' friend Digger, and Digger had admitted killing Carla Prentiss, and he might have killed Zina, too. Oh, and she'd found Chloe Manning, the actress—

Harper stopped, bothered by the look in Rivers' eyes. It was soft, like sympathy. Sympathy? It reminded her of the way she herself had looked at Burke when she'd thought he was nuts. Damn, didn't Rivers believe her? Did she think she was just ranting? Why wasn't Rivers calling for backup, taking off for Langston's with lights and sirens? Five, maybe ten whole minutes must have passed since she'd walked in, and every moment counted.

Sighing, Rivers got to her feet. 'Do you feel up to going back there, Mrs Jennings? So you can show me exactly where the body is?'

It wasn't until she peeled herself off the sofa that Harper realized exactly how drained she was. 'Of course.' She teetered as she started for the door.

'Going with.' Hank's beefy hand closed around hers. And suddenly, she wasn't quite as exhausted any more.

A patrol car followed them. Rivers didn't turn on the sirens; there was almost no traffic at this early hour. Harper sat in the back seat with Hank, leaning against his shoulder.

'Got dark out. Waited. Thought you mad still with me. Stayed out.'

Harper shook her head, no. She hadn't been mad.

'Got mad, too. Thought OK. Games. Let her play. Late got though. Finally, called you. Not answer.'

'But I wouldn't do that. I don't play games, Hank.'

'Midnight after. Worried. Tried to find house. Lang. Ston's. Didn't know. Where. Had to find. Came there. Looked for you.'

Wait. Hank had gone to Langston's? He'd been there?

'Drove there.' Hank's eyebrows furrowed. 'Window broken found. Looked whole house. Your bike. Your. Bag. Phone. Broken rel. Licks. Blood. Lots. And hole big in wall. No you.'

Harper's eyes filled. Hank had gone to look for her. She wondered – in the tunnel, had she really heard his voice? 'Did you call my name?'

He went on. 'Looked in wall. Yelled "Hoppa." Tried to go through hole. Arm. Leg. Caught, stuck. Couldn't get in. Help.'

'Your husband was quite alarmed, Mrs Jennings. He called us, and we went out about one in the morning, looking for you. When we saw the blood, we got concerned. Took samples. Made the third floor east wing into a crime scene. We sent an officer into that hole with a rope, so he wouldn't get lost. He got to the end of his rope, literally, and came back. Frankly, we were all pretty concerned. We were about to get a dog to follow your scent.'

Wait, the police had been to Langston's? Why hadn't they seen the thieves? And why hadn't the thieves seen them?

'Meantime, I took your husband back home and kept him company until your friends got here. He's had a hell of a night, and I didn't want him to be alone. When you suddenly showed up, you can imagine how relieved we were.'

Hank leaned over, planted a tender kiss on her forehead. Harper leaned up; her lips met his. She stayed tightly secured in his arms until Rivers pulled on to the road leading to the Langston house.

Then, Harper sat up, gazing out the window as they approached the spot where she'd found Zina. 'I came out of the tunnel somewhere in there.'

Rivers stopped; the patrol car parked behind them. Everyone got out.

Harper tensed, preparing herself to go back.

'OK?' Hank whispered.

She met his eyes, took a breath, and led the way into the thicket of trees and bushes, past the clearing where she'd had drinks with Zina's brother, looking for the opening in the ground. Damn. Why hadn't she paid closer attention? Why hadn't she marked the spot?

She walked in circles. The opening wasn't small, had been large enough for large men carrying packages to walk through. But then she saw a subtle path, crushed foliage leading to the road, and she followed it around a fallen tree trunk.

From the outside, hidden in the thicket, the ramp seemed small and harmless. Kind of like a large animal had burrowed there.

'He's down here,' Harper started into the tunnel.

Detective Rivers grabbed her arm. 'Mrs Jennings. Wait here.' She motioned the officers to go first, handing each a flashlight. 'Give us the all clear.'

One at a time, preceded by thin, white beams, the two men lowered themselves through the opening on to the ramp, guns drawn.

'We're clear, Detective.' The call came almost immediately. Too soon.

Rivers went in, Harper right behind her, leaving Hank to lumber behind.

'Do you see him?' Harper asked as Rivers entered the hollowed out room. 'He's in the back—' She stopped at the bottom of the ramp, and stared.

The room, except for a few broken crates and a couple of black and white bird feathers, was empty. Rick was gone, along with the altar that had held him. There were no lanterns, no pots of burning oil. All that remained of what she'd seen were primitive paintings on the wall: a deer, a dog, an owl, a jaguar, and a man with a jaguar head.

Harper was furious. If Rivers hadn't stalled, wasting precious minutes back at home, they'd have caught the men. But now, there was no proof of anything, not even of Rick's murder.

Harper showed them the opening to the tunnel. 'This leads back to the house. And all through the house. Chloe Manning's in there. I can show you.'

Hank's arm was around her. 'Tired too.'

Harper twisted, freeing herself. 'No. I'm not too tired. I should show you before these guys have time to make more evidence disappear.'

Rivers bristled. 'Look, Mrs Jennings. If you're implying that I—'

'We should have come right back here, like I said.'

Rivers stood tall, looked down a few inches at Harper's face. 'Listen, ma'am. When you came into your house, you were in no condition to go anywhere. You had a head wound and you were rambling. Before I moved, I needed to understand what you were saying, as well as to assess the accuracy – actually, the credibility – of your claims. I acted as quickly as I thought reasonable. Within a matter of minutes.'

'But we missed them.'

Rivers crossed her arms, met Harper's eyes. 'Mrs Jennings, if what you say is true—'

'*If?*'

'—then I'm pretty sure your relic traffickers had removed the body by the time you got home.'

The two women stared at each other for a moment, Harper steaming.

'I understand you're frustrated and exhausted, but I need to conduct an investigation, and I'd appreciate your calm cooperation. How about you show us exactly what happened back in the house?'

Hank had stepped close, silently took Harper's hand. Then, as a group, they went back to the cars and drove up to the house where they found two very agitated men, standing at the door.

Angus spoke first. 'What the hell's been going on here?'

'We were just about to call the police. We thought someone murdered you.' Jake glared at Harper.

She said nothing, was listening to their voices, wondering which of them was the relic thief.

'So you called the cops? What the hell went on up there!'

'I told you, Jake.' Angus grumbled. 'It's the damned university and all their publicity. Someone fucking broke in and robbed us. The collection's been in the news so much, we might as well have had an open house for burglars.'

'Gentlemen,' Rivers interrupted, 'can we take a look inside?'

On the way upstairs, Angus went on, 'Man, I wish I'd come by earlier. I'd have caught those sons of bitches.'

'Why did you come by, Mr Langston?'

'I come by every day. To check on the place.'

'What time was did you get here?'

'Dunno. Before six.'

'Awfully early, isn't it?'

'Not for me. I'm up at sunrise.'

By the time they'd arrived on the third floor, Angus had explained that he'd seen the missing windowpane and called Jake. Together, they'd gone into the house and found mayhem upstairs. A smashed wall. Broken artifacts. And blood.

'We thought it was your blood,' Jake moved closer to Harper.

Hank took a step forward, stood between them.

But Harper wasn't paying attention. She was concerned; the crates that had been stacked in the hallway were missing. Where were they? On an impulse, she peeked through the gash in the wall and in the dim light below saw a heap of mangled wood and packing boxes.

A sound – kind of a groan – escaped her belly as, oblivious to the others, she rushed to check the workroom. Thank God, the crates there remained unharmed. But there was damage there, too. Despite the stiffness of her leg, Harper knelt and carefully picked up the pieces, cradling a broken ancient bird.

It was a catastrophe.

Harper grabbed her stomach, felt the loss as physical pain. 'Oh my God. Oh God,' seemed to be all she could say. She stood, gently replacing the broken artifacts on the worktable and rushed back to hall where Angus and Jake were shouting, cursing, pacing in distraught concentric circles.

Hank had looked at the breakage. As had Rivers and the two officers. Harper shoved her head back through the hole, gawking at the devastation, baffled about what could have happened. Replaying the night before, her encounter with Rick.

She'd fallen through the wall and escaped into the tunnel. But she hadn't broken the wall, had she? No, it had merely given way.

So Rick must have tried bashing the wall in. And then found out how to open the door before throwing the crates down into the passageway? Why?

Rick had had no idea what the crates held. To him, they'd merely been big wooden boxes. So he'd dropped priceless, irreplaceable objects so he could climb down the boxes that held them.

'She was up here. She must know what happened.' Angus came at Harper from the left, Hank half a step behind him. 'Did you have anything do to with this?' Angus raised his hand to grab her arm; Hank's went up to intercept it. Angus wheeled around, swinging, his fist thudding into Hank's jaw. Harper leapt at his back, jabbing his ribs, but the officers pounced on her, one from each side while Rivers separated Angus and Hank, cautioning Jake against moving a muscle.

'Mother of God,' she breathed. 'What is wrong with you people?' She shook her head. 'No, don't answer that. Don't say a single word, anybody. Unless I ask you to.'

Harper went to Hank. His gum was bleeding. She glared at Angus, who glared back.

When the room was silent, Rivers looked at them, one after another. Then she said, 'So. Who wants to tell me what you all are fighting about?'

They all began talking at once. But Rivers made them take turns, and finally came to understand the significance of the smashed crates, that the treasures they held were part of Professor Langston's renowned, disputed, and controversial collection.

'It was Rick. The dead guy who wasn't there just now – the one who attacked me—'

'Hold on – a dead guy who wasn't there attacked you?' Jake rolled his eyes.

Rivers scowled, held up her hand. It made sense to her.

'Rick had no idea about the relics,' Harper went on. 'He came here for me. And when I fell through the wall, he must have smashed his way through and piled up the crates so he could come down after me.'

'After you?' Angus looked at Jake. 'She was in the passageway?'

'How'd you get in there? Actually, how did you even know about it?' Jake's head didn't move, but he glanced at his brother.

Again, Rivers quieted them. 'You guys interrupt again, I swear, I'll arrest you.'

'What the hell? We can talk if we want. We own this damned house and—' Angus began. Harper thought she recognized his whiny tone.

Rivers' gaze seared him, made him stop mid-sentence.

'So this guy broke in downstairs,' Rivers summarized. 'But he didn't know about the relics. So what did he want?'

Hank squeezed Harper's hand a little too tightly. Letting her know he had questions, too.

'Me.' She couldn't stop thinking about the broken relics. The incalculable loss Rick had caused. She heard him urging her to cooperate with Colonel Baxter, to work with them. But he'd known she wouldn't agree, had brought a gun. 'He came here to offer me a job.'

'A job.' Rivers looked skeptical.

'Job?' Hank echoed.

'The same "job" he'd offered Burke. Right before Burke jumped off the bridge.'

'Hoppa? What. Saying—' Hank began.

'Rick tried to bribe everyone from our special detail.' Harper tried to explain, had trouble knowing where to start. 'He wanted to keep us quiet about what happened in Iraq. See, turns out, Burke's conspiracy theories weren't totally delusional. I think he was correct that our detail unknowingly aided a superior officer in a heist – a theft of millions of dollars in cash.'

Rivers frowned. 'That superior officer was—'

'Yes,' Harper interrupted. 'Colonel James Henry Baxter. The Senate candidate.'

The frown deepened.

Harper continued. 'Pete Murray figured it out – maybe he knew from the start. Anyhow, I think Murray threatened to expose him. Maybe even tried to blackmail him. After that, the Colonel must have assumed that everyone in the detail knew; we were all liabilities. He couldn't afford a scandal – let alone prison – so he hired Rick . . . Rick was on the detail, too. And Rick's job was to pay the rest of us off. To convince us to keep silent. Suddenly, soon afterwards, Pete "committed suicide". Then Burke. Who knows? If I hadn't fallen into the tunnel, I might have "killed myself" too.'

For a moment, nobody spoke. Hank's nostrils flared and his breath was heavy, but he said nothing, containing himself. Angus cleared his throat, looking at his feet.

Finally, Rivers sighed, shook her head. 'OK. Clearly, this is going to take a longer, more private interview. Right now, I don't know what we've got here. The blood indicates that there might indeed have been a homicide. And we have a burglary, an assault with intent to kill by a person unknown. Destruction of property. For now, this whole house is a crime scene. Nobody comes in; after we leave, nobody goes out.'

'But we need to find—' Harper began.

'Don't worry, Mrs Jennings. If your buddy is anywhere in the house, we'll find him.'

Her buddy? Rick? Harper nodded and walked with Hank back to the car, not bothering to correct the detective. She hadn't been talking about finding Rick; she'd been talking about the relics. Hoping to find some that had survived the fall.

On the way home, Rivers said nothing, just drove. Harper leaned against Hank, struggling to stay awake. Wondering how many artifacts had been destroyed. Where Rick's body was. What the brothers knew about the stolen relics – if they had been the men with Joe. Her eyes flittered closed, and she saw the passageways again, the endless corridors of darkness, twists and angles. She saw Chloe Manning's skull fall from her fur coat. And Rick's dead eyes, his open chest.

Damn. She couldn't let herself sleep. Had to stay awake and tell Rivers about the men who'd been stealing the relics. About Digger, who'd killed Carla. About her certainty that Angus or Jake was involved. And about Joe, who seemed to be the leader. And she had to talk about the Colonel – who needed to be stopped.

But the steady rhythm of the car relaxed her, and a day and a half without sleep took over. When Harper woke up, she was in her bed, and the sky out the window was black. Night time again.

She bolted up, sank back, dizzy. Sat again, more slowly. 'Hank?' Her throat was dry. She got out of bed, started for the stairs.

Hank called from the kitchen. 'Awake?'

The aroma of roasted chicken wafted upwards. Lord, she was hungry. When had she eaten last? What time was it? How long had she slept?

Harper held the banister, descending slowly. Still off balance.

'Slept thirteen hours.' Hank answered her unasked questions. 'Now. Eight o'clock. Made dinner.' He reached for her hand, helped her down. 'First, something. Else.'

What? Hank led her down the hall to the bathroom. A bubble bath was steaming there, ready for her.

A bubble bath?

Since the war, Harper had taken only combat showers. Ninety seconds long, exactly. Divided into precise divisions for soaping and rinsing. But Hank had prepared this. How had he known when she'd wake up?

'Third one I made. You. Kept sleeping.'

Oh. He hadn't known. Had refreshed the bath again and again. How dear. Harper's eyes misted.

'Need wash, Hoppa.'

She glanced in the mirror, saw a clotted cut on her temple, lumps and bloody smudges, clumps of sooty hair.

Hank was undressing her, helping her into the water. Harper sank back, raw skin stinging, then soothed by the heat. She listened to bubbles popping. Felt warm water sway with her breath. Ninety seconds passed; she knew the duration. But she hadn't even begun to wash yet. Hank sat on the edge of the tub, reached into the water and retrieved one of her feet. He began to scrub her, tenderly, part by part.

When she stepped out of the tub twenty minutes later, Harper was shiny clean and refreshed. Not tired, but ready to go back to bed.

They didn't make it upstairs, only to Hank's office across the hall. Their love-making was spontaneous, wordless. Both desperate and tender. Full of apologies, of promises conveyed through touching.

Afterwards, Hank set out comfort food – roast chicken, mashed potatoes, green beans, apple crisp. He spoke little, made no allusions to their conflicts, the Langston relics or the deaths. Harper was relieved. She was ravenously hungry, didn't want to do anything but eat. She was almost through her second helping of apple crisp when the doorbell rang.

'Rivers.' Hank glanced at the clock, started for the door.

Rivers?

'Coming now. Tell.'

What? Had she made an appointment? Why hadn't Hank warned her? Harper wiped her mouth, started to get up. But Hank was already back, leading Detective Rivers into the kitchen.

'Coffee?' he offered. 'Crisp?'

'Coffee would be great. I seem to be eating here a lot these days.' Rivers took a seat across from Harper. 'You look better.'

Harper smirked. She was cleaner, but hadn't as much as combed her hair. 'I slept.'

'That's the best medicine.' Rivers thanked Hank as he handed her a steaming mug. 'I've had guys going through that passageway. Mrs Jennings, I got to tell you, that thing snakes all over. Hither and yon and back again.'

Harper nodded. She'd seen that for herself.

'I'd heard about the secret passages. Everybody's heard about them. That house has a hundred stories about it. But I never imagined anything this complex. It seems like every single room has a passageway wrapped around it. Separating it from the next room and the hall, sometimes from the room above. I see how you'd have gotten lost. You might have been looping around the same circuit, zigzagging, retracing your steps for hours.'

Harper's hand stiffened around her coffee mug. She recalled the darkness, the never-ending angles, divides, dead ends and turns.

'You're lucky you didn't get seriously hurt. Sections of the floors are rotted; you could have fallen right through.'

Actually, she had.

'But other sections are in good repair. In fact, they seem to have been maintained carefully. New floors, even ramps leading to the lower levels. Which indicates that they've been in recent use.'

Of course they had. The traffickers had snuck through them to pilfer relics, probably even while the professor was still alive.

Detective Rivers poured two per cent into her coffee. 'So. If you have a few minutes, I have some more questions for you about—'

'No, wait. Tell me, did you find Rick?'

Rivers swallowed coffee. 'No sign of him. Other than the blood.'

Harper nodded. Where had they put Rick? And why had they moved him?

'Apple. Crisp.' Hank put a dish in front of Detective Rivers, handed her a fork.

'Looks delicious.'

'I'm good. Cook.'

'What about Chloe Manning?'

Rivers hesitated, chewing. She glanced at Hank, then back at Harper. 'They followed your X marks and found some remains. Yes. Initially, they seem consistent with Chloe Manning – the fur coat has her initials in the lining.'

Harper played with her spoon. Saw a skull rolling, hair falling free.

Rivers was ready for Harper's statement, and Harper began, repeating much of what she'd already told them. In one non-stop burst, she repeated Burke's assertions about the theft in Iraq that had funded the Colonel's rise to power. She described how the Colonel had tried to buy off everyone who could threaten him. How he'd sent Rick to deal with her and Burke. Harper skipped over her time in the tunnel, didn't mention her terror or doubts about ever getting out. But she talked about finding the missing actress. And Rick's body. And hearing the men with the stolen relics, their discussion of the long-ago murder of Carla Prentiss.

Finally, she stopped, certain there was more to tell, not sure what it was. Rivers was making notes. Hank frowned and took her hand. 'Now?'

Now? What did he mean, 'now'? Now. Harper fudged. 'I don't know. I guess there will be consternation about the collection. And the police will try to find Rick's body.'

'No. You. Now. Danger still.'

What?

Rivers looked at Hank. Swallowed the last of her apple crisp.

'Colonel. Still.'

Oh. The Colonel.

'The allegations against this man need to be substantiated, Mr Jennings. Remember, he's a prominent figure, a leading candidate for the Senate, and the election is just a day away.'

Hank took a breath. 'Rick didn't. On his own. Come. See Hoppa.'

He was right. And if the Colonel thought she posed a threat, he'd send someone else to deal with her.

'What are you suggesting, Mr Jennings?'

'Wife my. Not safe.' He moved close, took her arm. 'Famous man. Crap. Stop him. Need to.'

Rivers responded with warnings about making premature conclusions and false accusations. She talked about suspicion versus proof, the importance of procedure and evidence. Harper wasn't listening. She didn't know how or exactly when it had happened. But the problems she and Hank had been having seemed unimportant, insignificant. At least for now, they'd disappeared. She and Hank were solid again.

Rivers didn't seem to think that Harper was in imminent danger. She packed up her notebook, getting ready to leave.

'A few more things before I go.' She folded her hands. 'I took statements from the Langston brothers today.'

Harper pursed her lips, wondered if she should mention her suspicions. But she had no proof that Angus and Jake were stealing the relics. No evidence at all.

'Those guys are pretty upset about their inheritance. They insist that the collection should be theirs. In fact, Jake's so opposed to the will that he said he'd rather see the pieces stolen by traffickers than taken by the university.'

Especially if he was one of the traffickers, Harper thought.

'He also said that, as boys, he and Angus used to play in the passageways. That they know how to get around in them, how to avoid the dead ends like the one where Ms Manning got lost. But he said, as far as he knows, he and Angus are the only ones who know how to get in and out of the passageways. So he doesn't buy the idea that traffickers have been using them.'

Harper met Rivers' eyes. Didn't the detective see what she was saying?

Hank finally said it. 'So. Maybe traff. Ickers. Are brothers.'

Rivers smirked. 'Again, Mr Jennings. That's an interesting theory. But we need evidence. We have none.'

'Find.' Hank suggested.

Rivers looked at him directly, then at Harper. 'And there's this.' She reached into her satchel, pulled out a plastic evidence bag containing a cell phone. 'We found this in the hall near your workroom. Recognize it?'

'No.' Was it Rick's? She reached for it, took a closer look.

'Seems several calls were made on it to your phone. And several more to a private number in Tennessee. Which happens to be the private line of your old friend, Colonel Baxter.'

Harper sat up straight. This was it: evidence to support her story. 'See? The calls prove that Rick worked—'

'All it indicates is that the owner of the phone had contact with both you and Baxter. You said Rick worked for him; it makes sense they'd talk. But working and talking don't mean—'

'Not by themselves. But Rick knocked the wall down to come after me.'

'Possibly to try to save you after you fell through. There are lots of interpretations possible, here, Mrs Jennings. I admit that your story is compelling, but like I've said, it needs to be substantiated. Right before an election, I can't go making wild accusations against a candidate.'

'What about after the election?'

Rivers started again, repeating her speech about the need for evidence, and Harper nodded as if paying attention while she lowered the phone to her lap, pushed a button through the plastic, turning it on. Pressed the send button. Saw numbers come up, recognized hers, memorized another. Shut the phone off and gave it back, repeating a phone number in her mind.

Vicki still liked newspapers, but Trent did his reading online. Both sat with Hank and Harper at their kitchen table, summarizing what the media were reporting as they munched bagels and breakfast scones. Tales of the Langston house were sweeping not just through Ithaca, but through the country.

'Says here that Chloe Manning was nude beneath her fur coat.' Trent seemed amused. 'Must have been quite a party.'

'Apparently, one to die for.' Vicki took a bite of cinnamon walnut.

'And you, my dear Harper, are the celebrity *du jour*.'

Harper's phone gonged again. It sat on the counter, had been ringing non-stop; Harper had stopped answering. Mostly the calls were from reporters wanting sound bites.

'Turn off?' Hank offered.

Harper shrugged. She didn't care. Hank stood, heading for the phone. The gong stopped.

Trent went on. 'Your ordeal in the passageways fascinates the public. Coupled with the discovery of the long lost starlet. Goodness, I'm amazed there was anything left to find. It's been, what, almost a century since she wandered off?'

'It must have been cool and dry in there.' Vicki offered. 'She'd be, like, mummified. Was she, Harper?'

Harper spread butter on to her scone, thinking again about Rick.

'Was she?' Vicki repeated.

'Hoppa. Tired.' Hank chided Vicki. 'Too much.'

'Oh, of course. Sorry. Trent, we are so insensitive. Are you feeling OK, Harper?'

Everyone looked at her, assessing her wellness. She put down the butter knife. 'Fine. I'm fine.' She glanced at the newspaper. 'What else does it say?'

'You're sure you want to hear?' Vicki looked at Hank.

'Hoppa. Not. Need. Now.'

'No, I'm fine. Tell me.'

'Well,' Trent drawled, 'the media seem to delight in the fact that as one corpse is found, another has vanished.'

Rick. Where was Rick?

'They make it sound like Langston's house has grabbed fresh meat, relinquishing Chloe Manning only after it swallowed your assailant, whom they say you've identified, but they don't give his name.'

Harper saw his open eyes, open chest. Had she mentioned his chest to Rivers? She couldn't remember, doubted that she had. Needed to remember.

'And Dean Van Arsdale is quoted, addressing the university's dismay at the damage to the collection. They quote him as being appalled and pained at the loss. He says that these traffickers have looted perhaps the most unique and enlightening collection of Pre-Columbian artifacts in the world. And on and on.'

'What did he say about the broken artifacts?'

'Broken artifacts?' Trent scanned his computer screen.

'It just refers to "damage".' Vicki rechecked the article. 'What got broken?'

Harper shrugged. 'Don't know yet.'

'More coffee?' Hank changed the subject.

Harper stared at her scone. None of the news items, directly or indirectly, had mentioned Colonel Baxter. Of course they hadn't. Rivers wouldn't have revealed anything, had insisted there wasn't any hard evidence against him. Baxter had led to the destruction of relics, the deaths of Pete, Burke and Rick. But nothing would happen to him? He'd be elected to the Senate. Then what? Amass more power, run for president? Burke had said the Colonel had bigger plans than she could imagine.

Harper tried to figure out how to stop him, but her thoughts disconnected, interrupted by questions. Who were the traffickers? Who was Joe? Or Digger, the 'priest' who'd killed Carla Prentiss? Where was Rick's body?

She tried to shove these thought aside; the election was less than twenty-four hours away. There was limited time to get to the Colonel. She needed to think, to be away from the chatter. Harper pushed her chair away from the table. 'I'll be right back.'

Apparently, she'd interrupted Trent in the middle of a sentence; he frowned, offended.

'OK? Hoppa? You?'

'Yes. Fine.' She pecked Hank's cheek, squeezed his shoulder as she passed.

'Want company?' Vicki started to get up.

Harper's, 'No,' was too emphatic. She added, 'Thanks, Vicki. I just need a second or two.'

Not certain what she was going to do, Harper headed for the hall. On the way, she grabbed her phone.

When he picked up the call, he said, 'Harper?' He didn't sound surprised to hear from her. In fact he sounded glad. 'I'm glad you called.'

'Rick's dead.' She closed the door, leaned against the bathroom wall.

Silence. Then, 'What?' His voice was thin.

'He's dead. They haven't found his body yet, but I saw him.'

'What the hell happened?'

'What do you think?' She snapped, had no patience for bullshit. He hesitated. 'I have no idea.'

'You sent him after me and Burke, didn't you?'

'What?' A pause. 'Harper, are you telling me that you killed him?'

'Me?' Why would he say that? 'No. But I would have if I hadn't fallen.'

'Look, I don't understand what you're saying. I asked Rick to bring you guys on board. I owe you – all of you. And I'm finally in a position to pay you back. Harper – I thought I explained all this last time we talked. Rick was supposed to convince you, Everett and Murray to accept my offers, that's all.'

The man was buttery smooth, sounded sincere, caring. No wonder voters loved him. Harper sat on the toilet lid. 'Well, Rick's idea of "convincing" us was rather forceful. It involved a gun.'

A slight pause. 'That's not – no, that's just Rick. He's carried since the war. It's legal; he has a permit – the gun has nothing to do with what he's doing for me.'

'Really? Because Rick stalked me, broke into my workplace, snuck up on me with his weapon. Tried to force me at gunpoint to accept your offer.'

The Colonel swore under his breath. 'Harper, I swear I have no idea what you're talking about. What you're describing is unbelievable. It's way beyond what we'd . . . I'd never have imagined . . .'

Really? 'Well, you better imagine it, sir. Because while he was attacking me last night, somebody killed him.'

Baxter didn't reply for a moment. Harper heard background voices. Papers shuffling. Machines whirring. The sounds of a political campaign in its final hours.

Finally, 'It's chaos here today, sorry for the interruptions. Now, tell me. How? Who?'

'How is still uncertain. But it was some guys who traffic stolen antiquities. He ran into them while coming after me.'

'Antiquities? What? Look – damn. Hold a sec.' His voice muffled as he covered the phone and spoke to someone. When he came back, he sounded shaken. 'Harper, this is terrible news. Terrible. Rick was like a kid brother. He was my go-to guy. I trusted him with my life.'

And with the truth about the money you stole? Harper couldn't help it; she had to ask. 'Sir, back in Iraq—'

'I'll never forget how the four of you saved my life.'

'Yes, sir – but—'

'I've told you, I'll never forget your courage. I'm deeply indebted.'

'It was our job to protect you. But, sir, that cargo we loaded. What was it?'

Oh God. Had she really just said that?

'The cargo? I don't remember. Supplies. Standard stuff. Why?' He didn't sound elusive. Not even a little shady.

Was he that good a liar?

'It wasn't money?'

'Money?' He let out a low whistle. 'What gave you that idea?'

Harper fudged. 'Just a rumor.'

'Great, wonderful. That's all I need. Another rumor. Ever since I started running for office, there's been one after another. Now, what are they saying? That I did what, stole a helicopter full of money? What's next? That I started the war? Who thinks this stuff up, anyhow?' He sounded indignant. Wounded. Honest.

Could Burke have been wrong? Had he or Pete invented the cargo story?

'Wait.' The Colonel changed focus. 'Didn't you say they haven't found Rick? So are you sure? How do you know he's actually dead?'

God. Did he think she didn't know dead when she saw it? 'Because, like I said, I saw him.'

More background sounds. Another interruption.

Then: 'Thanks for letting me know.' Colonel Baxter lowered his voice. 'The election's tomorrow, Harper.'

'Don't worry, nothing about Rick will hit the news before then. It won't interfere.'

'What? Oh. No. I didn't mean that, Harper. I meant I'm tied up completely today and tomorrow. After that, let's talk some more. You'll fill me in on what happened, what you said about Rick's odd behavior – his breaking in and so on; you'll explain the details, OK? So we can figure this out? Remember, I can put in a good word for you with Van Arsdale. Or fix your husband up with a new position. Maybe you'll reconsider my offer. I'd appreciate having you around, especially now that you're the only one left.'

When she got off the phone, Harper stayed in the bathroom, holding her head in her hands, trying to make sense of the conversation.

Colonel Baxter was blustery and pushy, but he'd almost convinced her that he was a stand-up guy. That the story of the theft had been invented by Pete or Burke. That the violence and deaths to members of their detail had been the work of Rick alone.

When she came back into the kitchen, the conversation stopped and three heads turned toward her.

'OK?' Hank folded the newspaper, slid it into the recycling bin.

'We've decided you need a diversion, Harper.' Vicki stood. 'How about a girls' day? A facial? Or a massage?'

'What?' Harper sat.

'I called my favorite spa. They have openings in an hour. A facial or a massage – aromatherapy, deep tissue. You choose, whatever you want. It's on Trent and me.'

'Go,' Hank urged. 'Relax you.'

'Consider it a sign of our love.' Trent refilled his coffee mug.

Really? Harper thought about it. A massage? Zina and Burke were dead. Rick, too. Relics had been ruined – what good was a massage?

Then again, it would only last an hour. Might help her release some tension. Besides, she had most of the day free. She had an appointment with Leslie later, but that was all she had planned. Still, what was the point? Harper stood, carrying plates to the sink.

'No, don't.' Trent put up a hand.

'Clean up. We'll.' Hank took the plates from her.

Harper went for her bag.

'Leave it. You won't need it.' Vicki grabbed her arm, led her out the door. 'I'll drive.'

'No, it's OK.' She headed for the Ninja. 'I'll take the bike. You won't have to drive me home.'

'I don't mind. The whole point is that you can relax.'

But Harper climbed on to her motorcycle, rolled it down the driveway to Vicki's car, following her into town.

The first day of November was brisk, the air refreshing. The sky bulging with blue-gray clouds. Harper sped along, trying to be in the moment, but kept seeing herself wandering an endless dark tunnel that led to Chloe Manning's skeleton. Zina's lifeless body. Rick's dead eyes. Or a mound of broken crates and smashed artifacts.

Her mind mimicked the passageways, tangled with thoughts that led nowhere, or into and around themselves in an endless loop.

A massage, she decided. She would have a massage and let go, stop thinking for an hour. A whole hour.

Ahead of her, Vicki turned right. The spa was just a few blocks away, on Audubon. Harper followed, was halfway through her turn when she noticed some pedestrians standing at the corner. One of them was Salih Salim.

Harper was surprised to see him; Rivers had said that she couldn't find him or his family. That they had disappeared. But there he was, right out on the street.

Harper pulled over to the curb. 'Salih?' She pulled off her helmet.

He turned, startled. 'Harper?' He seemed surprised to see her, but grinned, stepped over to embrace her. 'Good to see you again!'

'Where have you been, Salih? The police wanted to talk to you about your sister and—'

'No, no. I've been away.' His smile vanished; he looked away. 'With the family. It's been a difficult time for us.'

Harper nodded. Of course it had. Zina had been murdered.

'Our business is shaky at best.'

What? He was upset about business? Not Zina? 'And your sister . . .?'

'Well, of course.' His eyes didn't rest, kept moving. 'My sister. Despite my family's claims to the contrary, they all feel Zina's loss. In fact, that's where we've been. I convinced my . . . my father decided to provide for her funeral. We all went back home to bury her.' He paused, took a breath. 'I got back just yesterday. A quick trip.'

Harper nodded, didn't know what to say.

'So there's nothing to do for her any more. She's at peace. And now, I have to hurry and salvage our business or it will die, too.' His mouth formed a sad twisted smile. 'Good to see you again, my friend.'

They hugged, separated, waving goodbye. Then Harper remembered Zina's bracelet. It was back home, still in her bag. 'Oh – Salih? I have something to give you.'

'To give me?' He called as he walked away. 'What is it?'

'Something of Zina's.'

He stopped, turned. Met her eyes. Looked away, at traffic. Hurried. 'I can bring it to you.'

'Good, if you don't mind – I'm at the same hotel as before. Oh – I don't use my own name. I'm registered as Smith. Come by, say, around three?' He waved, turned, and, as the light was green, headed across the street.

Naked under a sheet, listening to music that sounded like water, Harper smelled scented oils that reminded her of the oil burning around Rick's body. She thought of seeing Salih, of how hurried he'd seemed. Of taking Zina's bracelet to him. But her thoughts wandered and waned, and gradually faded altogether as she paid attention only to the hands of Kara, the masseuse.

The hands worked steadily, slippery and lubricated, building friction, causing waves of heat to roll through her muscles, one by one. Soreness Harper hadn't known about rose up and fought, only to be vanquished, banished by Kara's hands. Aches she'd tolerated as permanent were soothed. Her left leg almost wept with sweet release. For an hour, the hands of a stranger pulled the tension from her tissues, and Harper was immersed in sensations, indifferent to time.

Afterwards, wrapped in a terry robe, she sat with Vicki, sipping water with lemon slices. Vicki's face was bright red, glowing.

'Was yours good?'

Harper nodded, closed her eyes, almost too relaxed to speak. 'Yours?'

'Mmmm.'

They sat, speechless. Sipping. Finally, forced themselves to shower and dress. Harper thanked Vicki. Hugged her. Reminded her of their Tuesday night dinner. And got back on the Ninja, almost too relaxed to drive.

But she did drive, floating on her Ninja all the way home. Hank was outside, working a leaf blower. He shut it down, beaming. 'Bought today this.'

Half the front yard was already clear, the rest a speckled sea of leaves, even though they'd raked just days ago.

Harper forced a smile, aware that, until recently, Hank would have discussed the purchase with her before making it. And would have wanted her to go with him to the mall. But never mind. Hank was his own man again, and that was good. She walked over, gave him a hug. He smelled like the outdoors, hard work.

She looked at the leaf blower. 'So you have a new toy.'

'More. Snow blower. Bought. On sale. And mower. Drill set. Saw, too. All.'

Really? He'd bought all that? Without even mentioning it? Harper felt stung, as if disenfranchised in decision-making. The tools would allow Hank to work around the property, but where would they get the money to pay for them? Hank's disability didn't provide much. And she had tuition debts to pay off. Harper bit her lip, didn't comment. Didn't want another argument.

'Massage? Good?'

'Yes. Very.' But tension was already building up in her shoulders, tightness in the small of her back. She pecked his cheek. 'I have to go – an appointment with Leslie.' Then, because she was practicing openness, she added. 'I ran into Zina's brother before. He's back in town.'

'From where back?'

'He said the whole family went home to bury Zina. Maybe he meant England? Or Syria? Anyhow, I'm going to stop by and drop off Zina's bracelet.'

'Bracelet?'

'Remember? She left it here that night—'

'Rivers no?' Or Rivers know?

Know? Oh right; she'd wanted to talk to Salih. 'I'll let her know he's back.'

Hank yanked the electric cord of the leaf blower, began winding it around his arm. 'With you go.'

'No, Hank. Stay here. Do what you're doing.' Her stubbornness rose, resisting him. Insisting that, if he could do things alone, she could, too. 'I'm seeing Leslie in an hour. I'll just stop by the Embassy Inn on the way.' She started for the house.

'Hoppa. Letter for you. Sad. Burke. Came,' Hank called.

'A letter?' Sad? Burke?

Hank had started the leaf blower again, couldn't hear her. So Harper went inside, where she saw it in the foyer. She picked it up, looked at the envelope, sighed. The name on the return address was Burke Everett. It had been sent Friday, right before Burke died.

She tore it open. Looked for a note, an explanation. Found none. Only a list of serial numbers, crate numbers, shipment numbers. Receipts dated the final day of their assignment with Colonel Baxter, all with his signature. Itemized accountings of parcels, crates and containers – the shipment her detail had nearly died to protect, the one that they had loaded on to a helicopter in Iraq.

The one Baxter had insisted was full of supplies.

And that Burke had insisted was full of cash.

Harper stared at the papers, picturing Burke in his last hours, desperate, unable to reach her, increasingly certain that he wouldn't survive. Managing to mail these papers to her, hoping that she'd act on them, since neither he nor Pete could. She recalled his jittery hands, his darting eyes. Burke had been unbalanced, paranoid. Might have invented the theft in his mind. Might have sent her a list of serial numbers of standard supplies. Did she really believe that this envelope contained proof of a major multimillion-dollar heist? And, even if she did, did she really want to create a scandal, embarrassing the Colonel – potentially ruining his political career by asking the army to confirm the contents of his shipment?

Harper rubbed her forehead, fighting a headache. The relaxation of her massage had evaporated; her legs felt heavy and her shoulders ached. She stared at the papers, uncertain about what to do. The possibility was undeniable that they might incriminate the Colonel in a huge theft, might even implicate him and Rick in Burke's and Peter's deaths.

Then again, they might not.

She walked in a circle, gazed out the window at Hank, pushed her fingers through her hair, looked again at the papers, the signatures. Finally, she came to a realization: she wasn't in charge of investigating either theft or homicide. And it wasn't her place to approach the army, not her job to launch an inquiry that could ruin a man's life.

Harper folded the paper, replaced it in its envelope, set the envelope back on the foyer table. She'd give it to Detective Rivers and let her follow up. Rivers could contact the army as part of her official investigation into Burke's death. The army would confirm the contents of the shipments, would determine whether a theft had actually occurred.

Relieved, Harper took her phone out of her bag and made the call, left a voicemail for Rivers. Told her that she'd received mail from Burke, asked her to call. Added that Salih was back, registered as 'Smith' at the Embassy Inn on Dryden Road.

Then at three o'clock, Harper grabbed her bag, went outside and climbed back on to her Ninja. When she shouted goodbye to Hank, the leaf blower was making a lot of noise. He didn't hear her, but he looked up and waved as she drove off.

The Embassy Inn was on the other side of campus. Harper got there about three fifteen, plenty of time to see Salih and make her appointment with Leslie. She asked at the desk for Mr Smith; the clerk made a call. In moments, Salih came into the lobby, still dressed in his pinstriped business suit, his red tie. He greeted Harper with a grin, a warm hug.

'Thank you for coming all this way.'

'No problem.' She reached into her bag, feeling for the bracelet. 'Let me give you—'

'No, no. Not so fast. First, you have to join me for a drink. I have a selection set up in my suite.'

Was he asking her to his room? 'Really – I have to get to an appointment.'

'So you don't have to stay long. And I promise not to make a pass.' He winked playfully, took her hand, tugged on it. 'Come, my drinking buddy. Just one drink. We'll catch up.'

Harper shook her head. 'I can't.'

Salih kept it up. 'When's your appointment? I'll have you on your way in plenty of time.'

Fine. What was the harm in one drink?

His suite contained a sitting room stocked with liquor. Stoli, Johnny Walker Black, Chablis. The fridge was full of beer. Salih had set up his own bar.

He poured her a Scotch, himself a vodka. Raised his glass in a toast. 'To friendship.'

They clinked glasses, sipped. Sat. She on an easy chair, he on the love seat. Cartons wrapped in brown paper were stacked along the far wall, as if ready for shipping.

'Tell me, Harper,' he eyed the cut on her forehead. 'What happened to you? Were you in an accident?'

'No, it's nothing serious.' She took a sip of Scotch. 'I fell at the Langston house.' It wasn't a lie.

'And how is it, working there?'

Really? He was asking how she liked his dead sister's job? 'Well, I don't like how I got the position.'

'Of course not. I didn't mean to imply that. I meant only what I asked. How is the work going?'

Harper thought of the missing pieces, the traffickers. Rick's body, the crates he'd dropped into the passageway. 'It's been complicated.'

Salih raised his eyebrows, tilted his head. 'Complicated?'

She didn't want to talk about it, couldn't bear to. So she changed the subject. 'How did your business meeting go?'

He crossed his legs. The cuffs of his slacks revealed unmatched socks. Both black, but of different fabric. Odd, for a man so meticulous. 'It's a difficult time. Did I mention it last time? What we do? We deal in fine art, sculpture and some antiques. But our passion is artifacts. That's how Zina first came to archeology. As a child, she tagged along with our father to auctions and such. But the problem today is that many countries are determined to repossess their relics. Even decades or centuries after they've been traded. Just recently, the Chinese filed a suit against us to prevent us from auctioning several exquisite pieces.' He uncrossed his legs, took a drink. 'But you don't want to hear about my troubles. Let's talk about you. The Pre-Columbian collection.'

'What do you want to know?' Harper swallowed Scotch. Checked her watch. She had to leave in a few minutes. But the Scotch had warmed her and it wasn't often that someone was really interested in talking about artifacts.

'Tell me about the collection itself.'

Harper shook her head. 'It's beyond description. It's vast. The collection includes pieces from South America through the southwest US. Some pieces are more than three thousand years old – and many are pristine.' Well, maybe not the ones smashed to smithereens. 'The other day, I held a three-thousand-year-old jaguar—'

She stopped at the sound of a key turning. 'Hey, Joe? I found that replacement.' The door swung open and Angus Langston walked in, carrying a small package. His mouth opened when he saw Harper, then he turned to Salih. 'Shit, Joe. How was I supposed to know you had company?'

Joe? Why was Angus calling Salih 'Joe'?

How did Angus even know Salih?

And why were they both staring at her?

Instantly, Harper flashed back to the tunnel, the traffickers, their voices. The argument about a relic worth $55,000; Joe scolding someone for breaking it. Threatening to make him pay for it out of his own pocket. Oh God. No question: Joe was Salih – and Angus was one of the traffickers.

'No need to look so confused, Harper.' Salih forced a smile. 'I go by 'Joe Smith' when doing business. I've found it easier to get along in this country if I use an American-sounding name.'

Harper nodded, feigning indifference. Told herself to be cool. After all, neither Salih nor Angus were aware that she'd heard them from the passageway. Or that she knew they were stealing relics. Or that they'd been involved in Rick's death.

'Hello, Angus.' She smiled, put her glass down and stood, trying to sound casual. Forgot about returning Zina's bracelet, the reason she'd come. 'Well, I'll leave you to your business.'

'What are you up to, Joe?' Angus snapped. 'What's she doing here?' He squinted, suspicious. 'Is she trying to undercut us? Are you two making a separate deal?'

'Good God, Angus. We're having a drink,' Salih finished his and set the empty glass beside Harper's. 'Not that it's your business.' The men glared at each other.

Harper cleared her throat, excused herself. 'Well. Thanks for the drink, Salih.' She started for the door.

Angus stood in her way, wouldn't step aside.

'Excuse me, Angus.' Harper looked up at him. He was a foot taller than she was, maybe ninety pounds heavier. She counted her options, ways to take him down as she stepped sideways, trying to get around him.

'This bitch is the reason half our stuff is broken.' He blocked her, moving with her to the side. A pas de deux. 'She cost us a fortune!'

'Wait just a moment, please, Harper.' Salih put up a hand. He addressed Angus. 'What are you talking about? Broken? What's broken?'

'You've been gone, Joe. Out of touch. You don't even know what happened. This broad and the guy Digger offed? Somehow, they dumped about twenty crates of relics into the—'

'I had nothing to do with—' Harper stopped. Replaying. *That guy Digger offed.*

Angus went on, telling Salih about the damaged and destroyed treasures they'd found in the passageway. But Harper wasn't listening. She was putting pieces together. Unbelievably, Salih must be – *had* to be – Joe. That he'd been there when someone named Digger killed Rick. That he was the leader of the traffickers.

Salih sighed, rubbed his eyes, reacting to the bad news. When he looked up, his gaze moved from Angus to Harper, back to Angus. 'This is disturbing.'

'Yeah, that's what I'm trying to tell you. She's even worse than your sister. This bitch cost us a fortune.'

Salih blinked at him. 'You really are an ass, Angus.' He turned back to Harper. 'My apologies, my friend. Professor Langston was

a long-time client of my family. Until his death, we dealt with him
with some regularity. But now, we seem to have inherited his sons.'

'What kind of bullshit is that?' Angus interrupted. '*You* came
to *us!*'

'Look,' Harper feigned indifference, frowned as if confused. 'I'm
going to be late. I'll go and leave you two to discuss whatever it is
you—'

'Don't think so, darling.' Angus stepped forward. 'You're what
they call a liability.'

Salih sat back against the love-seat cushions, sighing. 'Angus. You
aren't just an ass. You're a complete moron.'

'Well, what do you suggest we do, Joe? Let her walk out of here?
She's competition!'

'She has no role in this business whatsoever.'

'Yeah? Then ask her what she and that dead guy were doing in
the passageway.'

Salih's eyes darkened and he turned to Harper. 'Actually, it's a
good question. However, at this point, after all that's been said, the
answer is irrelevant.'

Harper assessed the situation, eyeing Angus. She'd do a one-two
move, knocking the wind out of him by slamming his solar plexus,
then, as he sank, she'd chop his neck. And dash for the door. She
drew a breath, ready, set—

And Salih called her name in a menacing tone.

Harper looked over her shoulder, saw the gun in Salih's hand.
Damn. Would he really shoot her? She doubted it. She met Salih's
eyes, debating whether or not he would. Whether she should test
him and take Angus down. Suddenly, though, her debate ended
unresolved as she went blank, dropping to the floor even before she
could feel the blow.

The smell was sickening. Musky and sweet, moldy and smoky. She
could actually taste it. Harper grimaced and turned her head, initiating
a sudden sharp pain in her neck. She groaned, waiting for the pain
to subside. Tried to sit up, couldn't move. Couldn't move an arm or
a leg. Nothing. Oh God.

Slowly, warily, she opened an eye. Saw a small flame inches from
her face. A candle? Then she inhaled the noxious scent. Recognized
it, though it was stronger now; she was closer to it. Some kind of
incense was burning. Or scented oils.

OK, she was stuck in a dream, a nightmare. One of those where she thought she was paralysed but it was just a phase of sleep. So she started over. Closed her eyes, tried again to sit. Couldn't move. And she felt restraints around her wrists, her ankles.

It wasn't a dream. Damn – where was she?

Harper lay still, squinting to focus and see beyond the flame. Gradually, in the dim light, she looked to her left. Saw a wall of stone and clay, like a cave. And pictures painted on it. A deer. An owl. A dog . . . Oh God. She was at Langston's. In that room at the end of the passageway, the one where she'd seen Rick—

Images surfaced. The hotel room. Salih. And Angus. Salih holding a gun. Lord. What had happened? Had Salih shot her? Harper closed her eyes again, carefully took an inventory of her body, searching for the pain of a bullet wound. The scent of fresh blood. Found none. So she hadn't been shot, but somehow, they'd knocked her out. She'd been unconscious. But for how long? Never mind – that was irrelevant. She needed to figure out how to untie herself. How to escape.

Something moved near her – softly, like footsteps, coming closer. Harper kept her eyes closed, playing possum. The steps stopped. She felt subtle swirls of air, and a man's voice chanting syllables she didn't understand.

Carefully, she opened her right eye a crack. Just enough to reveal a sliver of vision. At first, she saw shadows darting directly above her. Then something glimmering, reflecting the flame. She closed her eye, listening, trying to calm herself. But she sensed someone close to her, peeked again. And saw a man leaning over her. He was talking to himself, and suddenly, he pressed something – a rag? – over her mouth and nose. Harper smelled chemicals, wriggled and resisted, struggling to breathe. Fading, she realized that, no – it wasn't a man. It had a man's body, but it was covered with feathers like an owl. And it had a jaguar's head.

The Nahual was hungry. Not the kind of hunger known to men. This was the hunger of the jaguar, the hunger of mountains and of the moon. It was the hunger, also, of the hunt. And of the dead.

He'd finished with the man, taking his power in, engulfing his spirit. Had offered the remains, as was his calling, to the wolves, the ravens, the foxes and dogs. He could feel his strength even now, raging in his blood like the screams of a warrior. The man was completely unlike the trader's sister. She'd been meek; despite her superior intellect. Her spirit had been marred, defeated by the betrayal of her dying.

Having fasted and cleansed himself, he slipped into his owl form, becoming himself an omen of death. Again, he observed the woman on his altar. She was small but muscular, almost as firm as the man. She wore a wedding ring, and so was clearly not a virgin, but never mind. He'd incorporated purity decades ago. Now, his goal was to enhance his spirit, increase his potency. At times during rituals, soaring above earth, he felt godlike.

He took the form of the jaguar, preparing himself. Stepped beside her, beginning his incantations. Presenting her with the sedating drug, releasing her limbs to free her spirit.

Yes, this one would make an excellent addition. For one thing, she was still alive. If he acted quickly, when he began to take it in, her heart would still be beating.

That now familiar, sickening scent of pungent and sweet smoke was her first sensation. And second was nausea, not quite bad enough to make her retch. But bad. Harper didn't want to open her eyes. She was afraid to see that creature again. It must have been a dream. But how had it been a dream? It had been so vivid – she could have sworn that she'd actually seen a creature of many shapes. Maybe a Nahual. So she kept her eyes closed, not looking yet. She reached out for Hank, felt empty air. Where was he? What time was it? What was that smell? Her back ached, and she was chilly. She reached for the blanket. Found none. No Hank. No blanket. Oh God. Harper opened her eyes. Saw the vessels of burning oil. The paintings of animals on the wall. Remembered Salih and Angus. And waking up here with that creature . . .

Harper sat up, was overtaken by nausea. And pain in the back of her skull. She stayed still, waiting for the waves to pass. Damn. What had they done to her? She touched the back of her head, felt a mushy, golf-ball-sized lump. Her last memory was back in Salih's room. Trying to leave. One of them . . . Angus must have knocked her out. Maybe she'd been delirious from the blow to her head, imagining that strange bird-cat-man. Maybe she'd never even been tied up. Never mind. It didn't matter. She needed to get out of there, and her arms and legs were unbound now. She could move.

Slowly, she turned her head, looking around the dim cave-like room, seeing no one. She was alone. Fabric tickled her belly. Harper glanced down, saw that her shirt had been ripped open, her bra removed. Her chest exposed. Reflexively, without thinking, she gathered the torn fabric, covering herself. Pictured Rick lying dead in that same room, his exposed chest sliced open. She took a breath, recalled the creature she'd seen before she'd passed out, something – a knife? – glittering in his hand.

Oh God. She thought of the conversation she'd heard when she was lost in the passageway. A man claiming he'd learned the rites and rituals of the ancients. Bragging that he'd sacrificed Carla Prentiss. And the other guy mocking him, calling him The High Priest of Owl Feathers? Telling him he looked like a feather duster.

Harper closed her eyes, saw the feather-covered creature with a man's shape and a jaguar head. It hadn't been a dream, was not a trauma-induced hallucination. It had been a guy dressed in ritual costume. Wearing the head of a jaguar, the most revered of all beasts, the embodiment of power. And the feathers of owls, the messengers between the living and the dead.

Even before she'd processed these thoughts, Harper had hopped off the table and begun to run. But she'd stood too fast. Dizziness overcame her, and she buckled with nausea and pain. Bent over, she kept moving toward the door to the woods. Told herself she was almost there. Counted her steps to take her mind off her dizziness. When she got to seven, she stopped. Listening.

Men were talking. Just outside, on the ramp to the woods.

Damn. Harper hugged the wall, listening.

'You have to dispose of her anyway.'

'Thanks to this idiot, yes. We have no options.'

Salih? Was that his voice? Salih was agreeing to kill her?

'Me? How is it my fault you decided to—'

'Let's not waste more time going through it again.'

'Exactly. I need to continue the rite before she wakes up.'

'You're not going to lay a hand on her.' Salih insisted. 'It's enough you mutilated my sister. I won't let you—'

'I am not the one who killed your sister. You should thank me; I resurrected her strength.'

'Thank you? I should kill you!'

'Meantime, what did you do with the guy?' That voice was Angus'.

'The guy?'

'Where is he? Are the cops going to descend on us like last time?'

'No, it isn't like before. His remains are where no one but wolves and spirits will find them.'

'Except for the heart, right?' Salih's voice was a growl. 'What do you do with the hearts, you sick bastard – what did you do with my sister's?'

'What the hell difference does it make, Joe?' Angus tried to appease him. 'Let him get on with it. It's all the same to us. And to her – I mean when you're dead, you're dead.'

'How can I say this in a way you two morons will understand?' Salih spoke slowly and clearly. 'There are such things as human dignity, loyalty and honor. That woman has done nothing to defile herself or anyone else. She may need to be eliminated for practical reasons, but she deserves—'

'No.' The third man interrupted. 'The woman has exquisite power. It emanates from her visibly, like a corona. And I intend to acquire it through the practices of my predecessors. End of discussion.'

'If you as much as touch her, consider our relationship and business dealings finished. I mean this.'

'Cut it out, Joe. You aren't going to end anything.' Angus whined. 'We depend on each other.'

'Get out of the way, Angus. If he wants to cut her, he'll have to get past me.'

There was scuffling outside. The sounds of punches landing. Of grunting and cursing. Then, of someone coming.

Harper dashed back into the cave. Maybe she could get to the rope ladder, climb up into the passageway. But, no – not enough time. They'd grab her and yank her back down. She had to stay there. Take them on face to face? Or better – she could lie back on the table, feigning unconsciousness and, when the guy approached her, take him by surprise. Grab his weapon and turn it against him. Harper took her position, wounded, dizzy. Wondering if she'd be able to overpower him. If she were strong enough.

In the end, it didn't matter; it was the only plan she had.

The Nahual shoved the man aside, pummeling his face, slamming him to the ground. How dare he challenge him? This day would mark the end of their collaboration. The man had mere materialistic goals, had no concept of the real significance of their work. The acquisition of spiritual enlightenment and power were far more valuable than any tangible wealth. But Joe Smith would never understand.

He wasn't even worth sacrificing; his spirit was tainted and slimy. Incorporating Joe's heart might actually harm him, might stunt his growth.

But the woman was different. She glowed with life energy, moved catlike with power and purpose. She was a fighter, too, and of a fertile age. She lay along the wall under the images of death, of the souls of warriors, of the hunt, of the mountains. Her lungs would be filled with the mystical scented oils, the fires of priests. He'd never taken in a living organ, but, in moments, that would change. Her heart would be beating in his hands, in his mouth. Her life would enter his body, become his, uniting with his soul, joining the others – the dog, owl, bat, deer, butterfly, turtle, rabbit, toad. The young woman of his youth. The man from the tunnel. He remembered each of them, the surge of awareness each had brought. The struggle with the turtle's shell. The mottled skin of the toad. The bloody ribs of the virgin.

Slowly, he resumed the chanting that the others had interrupted. He readied his blade to open her chest, prepared for the soaking volcano of blood that would spew. He closed his eyes, repeating syllables he'd memorized decades ago at the professor's side. Words that praised the bravery, strength, spirit, beauty of the creature about to die. He touched her face, covered her eyes with his hand, spread his wings to cast a shadow over her body. Then, taking one last look at her, he held his weapon above her chest, silently taking aim.

The guy was standing beside her, mumbling syllables in a language she'd never heard. Careful not to lift her eyelids too far, Harper peeked at him. Saw the head of a wild cat on top of his, askew like a lopsided headdress or crown. And a jacket of feathers, speckled in red. Damn. Was this the Nahual that had scared Zina? Some guy dressed in feathers and stuffed animal parts? 'You look like a damn feather duster,' Joe – or, rather Salih – had said.

Harper watched through her sliver of vision as he waved his arms like wings and rotated in circles, swooping, whirling, spinning and chanting. Reaching up, bowing low. Spinning again.

She thought of jumping on him while his back was turned, but he moved quickly, unpredictably. She might miss him and land on the ground. So she watched, waiting for the right moment, legs tensed, ready to push off the wooden slab. Finally, he stopped dancing around and stood silent and unmoving, looking down at her, both hands poised above her chest, holding a long thin blade.

Harper roared, startling him as she flew off the altar, springing at him with all her hundred and twenty pounds. He was clumsy, off balance with two heads, unprepared for an assault, and he keeled over with Harper attached to him by all fours. The spines of feathers pricked her skin as she pounced on him, scratched her as he hit the ground and twisted to get free. Harper held on, looking for the knife, not finding it, feeling his empty fists instead as they pounded her sides. Still, she didn't let go, stayed on top despite his squirming body and dizzying blows. She hung on with her thighs as if riding a bull, punched his face, jabbed his ribs. Scanned the floor again for the knife. Saw it a few yards away. Too far to reach. Harper took a breath, shifted her weight and thrust her strong knee into his belly, winding him so she could crawl off of him to get it. But he grabbed her leg, yanked it, pulling her back as he rolled to his side, then up on to his knees. He clamped one, then both hands around her throat as he stood, lifting her by her neck. Holding her face in front of his, meeting her eyes.

Harper's feet left the ground. She couldn't breathe. She kicked, aiming for his gut. She punched like a machine, reflexively repeating her combat training. She poked at his eyes. But her clarity was failing, her vision spotty. Her mind was disconnecting from her body, not obeying its commands. Flailing, Harper glared, trying to focus, and just as she began to black out, oh God, she recognized his face.

Professor Wiggins? She blinked, saw him again. Staring at her with glowing, hot eyes. Watching her die. Harper's mind fought, kept thinking. Was Professor Wiggins the Nahual? Was he really killing her? Was his face the last thing she'd ever see? Their eyes locked. Harper scratched, pulled skin off his face, but he didn't even wince. He kept the pressure on her neck, and she felt the blood pulsing behind her eyes, pooling inside her head. The strength was draining from her limbs. For a moment, she thought of Hank. And then, the Nahual's eyes widened, his mouth opened as if to scream. Slowly, he released her neck and they both, in unison, dropped to the floor.

Harper rolled, coughing, gasping, struggling to breathe. Unable to get up. Unsure what had happened. Sensing that she was still in danger, she tried to get to her feet, to run. Someone else was there with her – maybe Hank? Had he come for her? A man knelt beside her. She strained her neck to turn her head and look. Saw not Hank, but Salih.

'Harper,' he spoke softly, touched her shoulder. 'Are you all right? I'm very sorry about this.'

His face was a mess. An eye was swollen half-closed, his lip and nose bleeding. Harper skittered away from him, still coughing.

'You don't have to be afraid. I'm a businessman, Harper, nothing more.' He smiled, revealing bloody teeth.

From the doorway to the ramp, Angus shouted. 'Jeezus H, Joe. What the fuck happened now?'

Still coughing, Harper followed Angus' gaze. Professor Wiggins lay on the ground, his ritual knife protruding from his back. Salih had stabbed him, had rescued her. She tried to speak, but provoked more grating coughs. Salih looked concerned.

'I wish I had something – water, maybe – to help you. But I don't. Angus? Do we have water in the van?'

Angus stood at the ramp, scratching his head. 'What did you do, fucking kill Digger? What in hell's the matter with you?'

'Go see if there's water.'

'What the fuck for? This is so fucked up. Let's just get this over with and clean up, OK?' Angus stepped closer to the body, gaping at Wiggins.

Salih sighed, shook his head. 'I'm sorry you got involved in this mess, Harper. I truly like you.' He got to his feet, rubbed his hands.

Harper eyed him, unable to talk.

'But sometimes, unfortunately, our own survival requires us to deal with unsavory people and to perform unsavory tasks.' Another sigh. 'And, once again, I'm charged with the wellbeing – indeed, the survival – of my family. Protecting both its honor and its business interests. Despite my personal feelings and attachments, I cannot let this mess be revealed. You understand?'

Harper shook her head, no.

Salih chuckled grimly. 'Just like Zina. Stubborn to the end.'

Zina?

'My sister also claimed she had no idea why she had to die. This, despite her own deliberate defiance and dishonorable actions. Her refusal to marry the man my father had chosen for her. Her refusal to participate in the family business – even after we managed to obtain that research position for her.'

Harper blinked, wheezing.

'All she had to do was compromise. If she had procured even a few items for us, I could have convinced my father to overlook the marriage issue and spare her.' Salih shook his head. 'But she was so incredibly stubborn. Zina threatened to expose her own family, to publicly shame us. What was I to do? It was my responsibility. But when she realized what was coming, she pretended to be surprised. She must have thought she was immune, that her actions would never provoke consequences.' He paused, misty-eyed. 'I loved my sister.'

Harper blinked, trying to clear her head and understand what Salih was saying. He had killed Zina? She was pretty sure he'd just admitted that he had.

'She knew her responsibilities from the start. We partnered with Wiggins to get her the position for the very purpose of obtaining artifacts.'

Of course. Professor Wiggins had openly favored Zina, had lobbied hard for her to get the assistantship. Now Harper knew why. She glanced at his body. Had his leg been extended before? Had he moved?

'Little Zina. She was my favorite sister.' Salih looked into the distance. 'It was painful. Still is. But I did what was necessary.' He turned to her. 'I hope you understand. If I would kill my own sister whom I dearly loved for the sake of the family, I must certainly not hesitate to kill you.'

'Digger's still breathing.' Angus stood beside Wiggins. 'What do you want to do?'

Salih rubbed his swelling jaw. 'He's an abomination. Leave him.'

'Leave him? What, here?'

Salih stepped over to Wiggins. Looked down at him. 'No, you're right. We should dispose of him. Go get a cart.'

Angus hesitated, frowning.

'Well, unless you want to carry him.'

'This is messed up, Joe.' Angus headed to the ramp. 'I don't like it one bit.'

'And now, Harper. I guess it's you and me.'

Salih reached into his jacket, took out a pocket knife. It wasn't big, wasn't fancy. But it was more knife than she had. Her neck throbbed and ached from Wiggins' choking grasp, but she braced herself for yet another assault. Salih stepped closer confidently, as if he thought she was too weak to fight, too defeated. But Harper had been trained for battle and, as soon as he was within reach, she drew a deep breath, centered herself and swung, landing her fist hard in his eye, the one that was already swollen closed; then, as he reeled, she aimed and slammed her right foot up hard between his legs.

The Nahual listened, waiting silently, gathering his fury and strength. Assessing the severity of his wound. Testing each limb, refusing the pain. He never should have gotten involved with these philistines. Never should have trusted that their lust for monetary gain could interface with his for spiritual growth. No, it had been a mistake, but he would correct it here, today.

He was bleeding, though. Leaking strength. He'd need to act soon, before the moron Angus returned with his cart. He wasn't sure, given a choice, with whom Angus would side. Angus had known him decades longer; they'd grown up together. And he'd been the protégé of Angus' father. But Joe had all the money. And Angus, being a fool, might go either way. Given his condition, he didn't want to risk facing two opponents.

Not to mention the woman.

He'd injured her throat, had felt her windpipe collapsing under his grip. But she was already recovering; he heard her ragged coughing. Heard Joe rambling, apologizing that he had to kill her. Talking about honor, about family. As if his family had such a thing as honor. As if anyone did in this era where the earth itself was spat upon and defiled, where revered beasts were slaughtered, starved or caged. Joe's family, indeed. How did this insignificant creature have the audacity to think that he and those who'd spawned him had the capacity to possess such a thing as 'honor'? Honor belonged to the ageless spirits, the creatures of death and sky and rivers and mountains and wind. It didn't belong to petty criminals and thieves. No, he should never have gotten involved. But Joe had offered – no, had *promised* – him access to the relics, that he could select among them for his studies.

The Nahual played dead, lying still as Joe finished simpering about murdering his sister. He watched as the woman bludgeoned him and ran for the rope ladder, as Joe moaned and stumbled, chasing after her. Recognizing his moment, the Nahual chanted softly, calling upon the spirit of Joe's sister, and he felt it stir within him, raging, seeking revenge. He called up the spirit of the dead male from the tunnel, too, and summoned all the creatures he'd ever embodied, and then he drew a breath, drawing fury from his own pain. Finally, he pulled the power of all those spirits together and leapt to his feet, hurling himself at Joe with a warrior's cry, landing a crushing blow to the base of his skull. Knocking him down. Standing over him with a triumphant bellow. Dragging him to the altar where he would take his life, his heart. And his spirit.

She was weak, sore all over, her neck felt sprained, and air scraped like dull razors in her raw throat, but Harper made it to the rope ladder and, by the time Salih had chased her to the bottom, she'd pulled herself up into the passageway. Spent and wheezing, she stopped to glance back. Damn – Salih was already halfway up the ladder. She turned, ready to run. But before she'd taken a step, she heard a shout, a thud, a groan. Harper stepped back, looked down the ladder once more. Salih lay flat on his back on the ground, staring up at her exactly as Rick had. And exactly as Rick had, Salih began sliding away. Someone was dragging him.

Harper couldn't see who it was. Angus? Had he gone after Salih and slugged him? She lowered herself on to the floor of the passageway, stuck her head out the opening. And saw the Nahual – Professor Wiggins – the knife still in his back, holding Salih by his armpits and pulling him across the cave.

Salih seemed conscious. His eyes were alert, open, fixed on her as Wiggins moved him. And when Wiggins stopped to rest, Salih rolled over and jumped to his feet, fists flying. Wiggins fought back with amazing vigor. Punching and grunting, they moved out of her view. Leaning further down, careful of her neck as she lowered her head, Harper saw them again; the Nahual costume now ripped, the jaguar head dangling loose, Wiggins stumbled toward the ramp with Salih close behind. Salih reached, took hold of the hilt of the blade and twisted it before pulling it out. A gut-twisting scream resounded through the cave as the Nahual fell to his knees, both of his heads bent, the back of his feathered jacket blood-soaked, his arms raised to the sky. Salih stood behind him, raised the blade high with both hands and unceremoniously shoved it down into the Nahual's back, piercing his heart.

Salih remained there, breathless and bloodied beside the pile of feathers until Angus came in with a wheelbarrow.

'Hey, how'd he get all the way over there? Shit, Joe. Your face looks like—'

Harper couldn't hear Salih's response. But she saw him pointing toward the house, gesturing emphatically, showing Angus where to go. Damn. He was sending him to the other end of the passageway, to Rick's broken wall. The only way Harper knew to get out.

'Shit. This just gets worse and worse, man. Jake's gonna find out and then we'll all be dead.'

Salih said something, gesturing again, and Angus rushed up the ramp, cursing and whining.

Slowly, Salih lifted his gaze to the top of the rope ladder, meeting Harper's eyes.

Faster, she told herself as she yanked at the ladder. Hurry. She tugged on the thick, heavy ropes, taking them up rung by rung, expecting at any moment that Salih would pull down from the other end. But he didn't. The ladder was difficult to maneuver and weighed more than she'd expected, but, sweating and wheezing, she managed to pull it all up and gather it into a pile. Favoring her neck, she lay flat beside the rope and peered down into the cave for Salih. Saw the wheelbarrow, the dead Nahual. The vessels of burning oil. The altar . . . And finally, Salih, apparently returning to the cave after stepping out for supplies. He was lumbering across the cave with his arms full, carrying an extension ladder and a flashlight. On his shoulder, she saw a holster.

OK, time to go. Harper got to her feet and turned, gazed into the passageway. Saw a well of total darkness. Damn. This time, she had no flashlight, would be completely blind. But Salih had a gun. She had no choice.

Harper plunged into blackness, her hands on the walls, feeling for the trail of X's she'd carved with a nail. Hearing the clunk of the ladder against the opening, Salih's heavy footsteps on the rungs. His panting as he climbed into the passageway. His voice calling, 'Harper?'

She kept moving blindly, cautiously, testing the floor with her feet, following the wall with her fingers. Was that an X? Or just a random scratch? She traced the line, touched the intersection in the middle – yes, it was an X! She wouldn't get lost if she stuck to the trail.

'Harper, stop. You'll get lost. Look, I'm a businessman; we can negotiate.'

Harper hurried away from the voice, deeper into the passageways, trying to remember the turns, the dead ends. Remembering with dismay that the X's didn't lead to an exit; they led to the spot where she'd found Chloe Manning. Following them was useless. Oh God, what if she got lost again, this time in the dark? Familiar panic bubbled in her belly. What a joke. After escaping against all odds, she'd come back to die here after all?

Shut up, she told herself. Stop whimpering and just go. Salih was not far behind; she could hear his steps. Imagined his bloody breath on her neck, his gun at her ribs. She hurried on, suddenly felt the air shift. Just ahead, her fingers felt empty air. A gap in the wall. Was this a turn in the passageway? She didn't remember one so close to the rope ladder, but she'd been exhausted, half-delusional and dehydrated, might not have noticed. And the wall definitely had a gap. So the tunnel turned. Except, no – she felt gaps on both sides. So the tunnel divided left and right. She stepped forward, arms outstretched. Found no wall ahead either. She was at a crossroads, could go straight, left or right. She couldn't take time to think; Salih was too close. Needed to choose and move. Oh God. Harper had no idea where she was. Taking a breath, she chose without a reason and turned right. Her hand skimmed the surface of the wall, feeling her way. Counting her steps in case she had to retrace them.

At the ninth step, Salih called again, his voice not as close. 'Harper – there's no point wandering. There's no way out for you. Come back. We'll have a bottle of wine and talk things out.'

A bottle of wine? Really? Harper kept moving. Counting steps, she turned and zigzagged blindly, feeling oddly calm. Gradually, Salih's voice became more distant. After a while, she didn't hear it at all.

She'd lost count of her steps somewhere after two hundred thirty. And she'd forgotten the sequence of her turns, even though she'd tried to make a marching song out of them: right, right, left, right, left. But she couldn't remember them, wouldn't be able to find her way back if she had to. Harper wandered lost, listening for Salih, not hearing him. But soon, she heard other voices.

'Mrs Jennings?' A man.

'Hoppa!' Hank?

And the barking of a dog.

A dog?

Harper stopped walking and shouted to them, but her voice was thin and hoarse. And using it, she began to cough again. Could they hear her? She waited until they called again, tried to identify their direction, to go towards them. Running, stumbling on the uneven floor, turning corners she wasn't sure would take her closer, she called out as loudly and often as her throat would allow until, finally, she saw a glow of light ahead. Squinting, shading her eyes from the brightness of flashlights, Harper stopped walking and let herself sink to the tunnel floor.

A golden Lab pulled on his leash, dragging the officer behind him; when he reached Harper, he sat beside her. Panting. And Harper sat panting in unison.

'Mrs Jennings?' The officer aimed his flashlight at her face, blinding her. 'It's OK, Mrs Jennings. We've got you.'

'Hoppa? Hoppa – OK?'

She couldn't see him, but Hank's winded voice came to her from somewhere behind the policeman. And then, as the officer talked into a radio, Hank was moving in front of him. And around the dog. And as he reached for her, Harper half jumped, half fell into his arms.

Hank handed her up through the hole in the wall to the EMTs who'd been waiting. He stood on Rick's pile of broken crates and smashed relics. They'd set up lights down there, illuminating a whole section of the passageway, but Harper couldn't bear to look. Didn't want to see the wreckage of relics on the ground.

The EMTs placed her on a stretcher. Began checking her out. Frowned at her face, her torso. Her throat. Conferred with each other then asked if someone had choked her. She started to nod, but the older one stopped her. 'No, no – don't move your head. Stay still.'

Harper kept still, but moved her eyes, searching for Hank. 'How'd you know where—' she started but her voice again broke, instigating a fit of coughing and alarming the EMTs.

'Leslie,' Hank said.

Leslie?

'Called. Said you. Shown up. Not.'

What? Shown up where? Harper tried but couldn't remember anything about Leslie. Couldn't even recall how she'd gotten to Langston's.

'Thank goodness you're all right, Mrs Jennings.' Detective Rivers climbed out of the hole in the wall, talking as she strained to lift a German shepherd out and helped an officer climb after her. 'We've been scared sick about you. Especially after we got to Mr Salim's hotel and saw what was in his room.'

His room? Harper pictured it, the suite, its well-stocked bar. Wait.

Her memories were resurfacing – she'd gone to Salih's hotel to give him Zina's bracelet, and he'd offered her a drink. 'Just one,' because she didn't want to be late. Wait – late? Oh – late for Leslie! Yes, she'd had an appointment with Leslie, but hadn't shown up.

Even so, why had Leslie called Hank? If Leslie had a concern, she should have called Harper. Except that maybe she had. Harper wouldn't have answered her phone, didn't even know where it was. And, given Harper's role in the headlines of the last week, Leslie would have worried when Harper hadn't shown up and wasn't answering her phone. Which would explain why she'd called Hank.

Harper's head hurt, resisted thinking. Something pierced her arm. She looked down, saw one of the EMTs – the younger one – inserting a butterfly needle into her arm. Damn. They were giving her an IV.

'I don't need that!' She started to sit up, tried to push him away. Didn't want to go to the hospital.

'Lie back, ma'am. It's just in case.' He connected a saline bag to her arm while his partner strapped cold packs to her torso.

Detective Rivers was still talking.

'. . . your motorcycle outside and your leather bag in his room. But that wasn't all.' She folded her arms. 'We found over a dozen relics in there, packaged and ready to go. Do you know anything about those?'

Harper tried to shake her head but couldn't. They'd put something around her head and neck, immobilizing her. When had they done that? How, without her noticing? Cold fluids streamed into Harper's arm. Breathing hurt. The detective talked on.

'. . . my untrained eye, Mrs Jennings, those relics look to be Pre-Columbian, and I suspect they might belong to the Langston collection. Given that Mr Salim's sister used to work with the collection, and that her body was found at the Langston house, and that these relics might have been stolen from there, I thought I should stop over there and see what was going on.'

Harper was still confused. How had they known to search the passageway? Why would they think she was in there?

'When we arrived, we saw a van parked outside that cave you showed us. We went inside, and, Mrs Jennings, there was a lot of blood in that cave.'

Blood? Wait. Not Wiggins' body? The EMT was checking her blood pressure, distracting her.

'Frankly, with so much blood, I feared the worst, but your

husband – he's a keen observer – he noticed something odd: the rope ladder to the passageway had been pulled up. So we thought – we hoped – you'd skedaddled up and taken it up with you.'

'Enough.' Hank put a hand up, scolding. 'Hoppa. Hurt. Talk later not more now.'

The older EMT nodded agreement. 'We're ready to roll.' He rechecked the stabilizing equipment around her neck.

'One minute.' Rivers stopped them. She eyed Harper. 'Mrs Jennings, please. If you know, tell me: where is Salih Salim?'

Harper pointed to the passageway, mouthed, 'In there.'

'In the passageway? He was with you?'

Harper tried, but couldn't shake her head, managed to croak, 'Following me.' And then something else occurred to her. 'Where's Angus?'

Harper woke up, full of painkillers, staring at an IV pole and bag of fluids. In the hospital. Again, she saw the explosion at the checkpoint, her patrol blowing up. Felt the thud of landing on a burn-out car, her leg . . . She reached down, felt her leg. No bandages. What? She tried to turn her head to look around, but couldn't move it. Wait – how come—?

'You up, Hoppa.' Hank stood above her, taking her hand. 'Feel how?' He leaned over, kissed her.

Harper closed her eyes, her memory spotty. 'I'm in the hospital.'

He explained that, yes, she was. And had been for two days under heavy doses of pain medicine. She'd been X-rayed, MRI'd, examined all over. Tests had shown that her neck was sprained, her larynx bruised, a couple of vertebrae dislocated. Her ribs were bruised, her hands raw from rope burn. From head to toe, she was banged up and scraped. While she'd been running from Salih, adrenalin had probably masked the pain of these injuries, but once she was safe, it had erupted hot and fierce. The pain medications had made her groggy, and, when she'd been awake, she'd had flashbacks of being injured in Iraq, of the explosion that had killed most of her patrol and nearly taken her left leg. She'd cried out, she'd fought. And then she'd slept again.

Hank held her hand. 'Hungry?'

Harper couldn't see the tray, but she smelled something sweet. Trying to sit, she reached for the control, couldn't find it. Hank pushed the button and raised the bed for her; sitting up, she regarded the tray in front of her. Hospital pancakes. A scrambled egg. Some kind of pink meat. Apple juice. Jello. Jello?

Hank pulled the tray over, cut the pancakes for her. Harper couldn't remember when she'd last eaten. Wasn't sure if she wanted food. But Hank held a syrupy blob to her mouth, and she ate.

'Good,' Hank beamed as if she'd finished a marathon. 'Good eating, Hoppa.'

She chewed in a haze. Felt grimy, wanted a shower.

'Mother your called.' Hank shoveled more pancake.

Oh God.

'Wants come out here.'

Harper almost choked. Her mother? 'Uh uh.' Her mouth was full, and her voice unaccustomed to talking. '*No.*' Harper's mother meant well, but required too much attention. Harper always took care of her, not the other way.

'Told her. Visit later. Better.'

Harper let out a breath, swallowed. On her own, she lifted the juice, pulled the top off with shaky hands. Lord, she was weak.

'Help you?'

'I got it.' Almost. She pulled, finally lifted the foil top from the plastic cup, took a drink. All without moving her head and neck, which were still stabilized in the brace. 'Can they take this thing off?'

'Soon.' Hank took the empty cup. Cut another slab of pancake.

Harper was still chewing when Detective Rivers came in. And that's when breakfast stopped.

'She better today? Think she's coherent?' Rivers addressed Hank.

'Eating.' Hank stood bear-like, blocking the detective. Protective.

'Good. So she can keep on eating. I won't stay long.'

'Not strong.'

Harper sat chewing, listening to them discuss her as if she weren't there.

'I'm not going to give her a workout, Mr Jennings. I'm just going to talk.'

'It's OK, Hank. Good morning, Detective.' She had a few questions for Rivers, was eager for the chance to ask them.

Rivers came around the bed, took a seat opposite Hank, beside the window. 'You look better.'

Harper hadn't considered how she looked. Knew it couldn't be good.

'You up for talking a bit?'

Harper swallowed. 'Sure.'

'Because you might have some insights about what's happened. After we sent you off in the ambulance, we found another body.'

Harper couldn't turn her head. Her eyes moved from side to side, Rivers to Hank. Hank to Rivers. Waiting. Whose body? Rick's? Salih's?

'Turns out he was a professor of Archeology. Frederick Charles Wiggins. He had deep scratches on his arms and face, bruises on his sides as if he'd been beaten up. And two knife wounds – one that pierced the heart.'

Made sense; Harper had fought him pretty hard.

'And he was posed, just like Zina. Leaning against a tree outside, right where she was.'

Against a tree? How had he gotten there? Maybe Angus moved him? He must have. He was the only one—

'He was dressed in some kind of costume. Feathers . . .'

'He wanted to be a shape-shifter. Recreating Pre-Columbian rituals.' Harper's voice was weak, still hoarse.

Rivers tilted her head. 'Mrs Jennings, did those rituals involve taking out people's hearts?'

Harper stiffened.

'If they did, he wasn't the only one recreating them. Because someone took his.'

Someone took Wiggins' heart? But who? And why? Wiggins was the guy trying to become a Nahual. He'd been the only one with even a remote reason to take hearts.

'I don't get it – Wiggins was the one taking the hearts.'

Rivers squinted. 'How do you know that?'

'Because I heard them talking about what he'd done to Zina.' She hesitated. 'And because he tried to take mine.'

Hank's mouth opened. 'Hoppa.' He took her hand, turned to Rivers. 'Upset now. Enough.'

'Just a few more things.' Rivers leaned forward so Harper could see her more easily. 'It's interesting what you've just said, Mrs Jennings. Because it's consistent with our findings. Wiggins's heart was removed, but not the way Zina's was. Zina's body had minimal damage. The cuts were neat and skilful. The breastbone opened with almost surgical precision.'

Or with the care of a Nahual.

'This one was ripped open, mangled. Looked like it got hacked with an axe. Clearly, not the work of the same guy.' She paused. 'So do you have any idea who could have done it?'

Maybe. 'Angus Langston was the only other person there.' But she couldn't figure out why Angus would mess with Wiggins' body, let alone take his heart.

'Interesting. Because Angus took off. He tried to split.'

Tried?

'We picked him up for a DUI yesterday. He was speeding out of town.'

Had Angus taken the time to cut out Wiggins' heart before he ran? Harper couldn't picture it. Didn't want to.

'That it?' Hank asked.

'It'll do for now. It's good to see you getting better, Mrs Jennings.' Rivers stood, started for the door. 'I'll be in touch.'

As she was leaving, Harper remembered what she'd wanted to ask. 'Detective – wait. Have you found Rick Owens? And what about Salih?'

Neither had been found.

The police had looked for Salih in the passageway, had watched the house and the ramp exit to make sure he couldn't leave. They'd scoured the tunnels with dogs. But the dogs ran into dead ends or seemed to lose the scent. Two days after he'd entered them, Salih hadn't emerged from the passageways. Harper wasn't surprised. Chloe Manning's body had gone undiscovered for almost a hundred years. The secret corridors were too twisted and gnarled to be untangled so quickly by a few men and dogs.

Harper came home the next day with a cervical collar and pain pills that made her mind foggy. She disliked dozing off, disliked more the shuddering pain that radiated through her body without them. Despite her loopiness, Harper played hostess to a stream of visitors. Detective Rivers and her sometime partner, Detective Boschi, checked in, reporting that Angus had confessed to stealing relics, but vehemently denied having anything to do with killing Wiggins, whom he called Digger, or anyone else. He admitted that he had information about other crimes, but, hoping to make a deal, he refused to give details until he could negotiate.

Vicki and Trent came with flowers, balloons, bonbons and Scotch. The Archeology Department sent a fruit basket. Professor

Schmerling and Dean Van Arsdale came by with chocolates, awkwardly apologizing for Professor Wiggins, muttering that they'd known he'd been eccentric but had never dreamed he'd been so disturbed. Phil and Stacey arrived with questions and a huge tin of candy corn. The press called often; Harper's mom called even more often, still wanting to fly out, refusing to believe that Harper was 'fine' as she claimed. Hank stayed steadfastly by Harper's side, answering the phone, limiting the number and length of visits. He seemed to relish his role of caretaker, making decisions, taking control.

Harper's throat began to heal, but she still didn't speak much. Found herself listening more, thinking that most of what people – even her friends and professors – said was blither. She wondered if Hank, unable to converse well, felt the same distance as she did from others. She thought of them as 'talkers'. Of herself and Hank as 'watchers' and 'listeners'.

The first few days home passed in a haze of medication. Harper saw the news reports about the murder at Langston's, heard reporters' references to the election held earlier in the week. Even with the references, she didn't think of Colonel Baxter right away, and she didn't remember Burke's letter. She didn't think of the letter even when she watched a feature about the landslide victory of an Iraqi war veteran, a former army colonel elected to Senate from the state of Tennessee. That news upset Harper, but it wasn't until Friday, walking past the front door, that she actually saw Burke's envelope under a paperweight on the foyer table. That was when she remembered the list of shipment dates and serial numbers. And it was when, with Hank hovering and telling her not to lift her heavy leather bag by herself, she went to get her phone.

'You said you needed evidence of theft,' she said. 'These shipment numbers will prove that Baxter stole millions.'

'Mrs Jennings,' Detective Rivers sounded tired. 'The man is now a United States senator. He just won by an overwhelming majority. And, frankly, this alleged theft occurred years ago, while I have more than a couple of open homicides to investigate.'

'I hope those include Burke Everett's. Because I think these papers will show motive for his murder, evidence that it wasn't suicide. And they'll show why Rick Owens was coming after me.'

'Mrs Jennings, maybe you should—'

'Baxter sent Rick.' Harper's voice was hoarse and strained. 'To silence Burke and me. About Iraq. Ask Angus – he was there when Wiggins killed him.'

'Hoppa. Calm down.' Hank stroked her back. Hovering.

'Detective, Rick killed Burke – I'm sure of it!'

'Hoppa – stop.'

Harper scowled, pushed Hank's hand away. 'And Wiggins killed Rick after he chased me through the passageway, and—'

'Whoa. Settle down, Mrs Jennings – your husband will have my hide.' She paused, sighed loudly. 'All right. You win. I'll stop by and check out the letter.'

Relieved, Harper ended the call and set the envelope back on the foyer table under the paperweight. And noticed Hank glowering.

'What's wrong?'

He simmered. 'You. Don't listen. Need rest.'

'I'm fine, Hank. You don't need to stand over me every second.'

As soon as she said it, she was sorry. Lord, how ungrateful was she?

'I didn't mean that . . .'

But it was too late. Wounded, Hank turned away, started for the door. 'Super. Market. Going. Now. OK?'

Harper went after him, called to him, but he didn't stop. Who could blame him? All week, he'd helped her eat and bathe and dress and move. And now, she'd snapped at him? What was wrong with her?

When he came back, she'd apologize. Meantime, it would be good for Hank to take off for a little while. It would be fine.

Harper dozed on the den sofa, felt someone standing beside her, assumed it was Hank. She opened her eyes and saw not Hank, but Angus, staring at her. Smiling. Harper froze – when had Angus been released? Slowly, cautiously, she sat up. Looked around for Hank, remembered he was gone . . .

'Sorry. Didn't mean to startle you – the door was open.'

It was? Harper didn't remember it being open. But she felt relieved. And foolish. It wasn't Angus who'd come to see her; it was Jake. She greeted him, moved to the end of the couch. 'Come sit down.'

'So. You doing OK?' he sat, studying the cervical collar, her bruises.

'Better.'

'Look. I want you to know. I had no idea what my brother was doing. He knew better than to tell me.'

Harper still couldn't turn her head much, so she twisted her body to face him.

'Angus.' Jake shook his head. 'He probably started selling relics after he found out about the will. Probably thought that by ripping off the collection, he was taking what was rightly his. But the killing? Zina?'

'Angus didn't kill her. That was Zina's brother,' said Harper.

'What about Digger? You must have seen him. You were there, right? The guy in the feather jacket with a stuffed cat on his head. Wiggins.'

Oh. Wiggins, Digger, the Nahual. All the same person. 'Salih Salim killed him. Not Angus.' But it struck her that the detectives hadn't mentioned Wiggins' cathead. Maybe they'd thought it unnecessary, too much gruesome detail.

Jake paused, took a breath. 'You know, Angus and I – we've known Wiggins for just about always. Digger. His dad was our dentist. And his mom was a drunk, so he hung around our house until he became part of the family. Went on digs with us – that's how he got the name. Growing up, he was like a brother.'

Really? Wiggins?

'After a while, my father spent more time with Digger than he did with us.'

Harper didn't know what to say. 'Maybe it just seemed that way.'

'No. He did. Digger became father's protégé. They were always in the study, talked about research, spiritualism, symbolism. God knows what all. My father brought him to conferences. To South America. Utah. All over. Until that girl died. Carla.' Jake looked into the air. 'After that, Digger went away for a while.' He looked at Harper, smiled oddly.

'All this time, you knew?'

'Yep. She wasn't his first, either.'

Jake's grin was crooked. 'We had a dog. Aubrey. I found him behind the house. His chest was ripped open.'

Harper recoiled.

'There were also birds. A cat. Even a deer. Over the years, all over the property, animal corpses would show up, *sans* hearts. The owls were the messiest. He plucked out their feathers.'

'You're saying Wiggins—?'

'Oh, for sure. I told my father about it. Know what he did? He laughed. He shook his head, but he laughed. He told me not to worry, that long ago, spiritual men sacrificed the hearts of creatures for their religions. Probably someone was doing that again. He said he'd talk to the person.'

Harper sat silent.

'But my father didn't do anything. Not even when Digger killed Aubrey. So when Digger went on to Carla, it was my father's fault.' Jake's eyes became steely. 'I was mad – I liked Carla.'

'What did you do?'

Jake's jaw rippled. 'Told my father what I knew. This time he didn't laugh. But he didn't go to the police. He arranged with Digger's family to send him abroad. Supposedly to get help. But I don't know about that. Because some years later, all educated and grown up, Wiggins came back with his PhD. I think he expected to be welcomed home like a prodigal son. My father got him a position at the university, helped him get a start. But he would have nothing to do with him. Wouldn't let him near the relics. Hell, he wouldn't let him in the house.'

Harper listened, chilled. And wondered why Jake was telling the story to her, not the police.

'Thing is. Once he was back, dead animals started showing up again, without their hearts. This time, I was a grown man. I went to him, told him what I knew. He denied it. He said it wasn't him, that it had been Angus all along. That Angus had killed the girl. He'd just taken the fall.'

'Jake. This is—'

'Unbelievable? Is that what you were going to say?'

She'd been about to say: '—something you should tell the police.'

'Well, it is. Meantime, the cops have Angus in custody. But Angus is no killer. He's spineless. And a sneak. My own brother, and he was ripping me off. With Wiggins. I can't figure out when it started. But they got together and decided to steal pieces from the collection. Which meant from me – because that will won't stand up. Wiggins took my dog, my father, and now he's taken my brother and my inheritance from me.' He closed his mouth, clenched his jaw, and slid closer to Harper on the sofa.

'You know why I'm telling you this?'

She didn't. But she didn't like the look in his eyes. Or the nearness of his body.

'Fact is, nobody but you can testify against Angus in any of this. Not the thefts. Not the killings.' He met her eyes. 'Angus is a pussy, but he's all I've got left.'

For a moment, neither spoke.

Harper stood, her eyes still on his. Jake stood smoothly, like a jaguar about to spring. She spun around, headed for the foyer, the door.

Jake followed, unhurried. 'Wait, I'm not finished – don't you want to hear what he did with them?'

She broke into a run, made it into the foyer, to the table by the door. Saw Burke's letter, the paperweight.

Jake grabbed Harper's shoulder, spun her around. Leaned close and spoke softly. 'Wiggins thought that a creature's heart contained its power and spirit. So that each heart he ate made him more powerful.'

Harper felt his breath on her face, tried to turn away, but couldn't move her neck. Inched her arm toward the table.

'I finally got him, though.' Jake smiled. 'My dog. And all those "spirits" he spent years gathering – all his so-called powers. Who's got them now?' He licked his lips, tightening his grip on her. 'Guess who's the Nahual now?'

Harper swung the paperweight.

When Hank came in with his arms full of grocery bags, he found Jake hog-tied with duct tape in the foyer, Harper calmly watching, reading in the living room, waiting for Detective Rivers to arrive.

The search for Salih continued. His family offered rewards, but he remained missing, apparently lost in the twisted bowels of the Langston house. Angus traded information about the murders of Carla Prentiss, Zina Salim, and Rick Owens to reduce the multiple charges against him. Rick's bones were found in the woods, his flesh devoured by scavengers. Jake was charged with abusing Wiggins' corpse and assaulting Harper with intent to kill, even though he'd never actually laid a hand on her.

The Tuesday before Thanksgiving, Rivers stopped by. She turned down the offer of coffee, said she couldn't stay. 'I heard back about those serial numbers you gave me. The FBI and the Army – all the powers that be – say that the shipment list isn't enough to launch an investigation. They don't even want to bother checking the numbers, because merely loading cargo on to a helicopter – well, that wouldn't prove that there was a crime or even misconduct. And there's no other evidence to indicate wrongdoing. Not even any witnesses.'

No. Except for her, all the witnesses were dead.

'Anyhow, it's a good thing you didn't try to sabotage Baxter's election over this, Mrs Jennings. There'd have been hell to pay. They say he's a rising star – there's already talk about him running for president.'

She handed Harper a file folder. Inside was a copy of Burke's letter and a pile of correspondence going up the chain of command from Rivers to her boss to the FBI, the Army and the Justice Department.

After Rivers left, Harper put the file aside, didn't want to think about Burke, Rick, Pete, the Colonel, his election or a theft that might or might not have happened back in Iraq.

The next day was gray and wet, but she walked to the bridge where Burke had died, spent some time just standing in the rain, remembering.

'How was Thanksgiving?' Leslie's office smelled of cinnamon. She sipped tea, curled on to the green leather sofa beside Harper.

'My mother came out.'

Leslie nodded. 'Got it. How bad?'

'Pretty bad. But she means well. She's just high maintenance.'

Silence. Harper didn't know what to say, where to begin. Avoided the Big Stuff. 'I'm back working on my dissertation. It's going well.'

'Good.' Leslie's voice was like silk. Or maybe cotton balls.

Harper nodded. More silence. Tell her, she thought. But she didn't. Instead, she said, 'The department asked if I wanted to be part of the relic assessment. To identify all the damage. I declined.'

'I'm sure they understood.'

Harper nodded. 'Professor Schmerling said they did. It's kind of funny – I mean, in a terrible way: after everything that's happened so they could acquire that collection, the university isn't even keeping it.'

'Seriously?' Leslie put her mug down. 'Why not?'

'Most of the pieces are going back to the countries of origin. After all the attention in the press, countries requested their return. I guess the university wants to avoid more trouble.'

Silence again. Tell her, Harper thought. But she didn't.

'You're all better. Physically?'

'Pretty much.' Harper demonstrated, turning her head just a little.

'And how are things with Hank?'

Harper sipped tea, stalling. The truth was that she and Hank were still cautious. Dancing around each other, not sure how tightly to hold on, how much to let go. 'Better.' Maybe.

'Is he more comfortable with independence?'

With his independence? Or with hers? 'He doesn't like me to be out of his sight. He worries about me. It's the opposite of how things were – I used to be the one worrying, taking care of him. Now, he's helicopter husband, always hovering.'

Leslie smiled. 'Have you told him how you feel about that?'

No. She hadn't. She would, but not until she was sure she wanted him to stop. Harper still had nightmares about endless corridors, men with bloody grins. Or feathered creatures feasting on beating hearts. In the night, she often climbed on to Hank, clinging to him in her sleep.

Or waking him up to make love.

Often without birth control.

Tell her, she thought. But she didn't, wasn't ready to talk about that. Not even to Leslie.

Not even to Hank.

Leslie was talking, assuring Harper that she and Hank were solid, just finding their way. Going through a new phase.

Harper toyed with the bangle bracelet on her wrist, thinking about new phases. About the name Zina. About what to buy Hank for Christmas. About the nursery. About her dissertation. About the changes the New Year would bring.